MAJOR CRIME UNIT

BOOKS 1 - 3

IAIN ROB WRIGHT

ULCERATED PRESS

NOWHERE IS SAFE

When a quaint town in the United Kingdom is struck by a suicide bomber, a once proud nation is brought to its knees. Yet this first attack is just the beginning of something much greater and far worse. Something that nobody could have predicted.

The days to follow will determine if the UK has a future, or if it will be reduced to anarchy and ashes.

Only one person stands between the people of the UK and their complete destruction. Too bad it's an angry, damaged ex-solider named Sarah Stone. Sarah despises her country for what it did to her, and that's what makes it so hard when she is forced to save it.

SOFT TARGET is the first in a series of books featuring acerbic protagonist Sarah Stone. It is a non-stop action thriller in the same vein as 24.

Dedicated with those with scars.

With Thanks to:

Sean Ellis
&
Chris Kirk

Everything I got right, I got right because of them.

"Great Britain has lost an empire but has not yet found a role."
– Dean Acheson

"Terrorism has no nationality or religion."
– Vladamir Putin

"Damn it!"
–Jack Bauer, 24, Fox Network Television

1

PROLOGUE

Birds flocked above the town square as young and old alike scoffed popcorn and candy floss. Shuffling bottoms filled every bench while an exuberant rock band assaulted the airwaves. Those who could find no seat, stood and raised their plastic beer cups along to the music. Stretched between a pair of gnarled oak trees, a banner painted with bright red letters declared: **APRIL 25th SPRING FETE: Getting nutty in Knutsford.**

Carnival games and food stalls had sprung up everywhere in the last twenty-four hours, their licensed operators as ruthlessly efficient as German car factories.

Jeffrey Blanchfield stood beneath some sagging blue-and-white bunting, gazing up at the azure sky. The scent of freshly cut grass and the cooing of pigeons signalled the start of a lovely afternoon. The bright sun blazed behind one single cloud.

Fresh air was something Jeffrey had enjoyed ever since his childhood on granddad's farm. He'd tried to take Margaret to see the old place once — on their fourth anniversary — but it had been paved over to make way for a trading estate. He hadn't realised then, but a part of him had died that day. The memories of him standing amongst the cows as a boy, breathing in the heady aromas of country air and fresh dung, were now melancholic and painful. Nowadays, thirty-five million cars fouled the country air, and the cow dung had been replaced by minefields of dog shit.

Jeffrey's worn kneecaps groaned, and he let out a shiver as his bones struggled to retain the sun's warmth. Even today, in the bright sunshine, he had needed to wear his long grey anorak.

When had he got so old?

A young girl moved in front of him. She had sapphire ribbons tied in her pigtails and a stuffed bear tucked under one arm, and a mongrel on a lead. She was alone, and watching the fete with curious interest while her scruffy pet cocked its leg over a flowerbed. Jeffrey knew it was wrong to approach the girl, but he always found the young ones so insightful. Their opinions were indicative of the current state of society, and he wanted to know where things currently stood. He wanted to make sure, one last time, that what he was planning to do was the right thing.

The only thing.

He and Margaret had never managed children — Jeffrey's fault if you asked the doctors, thanks to a 'low sperm count,' — and perhaps if they'd been able to have a family, things would have turned out differently.

Jeffrey would have enjoyed being a father.

He moved close enough to pick up the young girl's scent — Mummy's perfume mixed with sugary sweets. The smells of childhood mixed with an impatience to grow up. Jeffrey wondered if he'd ever tried to wear his father's aftershave as a child, but couldn't remember. It was so hard to remember anything these days.

The little girl turned and noticed Jeffrey standing over her. "Hello," she said warily.

"Hello there, young lady. How are you today? Enjoying the fete?"

"I won a teddy bear," she pointed to a badly stitched gypsy prize tucked beneath her arm. "On the darts game."

"How splendid!" Jeffrey knelt to pat the girl's mongrel on the head.

It was some kind of diluted beagle, a half-breed like most the world nowadays. "And what is this little fella's name?"

"Ruby. She's a girl."

"Ruby? What a pretty name."

"I called her it 'cus it's my favourite stone. When I get married, I'm gunna have a big ruby on my weddin' finger." She raised her hand and wiggled her ring finger at him.

"Don't you dream of doing something besides getting married and having an expensive ring? Don't you want to do anything special?" Jeffrey's voice had unwittingly taken on a disapproving tone which obviously upset the girl.

"I... I'd like to help animals. I like animals."

Jeffrey smiled. "A vet perhaps? Now, that's a good profession. Your mummy and daddy would be very proud."

"I don't have a daddy."

Jeffrey sighed, and for a moment he retreated into despair and anger. "Another careless pregnancy, no doubt. So many of them nowadays. Women have no self-respect anymore, and the men are no better — work-shy thugs. Sluts and thugs. That's the United Kingdom of the twenty-first century for you." He realised his lack of manners and covered his mouth with a withered old hand. "Forgive my rant, young lady. The internal filters start to go at my age."

"Mummy!" The little girl scanned the crowd, yanking at the poor mongrel's neck. A heavyset woman emerged, grasping a beaker full of cider in one hand and a greasy burger in the other. Her flabby breasts spilled from an undersized halter-top, and she sported a ghastly tattoo of a flower on her calloused right foot.

"Was up, bab?" the woman asked. "Was wrung?"

Ugly way of talking, Jeffrey thought to himself. *If ever there was a region so proud of sounding stupid, it was Birmingham.* Jeffrey had visited Smethwick once for a football match a colleague had invited him to. Never again. It had been a dirty, grimy, uncivilised place, full of people spitting and snarling. There had been a pub by the stadium with boarded-up windows and peeling blue paint. The North was a much nicer region of the country, but that too was going down the lavatory.

The little girl pointed an accusing finger at Jeffrey. "He's scaring me, Mummy."

The fat mother glared at Jeffrey, narrowing her heavily made-up eyes. Jeffrey hid his disdain behind a polite smile. "Your sweet daughter has already had my apology, but I offer one to you too. Forgive my manners. Mind wobbles at my age, I'm afraid."

The woman wrapped a chubby arm around her daughter and pulled her close. "Nay problem." But as she moved away she muttered something else: "Dirty old perv."

Jeffrey rolled his eyes. You couldn't hold a conversation these days without somebody accusing you of something, it seemed.

Nearby, a teenage girl writhed against an older boy while a group of lads leered at the bright pink thong peeking out the back of her jeans. Nobody took exception to the lewd display. Things that had once been private and respectful were now frivolous and undervalued. Where it would end? Would people rut in the street fifty years from now? Would they take animals into their beds? Mankind was on a trajectory to Hell.

Jeffrey remembered the green and pleasant land of his childhood and missed it dearly. He remembered when a foreigner was a novelty instead of an entitled parasite or potential criminal. He remembered when women, like his beloved Margaret, were gentle and kind, and men knew what hard work was. It had all turned to shit. It left him sick.

He pushed his way through the crowd, receiving a drenched elbow from a carelessly held cup of cider. He winced as cuss words flew over his head like fluttering sparrows. Exposed cleavages sullied the scenery along with great puddles of alcohol and half-eaten food. All around, people danced in their own tawdry filth.

Jeffrey made his way to the bandstand, suffering the glancing blows and drunken shoves, the reckless swearing. He was Jesus walking the *Via Dolorosa*, disregarded and misunderstood, but history would show that he was righteous. It was everybody else who was damned.

By the time he reached the bandstand, his arthritic knees were hot coals beneath his skin. The tribute band had just finished their latest racket and were now interacting with the crowd. "Who's enjoying themselves?" the lead singer crowed.

The audience cheered. Beer and cider flew from cups and spattered the ground in a foul baptism of cigarette ash and alcohol.

"Is everybody ready for a rocking summer?"

More cheers.

"Now, before we play our next number, me and the band would just like to thank you for being such a wicked audience."

'Wicked' is the correct word, thought Jeffrey. And it's 'the band and I'.

"You people really know how to have a good time."

In case Jeffrey had any doubts about what he was about to do, he studied the crowd one last time and spotted a couple his own age gyrating and snogging like teenage lovers. Disgusting.

Hatred had led Jeffrey there, but all he felt now, at the final moments, was pity — pity for these doomed, unworthy souls. Surely, Heaven did not await them

His mission had begun the moment his beloved Margaret had died at his feet, clutching her chest and pleading for life not to leave her. But it had left her. There had been nothing he could do but watch her die on the worn carpet of their cold living room floor.

The heart attack had been inevitable as soon as the Government had started housing benefit seekers and minorities in the houses either side of theirs. He and Margaret had broken their backs working to pay-off the mortgage on their humble three-bed semi, had worked their entire lives so they could enjoy retirement together. But when their twilight years had finally arrived, they were filled with stress and aggravation. Petty crime had taken over his town — theft and vandalism on every corner. Eventually, Margaret became afraid to leave the house, unwilling to risk the haranguing of local youths gathered in every underpass. The constant fear and worrying had eventually burst her poor, gentle heart. His dear Margaret had gone to a better place while he was stuck in this cesspit.

But no more.

Jeffrey took a step towards the bandstand. The lead singer noticed him immediately. "Ay up, we've got a new member of the band. You lost, old fella?" Jeffrey ignored the musician and started up the steps. This amused the man even more. "'Ere, looks like he's coming to sing one with us. Would we all like to see the old fella sing us a song? I'm not sure we have anything by George Formby. How about *When I'm Sixty-Four?*"

The crowd bellowed with laughter.

Jeffrey made his way up onto the bandstand's wooden platform, taking advantage of the band's confusion. He was able to stroll right up to the mic stand. Once there, he said what he had come there to say. "You people disgust me."

Jeffrey pulled open his anorak and detonated the bomb strapped around his waist.

2

FALLING DOWN

Summer was nearly here, but the bugs were early. Sarah hopped from the '64' bus and landed on the sticky pavement. Immediately, as if to greet her, a wasp darted at her face. She swatted at it, and when the buzzing menace refused to flee, she gritted her teeth and snarled. As it dived at her face a second time, she snatched it out of the air and crushed it in her fist. The little bastard got off a parting shot though, and the piercing pain in her palm reminded her of the virtue of calmness. Getting angry only ever seemed to hurt *her*, yet it was her default emotion — the one she always grasped at first.

Sorry, Mr Wasp, but you were the one who made it personal.

She threw the crushed wasp carcass to the pavement and resumed her journey. As she marched through the high street, she might have ignored the gawking strangers glancing at her in disgust, but instead she met their stares head-on. If they wanted to gawp, she had every right to glare right back at them. Either that or they could pay for the freak show.

The bank was in the middle of Birmingham's busy Corporation Street, and it didn't take her long to reach it. She joined the winding queue inside and cursed beneath her breath. Out of the six serving windows, only two were manned. "Are you kidding me?"

She glanced at the gaping arse-crack of a woman queuing in front of her, and at her snot-nosed toddler running around and making a racket. The toddler stopped its screaming when it spotted Sarah's face, but Sarah wasn't about to offer any comfort. She bared her teeth and the child whimpered. Its mother was too busy with her iPhone to give a shit.

Sarah utterly hated the bank, and if she could've helped it, she'd do away with these monthly visits. Other aspects of her life could be dealt with via the Internet or over the phone, but there was no choice when it came to the bank. She needed to visit the city once a month to pay in her cheques.

"Come on," she mumbled as the queue moved forward by a single body. Her wasp sting was itching. She ran her ragged nails over her throbbing palm to ease it. It had been a mistake crushing the wasp. They were alike. People flinched at the sight of Sarah too.

A well-kempt businessman strolled away from the tellers after having concluded his business. He smiled at Sarah as he approached, but once he got close enough to see the far side of her face, his eyes fixed on the floor and he sped up.

Men often gave Sarah a smile if they caught her good side — from that angle she was a shapely blonde woman — but as soon as they glimpsed the scarred left side of her face, their stomachs turned and they acted as if they'd suddenly realised they were in a hurry.

The queue inched forward. It was a Monday morning. Didn't the bank expect to have this many customers? What made things worse was that there were another three members of staff in the back, hanging around in the office right behind the serving windows. One guy was swigging coffee and laughing, oblivious to the waiting customers.

Sarah thought about the bomb that had gone off yesterday in the town of Knutsford, and whether people had been hanging around like this? Did they even see it coming?

She'd visited Knutsford once. A place just outside Manchester with a cosy Italian restaurant that served the best ravioli she'd ever tasted. She and her husband, Thomas, had eaten there one night before they had boarded a military flight out of Manchester Airport. Thomas had ordered spaghetti and made her leak wine out of her nose by letting the strands hang out of his mouth like a monster. Knutsford was a nice place with nice memories. Sarah had been shocked to see it littered with bodies on last night's news.

The BBC had claimed some disgruntled pensioner was behind the attack, but that just raised more questions than it answered. Like, how did a retired postal worker learn how to make a nail bomb? And why attack a small town like Knutsford?

The queue shuffled up another half-step. Four of the six serving windows were still unoccupied while the dickheads in the office continued sipping coffee.

Okay, enough's enough.

Sarah exited the queue and marched on up to one of the empty serving windows. "Hey, do you think you could come out here and do your job? There are people waiting, in case you hadn't noticed."

A few chuckles erupted from the people standing in the queue, but mostly there was awkward silence. The young guy with the coffee ambled towards the other side of the window, as if he'd just been summoned by a naughty child. He wore a cheap suit with garish cuff-links that he clearly thought were stylish. His badge read: '*Assisant* Branch Manager.' Sarah wondered if he knew about the spelling mistake. When he noticed the scars on Sarah's face, he stumbled mid-step, but recovered well enough to pretend he hadn't noticed. "Ma'am, you need to join the queue."

"I *did* join the queue, but I'm worried that by the time you people get to me, I will have joined the afterlife."

"Ma'am, if you won't join the queue and wait to be served, I will have to ask you to leave."

"And I'll have to ask you to kiss my arse. All these people are waiting, and you're standing around like a monkey with a hard on."

More guffaws from the people in the queue.

The 'Assisant' Branch Manager adjusted his tie and looked down his nose at Sarah. "I'm now asking you to leave, ma'am."

Sarah folded her arms. "So you won't let me cash the cheque I get from the US Army for my dead husband? He was blown up in Afghanistan, in case you're wondering. It was so bad they couldn't even put his body back together. And what about the money I get from the British government for losing half my face fighting for this country? Look, I understand you like to drink your cappuccino in the back and pretend you're a real businessman, but I need my money to live. I'm fussy like that."

"I-I'm very sorry to hear that, ma'am, but I'm afraid you'll have to leave if you're going to be difficult. Please call our customer service number if you'd like to make a complaint."

Sarah moved her face right up to the glass so that the prick could get a good look at her. "I'm not the one being difficult. Don't you people get paid enough not to treat your customers like a nuisance? We give you our money and you act like it's yours. You fine and charge us every chance you get, then refuse to explain why, as if we should just accept that you make the rules. Well, let me tell you something, Mr Assisant Manager, I got my face blown off fighting in a foreign country for entitled idiots like you, so when I say get your bone-idle backside out here, I think I've earned the right."

There was an outright cheer from the queue of customers, and they were now solidly behind Sarah. The *Assisant* Manager nodded over her shoulder as if he were Augustus Caesar having a dissenting peasant dragged away to be executed. Sarah spun around to see a wide-shouldered security guard stomping towards her. With his bald head and tattoos, he looked absurd wearing a smart blue uniform. "You've been asked to leave, luv."

"And yet I'm still here."

More chuckles. The crowd was egging her on, eager to see what happened next. Sarah just rolled her eyes. They were happy to let a disfigured freak entertain them for a while, but she doubted any of them would step in and help her if she needed it.

"You need to leave," the guard commanded, giving her his best impression of a snarling bear.

Sarah waved a hand in front of her nose. "You need to take a breath mint, mate."

"Okay, don't say you weren't asked politely." The guard reached out a hand to grab her by the shoulder, and without thinking, Sarah grabbed the big man's wrist and twisted, yanking him one way and then the other. It was a basic Aikido throw, but it worked like a charm. The guard flipped and hit the ground like a sack of potatoes. He was unhurt, but more than a little surprised.

Sarah stood over him and snarled. "I'd advise against standing up, or I'll make a deposit up your backside with my foot."

The customers cheered. The violence had excited them. Sarah knew enough about mob mentality to know how people's morals changed when their neighbours acted up. It was time to leave. She'd made her point.

Sarah looked back at the stunned Assisant Manager, still safe behind his glass barrier, and pointed her finger at him. "Get your name badge replaced, you moron. It shows what an idiot you are." She then strolled out of the bank and into the crisp air of early May, wondering how the hell she was going to get by without her cheque being cashed. Maybe if she came back tomorrow, they wouldn't remember her face.

Yeah right!

Sarah picked up her pace and hurried away from the bank. If they called the police, she would be easy to identify. Heavily scarred women wearing jeans and work boots were easy to spot. Sure enough, it didn't take long before she was certain she was being followed. Her pursuer stayed back, slinking behind pedestrians, and every time Sarah glanced back, the man pretended to be busy with his phone or the produce of a nearby market stall. He wore the long grey coat of a middle-class car salesman.

Sarah slid into an alleyway between two estate agents, then headed for the rear of the high street where she found nothing except a car park, pizza place, and dingy salon. The man could make no secret of pursuing her now. His footsteps echoed on the concrete behind her, keeping pace rather than catching up. He was apparently in no rush to catch her.

Sarah rounded a brick wall that sectioned off a small parking area belonging to the bank of all places, and then slid herself behind a large steel wheelie bin.

The stranger approached, footsteps growing louder.

Sarah crouched and waited.

Clip clop clip clop.

Clip clop.

Clip.

Sarah leapt up from behind the wheelie bin and swung her leg in a flying roundhouse. It was a knockout blow, designed to end the confrontation before it began. The stranger ducked and swept Sarah's feet out from under her as soon as she landed. Her head struck the concrete and left her lying in a daze.

"Captain Stone," said the stranger. "I prefer to shake hands upon meeting but I'm open to other customs. Would you like to get up and try something easier?"

Sarah gazed up at the man and saw he was clean-cut and handsome. His chin jutted out like a superhero's, and his dark sideburns might've been shaped by a laser. Not a single crease found its way onto the tailored shirt beneath his grey coat.

This guy ain't Old Bill.

Sarah sprang to her feet and leapt at the man again, this time opting for fists. Her first blow missed, glancing sideways off a blocking fore-arm, and her follow-up blows struck thin air. Her humiliation was compounded by her legs being swept out from under her once again.

As soon as she hit the ground, she sprung up and launched a third attack. This time the man pulled a gun from inside his coat and pointed it at her forehead. "You're testing my patience, Captain Stone. Please, calm down."

Sarah let her fists drop to her sides, but kept them clenched. "Who the hell are you?"

"You can call me Howard."

Sarah frowned. The man didn't look like a Howard. "What do you want with me, Howie?"

"An afternoon of your time."

Sarah went to turn away. "Sorry, I'm busy."

"Busy with what? Cashing the pittance the US Government begrudgingly pays you in widow's benefits, or the marginally more generous giro the British Government gives you for taking half your face?"

Sarah snarled. The mention of her scars made them tingle, and her left eye blinked sorely where the thick tissue met her eyelid. "You don't know anything about me."

"I know you made a fine Captain until you hit that IED. I know you've been slinking around for the last five years like a feral fox, snapping at anybody who gets close. You're angry, Sarah, and I don't blame you."

Sarah snorted. "So what? Half the world is angry. The other half are pushovers. What do you care?"

Howard looked at her. It'd been a long time since any man had kept his eyes on her for more than a few seconds. "I can give you the chance to do some good again, Sarah. I want to give you the opportunity to pull yourself out of this quagmire of despair you've found yourself in."

Sarah was growing tired of the vague talk. "Who do you work for?"

"An agency you've never heard of. An agency whose job it is to keep this country safe. I work for the Government."

Sarah smiled. "You work for the government? Well, why didn't you say? You can go to Hell."

She tried to walk away.

"The bomb that went off yesterday..."

Sarah stopped and turned back. "Yeah, good job protecting the country there, mate. How many died?"

"Forty-two. The people responsible have owned up to it."

"People? I heard it was a geriatric with a grudge."

"It was," said Howard. "The bomber was Jeffrey Blanchfield. Sixty-eight years of age and a retired postman, just like the news reported, but there's more. The grudge may have been his, but the bomb came from Shab Bekheir."

Sarah froze. For a moment, she couldn't move or speak. "Y-you're telling me that a terrorist cell in Afghanistan is responsible for a pensioner blowing up a town in Cheshire?" She couldn't help but laugh, it was ridiculous.

Howard was apparently serious though. "We received a videotape this morning taking credit for the attack. Al Al-Sharir made the claim himself."

Sarah's eyes widened, stretching out her scars and making them itch. Her heart was thumping. "Al-Sharir?"

"That's right. Al-Sharir, the man responsible for the IED that hit your squad. You're the only one who survived, right?"

"No one made it out alive that day."

"Fancy a chance at getting even?"

"By going with you? I don't even know you."

"No, but what do you have to lose by trusting me? I didn't go to the trouble of tracking you down just to pull your leg. You have experience we can use, Sarah; so help us."

"Where do you want to take me?"

"To a place that doesn't exist."

Sarah was about to ask what the hell that meant when a door opened at the back of the parking area. A man stepped out of the bank's rear exit and lit a cigarette. To Sarah's surprise, it was the *Assisant* Manager of the bank, taking a break while the bank's queue probably still trailed out of the door.

Sarah looked at Howard and said, "Just let me deal with something and I'll be right with you, okay?"

Howard looked confused, but he shrugged and nodded.

When the *Assisant* Manager saw Sarah stomping toward him, he seemed at first surprised and then worried. As she got closer, he stood his ground, puffing up his chest like a peacock. Sarah grinned. Men never ran from a woman. They always thought they were the ones with the power.

Sarah kicked the smug git right in the bollocks before walking back to the shocked Government agent. "Okay, Howie," she said. "Now we can go."

3

THE GAME

"Where are you parked?" Sarah asked the stranger she had decided to trust.

"Nearby. My colleague is waiting for us."

"It's not Will Smith, is it?"

"What? No."

"Pity. I thought you might have been the men in black."

"I'm not wearing black."

"Good point."

Howard kept them to the back streets, heading away from the city centre. It was a part of town Sarah hadn't visited before, and it was none too pretty. The well-kept Victorian buildings of Birmingham's nucleus gradually gave way to rundown terraces, oily tyre-fitting garages, and ethnic food stores. They walked for twenty minutes before she became impatient enough to say anything else. "Where the hell are you taking me, Howie? Maybe you should show me your badge or something before we go any further."

"We're almost there," was all he told her. It was only Sarah's curiosity that spurred her on.

When they crossed over a one-way street, to the chagrin of a beeping van driver, Howard explained more. "We couldn't arrive directly in the city centre. We had to touch down on the outskirts."

"Touch down?"

Howard smirked, his default expression, and his hero's chin jutted out every time he did it. "Come on," he said, "just inside here."

Sarah spotted an old scrapyard. Its gates were hanging wide open. Wicked spikes lined the top of the surrounding fence. "Oh, hell no," she said. "You're not getting me in there. This is feeling like a mob hit."

"Are you always so dramatic?"

"Look at this face," Sarah pointed to her scars. "I'm the Phantom of the bloody Opera. I can't help being dramatic."

Howard kept his smirk and forged ahead without comment. He passed through the open gates and headed inside the scrapyard, leaving her no choice but to follow. She hated to admit it, but this was the most excitement she'd had all year. After avoiding people for so long, she had suddenly found herself involved in some kind of intrigue with a man she'd just met — a man who could take her in a fight, which was intriguing enough by itself. Sarah might have been rusty, but she was a seasoned practitioner of Aikido, Muy Thai, and Krav Maga. There weren't many people who could put her on her back so easily.

They headed deeper into the scrapyard, passing engine-less car frames and other machinery carcasses. Nobody else was around, which was weird. With the gates hanging wide open, Sarah had expected to see a couple of employees at least.

"We're just around here," said Howard, and slipped behind a rusty shipping container, disappearing from sight. Sarah slowed, her body tensing. She knew nothing of this Howard, but she'd come too far to turn back.

What's the worst that can happen? He kills me? I'm okay with that.

Sarah took a deep breath and sprang around the side of the rusty container, ready to fight at the first sign of danger.

"Hop aboard," said Howard, pointing to an idling helicopter as if it were the most normal thing in the world. The Griffin HAR2 was painted a solid black instead of its typical earthen hues, and the RAF insignia had been scrubbed from its tail boom. Sarah hadn't seen one of the plump, twin-engine helicopters since a training mission in Cyprus ten years ago, so seeing one now made her think of the Mediterranean Sea. She almost felt the sun and salt on her skin. Of all her memories of the Army, it was one of the better ones.

"I'm not getting in that helicopter unless you tell me where we're going."

Howard gave a hand signal to the helicopter pilot and then turned back to face her. "Sarah, your father is a major in the SAS, is he not?"

Sarah flinched. "I don't know what you're on about. My dad is a major in the Royal Logistics Corp. He's in charge of ordering regimental bog roll."

Howard chuckled. "I know everything about you, Sarah, so there's no point in lying. Your father is Major Curtis Stone, and you're the only female in the history of the British Armed Forces who has taken and passed the SAS selection test, despite not being accepted into its ranks afterwards."

Sarah couldn't help but snarl at the recitation of that grim fact. She'd outperformed and outlasted all the men in the SAS selection tests, but she'd been denied entry anyway. The only reason they'd even let her try out in the first place was because her father had pulled some strings, but he had only agreed to do so because he'd been so sure she'd fail. She had proved she was as good as any man, but they turned around and reminded her that it didn't matter. Cocks and balls still ruled the world. She'd gone through two weeks of the grimmest hell imaginable for nothing.

Howard folded his arms. "The Government keeps secrets, Sarah. You know that as well as anyone. I can't give you the location until you've been given the proper clearances. I promise, that at the end of a short helicopter ride, all shall be revealed. After that, you can choose whether to help us or not. A quick signature on an official secrets document and you can leave at your leisure."

Sarah chewed her bottom lip. She was distrustful of anyone with a

Government stamp on their pay cheque, but she had to know what was going on. Why did Howard know so much about her?

"Okay," she said, "but you try to stick a blindfold on me and I'll bite your nose."

Howard raised an eyebrow. "There won't be any need for that."

And there wasn't. When Sarah climbed into the rear of the helicopter, she found that the windows on both sides had been completely blacked out. All she could see was the passenger cabin and the cockpit ahead. The man behind the controls was a giant. His shoulders were twice the width of the seat and bulged out on either side. His neck was as thick as Sarah's thigh, and when he turned to look at her, his face was almost as ugly as hers.

"This is Mandy," said Howard, getting into the co-pilot's seat beside the large man.

"Mandy? Isn't that a girl's name?"

"His name is Manny Dobbs," said Howard. "Mandy is just a nickname. Yours is going to be 'brat' if you don't start being nicer."

"Scarface would suit me better."

"Bit cliche, don't you think?"

"Oldies are the goodies."

Howard turned back to face the front and exchanged a few quiet words with Mandy. Soon the engine started up and the rotors began to spin. The gentle rocking gave way to a sudden lurch and then they were off, airborne.

"The flight will take forty minutes," Howard shouted. "Take a load off and I'll tell you when we're near. There's some earmuffs under your seat."

Sarah put on the earmuffs and eased back into her seat. As she glanced around, she noticed that much of the interior differed from the utilitarian RAF model she knew. Nylon rigging and handholds lined the cabin's roof and additional compartments and cabinets filled the walls. Even the cockpit was sleeker than normal. The stark dashboard had been replaced by something akin to a modern-day 4x4.

Once again, Sarah wondered who she'd agreed to ride along with.

Whoever Howard was, he belonged to no branch of the Military she knew. Perhaps he was a civvie or a member of a private organisation, but the way he fought, and the fact he carried a concealed weapon, made her wonder if that could be true either.

All of the thinking tired her, and the comfort of the chair was sucking her inward, swaddling her like a colicky babe. The vibration of the engine massaged her back. She couldn't help but close her eyes just a little.

AFGHANISTAN, 2008

The heat in Afghanistan was like everything else in Afghanistan: out to kill you. It burned your skin without you realising it, until you took a shower and gritted your teeth as your whole body screamed in torment. While parts of the country were green and pleasant, others were nothing but mud and desert or mountainous rock and shale. When the wind was up, you couldn't open your eyes for fear of getting grit in them. But all that paled compared to the people. There was no difference between the civilians who wanted to help and the Taliban who wanted blood. Both looked and dressed the same. Both waved and smiled whenever they saw British soldiers. It was like fighting shadows — impossible to tell friend from foe.

That was why Sarah was glad she was getting out. She'd entered Sandhurst Military Academy because that was what members of her family did — at least that's what the men did. The Armed Forces were an esteemed tradition in the Stone family, and joining had seemed like a good way to impress her father. Yet it had only horrified him. He had sent her to university to become a lawyer or a doctor, not a butch Jane with a rifle she was too dainty to handle. Her father, most of all, would have been pleased to know she had decided to leave the Army to play homemaker.

Sarah had met her husband Thomas Gellar at Camp Bastion, a British military base the size of Reading. The US Camp Leatherneck adjoined it, and their personnel often strayed onto British turf to share intel, play sports, or take advantage of the softer alcohol restriction, which was why it was no surprise that she had met and fallen in love with an American. While there was always a 'them and us' mentality between the two camps, there was also a mutual respect and admiration. While they might not have been family, the US and UK soldiers were most certainly 'friends'.

Thomas was an officer with the 75th, and the day they had met, he had been visiting with information about a Taliban enclave his squad had surveyed in a surrounding village. He didn't have the forces to handle it himself, and there were no significant US reinforcements in the region. As the village fell under the purview of British patrol routes, Sarah had to hear him out and act on his intel. His offer of sharing a bootleg bottle of wine with her in the Officer's NAAFI that same evening had been above and beyond what was expected, and his wide smile and Floridian drawl had won her over. Eight months and several sneaky bottles of wine later, they had wed in a modest ceremony in front of Camp Bastion's chaplain. She and Thomas had then flittered between bases as often as they could, until their romantic liaisons had eventually led to something unexpected. In the harsh, rocky plains of Afghanistan, Sarah had fallen pregnant with an American Lieutenant. They were going to be a family — albeit, one surrounded by gunfire, hostile territory, and nationality.

Thomas had decided the only way to be together was to quit the Army. Surprisingly, Sarah had been more than happy to oblige. She had never truly wanted this life. Violence and danger were not something she sought, and as she considered raising a family under the Florida sunshine, life in the Army grew more and more undesirable. Her future was elsewhere. The only thing she had left to fear was informing her CO that she'd gotten pregnant in the line of duty. It was frowned upon, to say the least.

But that was a problem for another day. Maybe tomorrow.

Definitely tomorrow.

"Eyes on," said Hamish, her Glaswegian corporal. The hulking lad, with the beaten face of a regimental boxing champion, had the wheel of the Land Rover Snatch-2 between his thick hands. Sarah sat beside him, while in the back were three privates still in nappies. Sergeant Ernie Miller knelt in the rear, cursing at every bump and dip.

The Helmand village of Larurah lay ahead — a confirmed 'friendly' village, but that meant little out here in the desert. In Afghanistan, allegiances shifted overnight with the sands.

They were on their way to meet the village elder and his wife, who had potential information about an influential Taliban leader, Al Al-Sharir. Sarah had been sent as a liaison because she spoke Pashto and had a knack for sorting out lies from the truth. She was to meet up with the female engagement squad at the far side of the village, along with two patrol squads to keep them safe.

Female soldiers couldn't go anywhere in the desert without an escort. Strictly speaking, the British Army didn't like sending women into the field at all, but Sarah had a way of interacting with the locals that forced an exception. She had a talent for prodding at people and making them drop their guard. Her CO, Major Burke, was enlightened enough to treat Sarah based on her ability, not on her sex, so she would often travel alone with only her squad as protection. She guessed her father's name had something to do with that special treatment as well.

Little was known about Al-Sharir, but the native Afghan had taken responsibility for a host of recent attacks against British and American personnel. He hadn't claimed association with the Taliban, yet he'd been spotted with several known members in the region. One week ago, Al-Sharir had commanded a small insurgency that had resulted in an American transport truck being flipped by an antique soviet RPG-7. Three servicemen had died, and a fourth had gone back to his family without his left arm. Finding Al-Sharir had become one of the campaign's biggest priorities after finding Bin Laden himself.

Up ahead, several villagers gathered in front of a banged-up Toyota Corolla. The vehicle's white paint had rusted and the front wheels were missing. The villagers were using the wreck as a place to sit around and chat. Having been 'liberated' from the Taliban, the village was now supposedly safe, but many still felt the constraints of fear. The Taliban was a looming presence over the country and many feared reprisals. The people here weren't free, even after being liberated.

"Slow up," said Sarah.

An overturned watermelon cart blocked the middle of the road, and a lone woman in a cumbersome burka was scurrying to pick up the spilled fruit. No men offered to help — because she was a woman.

"Halt here," said Sarah. "We're going to lend assistance."

Hamish glanced at her and frowned.

"Just do it," she barked. She hadn't fought her way to the rank of Captain to watch ignorant men ignore a woman in need.

"Is there a problem, Captain?" Sergeant Miller stepped out the rear of the Snatch and joined her on the road. He looked concerned.

"Help me get this fruit cart back on its wheels, Miller."

"Do we have the time?"

"We'll make time. Now come on!"

With a sigh, Miller moved up beside the cart and took hold of one side while waiting for Sarah to grab the other. The villagers watched them from a dozen nooks and crannies. There were no children playing, which was strange. Local kids were always interested whenever soldiers arrived.

The woman in the burka bowed and stepped out of the way. She moved over behind an old well, and as Sarah glanced at her, she noticed a missing left hand. Had one of the men in this village taken it from her? Her father, her brother, or some random male who felt he had the right to maim a woman? Did she have to face that man every day?

Sarah hated this country.

"You ready?" asked Miller. "This thing looks like it weighs a tonne."

Sarah grabbed the other side of the watermelon cart. "Let's just get it done."

Miller started a countdown. "After three, ready? One... two..."

Sarah glanced at the woman cowering behind the well, and saw her eyes narrow, crinkling at the edges as if she was flinching.

Or preparing for a loud bang.

"Three!"

"Wait!" Sarah leapt back, but before she had a chance to warn her sergeant, Miller had lifted the watermelon cart all the way up.

Something clicked and Sarah felt herself take flight. Her body became weightless, her senses a confused blur. The world rushed around her in a maelstrom of colour and sound. She hit the dirt but couldn't get up. She saw the watermelon cart ablaze. She saw Miller lying a dozen yards away, both legs missing and a pool of blood soaking the ground beneath him.

Gunfire — *clatter clatter* — filled the air.

Sarah felt weightless again as she began moving backwards. At first she thought she'd been captured, heading towards some nightmarish fate, but then she heard Hamish's reassuring voice in her ringing ears. "You're gun' be right, Captain. Everything gun' be right."

Sarah Groaned. "Miller?"

"He's gone. We need to bolt."

Hamish dragged Sarah over to the Snatch where the three privates were nervously returning fire at unseen enemies. Sarah remembered she was in charge, and that these young men needed her to get them through his safely. It was her fault they were in this situation. It was her fault Miller was dead.

She struggled to get to her knees. "E-Everyone, back inside the Snatch. We're getting out of here, right fucking now."

The three privates fired off a short burst of gunfire from their SA8os, then threw themselves into the rear of the armoured Land Rover. Hamish slid in behind the wheel while Sarah pulled herself in beside him. Before he started the engine, he gave her a concerned look.

"Everything will be fine," she told him. "We'll be sharing a pint down the NAAFI before the day is through, I promise."

Hamish cleared his throat and nodded, but his craggy face was pale as he looked at her.

Sarah thumped the dashboard. "Sodding move it!"

Hamish gunned the engine and shot the car into reverse. He pulled on the handbrake and spun the vehicle around. By the time he shifted into first, ready to speed away, insurgents had lined the road and blocked their exit. They fired AK-47s and a swarm of bullets hit the Snatch's reinforced windscreen.

Sarah clenched her fists. "Shit! They'll rip us to pieces. Turn us the fuck around! We'll head through the village. Anyone gets in the way, run 'em down."

Hamish spun the Snatch around again, giant tyres crunching over watermelon and splintered wood. From the top hatch, one of the privates returned fire.

A cloud of dust coughed up behind the Snatch as they picked up speed. "Watch the well," Sarah shouted as Hamish drove within feet of the crumbling brick reservoir. The woman who'd tricked them was now firing a hunting rifle at them with careful aim. She used the stump of her left arm as a rest for the barrel.

I'll get you for this, you bitch! I was trying to help you.

The woman faded into the distance as Hamish brought the Land Rover up to sixty. Sarah's hands were shaking, and blood dripped down her shirt and onto her bare forearms. She reached up and unfolded the Snatch's sun visor and mirror. A wounded stranger stared back at her. The left side of her face was blackened and bloody. Muscle and tendon glistened within a deep crevice of flesh. A shard of wood lay embedded in her cheek, too deep to extract. She fought back revulsion and tried to stay focused. It was a nasty wound, sure to leave a scar, but it wasn't as severe as it could have been. She could have died. Miller had.

The thought of death made her woozy, and her hand shot to her belly. An overwhelming horror took over her — fear for her unborn child. Hamish's voice brought her back from the brink of panic. "Which way?" he demanded. His usual gravelly voice was now high-pitched and overwrought. "Captain, which way?"

Sarah searched ahead. The village was a maze of alleyways and crumbling, flat-topped buildings, each one a perfect hiding spot for an RPG or high-powered rifle. Death could come a dozen different ways. "Go... um... go left. Damn it, go left!"

Hamish spun the wheel and whipped the Snatch around to the left, slotting the vehicle into an alleyway between a mosque and a two-story domicile. Villagers leapt into the cover of doorways, yelling out insults as they narrowly avoided the Land Rover's giant tyres. Some threw stones which bounced off the bonnet. Hamish put his foot down.

The gunfire faded behind them.

The private pulled himself back inside the Snatch's rear cabin and sat down, panting and gibbering with relief. The battle was over. They were home free.

Sarah put her fingertips to her face and winced at the pain. Now that the danger was over, she started freaking out.

I need to know that my baby is okay.

She clutched her stomach and sobbed.

Hamish glared. "Get your shit together, Captain."

Sarah choked back a sob and nodded. "I... I screwed up. This is all my fault."

Hamish kept his eyes forward, concentrating on the dirt road. "Way I see it, the bitch with the watermelons is to blame. I dinae know bout you, but I'm coming back here with the Second Royals to flatten this place to dust. Focus on that, not on what you coulda done."

Sarah nodded. He was right. There was nothing to be done now except respond to the situation. She needed to get back and report. Camp Bastion awaited less than two hours away. "Step on it," she yelled, gritting her teeth as shock gave way to lucid pain and rising agony. "The sooner we get out of here, the sooner we can come back and rain down hell on this goddamn village."

"Amen to that," said Hamish, flooring the accelerator. He pulled right, putting the village behind them.

She heard another click.

The last thing She saw was the horizon disappearing from the windscreen as the nose of the Snatch rose into the air, riding on a blanket of roaring flames.

4

THE CUCKOO'S NEST

Sarah bucked forwards and gasped. For a second, she thought she'd been struck by that IED all over again, but when she saw Howard staring back at her from the cockpit, she registered where she was.

"You okay?" Howard asked.

"Just a dream."

"Good timing. We've arrived."

Sarah went to look out the window, then remembered they were blacked-out. "Where are we?"

Howard smirked. "Not until you sign the paperwork."

Sarah rolled her eyes. Her cheap, yet ever-reliable, Casio watch informed her she'd been asleep for thirty minutes. Not bad, for her.

The helicopter tilted forward and rotated, losing altitude. Despite his lumbering appearance, Mandy kept impressive control over the aircraft and brought them down smoothly. When they touched earth, Sarah barely felt it.

Howard hopped out of the front passenger seat and slid the rear passenger door open. Sunlight flooded in and Sarah shielded her eyes as she got out and removed her earmuffs.

"Good day for it," said Howard.

"That remains to be seen." Sarah looked around. Green fields and trees stretched for miles in every direction. "We're in the middle of nowhere," she noted.

"Not as far from civilisation as you might think, but we have our privacy, that's for sure."

Sarah turned another circle, hoping to catch something she might have missed the first time, but there was nothing. "Why have you brought me to an empty field?"

Mandy stepped out from behind the helicopter and stood beside Howard like a marble statue. Howard pulled a small tablet from inside his jacket and held it to his mouth. "We're here," he said and ended the call.

A sudden vibration shot through the ground beneath their feet followed by a loud *clunk*. Howard moved to a patch of weeds, kicking them flat, and after a few moments, he reached out and grabbed something — a metal handle. He yanked up a hatch hidden in the ground, Scraps of soil and clumps of mud slid off of it as it lifted, and a gaping hole revealed itself.

"Welcome to the Earthworm," said Howard.

Sarah raised an eyebrow. "Earthworm? What the hell is that?"

"It's just what we call this place. Its real name is MCU Facility One."

"How many other facilities are there?"

"None."

Sarah cleared her throat. "So why give it a number?"

"Originally, there were going to be more."

"So what happened?"

"The economy collapsed. We had two more sites halfway-built, but the recession caused the funding for the projects to fall through. MCU Facility One is the only site that got built to completion."

"So, this hole in the ground is... what? A secret base?"

Howard smiled. "Why don't we find out?"

"Sod it, I came this far."

Howard led her over to the opening while Mandy stayed behind with the helicopter. There was a long staircase inside the hole, and it descended deep into the earth.

Howard waved a hand. "After you."

Sarah stepped inside and started down while Howard pulled the hatch back into place above their heads. The sunlight disappeared and LED strip lighting flicked on and illuminated the staircase. It seemed to go down forever.

It got colder as they descended, and Sarah began to feel claustrophobic. A hundred tons of soil could bury her at any moment.

Howard caught up to her on the staircase. "You okay? You looked a little—"

"I'm fine. Just not a fan of confined spaces."

"We'll be at the facility soon."

"Why is this place buried underground, anyway? Even MI5 has an office on the Thames."

"MI5 is known to exist. Our agency is not. The MCU was set up in response to the 9/11 terrorist attacks as a joint enterprise between the US and UK governments. Its purpose is to provide a joint-run task force that can follow up leads on both continents rapidly and cohesively. The US had three facilities of its own until recently, but this is the only one we have on our side of the Atlantic. We share whatever intel we have with the Pentagon, and they with us. There are no secrets between our two governments under the purview of this task force, and we are a united front against all known threats to our nations."

Sarah clip-clopped down the steps, hoping to reach the end soon. How much deeper would it go? "So, it's kind of like a US-UK bromance."

"I suppose you could call it that. One thing we learned after 9/11 was that much could be gained by working in tandem, rather than pursuing only our own interests. President Bush and Prime Minister Blair agreed to commission the MCU and give it autonomy to act as it saw fit, answering only to the president and prime minister themselves. Nowadays, we answer to President Conrad and Prime Minister Breslow."

Sarah whistled. "Those are some swanky connections. You can probably tell me if Elvis is still alive, huh? What about Benny Hill? Who did he leave his millions to? What's the deal with Kim Kardashian?"

Howard ignored her and they came to the bottom of the long staircase. Sarah let out a sigh of relief. Howard stepped up to a keypad and thumbed in a code. The console chirped at him and a round door slid aside into the earth.

For once, Sarah had nothing to say. The vast open space before her was the size of a football stadium. Her claustrophobia disappeared.

"Told you it opened up," said Howard, patting her on back and making her stumble forward with her mouth wide open.

"Welcome to the Major Crimes Unit."

5

TAKING THE TOUR

"Welcome to the Major Crimes Unit." Howard pressed a button on the wall and closed the hatch behind them.

Sarah continued staring in awe. The ceilings were fifty-feet high with massive vents in them. Banks of computers lined every wall, and a desk large enough to seat twenty people took up the centre of the room. At one end of the desk was a large monitor.

Sarah looked around for people, but there weren't any. All the computers were switched off. "Where is everyone?"

"We have offices in the back. Come on, I'll take you there now."

Sarah followed Howard, taking it all in, but the more she concentrated on her surroundings, the less impressive they became. The equipment was not high-tech, as she'd first believed. The monitors were old CRT units, and the computers were square and clunky. A thick layer of dust covered everything.

"When was this place built?"

"It was commissioned after 9/11, so it's over ten years old."

"And when was it last used?"

Howard understood Sarah's confusion. "The facility is bigger than we need. The team confines itself to a smaller section at the front.

Reason we call this place the Earthworm is that it's long and narrow — makes it harder to bomb. We just entered through the tail, but we do our work in the head."

"Right..."

At the far end of the room was another hatchway. A lone security guard in black fatigues stood next to it, and Howard nodded to the man as they drew near. The guard nodded back.

Sarah looked the man up and down. "What do you do if you want the toilet? Do they give you a bucket?"

The guard said nothing.

Sarah shrugged her shoulders. "I'm getting the impression people don't like talking to me."

Howard inputted another code and the next hatchway opened. The area that followed was much more confined, just a narrow corridor branching off in several directions and leading to various doorways. Many of the adjacent rooms had glass partition-walls, allowing one to see inside, but Sarah was concerned to see that most of them were as the previous rooms had been.

"We're still not at the head yet, I take it?"

"No. This is the middle. It's mostly offices and research rooms here, and the infirmary is just up ahead. We have a doctor on-site who works there. Dr Bennett. You'll meet her later."

"Can't wait."

The Earthworm was huge, admittedly, but vastly under-utilised. The middle section must have contained four-dozen empty offices, and while they passed by it only briefly, the infirmary was large enough to handle a minor epidemic. The place must have cost a fortune.

So why not make use of it?

They came to yet another hatchway, but there was no guard at this one. Instead, a bulky CCTV camera kept watch. Howard inputted another code and the door slid away. They then headed into what Sarah suspected was the Earthworm's head section. This part of the facility was warm, and scented with the heady pong of bleach and air freshener. A corkboard affixed one wall with multi-coloured pins spearing notes and memos in places.

"Some of us pretty much live here," said Howard as they progressed. "There are dorms for those of us who want to use them."

Sarah frowned. "Bit unusual for a bunch of civil servants. Do *you* stay here?"

"Not usually. I keep a place in the city about a thirty minutes away. Sometimes I stay here, if circumstances require."

"We're near a city then?" said Sarah. "Interesting. We travelled forty minutes from Birmingham by helicopter so, assuming we flew around 130mph on average, that would most likely put us either in Greater London or Manchester, probably London. Someplace rural on the outskirts maybe. The drive here takes you thirty minutes so, with traffic in and out of the city..." She put her finger against her lips and thought for a few seconds. "My best guess would be that we're in Uxbridge, or maybe as far out as High Wycombe."

Howard's lip twitched, which let Sarah know she was right — or at least close enough. For once, she was the one smirking at Howard.

Howard changed the subject and ushered her onwards. "I suspect everybody is in the briefing room waiting for us."

Unlike the rest of the facility, the following room was high tech and in obvious use. Paper-thin flat screens lined the walls and blinking apparatuses sat on desks.

Three people sat around a glass table in the centre of the room, but they all stood when they saw Sarah. The largest of them was a middle-aged Asian man with a shiny bald head. From the steel bracelet around his right wrist, Sarah suspected he was Sikh. Beside him was a diminutive brunette with impeccable make-up and a clean, white lab coat. The third person was a young man with mousy hair and the gleaming bright blue eyes of a child.

They all flinched — a nearly imperceptible flicker in their eyes — when they saw Sarah's scars, but she was so used to the reaction that she didn't let it worry her.

The Sikh offered his hand. "Ms Stone, thank you for coming."

Sarah shook the man's hand but said nothing.

"I can't say she came entirely willingly," said Howard, "but we got there in the end, didn't we, Sarah?"

Sarah watched the Sikh man, clearly the one in charge. "Why am I here? I'd like some answers."

"My name is Director Palu and I am in charge here at the MCU. I assume Howard has shared at least a little about why you've been brought here."

Sarah shrugged. "He told me we were somewhere outside London, near High Wycombe."

Howard spluttered. "I... I never— She guessed!"

Director Palu waved his hand dismissively and smiled at Sarah. "Your guess was correct. We're beneath some fallow farmland owned by the Government. It's considered a patch of wasteland to the public, so we're relatively undisturbed."

Sarah was astounded such a place existed, but she wasn't about to reveal her surprise. These situations were a power-play. The more she could keep them off their game, the better the advantage she'd have.

"Please, take a seat, Ms Stone. Officer Hopkins and I will conduct a quick debrief and be right back with you. In the meantime, please fill out this official secrets document. I'm sure you're familiar. I'll leave you with Agents Jacobs and Bennett."

Howard and Palu left the room.

Without being asked, Sarah took a seat at the table opposite the young man, and scrawled a signature for one *Sybil Fawlty* on the OFS document before swatting it aside.

"So, are you here for work experience or somethings?"

The young man's bony cheeks went bright red. "N-No, Captain. I work for the MCU. Well, sort of. Today's my last day."

"Bit young for a career change already, aren't you?"

"I'm twenty-four!" He glanced at the table. Sarah wondered if he couldn't face her scars. "I'm not cut out for this place," he muttered. "I tried, but..."

"But what?"

"But he screwed up," said the brunette in the lab coat. She had an American accent that reminded Sarah of her late husband's Floridian drawl. Not quite the same. "He screws up a lot."

The kid blushed a deeper shade of red.

"What's your name?" Sarah asked.

"His name is Bradley Jacobs," answered the American woman.

"And what's *your* name, sweetheart?"

"My name is *Dr* Jessica Bennett, not *sweetheart*."

"Oh, so you're Bennett? Look, Doc, I understand that being a git is all the rage in medicine since Hugh Laurie moved away from comedy, but I'm trying to have a conversation with Bradley here, and all I can hear is your yap."

Dr Bennett shot up from her chair and slapped her palms on the glass table. She glared at Sarah, but couldn't hold her gaze for more than a few seconds. So she stormed out of the room.

Sarah returned her gaze to Bradley. "Do my scars frighten you?"

"What? No! Why would they?"

"Because it looks like someone lit my face on fire and wiped their arse with it."

"No, it doesn't. You just look... different. Anyway, your scars don't bother me. They obviously bother *you*."

Sarah smirked, surprised by the comeback. The kid had deflected her button-pushing and prodded back at hers. "Why are you leaving? Did you screw up that badly?"

Bradley nodded. "I froze in the field. I was with Agent Hopkins, trying to find intel on a target. We were investigating an old warehouse when a group of men drew on us. I froze, and was too late shouting a warning. If it wasn't for the strike team, Howard would've got shot."

Sarah shrugged. "It happens. Especially the first time."

"It was my second time. I've frozen twice when it matters. I'm going to get someone killed if I don't leave. Just waiting for the clearance to come, but today should be my last day."

Sarah felt sorry for Bradley. The kid had a moral centre clear for all to see, but he lacked confidence. Maybe *his* dad was an overbearing bastard. Or maybe his mum had been too affectionate. "How did you ever end up in a place like this?"

"My father."

Sarah rolled her eyes. "Thought so."

"He was a physicist; worked on some of Britain's first nuclear power plants. He wanted me to do Physics too, which I did — at Cambridge. I specialised in nuclear physics and wrote a paper. It was about the application of nuclear components for the purposes of terrorism. Long story short, the paper raised questions with the Government's counter-terrorism officers and I was headhunted to join the MCU as a theoretical consultant. At first, I thought I would be like James Bond, but it soon became clear that the last thing I am is a hero."

"There's no such thing as heroes, kid. Heroes exist in storybooks to convince us that humanity isn't a cauldron full of shit."

Bradley shook his head. "I don't believe that. Deep down, I don't believe you do either, Captain."

Sarah stared at him, and couldn't help but laugh at his defiance. "All I have deep down, kid, is an ulcer. You should stop trying to find the best in people. An attitude like that won't do you any favours. Especially not in national security."

Bradley shrugged. "Probably best I'm getting out of here then. You'll make a good replacement."

Sarah blanched. "What?"

"I assume Howard brought you here to replace me. Today is my last day and they've got *you* here. I don't imagine it's a coincidence."

"I came here to help with a single matter. I don't plan on giving you people more than an afternoon of my time. Forgive me if working for the Government isn't exactly an appealing prospect."

"Maybe I'm wrong," said Bradley with a shrug. "To tell you the truth, nobody tells me anything since I decided to leave."

Sarah's expression softened, at least as much as her scars allowed. She knew how it felt to be abandoned by superiors.

Director Palu and Howard re-entered the room and took a seat at the table. When Palu realised someone was missing, he frowned. "Did Dr Bennett introduce herself before leaving?"

"Yeah," said Sarah, "right after she showed me pictures of all her cats."

Palu chuckled. "Yes, Jessica does love her cats. Her little children, she calls them."

Sarah grinned. "Are you going to tell me why you dragged me here like a bunch of cold war spies, or do I need to beat it out of someone?"

"Don't think that worked out too well for you the last time," said Howard, smirking at her. "How many times did I knock you down? Three times, was it?"

"Twice. Anyway, I like to go a few rounds before knocking the other guy out. You'll learn that about me, *Howie*."

Palu let his meaty hands drop to the table with a thud, recapturing their attention. "Perhaps we should get to the main thrust of things. You're no doubt curious as to why we brought you here, Ms Stone."

"Your powers of deduction astound me. I can see why they put you in charge."

Palu sniffed, and a brief glimmer of frustration shimmered on his face. It pleased Sarah that she was getting on his nerves. Authority, in all its forms, needed challenging.

"You're aware of the explosion in Knutsford this past Sunday?"

Sarah nodded.

"The man responsible was an ex-postal worker named Jeffrey Blanchfield. It is believed he had some kind of grudge. He was recently widowed, and police reports suggest he and his wife were having ongoing issues with their neighbours. There were reports of vandalism, threats, noise complaints... After Jeffrey's wife died, he seemed to blame his neighbours. He confronted them, and they responded by cracking his jaw and leaving him with a broken hip. Six months later, Jeffrey gassed his neighbours in their sleep and then blew up a village fete two miles from his home."

"Good for him," said Sarah, but regretted it. Even Bradley moaned at the insensitivity. It was bad, even for her.

Palu stared at her. "Forty people died, Ms Stone. Another eighty were injured. It was one of the worst terrorist attacks in our country's history. Everyone was packed together in a confined space."

Sarah nearly apologised, but decided there was little to be gained from it. "An old man with a vendetta does not a terrorist make. He had no agenda other than revenge. Revenge on the world."

Howard leant forwards on his elbows. "That's where you're wrong, Sarah."

Palu nodded his agreement. "I think you better watch something we received this morning." He produced a tiny remote control from the breast pocket of his shirt and pointed it at one of the television screens. The TV blinked to life and a grainy video played. A man with good, yet accented English appeared, flanked by two others — a stocky man with hairy arms and a smaller figure hiding in the shadows to the left.

The man in the centre began to speak. "People of the United Kingdom, today you have been struck by a warrior. A martyr in the battle for mankind itself. Through Jeffrey Blanchfield's sacrifice, all of you have been given a chance to reflect upon your nation's depravity. Many were taken this day, and soon more, but if you seek the holy path, all may not yet be lost. I am Al Al-Sharir, and Allah has given me a divine mission to save you from your own moral annihilation."

Sarah stared hard at the screen. The video feed was grubby, possibly from a VHS cassette tape or filmed with a low-spec mobile phone. The man who was delivering the message was wearing *shalwar kameez* — loose pyjama-like trousers beneath a long tunic. He was also wearing a red and white *shemagh* — a checked headscarf. A symbol of a scimitar emblazoned his right wrist, inked in henna so as not to permanently alter the temple of his flesh. The symbol of the sword was something all members of *Shab Bekheir* wore.

Sarah turned to Palu and shrugged her shoulders. "They're just trying to capitalise on a tragedy. It's terrorism 101."

Palu shook his head. "Just keep watching."

The man on the video was still talking. "In twenty-four hours, your nation shall be struck again. Jeffrey Blanchfield was avenging his dead wife who was murdered by your decadent ways. The next attacks will be greater, and will not stop until Prime Minister Breslow denounces the people of the United Kingdom as heathens and sinners. Only then may you all be saved. *Shab Bekheir* will show you the way."

Howard tapped his fingertips against the glass desk and said, "The videocassette was sent to Downing Street from the Knutsford post office. The postage date was two days before the attack."

"I tried to track down the sender," explained Bradley, "but the post office doesn't have CCTV. The fee was paid in cash."

Sarah leant back in her chair and released a long, lingering sigh. There was lots to consider. Many things that made no sense.

"What are your thoughts?" Howard asked her. "The reason I brought you here is because you've dealt with Al-Sharir before, firsthand."

"Yes," said Palu. "What do you make of the videotape, Ms Stone?"

Sarah chewed at the inside of her cheek for a moment, then said, "My first thought is that it's fake."

6

LEARNING THE ROPES

"**W**hat do you mean it's fake?" Howard seemed angered by her assertion. "I verified it myself."

"Do you people do this for a living?" she asked. "No wonder terrorists think they can win."

Howard glared, but Palu took over the conversation. "Why do you think it's fake, Ms Stone?"

"I don't think it, I know it."

"How?" Bradley shook his head. "It looks real to me. We've identified the accent as Pashto, which is consistent with members of *Shab Bekhier*. Their origin is the southern regions of Afghanistan where you served, Captain."

Sarah, for a brief second, doubted herself. It had been a long time since she'd been in the game, and even longer since she'd been in Afghanistan. Did she have cause to be so confident?

Hell yes, I do.

"The first thing telling me this wasn't Al Al-Sharir, is the red and white headscarf that is more common to Jordanians. Al-Sharir and his men operate in Afghanistan. They would wear *Pakol* or *Lungee*."

"That's a bit of a stretch," said Howard in a voice patronising enough that she wanted to punch him.

"Fair enough. Then how about the fact the man standing to the right of the frame is white? His hands and wrists are visible and you can see tufts of fair hair on his forearm. Al-Sharir might take advantage of a grieving old man to blow up a village, but I doubt he would work closely with a westerner. He's too much of an extremist. To him, we're two different species, two different animals fighting for supremacy. He wouldn't trust someone he considered part of another tribe."

"That's another big jump," said Palu. "The white man could be a Muslim of mixed birth."

Sarah nodded. "You might be right, but the main reason I know that the man delivering the message is not Al Al-Sharir is because the scimitar on his wrist is pointing the wrong way. The tip should be pointing *at* him, not away."

Howard tutted. "It's a henna tattoo. I'm sure Al-Sharir pays no attention to a bit of ink on his arm."

Sarah groaned. Was he really this much of an idiot? "That only proves how incompetent these impostors are and how little you people know about the man you're blaming this on. That tattoo means everything to members of *Shab Bekheir*. Al-Sharir would only ever have the scimitar pointing at himself because it signifies his willingness to die for Allah. It signifies him being a willing martyr. If it pointed the other way, at his enemies, it would signify that *they* were the ones dying for a righteous cause." Sarah folded her arms in front of her chest. "You've been played. This whole thing is some kind of dupe. The small details are the ones that matter most."

Palu remained still. He seemed more willing to believe her now, but there was still a degree of obstinacy in his tone. "How can you be so sure?"

"How can I be so sure? Maybe because I've met Al-Sharir and I know his way of doing things. He pays too much attention to detail to be the guy in that video. I don't know who's behind the attack on

Sunday, if it was more than just an angry widower, but I'm telling you it was not Al-Sharir."

Palu rubbed at his forehead and stood up. "Okay, let me check a few things out. Howard, Bradley, a moment, please?"

All three men left the room.

Sarah was then left alone for more than an hour. For all she knew, they were planning on leaving her there all day. Patience wasn't a virtue of hers, so eventually she decided to interrupt them. She had a life to get back to — a shitty life, maybe, but one she preferred to waiting around for a bunch of Government pricks to take her seriously. She'd already helped more than she'd intended.

She headed in the same direction as the men and found the door they had passed through unlocked. In the next corridor, she was faced with half a dozen doors leading off to various rooms. It was a maze. The sound of voices, however, led her to the second door on the left. She was planning to just shove her way inside, but then she realised she could gain a lot more by listening. She knelt and placed her ear against the door.

"She's a liability," said a voice she decided was Palu. "It was a mistake bringing her here, Howard. I should never have authorised you to bring her here."

"I know," said Howard. "I assumed she'd jump at the chance to get away from her pathetic life, but she's done nothing but fight me the whole time. She's not the woman she was in the Army. She's a train wreck."

"Guys, you're missing the point," said Bradley. "Captain Stone was right. The man in that video isn't Al Al-Sharir. You brought her here to offer her expertise on Shab Bekhier and that's exactly what she's done. I think she'll make a great replacement for me. You need someone that's faced these monsters on their own turf, someone with real experience."

Palu grunted. "What are you talking about, Bradley? She's not going to replace you. We needed her expertise and we've had it. The sooner we send her on her way, the better."

"Oh." Bradley sounded deflated. "Who will replace me then?"

"No one," said Palu. "The cost to train another officer is too high. It's unfortunate things didn't work out with you, Bradley, as we're now left even more shorthanded."

"Sorry."

"Nothing that can be done about it now. Your clearances have come through, so you're free to leave as soon as we finish with Ms Stone."

"Captain Stone," Bradley corrected. "I think if you showed her some respect she'd be more helpful. She's given up a lot for her country and has nothing to show for it. Asking for her help isn't enough, we need to earn it from her. She was a Captain in the British Army, and got wounded fighting for our country, facing the very enemy we're trying to stop. Don't you think her help will come in useful?"

Howard disagreed. "We don't need her help. It was a mistake bringing her here. She's been nothing but a pain. I thought she'd be... different."

"You mean you thought she'd be grateful," said Bradley. "That's the problem. You're acting like you're the one doing her a favour when really it's the other way around."

"Bradley, you have awfully big opinions for a guy who's about to walk out the door."

"Let's just get back to the conference room," said Palu. "We've already been too long."

Sarah flinched back from the doorway, then rushed back to the conference room before she betrayed that she'd been listening. The more she knew and the less they did, the better.

The office door opened, and Sarah slipped back into the conference room just as Palu and the others exited. By the time they returned to the conference room, Sarah was sitting with her boots up on the desk. "You chimps finished with your tea party?" she said.

Palu cleared his throat and remained standing. "It appears you were right... *Captain.* We have accessed existing surveillance footage of

Al-Sharir and reviewed previously verified footage of Shab Bekhier. The small details don't match. Based on that, we're assuming Sunday's attack was the work of somebody else. Perhaps the videotape itself is the act of terror, hoping to put us all on high alert."

"Probably," said Sarah. "If a suicide bomb in Cheshire wasn't enough."

Palu sighed. "With all of our technology and surveillance, the one thing we can't do is police every person on the planet. The fact the bomber was an elderly white man meant we were unprepared. He didn't exactly fit our profile of an extremist."

"One thing I know about crazy," said Sarah, "is that it doesn't wear a uniform or keep set hours. You can't profile hate. It can infect anyone."

"Do you think there'll be further attacks, Captain?" asked Bradley. "What's your gut feeling?"

Sarah pulled her boots off the desk and looked at them. "I'm not sure. If the men in the video are organised enough to be behind Sunday's attack, then perhaps there's a larger threat. Why the charade though? Why pretend to be Shab Bekhier? If the real Al-Sharir finds out somebody's using his name, they'll be signing their own death warrants within the terrorist community. Best case scenario, it's some-body trying to exacerbate an already distressing situation. Maybe a small group of extremists talked Jeffrey Blanchfield into blowing himself up. Perhaps that's all there is to it."

Palu cleared his throat and seemed to think. "I thank you for your help, Captain. It was enlightening."

"Yes," said Bradley. "You definitively know your stuff."

"Thank you." Sarah couldn't be a bitch to Bradley anymore, not after she had heard him go to bat for her in the other room.

"I'll take you back up top," said Howard. "Mandy will take you wherever you want to go."

"I've always wanted to go to Disney World. I hear they have a giant golf ball you can ride around in."

"Domestic flights only, I'm afraid," added Palu.

"Come on, then. Sooner I get out of this place, the sooner I can get the Government stink off me."

There was a sudden electronic chirping, and everyone looked to Palu. He plucked a small tablet from his trouser pocket, and then with his free hand motioned for Howard and Sarah to get going. Sarah was more than happy to oblige. Her claustrophobia was returning.

Palu's face suddenly turned horror-stricken.

Howard tried to pull Sarah away, but she shrugged him off. She remained standing by the glass conference table, watching Palu and trying to work out what had got him so concerned. "When, sir? Yes, I understand, sir. We had no intel concerning that. I... yes, I agree, sir. I'll await your instructions." He hung up.

Howard seemed to realise something was up now as well. "Who was on the call, sir?"

Palu lowered his head as though he was going to throw up. "That was the Home Secretary. There's been another attack. Another suicide bombing."

Howard kicked a nearby chair. "Damn it! Where?"

Palu closed his eyes and pressed a palm against his temple. "Three more villages — Studley, Dartmouth, Arborfield — all hit within ten minutes of each other. Downing Street is still getting all the information. They'll forward it to us."

Sarah bent forward using the desk for support. Three villages all at once? The country was under a full-scale attack.

Bradley looked close to tears. He was shaking his head in disbelief. "It makes no sense, hitting tiny villages instead of bigger targets. What's the significance?"

Sarah knew right away. "It means nobody is safe. It means you don't have to live in London or Manchester or Birmingham to be the target of a terrorist attack. You can live in the smallest hamlet and still get blown to smithereens. It's smart, if you think about it. Terrorists want to cause terror. What better way than to make the entire country afraid of being attacked? No place is safe anymore. The whole of the United Kingdom is about to become terrified."

"Shit," said Bradley.

"Yeah," said Sarah. "Shit is the right word because it just hit the fan."

7

SITTING THE TEST

Palu turned on the television and a breaking news report came on. A BBC journalist stood before a scene of devastation. The quaint fishing village of Dartmouth was burning. Its picturesque harbour had become ground zero of a devastating attack. Bodies cluttered the marina, floating face down in the water. Further out, a blackened ferry sank into the River Dart's estuary. Yachts and pleasure cruisers sank around it. Dogs howled while shell shocked survivors wept on the quayside. An ash-covered child wandered around with no parent or guardian to watch her. The little girl cried out for her mummy.

The reporter wiped a tear from his eye and cleared his throat before speaking. "T-Today, as I report to you, I am lost for words. After the events of this past Sunday, Britain was a nation already in mourning. Today, the tragedy has gotten even worse as yet another mass killing has occurred. Worse still, the village of Dartmouth behind me was not the only target. The villages of Studley and Arborfield have also been hit by what appears to be a co-ordinated terrorist attack against small population centres. The death toll and devastation Britain has witnessed in the last forty-eight hours is unparalleled. The Prime Minister is due to give a speech within the hour, but right now the question on everybody's mind is, who is behind this? I'm Jack Millis, reporting to you from the village of Dartmouth, Devonshire."

Sarah felt winded. If anything, Britain had finally started to put the fear of terrorism behind it. Bungled attempts at carrying bombs aboard planes in shoes, and other useless attempts, had made the modern-day terrorist a cartoonish villain foiled at every turn. They had become fodder for South Park and stand-up comedians — a joke, not a threat.

Someone had screwed up here though. Sarah clenched her fists as she glowered at the three men in the room. This was their job. They were supposed to stop things like this from happening. "Did you people know anything about this? Was there anything you could have done?"

Palu answered the question with a firm, authoritative *no*. "If there was anything we could have done, we would have done it."

Sarah shook her head and tried to understand. "You told me your job is to catch terrorists, so how the hell did this happen?"

Bradley still had tears in his eyes. "Captain, I promise you we do all we can."

"Shut up!" Sarah shouted. "People are dead because none of you caught this. Why did you people even bring me here? You're a bunch of idiots."

Palu strode towards Sarah. For a moment, it looked as though he might strike her, but instead he looked her square in the eye. "If you think we're a bunch of idiots, Captain, then help us. Help us find who's responsible."

"No," said Sarah. She couldn't help these people. They were under-manned and ignorant. And she was broken and of no use to anyone. They called her Captain, but the truth was she was nothing. The thought of diving back into the dangerous world, filled with murderous men and their monstrous activities, was enough to make her feel faint. Her father had warned her not to get involved in such serious business, and she had paid the price for defying him. She wasn't stupid enough to do it a second time. She turned towards the door.

"Sarah!" Palu shouted. "Before you leave, let me show you something."

Sarah turned. "You people don't even want me here. I heard you talking about me in the other room."

Palu stared her right in the eyes. There was sadness there, but something much darker bubbling beneath. "I just got the stats on the latest attacks. You should see them before you decide to leave." He pointed the remote at the television. "I may have wanted you gone, but right now we need all the help we can get. You have knowledge of Shab Bakhier that we can use. Can you really walk away, knowing you could help us?"

Sarah stared at the figures on the screen.

UK TERRORIST ATTACKS, MAY 2014

Knutsford: 40 fatalities (6 children), 86 injured
Arborfield: 36 fatalities (2 children), 47 injured
Dartmouth: 94 fatalities (19 children), 119 injured
Studley: 12 fatalities (2 children), 4 injured
— Total deceased: 182 (29 children)

"Okay," she said. "I'll stay."

8

READY FOR ANYTHING

Everybody took a seat at the conference table. Palu recalled Dr Bennett from the infirmary and she didn't look happy about it. According to Palu, the American was an expert in bioterrorism, psych profiling, and combat casualty care.

Bradley was told to collect his things and leave. His duty had expired, and they could no longer share classified information with him. That didn't sit well with Sarah. She knew that resigning from active service was a long-winded affair — it had probably been in the works for weeks — but without the option of replacing Bradley it seemed wasteful letting him go. Palu had said he needed all the help he could get.

Palu's tablet hadn't stopped chirping since they'd looked at the statistics on screen. Every message he received seemed to make him more anxious. Sarah felt sorry for him. He may have been in charge of MCU, but he was clearly a mutt with many masters.

"Prime Minister Breslow has just given a speech from Downing Street," Palu informed them. "She's halted the exit-strategy for Afghanistan and is even reinforcing the number of troops in the region.

She's keen to display Britain's strength. A request for aid has been made to President Conrad."

Howard huffed. "The Yanks won't go for it. The American people are tired of war. Conrad will leave us hanging, I guarantee it."

"That's a little unfair," said Bradley, re-entering from the back of the room with his things in tow. "The Americans have aided us countless times."

"Really?" said Howard. "So where are they now? MCU is supposed to be a joint enterprise, but it's been over a year since they made any contribution to the cause."

"They gave you *me*," said Dr Bennett snippily. "That's hardly *nothing*."

Howard rolled his eyes. "You were a token gesture. The US closed their own MCU facilities and their funding has dropped through the floor. We've been abandoned."

Bennett folded her arms, and when she spoke again, her tone was angry. "Do not refer to me as a *token*. I'm the most qualified person in this whole darned facility. I'd sooner be back home if y'all have no further need of my services."

"You are highly valued," said Palu. "Now more than ever."

Dr Bennett nodded, apparently satisfied.

"What's the deal here?" Sarah butted in. "I mean, why is this place empty? Why is there a skeleton crew inside a place that must have cost hundreds of millions? A single guy guarding the entrance, for Christ's sake."

"They're closing us down, Captain," said Palu. "Not this minute, not this month, but the writing is on the wall. After 9/11, the CIA, FBI, Police, Interpol, MI5 & 6, Scotland Yard, the Army... they were all given huge additional funding and free-reign. It was messy and uncoordinated. The MCU was supposed to bring everyone together; to stop the in-fighting and bring cohesion to the US and UK counter-terrorism operations."

Sarah's eyes narrowed. "So what happened?"

"The economy happened. Other agencies resented our funding

and held back their intel, refusing to co-operate. The MCU became benign and costly. In the last six years, we've been scaled back by nine-tenths and stripped of most of our authority. Now, the only intel we get is when other agencies throw us a bone. We live off their scraps. The initial plan was for MCU to be at the centre of everything, but now we're seen as a joke. Regardless, we still do everything we can to help protect this country."

"So why the hell are you letting Bradley go? Having a member of an already under manned team quitting is bullshit."

"It's already done," said Palu, eyeing Bradley who was still lingering by the door.

"Then undo it," said Sarah. "You want my help, Bradley stays. The more able bodies you have, the better. Wouldn't you agree?"

"Fine," muttered Palu. "Bradley, I hereby deny your resignation. You are to return to work immediately until such time that the current crisis ends. Sarah, you too are operating on a limited mandate. We will discuss your role here in greater depth once we deal with the current situation."

Bradley took a seat back at the table, looking nervous but committed.

Howard tossed his head back and let out a sigh. "So what do we have so far?"

"Not much," said Palu. "The Army has bomb specialists going through each location as we speak. It looks like more suicide vests. The Upper Ferry was the target in Dartmouth; a local pub in Studley; and in Arborfield, a supermarket was hit. I'm getting statements for all three attacks and CCTV footage from the pub in Studley."

Sarah frowned. "You did all that from your phone?"

Palu nodded. "It's a mobile sat link with a proprietary operating system. We've been scaled back, but I can still access the Government's internal systems. Anything the police or other UK agencies have that isn't restricted, I can get. We even have limited access to the FBI and CIA. Our biggest asset, however, is our liaison at Downing Street."

Sarah was impressed. Most of what she'd seen of the MCU had

been pitiful, but these people were slowly gaining her respect. "Do we have any files on this Jeffrey Blanchfield?" she asked. "We need to know if he had any connections with known terrorist groups."

"Maybe he was part of Al-Qaeda's over-60 cell," Dr Bennett quipped.

"Maybe," said Sarah, acting as if she hadn't noticed the American woman's sarcasm. "There's a chance this here attack was connected to today's commotion, y'all. Old Jeffrey may have done rubbed shoulders with some mighty wrong people."

Dr Bennett scowled.

"I agree," said Bradley, oblivious to the cold war going on between the two women. "We need to know if there's a link between Sunday's attack and today's. I'll get on it right now." He pulled a wafer-thin laptop out of his satchel and started typing away.

"Bring up the CCTV footage for the pub in Studley," said Palu. "Apparently there's clear footage of the suicide bomber."

Something on Howard beeped. He pulled out a phone the same as Palu's. "There's been another video. Released on the Internet, this time. Already has a million hits on Clip Share."

"They must be angry we kept their first video secret," said Dr Bennett. "They want to make sure they get credit this time."

Sarah sighed. "Now they can claim the Government kept the cause of Sunday's attack secret. It's a good way to sow even more discord."

"Put the video on the big screen," Palu instructed. "It's the best thing we have to work with for the moment."

Howard put the video up on the television and tapped the play button. This time, the three men in the video were not wearing head-scarves. They wore red bandanas over their mouths instead. Each wore matching army fatigues. Sarah couldn't be sure, but the uniforms looked like British Army, issued in the eighties perhaps. Her father had worn something similar during the Falkland's conflict.

In the background of the video, a single wooden desk held a dusty old lamp. There was nothing else to see except for a brick wall and an unidentified light source overhead. A ceiling bulb swinging back and forth.

The man at the front of the shot began his speech, his voice gravelly and thick beneath his bandana. His eyes were dark and soulless. "People of the UK, today begins your reckoning. Your villages burn like those set aflame by your own corrupt Government. The time for you to taste your own medicine has arrived. Your trinkets and idols will be taken, death and misery left in their place. You will suffer, as innocent people around the world have suffered beneath your country's amoral boot-heel. We are watching your soldiers, your agents, and your murderers-for-hire. Every time they take a life, we shall take more, that is our pledge. The four villages set ablaze are payback for a decade of murder in Afghanistan. You kill, we kill. Remove your soldiers from our homelands and the killing will stop. Have your Prime Minister renounce Britain's imperialistic past and its greed-soaked present, and we shall disband. Until such time, we are humanity's army. *Shab Bekheir* will show you all the way. *Sometimes only death can save life.*"

There was silence in the room for several minutes while they let things sink in. Palu's phone beeping broke the silence. "The Prime Minister just responded to the most recent tape," he said. "She promises the terrorist's actions will not go unanswered and that Great Britain does not bend to threats." He shook his head and sighed. "The media are in uproar, warning against a war on UK soil. They've caught wind of the first tape being suppressed and are citing the Government's incompetence as the reason three more attacks were allowed to happen."

"There'll be panic in the streets," Bradley said in a strained voice.

"I need to contact Homeland," said Dr Bennett, standing to leave the room. "I'll see if President Conrad will make a statement of support."

Palu nodded to permit her.

Bradley zapped something else over to the television screen and asked for their attention. It was the black and white CCTV feed from the pub in Studley. It showed a middle-aged woman wearing a long black cardigan standing in a bar lounge of a typical bistro pub — a place more eatery than boozer. It made a strange target for a terrorist attack.

Howard squinted at the screen. "What are we looking at, Bradley?"

"This is CCTV video footage taken from the Barley Mow pub in Studley. The local police have cleaned up the image as best they could and cut the footage down to the two minutes leading up to the explosion. We have everything except sound."

They watched the woman in the video wander into the middle of the pub's dining area. A few seconds later, she ripped open her cardigan and shouted something. The video's resolution was too low to make out what was around her waist, but it was obvious from the frightened screams of the diners that it was a bomb. The image on screen exploded. The CCTV feed ended. Everybody in the conference room groaned, even Sarah.

"An initial background has been compiled," said Howard. "The bomber's name was Caroline Pugh. She was white, middle-aged, and worked full-time job as a legal secretary. I'm trying to get a deeper background, but so far she doesn't appear to be a typical terrorist."

"What is a *typical* terrorist?" Sarah asked. "Asian, I suppose?"

"I'm not being racist, Sarah, just realistic. At the very least, you would expect a terrorist to be from another country, or part of a group with an agenda. Jeffrey Blanchfield and Caroline Pugh were average citizens. It makes no sense at all. How do they connect to Shab Bekhier and the men in the videotapes?"

"I don't know," Sarah admitted, "but I know who the man in the videotape is."

Everyone stared at her. Bradley stopped typing.

Sarah hadn't been positive of the man's identity until he'd spoken his final words. *Sometimes only death can ensure life.*

"The man in the tape is Wazir Hesbani. I'd know his face anywhere because he's the man who took mine."

AFGHANISTAN, 2008

Sarah blinked and took a deep breath, but instead of oxygen she got smoke and fumes. A rising pressure threatened to split her skull open from the inside, and she realised she was hanging upside down, held in place by a seatbelt.

Everything came rushing back at once. The woman. The watermelons. Miller getting ripped apart by an explosion. The white light followed by utter darkness.

They had hit an IED.

Sarah craned her neck and glanced around inside the Land Rover. She saw shapes in the darkness. "Hamish? Hamish? Anyone? Sound off."

There was nothing in reply, just silence and smoke. Sarah needed to know which of her men were still breathing and get them the hell out of there. She pulled out the small flick-blade that she kept on her belt and wished it was a machete. It would have to do because it was all she had. She used it to saw at the seatbelt, gritting her teeth as she did so. There was a white hot burning in her left thigh but, in the darkness, she couldn't identify the cause.

Voices.

For a moment, Sarah thought one of her squad had awoken, but then she realised the voices were coming from outside the vehicle. The approaching strangers were most likely enemies. She swore through pursed lips as either sweat or blood irritated her eyes. Her face throbbed as badly as her leg, and the memory of her reflection in the Snatch's visor came back to haunt her. There had been an open wound beneath her left eye, halfway down her cheek.

"Hamish... anybody? If you're breathing, argh, now is the time to... to look lively."

Silence.

"Damn it!" She managed to slice halfway through her belt, but the voices outside were getting close. They were about to be right on top of her. She sawed frantically, trying to cut through the last of the belt. Finally, the nylon snapped. Sarah fell free. Her head struck the

Snatch's roof panel and her teeth clacked together. She shook away the stars and locked her jaw.

The voices were right outside.

Sarah snapped into action. Her training and instincts made her focus on the task at hand instead of the pain and fear. There would be time to cry later. Lowering her hand to her waist, she slid her sidearm out of its holster — a SIG Sauer L105A1 9mm — and thumbed the safety off.

One last time, she shouted for her team. "Hamish! Hamish, are you with me?"

Still no answer. She thought she heard a shuffling behind her, but there was no time to investigate. She straightened out her legs and shuffled towards the opening where the Snatch's windscreen used to be. Glass shards and jagged stones bit into her knees and forearms as she crawled, but she moved fast. Even now, she could hear the strangers outside chattering to one another, kicking up sand as they hurried towards her.

Coming to claim their prize.

Sarah rolled onto her side and clutched her SIG, ready to start popping shots at whomever looked like they deserved it most. She clawed her way through the last of the broken windscreen and made it out onto the dusty road. The heat hit her back and she started sweating. The body of one of her men lay ahead. Was it Hamish? The dead soldier lay on their stomach, one arm missing and a hole in the side of their head. Death was a mercy compared to the screaming agony such wounds would have caused.

Sarah dragged herself to her feet just in time to meet the approaching crowd. She raised her SIG and prepared to pull the trigger, but her burning legs wobbled beneath her. Blood ran down her face.

Dark-haired children made up part of the crowd, eyes wide and mouths gawping. Their innocence was still intact — clear from their frightened faces — but that innocence would faded fast. It was about to be washed away with the blood of Sarah and her squad. This was how children got baptised in the desert.

A man stepped out of the crowd, putting a hand up in front of him as he approached Sarah. "Please, we are not here to hurt you. You are British, no?"

Sarah nodded. "Y-You speak English?"

The man nodded and smiled. He had a long, fuzzy beard and thick black eyebrows. "I study at your Oxford University. Economics, yes?"

"I need to get back to Camp Bastion. If you're friendly, let me go on my way."

"Your Camp Bastion is sixty miles away. Sun is hot. Your face and leg are bleeding. You will not make on your own."

Sarah glanced at her thigh and saw the top of a twisted nail sticking out of her muscle. It must have come from the IED. Lucky it hadn't entered her skull. Seeing the cause of the pain in her leg somehow made it worse, as if she could feel the nail clawing its way into her sinewy muscle. The stranger was right, she'd never make it back to camp on her own. "Give me a car," she said. "It will be returned later, along with a reward for your assistance."

The young man tilted his head and looked at her like she was a child. One of his thick black eyebrows curved into an arch. "You think we have car? No, we have nothing. You think we want British reward? British only give death and suffering to my people. If we help you, Taliban kill us. If we help Taliban, British kill us. You are not friend, and you do not offer reward. Only Allah can provide reward for our actions. We get what is deserved, yes?"

Sarah stumbled, and had to fight to right herself. "If you don't help me, I'll die. Will Allah reward you for murder?"

The young man continued to smile, but there was something predatory about the way he was looking at her now. "Sometimes death is the only way to ensure life."

Sarah felt her knees weakening, straining to support her. Her arms were tiring too, making it harder and harder to keep her SIG aimed ahead. "I'm sorry for what you people have gone through, but we *are* here to help you."

"Afghanistan does not need your help."

Sarah noticed blood dripping on the sand next to her foot.

"Your face is bleeding," said the young man. "Let me help you."

Sarah staggered backwards, struggling to keep her aim on the man's chest. "No! I need to get back to camp."

"You need rest. Tomorrow, you think about returning to your camp." The man took a stride towards her, closing the gap between them to only a few feet. The crowd behind him muttered and mumbled. If Sarah fired a shot, they'd be on her in seconds.

"G-get away from me!"

"Let me help you." He spoke softly and reached out to her, revealing the image of a dagger on his forearm. "You are bleeding."

"No! Step back or I'll shoot."

"No, you will not, I think."

Sarah almost called his bluff. She felt the trigger give a little beneath her finger, but pulling it all the way required a strength she didn't have. Her legs folded and she crumpled. The battle to stay on her feet was too much, and it was a relief when she hit the dirt.

The young man was on her right away, yanking the gun out of her hand and ejecting the magazine. He tossed the pistol aside but kept hold of the ammo. "Your face is very bad," he said. "We need to close wound or infection kill you, no?"

Sarah struggled, but the man straddled her waist and was too heavy to move. "Let me go," she begged. "Who are you?"

The young man held a brass bullet casing in front of her face. "My name is Wazir Hesbani, and I am going to help you, English. Close wound, stop infection." He placed the rear end of the bullet between his teeth and clamped down, twisting at the jacket with his fingers and unscrewing the cap. Sarah blinked as blood from her face made her vision red. With the man sitting on her chest it was hard to breathe.

Wazir spat the brass cap into the dirt, then stared at her with soulless brown eyes. "This might hurt a little." He upended the bullet casing over her face. Sarah spluttered and moaned as gunpowder covered her wound, stinging and burning; but the pain was nothing compared to what followed.

Wazir pulled a lighter from his pocket and ignited the powder on her face. The entire left side of her skull crackled and, for a moment, all she could see was flashing whites and flaring yellows. The agony was immense, a thousand pins shoved into her exposed flesh.

Finally, a numbness settled upon her and everything faded to grey. Sarah knew she was about to pass out and wished she could fight it, but it was impossible. Like trying to fall upwards.

Wazir levelled his face with hers, his long beard tickling her cheek. "There," he said. "It is not pretty, but at least bleeding has stopped." He stood and turned to the crowd. "Take her to Al-Sharir. He will want to talk with her."

9

BY STRENGTH AND GUILE

"You're sure the man in the video is Wazir Hesbani?" asked Palu.

Sarah nodded. "Hesbani was Al-Sharir's right-hand man in Afghanistan."

"As part of a terrorist cell?"

"Yes, *Shab Bekheir*. Although, this still doesn't feel like Al-Sharir's work. Bombing innocent civilians, working with westerners... it's not who he is."

Howard frowned. "The man is a terrorist."

"He's also a man of rules and principles."

Dr Bennett hissed. "A terrorist has no principles."

Sarah expected nothing less from an American. To them, the world was full of good guys and bad guys, just like their movies, but this was real life, where there were points of view other than the white Christian hero's. "Most terrorists believe themselves to be warriors," she said. "Principles are *all* they have. We may not understand them or agree with them, but they believe their actions are just. To them, *we* are the terrorists."

Dr Bennett rolled her eyes. Sarah ignored it.

Bradley looked at her. "What do you know about this Hesbani?"

"He's a monster. As much as Al-Sharir has principles, Hesbani has none. His role in Shab Bekhier was to do the things that Al-Sharir would not. Hesbani is not a terrorist, he's a psychopath."

"What's his motivation?" Dr Bennett asked. "Typical psychopaths lack the ability to plan and calculate. There seems to have been a lot of thought put into these attacks."

"Do you think Al-Sharir might still be pulling Hesbani's strings?" Palu asked.

"I don't know. Hesbani and Al-Sharir often disagreed. Al-Sharir only wants to nullify the West's presence in the Middle East. He believes in the rules of war — he wouldn't intentionally attack civilians — but Hesbani lives for revenge. He wants to hurt the West and have the Middle East rise as a consolidated superpower. He sees himself fighting a great war and emerging as the first true Muslim leader since Saladin. Perhaps the cell split up. "

"But that doesn't tally with what he said on the tape," said Bradley. "He wants the West to withdraw. It sounds like he's trying to *stop* the violence."

"The only way the Middle East can rise," said Howard, "is if the West relinquishes its hold on the region first."

Palu nodded. "So do we believe that Hesbani's goal is truly what he speaks of? He wants Western forces to withdraw from the Middle East?"

"I think so," said Sarah, "but it wouldn't end there. Hesbani was raised on hatred for the West. Even if he got what he wanted, he could never live a peaceful life. Without violence, he is nothing. Killing is all he knows. It's his philosophy — sometimes death is the only way to ensure life."

"Then how do we stop him?" asked Bradley. "Do we know where he is?"

Sarah shrugged. "He's here in this country."

"How do you know that?" asked Palu.

"Bring up the video again. I'll show you."

Bradley played the video on the big screen again for them.

Sarah pointed at the television. "Look in the background, next to the lamp."

Palu shrugged. He obviously didn't see it. "What?"

Bradley tutted, probably annoyed at himself for not spotting it sooner. "The plug socket. The lamp is plugged into a three-pronged socket."

Sarah nodded. The three black holes were a familiar sight in Britain, but you would struggle to spot them anywhere else.

Palu smiled as he saw the value of such an observation. "I would say it's likely a safe bet that Hesbani is in the UK. We need to check flight manifests and Interpol records. Bradley, see if we can find out when he entered the country and under what name."

Bradley nodded. "Before I do that, I've got some additional background on Jeffrey Blanchfield."

"Let's see it."

Bradley zapped his laptop display over to the television screen and went through the information. "After his wife's death, Jeffrey Blanchfield was involved in several escalating altercations, including assault of a minor, public affray, and reckless endangerment with a motor vehicle. There are numerous reports of him lashing out, particularly at the neighbours he blamed for his wife's death. He and his wife had filed many reports of anti-social behaviour around their home prior to her death, but the police were unable to assist."

Despite his monstrous actions, Sarah felt badly for Jeffrey Blanchfield. Sometimes anger could consume a person until there was no room left for things like compassion or remorse. Sarah knew too well.

Bradley opened a new screen. "This is where it gets interesting. Jeffrey was brought before the courts for his consistent offending and ordered to attend grief counselling."

Dr Bennett frowned. "Why is that interesting?"

"Because Caroline Pugh was in court-mandated grief counselling too."

Palu leant on his elbows and raised an eyebrow. "Excellent work, Bradley. Do we have anything more on the woman?"

"Yes, Caroline Pugh, thirty-eight. Lost her daughter to a drunk driver, then picked up a drug habit. Eventually, she was arrested for making a scene at a local pub..." he looked up from his screen, "the Barley Mow — same one she blew up."

"The threads are untying," said Dr Bennett.

Bradley continued. "In a prior incident, the pub's barman called the police after Caroline Pugh collapsed in the toilets after a cocaine bender. When she refused to get up, he allegedly kicked her so hard that he broke her ribs. He dragged her outside in front of the whole pub, but only got a slap on the wrist for his callous behaviour. Caroline Pugh, however, was ordered into grief counselling to help end her drug addiction — the same court-appointed psychiatrist that Jeffrey Blanchfield attended."

Palu struck the desk with his fist. "And there you have it! What's this doctor's name?"

Bradley brought a medical license up on screen. "Wesley Cartwright, MD, Ph.D. He works out of an Oxford address — I have it here — but he also conducts court-appointed grief clinics up and down the country. His file is squeaky clean. No misdemeanours, no points of interest."

"I don't get it," said Howard. "Why would a psychiatrist be involved with terrorists?"

"Perhaps he doesn't realise he is," said Sarah. "We can't assume anything yet."

"It may just be a coincidence," said Dr Bennett. She pulled a notepad out of her breast pocket and jotted a few things down. "The link may be that both suspects were angry and in trouble with the law."

"Perhaps," said Howard, rubbing a finger across his square jaw, "or else somebody deliberately got Jeffrey Blanchfield and Caroline Pugh involved in this. Somebody who is bringing damaged people together and brainwashing them into blowing themselves up. Who could be behind something like that? Who's responsible?"

Sarah studied her chipped fingernails. "I think the United Kingdom is. Terrorists didn't make Caroline Pugh and Jeffrey Blanchfield broken and angry. *We* did that. *Society* did that. Terrorists are just taking advantage of what was allowed to happen to these people."

Dr Bennett scoffed. "Nobody did anything to these people. Life is life. We all have the same hardships to deal with. If we all went and blew ourselves up, there'd be none of us left."

"Pain can make people do bad things," said Sarah, "and contrary to popular belief, some people have it worse than others."

"I don't believe that. These people are just insane."

Palu waved his hand. "It doesn't matter why these people have done what they've done. Our only focus right now is making sure nothing else happens. Howard, I need you to track down this Dr Cartwright at his office."

"I'm going too," said Sarah.

Palu likely wanted to argue, but he didn't. Maybe it was the look on her face that told him not to. "Fine, you and Bradley can provide support if Howard needs it, but you're to stand down until then."

Sarah snapped off a mock salute.

Palu waved hand to dismiss them. "Dr Bennett and I will work intel while you're gone. Stay on the wire."

Howard exited the room with Bradley and Sarah. En route, he slipped out his mob sat and made a call. "Mandy? Get us two road warriors ready in five."

Sarah caught up to Howard and looked at him. "Road warriors? Do you have a fleet of tanks here that I missed?"

"Didn't anybody tell you? The Earthworm has arms."

Howard and Bradley led Sarah into the Earthworm's middle section and then into a side corridor. "Follow me."

They made their way up a narrow staircase. The size of the place still shocked Sarah. It could have housed a thousand employees, probably more. A person could die inside the Earthworm with the way things were and never be found.

The long staircase wound back and forth on itself, a coiled python, and by the time Sarah reached the top, she was sweating. Howard and Bradley were waiting for her on the top landing — having made the climb quicker — with subtle grins on their faces. "You get used to it," said Bradley. "There was supposed to be a lift, but then…"

"Yeah, I know," said Sarah, panting. "Funding cuts. How is this place not falling apart? It's huge. And empty. Is it really just you lot?"

Bradley held open a door and daylight bled into the stairwell with a gentle Spring breeze. It felt good to get out of the pit and back into open air.

"Sergeant Mattock's strike team comes and goes," Howard said, "but we feel he's better placed out in the field."

Sarah was still panting. "I look forward to… gah… meeting them. Jesus, I'm knackered."

The men chuckled.

They had emerged inside a rickety shelter. Sarah glanced around at various outbuildings and empty livestock pens, then quickly deduced she was at some kind of farm. A rusty tractor sat parked up against an old farmhouse which was missing both its roof and one wall. Rocks and weeds jutted out of the ground where there might once have been crops.

"It's our disguise," said Bradley.

Sarah nodded. "It's a good one. I wouldn't want to go snooping around this place. Looks like Old MacDonald haunts it."

"It's more high tech than it looks," said Howard. "There are cameras hidden in a dozen places." He pointed to the tractor and Sarah saw the glint of a lens hidden inside the exhaust pipe.

She put her hands on her hips. "So do you plan on walking to Oxford? Because I didn't wear the right shoes."

Howard trudged through the mud toward a slanting feed shed. Its entrance had been fitted with a collection of padlocks, but they had all been popped open. Howard pulled open the corrugated metal doors and revealed Mandy standing inside. The big guy nodded at Howard and Bradley as they entered, but gave Sarah only a cursory glance.

"Good to see you again too," she grunted.

Inside the feed shed, a group of powerful super bikes sat beside two sleek saloons. Behind them, two jet-black Range Rovers idled. The two

4x4s made Sarah think of the Snatch Land Rovers used in Afghanistan. She shuddered.

Bradley studied her. "You okay, Captain?"

"So these are our rides, huh? Way things were downstairs, I was expecting a couple of Mini Metros."

Howard rolled his eyes. "We do the best we can with what we have. Didn't they teach you that in the Army?"

"Naw," said Sarah in a dopey voice. "They just teached me what end of the rifle to point at the baddies."

Howard opened the passenger door of one of the two Ranges and glanced over at the other. "Bradley, you take Two and follow me and Mandy in One."

Mandy gunned the engine and took off in the first Range Rover while Bradley waited for Sarah to get into the passenger seat of the other. Instead, she went around to the driver's side and elbowed him. "Shove over. I'm driving."

"But—"

"Just move over!"

Bradley climbed awkwardly into the passenger seat, allowing Sarah to take the wheel. She shifted into first gear and the engine grumbled as she brought up the clutch. Then she put her foot down, taking off after the other Range which was already a hundred metres in front. Poor Bradley slunk down in his seat as they picked up speed, and within two minutes they were side-by-side with the other vehicle. It was a rush, and sure as hell beat taking the bus.

Bradley directed Sarah to a gate at the edge of the field which caused her to slow down and eventually skid to a halt.

Mandy parked up next to her and Howard leapt out. He marched right over to her driver's side door. She lowered her window and looked out. "Problem?"

"Do you think this is a game? We're trying to catch the people responsible for four terrorist attacks and you're racing around like you're on bloody *Top Gear*. I told Bradley to drive."

"He said he couldn't concentrate with me sitting next to him. He asked me to take the wheel so he could touch himself."

Bradley turned bright red. "I-I didn't..."

Howard grunted. "Look, Sarah, I understand the whole attitude thing — it comes with the scars, I suppose — but can I rely on you?"

Sarah gripped the wheel tightly and snarled. "I can handle my shit. You just handle yours."

"I'm taking lead, so follow me — and keep that Mario Kart shit to a minimum."

Sarah snapped off another mock salute. "Roger that, Howie."

They got moving and drove out through the gate, pausing while Bradley closed it behind them. "What's Howard's deal?" Sarah asked Bradley once he climbed back inside the car.

"What do you mean?"

"Why's he got such a bug up his arse?"

Bradley shrugged. "Just the way he is."

"Bad childhood?"

"Nope. Howard was an Assistant-Lecturer at Nottingham. He was teaching Terrorism and Security studies when MCU recruited him. Before that, he almost made it as a professional tennis player. His father was a carpenter and his mother stayed home. He has the least baggage out of everybody at MCU."

"What, all five of you?"

"There are more of us than that. Sergeant Mattock leads our strike team. He's ex SAS."

Sarah's heart skipped a beat. If Mattock was SAS, he would know her father. "Another thug with a beige beret, right?" she said. "Shoot first, ask questions later. I've met the type before."

Bradley looked out the window. "You'll be glad to have him if you need him. He's the only reason Howard didn't die when I froze. It might be MCU's job to protect the country, but Mattock's job is to protect us."

"I don't need protecting."

"Good for you. The rest of us aren't so perfect. It's nice to have a little help when we can get it."

They sat in silence for the next twelve miles. The roads were quiet for a Monday afternoon on account of the brutal terrorist attacks. People wouldn't want to leave their houses for fear of getting blown to pieces by maniacs. Sarah wondered how many people had left work early this afternoon after the attacks. The economy would already be suffering.

Howard spoke over the radio, breaking the silence. Sarah hadn't realised it, but the Range Rovers were comm-linked. "I just got an update from Palu."

"Cartwright's receptionist says the doctor is with patients today. He's at his office right now. Mission to extract is green, but we need to go in soft. We can't afford to endanger civilians."

"Civilians are in danger every time they cross the street," said Sarah. "What's the plan?"

"I'll go in alone and speak with the doctor. If I feel he has information on the attacks, I'll bring him in."

"Alone?" Bradley asked.

"I can take a lone civilian easily enough, Bradley. If I need help I'll give the signal. Keep the line open."

"Roger that."

Sarah sniffed. "So our orders are to sit in the car and do nothing? Not very James Bond."

"Don't worry," said Bradley. "I play a mean eye-spy."

Sarah didn't know for sure that Bradley was joking.

So far, the entire day had been something out of a contrived espionage novel. It was as if the ghosts of her past had teamed up to haunt her all at once. Hesbani. Al-Sharir. Her father. It was all getting a little too difficult to process.

Sarah lowered her speed, suddenly not in so much of a hurry.

10

WHO DARES WINS

They entered the city of Oxford forty minutes later, driving through the high street and cutting between the Norman, Gothic, and Victorian architecture that mingled with the grand buildings of the world's oldest English-speaking university. It was a city that cried 'England,' but at the same time, it was undeniably cosmopolitan. As Sarah moved through loose traffic, she spotted students of various nationalities talking, hugging, and crying as they no doubt discussed the day's terrible events. It was a microscopic example of how the world could be when petty differences were set aside. It nearly restored Sarah's faith in humanity, but then she remembered that Wazir Hesbani had also attended Oxford University. How many of these kids would grow up to be monsters?

Howard came over the radio again. "The clinic is a half-mile from here. Stay close, but keep a little distance. When I park up, find a place nearby and wait for my signal. Mandy will be on standby in case I need to make an extraction. Bradley, you and Sarah are to remain in a support role."

"Roger that."

The radio went silent.

"The only thing with a support role in this car is my bra," said Sarah. "Any sign of trouble and I'll go get the doctor myself."

"We don't know the doctor has anything to do with the bombings."

"For his sake, I hope not."

Howard took a series of side streets that led into an office district. The buildings were modern and red-bricked, contrasting with the darker stone buildings of the city centre. Sarah followed behind until he pulled into a small car park in front of a three-story building. Instead of following, she overshot the car park and came to a halt around the corner in front of a newsagent.

"I'm entering the building now," Howard said over the radio. "Stand by."

Sarah pulled on the handbrake, "Ten-four, Captain Badger."

Howard didn't reply, but she heard him sigh before the radio cut off.

"Why do you like winding people up so much?" Bradley asked her.

"I can't get laid. What else am I supposed to do for kicks?"

Bradley blushed, but he kept on at her. "Do you mean because of your scars? That puts men off?"

"What d'you think?"

Bradley shrugged. "I don't know. I imagine people would stop noticing after a while, but I don't think it's as much of a problem as you think. My sister has *spina bifida,* but she never lets it hold her back. She's happy. It's all about how you see yourself, not how other people look at you."

"Your sister is unhappy, trust me. The brave face she puts on is just for you. She knows that if she feels sorry for herself, you'll all grow tired of her. Every time she smiles, she dies a little more inside, trying to make herself less of a burden to the rest of you. Your sister might be brave, but she's not happy."

"You don't know anything about her, so just... shut the fuck up."

Sarah grinned. "There you go. Knew you had balls somewhere in those girl's trousers."

Bradley stared out of his window in silence while Sarah glanced around, checking out the area they'd parked in. It was a nice part of town, with new buildings nestled between patches of grass and shade-giving trees. The kind of place you'd expect to find a psychiatrist's office.

Sarah noticed a grungy-looking girl inside the newsagent staring at them from behind the counter. She was talking on a phone while eyeing up the Range Rover. Something about her reeked suspicious.

Something was off.

Bradley noticed Sarah frowning. "What's wrong?"

"We have a nosy parker. Wait here." Sarah got out of the Range and climbed the single step in front of the newsagent's front entrance. It was a warm day, so the door was open. When the girl behind the counter saw her coming, she muttered something into her phone and ended the call. She then gave Sarah a wide, welcoming smile which revealed a small, silver ring through her bottom lip. "Hi there. How are you today?"

"You okay with me parking out front, sweetie?"

The girl noticed Sarah's scars and became flustered. "Oh, um, yeah, no problem. You're welcome to park there."

Sarah strolled around the shop, glancing at stacks of newspapers as if they were the most interesting things in the world. Eventually she turned back to the girl, making sure to keep the bad side of her face visible. "You here all by yourself?"

"I... yes, for the time being. Why do you ask?"

Sarah shrugged. "I used to work in a shop like this at your age. I remember how my boss used to leave me holding the fort too. Sucks being all alone. Hours go by slowly." She walked up to the counter and placed both hands on it.

The girl swallowed.

Sarah grinned, knowing that doing so would distort her gruesome scars. "Try to mind your own business, sweetie, okay? I would hate it if we were forced to become better acquainted."

Sarah left the newsagent and rejoined Bradley in the car.

"Everything okay?" he asked.

"Something's off about that girl in that newsagent. Don't ask me why."

"You think she knows something?"

"Most shop workers don't even give the time of day to customers standing in front of them, let alone a car parked on the curb doing nothing. I'll give her the benefit of the doubt, but she's got my spider senses tingling. Heard anything from Howard?"

"Nope, all's quiet. Sorry." By Bradley's tone, it was clear he was still upset with her. When Sarah thought about what she had said about his sister, she could understand why. It had been cruel, even for her.

"Look, Bradley, about what I said. I'm—"

The radio squawked and Howard's voice rang out. "Target has flown the nest. Repeat: target is gone. Be on the lookout. Suspect is a middle-aged man, with receding brown hair, shirt, tie, trousers. May be wearing spectacles."

"Somebody must have warned him," said Bradley.

"That bitch." Sarah leapt back out of the Range and raced into the newsagent. The girl had gone. A door in the back was hanging open. "I'm gonna kick your skinny little ass," Sarah shouted as she bounded through the shop and out into a bricked-up yard. There was no sign of the girl.

But there was the sound of an engine.

Sarah saw a sky-blue Citroen speeding towards her and shouted for it to stop. The driver stepped on the brake and the car lurched to a halt right in front of her. Sarah rushed to the driver's side door, snarling and shouting. She discovered a startled old lady behind the wheel. "Oh, sorry, ma'am. I thought you were a friend of mine."

The old lady spluttered. "That's how you treat your friends?" Then she sped off, no doubt wanting to get as far away from Sarah as she could.

That ten-second delay might have been all it took for the shopgirl to get away, so Sarah got moving. She heard racing footsteps in the distance and took off after them. She picked up speed, wishing she'd kept herself in better shape. The old wound in her thigh throbbed.

She rounded a corner and caught sight of her target. The grungy girl was racing towards the office buildings, chains dangling from the pockets of her black jeans. The doctor's clinic was right in front of her, and Sarah spotted Mandy parked up in the other Range Rover. The girl was making a play for the doctor, Sarah was certain of it. Somehow, the shop girl was involved in this.

Sarah tried to shout a warning to Mandy, but she was too late. Her teammate was forced to duck down in his seat as the shop girl suddenly pulled a gun and opened fire. Sarah should have leapt into cover, but instead she kept up her pursuit.

Mandy slipped out of the Range Rover and popped up over the hood to return fire with his own weapon, but the girl had him pinned. His shots were blind.

Bradley appeared from the left, running along the road and adding another gun to the party. Mandy held his cover behind the car while Sarah rushed to join the fray.

The clinic's main entrance sprung open and Howard exited. The whole team had arrived, positioned on all sides.

The girl had no place to go.

Howard hadn't exited the building alone. A man fitting Dr Cartwright's description was with him, holding a syringe full of something against his jugular and prodding him in the back to keep him moving. "L-Let me leave," the man demanded, all three of his chins wobbling, "or I'll fill him full of enough diazepam to kill a buffalo."

"Take the shot, Mandy!" Howard yelled. "He's got no place to go."

The shop girl fired at Mandy again and kept him pinned behind the Range Rover. Sarah tried to come up behind her, but narrowly avoided getting a bullet in the face. She skidded on her heels and put her hands up, wishing she'd asked for a gun before leaving the Earthworm. How the hell had her day ended up like this? She didn't even know these people

Bradley stood in a firing position to the left, his face pale and sweaty. The shop girl scowled at him. "Everybody, chill the fuck out. Dr Cartwright, are you okay?"

The fat doctor nodded. "I-I took him by surprise. If you hadn't warned me, Ashley..."

The girl winced at the sound of her name being given away so cheaply. "You can thank me later. We have to get you out of here."

"Nobody's going anywhere," said Howard, absurdly defiant seeing there was an arm around his throat and a needle against his jugular. "We can talk this through."

"Excuse me, handsome," said the girl obviously named Ashley, "but you're not in a position to negotiate. I'm the one with the testicles here."

Mandy tried to creep up and let off another shot, but Ashley aimed at him and shook her head to warn him off. Sarah eyed Bradley and tried to signal him to shoot. Somehow, he had remained on the fringes of the gunfight — the only one of them not pinned down. He had a bead on the girl's flank and could end this right now. But he had frozen on the spot. His gun was trembling in his hands.

"What do you want?" Sarah asked the girl, stalling while Bradley hopefully got his shit together and pulled the trigger. "Why are you working with terrorists?"

Ashley turned to face Sarah. "Sweetie, him and me *are* terrorists."

"We are no such thing," Dr Cartwright argued.

Ashley rolled her eyes. "Keep telling yourself that, Doc. We've all taken a hand in what's happening, but don't worry so much. Today's terrorists are tomorrow's freedom fighters. Future generations will thank us, even if this one doesn't."

"Ashley, I'd like to get out of here, please."

Ashley switched her aim between Mandy and Sarah, keeping them both in place. "Doc, if anybody moves, inject that son-of-a-bitch with whatever it is you have in there, understand?"

"Y-Yes, I understand."

Ashley slid between a pair of parked cars and fumbled in her jeans pocket with her free hand, keeping the gun raised with the other. Sarah thought about trying to rush her, but the risk to Howard was too great. So, instead, she crept forward inch by inch. Bradley finally got moving and followed her lead, shuffling closer to join her in the car park.

Ashley thumbed a button on a key fob and a blue Ford Focus flashed its lights. "Get in," she yelled at the doctor.

"What about him?" The doctor was referring to Howard, still held hostage by his needle.

"What do you think? He comes with us."

"No," said Sarah. "Hand him over and we'll let you leave."

"I'm leaving anyway," said Ashley. "So keep your compromises to yourself, freak."

Sarah wanted to kick the girl's teeth in.

"Get in the car," Ashley ordered the doctor once more. Cartwright reached around Howard with a shaking hand and yanked open the Ford's rear passenger door. He then awkwardly tried to shove Howard inside. Doing so while keeping the syringe against his neck was impossible. Howard spun around on the back seat and yanked the doctor down on top of him. Then he head butted the man in the face.

Cartwright yowled and collapsed forward into the Ford's rear footwell. Howard clambered over him and made it back out of the car. He bolted across the tarmac and threw himself down behind a Toyota minivan just as Ashley opened fire. Sarah saw her chance and rushed the girl from behind. She only made it halfway before something stung her shoulder. The force spun her around and she stumbled onto one knee. Her vision tilted and she suddenly felt sick.

Ashley kept firing. Once at Mandy, and several times at Bradley. Who the hell was this girl, and who trained her? Sarah couldn't get up off her knees. She slumped forward onto her hands and groaned in pain. Ashley approached, an animalistic expression on her face. Her gun was pointed right at Sarah's forehead. "You idiots have no idea what's happening, do you? We will bring this whole country to its knees. Too bad you won't get chance to see it."

Sarah closed her eyes and waited for the bullet that would end her life. She had expected death many times before, and part of her was a little glad it was finally here.

Blam!

Sarah flew backwards, but it was out of fright, not pain or impact.

She saw Ashley still standing in front of her, but the girl was now clutching her right hand and cursing as blood spewed from her fingertips. Her gun lay several feet away on the concrete.

Bradley took another shot and Ashley sprinted for the Ford as the bullet sailed past. Mandy let off several shots as well, but none hit the target. The girl managed to leap in behind the steering wheel and turn on the engine. She threw the vehicle back in reverse, and then squealed out of the car park with her head ducked down in the driver's seat. The Ford Focus disappeared around the corner before Sarah and the others had chance to regroup.

Rather than chase the target, Howard rushed over to Sarah. Bradley came too, and knelt beside her, pressing hard against her shoulder and causing her a shitload of pain. "You've been shot," he said, "but you're going to be okay. We're going to get you help, Sarah."

"It's my fault," said Howard. "I let the doctor get a jump on me."

"No," said Bradley. "I should have taken a shot earlier."

"You're letting her get away," said Sarah, feeling herself fading. Was she dying?

Howard stroked her hair in a way that was far too familiar for her liking. "She's already gone," he told her. "This whole thing has been a bust. Mandy, get Sarah to the car, we need to get her to Dr Bennett."

"I'll call Mattock," said Bradley. "See if he can reacquire the target."

"Do it fast!"

Sarah felt herself being lifted into the air, and closed her eyes to dream.

11

THE BLUE PILL

AFGHANISTAN, 2008

When Sarah opened her eyes, sweating stone walls surrounded her on all sides. Sunlight scorched a small patch of ground, cast from a narrow opening near the ceiling. It was like waking up inside a kiln.

A wooden door broke up one end of the room, and Sarah crawled over to it. Dirt and stone bit at her palms, and her right leg dragged behind her uselessly. When she reached the door, she pulled herself halfway up and shouted. "Let me out of here!"

But no one came to help. She had known nobody would, but something inside of her wouldn't allow her to just sit there and rot. It was important to do something.

A bandage covered her right leg, but her face was raw as she brushed it with her fingertips, every touch broken glass beneath her skin that brought tears to her eyes. She beat her fists against the wooden door, but it barely moved. Ancient and thick, it had most likely been cut from a tree a hundred years old. Nothing of any use lay inside her pockets. They had taken everything from her; even her dog tags.

Sarah thought about her father and how ashamed he would be of her right now. Being captured was worse than death in his eyes. Better to eat your own bullet than let the enemy take you. If the enemy caught you, it was because you'd stopped fighting, and when you stopped fighting, you deserved everything you got.

Thomas was the one who worried her most. What would he do when he heard she'd been captured? If they buried her in the desert, would he ever know for sure that she was dead? Would he spend the rest of his days wondering if he would ever see her again? Or the child she was carrying?

Sarah couldn't help it; she wept. With her legs spread out in the dirt, she slumped against the wall and sobbed. She was alone, which was awful, but she knew that when company arrived things would only get worse. Torture and death awaited her, and the best she could hope for was that her body found its way home.

She thought about her men, Hamish, Miller, and the young privates. Were they all dead? Had any of them been taken prisoner? She couldn't believe how badly she'd failed them. Their lives had been in her hands. "Just kill me," she shouted at the door. "You hear me? I have nothing to give you, so just kill me and be done with it."

The wooden door opened and a man stepped inside. Middle-aged, he wore full Pashtun dress with a *Taqiyah*, a short, rounded skullcap. He smiled at her in the doorway's glow, and for a moment he looked angelic. "If I wish for you to be dead, Captain, then dead you would be."

Wazir Hesbani, the one who'd burned her face with gunpowder stood behind this new man, glaring at her, but he did not enter. Like Hesbani, this new man had a tattoo of a dagger on his forearm. Sarah shuffled in the dirt trying to get away.

"Relax," said the unknown man. "I bring only bread and water, and a willingness to chat."

Sarah tried to speak firmly, but her voice quivered. "I-I won't tell you anything."

"That is up to you, Captain. I am not here to force you to do anything. You are my guest."

"Then let me go."

"In time."

"What do you want?"

"To chat."

"My mission was to speak with a village elder," she said. "That's the only intel I have. You should already know that because everything that happened in the village was a trap. Well done."

The man placed the tray on the floor and knelt in front of her. "The elder you came to speak to is dead. Taliban took the village many days ago. Your great Army didn't even know it. What happened today was because of your own failings. It is your own weakness that allowed your enemy to best you."

Sarah frowned at the man. "Are you not Taliban?"

"My name is Al Al-Sharir and I am just a man born of Afghanistan. I made no choice to be here instead of there, or to be Muslim instead of Christian. I am not Taliban but neither am I an ally to the West. Taliban is just one group of many that fight for what they believe is right. You fight for what you believe is right, yes?"

Sarah nodded.

"Then you are no different than the Taliban. A coin has two sides, but both are equal. Your right does not make other rights wrong."

Sarah struggled to understand. "What do *you* believe is right?"

Al-Sharir smiled. "That all of us are wrong and that there is no right." He held up his wrist to show her the tattoo of the dagger. Sarah shook her head in confusion. "It is symbol that my will belongs to Allah," he explained. "There is no place for my own selfish desires. My life is on the tip of a dagger and I can die at any moment. Allah allows life and only He has the right to take it. We are not here to rule in his place."

"We're just trying to help you people."

"Then why enter our country after events of 9/11? Is it not anger and fear which brought you here? What is it about now that makes your help necessary? Do not fool yourself, Captain, you are uninvited guests."

"But by killing us, you're just keeping us here longer. Where is the sense in that?"

"I make sense of the world in my own small way, as must we all."

Sarah felt more tears spill down her cheeks, stinging her wounds. "P-Please, let me go."

Al-Sharir sighed. "I will send you back, yes, but I am afraid I must first do what you expect me to do."

Sarah's heart beat against her ribs. "You're going to torture me?"

"Not me, but someone, yes. We must do unto you as you do unto others. It is the only lesson we have here to teach. My friend, Wazir, is a keen teacher. He would prefer you do not talk easily."

Sarah could sense Wazir lingering in the doorway, and when she looked, he was staring at her hungrily. "You sound like a good man, Al-Sharir. You don't have to do this."

"I am not a good man. You must stop thinking in such false ideals like good and bad." He reached for Sarah, grabbed the thumb of her left hand and twisted. Sarah screamed as her knuckle dislocated and fire shot up her arm. She tried to speak, but couldn't catch her breath, so she sobbed like a child.

Al-Sharir sighed. "You see? I am not a good man. But neither am I bad. If you were an innocent woman, I would let you go home, but you are not an innocent woman, are you? You are a soldier, willing to take a life, and so you must be willing to give one also." He pointed to the dagger tattoo on his arm. "The dagger points towards my heart because I am willing to die for what is right. That badge on your uniform is your dagger. It says you are willing to die for what you think is right. That is the truth, no?"

Sarah looked at the captain's bands on her dirty uniform and wept. She managed to splutter out one final plea for mercy. "I-I'm pregnant!"

Al-Sharir's eyes flickered as he studied her face. "A clever way for you to beg me, but it is a game I will not play."

Sarah grabbed the man by his wrist. "I swear to you, I'm pregnant. I don't want to be a soldier anymore, I want to be a mother."

Al-Sharir stared at her for what felt like an eternity. Eventually, he nodded. "I cannot harm the innocent life inside of you, so I shall release you in the morning. If you are lying, your punishment will be great and everlasting."

Sarah's eyes flooded with tears as she nodded. "I'm not lying, I promise."

"I hope not." Al-Sharir rose to his feet. "Because if I have judged you wrong in this life, Allah will correct my mistake in the next. I shall see you again in the morning, Captain. Until then, you shall have company."

Al-Sharir headed for the door, while his colleague, Wazir Hesbani, came inside. He snarled at Sarah like a jackal. "Don't worry, English. I will not hurt you. I am tired after spending so long with your friend."

Sarah frowned. "My friend? What–"

Hesbani booted Sarah in the face, cutting off her words and splitting both of her lips wide open. She tasted blood.

"You do not speak, English." Hesbani spat and then left the room. After a moment, two more men entered and tossed a body to the ground beside Sarah. Once the wooden door closed, Sarah crawled over to the body and realised the beaten, semi-conscious man was a British soldier. He looked up at her with swollen eyes and tried to talk, but he could only wheeze.

Sarah cradled the injured man in her arms as more tears spilled from her eyes "Oh, Hamish," she said, through swollen, bleeding lips. "What have they done to you?"

MCU, ENGLISH COUNTRYSIDE, 2014

Sarah let out a moan as past miseries jolted her awake. She tried to move, but couldn't. Her body floated through the air, legs dangling in nothingness. At first, she couldn't hear anything, but then all sound came rushing back.

Mandy looked down at her as he carried her in his arms. His face was pained, and beads of sweat ran down his nose. Sarah didn't mind being carried by him. She felt safe in his massive arms, like a baby. Fluorescent lights hummed overhead, hurting her eyes. The smell of chemicals bleached the air.

"Put her down on the table, quickly!"

Mandy placed Sarah down on something hard. Her legs straightened out and her head lolled to one side. Dr Bennett appeared and placed a hand on her cheek. "You're going to be okay, Sarah. You're back at MCU and I'm going to take care of you. Just lie back and relax, okay?"

Sarah lay still. There was a subtle pinch at her wrist followed by a tugging sensation.

"How long ago did this happen?" Bennett asked someone else in the room.

Howard answered. "Just under an hour ago. I kept pressure on the wound, but she's lost a lot of blood."

Bennett hissed. "You should have called an ambulance."

"We're not supposed to advertise our existence, remember? Also, she's still technically a civilian and we don't need that heat."

"I don't give a damn. You risked her life bringing her all the way back here. I ought to put a bullet in you."

Sarah felt light-headed, and wanted to tell them to stop bickering, but no words would come out. Her eyelids drooped and she couldn't feel her face. Even the familiar tightness of her scars had deserted her.

"Sarah, I've given you a painkiller," said Bennett. "You're going to feel very sleepy. Don't fight it. You will be fine."

Sarah closed her eyes.

When she opened them again, she was tucked beneath several sheets. She tried to sit up, but grunted from the pain and flopped back again. Her shoulder ached, and she could feel a thick bandage beneath her chin. She was in pain, but that was nothing new. Not a minute passed without her face throbbing and burning. The wound in her shoulder just added a little variety. Her most pressing concern, right now, was that she was stark-bollock-naked beneath the sheets.

She spotted a small red button attached to a wire beside her arm. It was close enough that she was able to thumb at it several times, and she hoped an irritating alarm was sounding somewhere. Sure enough, Dr Bennett entered the room less than a minute later.

"Sarah," she said, "you're awake. How are you feeling? Any pain?"

"Not too much. How long have I been out?"

"Eight hours. You're still under sedation so you might feel peculiar for a while. The bullet lodged beneath your collarbone. There was a small fracture and some tissue damage, but nothing you won't get back. You lost two pints of blood, so you need to rest."

As the doctor spoke, Sarah's vision tilted back and forth. "You sure it was only two pints?"

Bennett smiled. "A tad more perhaps, but you'll be just fine. Like I said, you need rest."

Sarah slid her legs over the bed rail and lowered herself until her bare feet slapped the floor. "No can do, Doc. I'm not the bed-rest type. Where are my clothes?"

The door at the back of the room opened and Bradley entered. He saw Sarah naked, and skidded on his heels, putting his hands over his face and turning around. "Jesus, Captain, I-I'm sorry. I came to get Dr Bennett."

Sarah remained standing. She wasn't shy about her body. With a face like hers, dignity went out the window. "Is something the matter?"

Bradley couldn't face her. He shielded his eyes like he was trying to avoid the blazing sun. "Maybe you should put some clothes on."

"Nah, I'm good."

Howard entered the room next, and when he saw Sarah standing naked, he acted exactly like Bradley did. "Sarah, I'm sorry. I came to check on you."

Dr Bennett rolled her eyes. "Captain Stone, there are clothes for you in the wardrobe. Perhaps you should put them on if you insist on staying out of bed."

Sarah limped over to the wardrobe, trying to disguise the weakness in her legs. It felt like she'd just run a marathon, followed by a mountain hike, followed by a pie-eating contest. She struggled to breathe. Inside the wardrobe, she found a pressed grey suit.

"It's one of mine," said Bennett, "but you're welcome to have it."

"Thanks." Sarah pulled the clothes on gingerly, buttoning up the shirt with clumsy hands. When she bent to lace the shoes, she crashed to the floor. Bradley and Howard rushed to her aid.

Dr Bennett growled. "I told you you needed rest, you silly girl."

"I-I'm fine. Someone just give me a hand."

Bradley helped tie her shoelaces and Howard eased her onto her feet. "Don't push too hard, champ."

"We're going with 'champ', are we?"

"Can you manage?"

Sarah took her hands away from Howard and nodded. "I'm good."

"What did you want me for?" Dr Bennett asked Bradley. "You said you came here looking for me."

Bradley cleared his throat. "Oh, um, yes, that's right. Director Palu wants all of us in the conference room ASAP. We've found out who the girl at the clinic was."

"Good," said Sarah, "because I'm going to kick her bloody arse."

Howard patted her on the back. "You'll get your chance."

Sarah smiled and tried to pretend that the pat on the back didn't just nearly floor her.

12

DOWN THE RABBIT HOLE

Sarah eased herself into a chair at the conference table. When she checked her watch, it was two-thirty in the morning. Did anyone sleep around here?

Palu was weary and pale as he nodded to her. "Captain Stone," he eyed her change of clothes. "I'm relieved to know you're okay. The paperwork would have been a nightmare if you'd died on us."

"I didn't know you cared."

"I advised the patient to remain in bed," said Dr Bennett, "so please let it be noted she refused."

"Noted," said Palu. "Can we get to business?"

Bradley placed his laptop on the desk and opened it. "What do we have?"

Palu opened his own computer and clicked through the files while giving them some preliminary intel. "I had the Home Office run employment checks on the newsagent. The suspect who snatched Dr Cartwright was legitimately employed there. We have National Insurance records, Income Tax reports... It's almost like she didn't care about being discovered."

"Or she expected no one to look for her," said Sarah. "She was just a kid."

"Her name is Ashley Foster," said Palu. "And you're right, she seems like an ordinary teenage girl on the surface."

Sarah folded her arms and winced at the flash of pain in her shoulder. "An ordinary teenage girl doesn't throw her life away, firing guns at... who are we exactly? I want to say the Justice League."

"We are the Major Crimes Unit," Palu stated, "and we take our job very seriously. If being shot hasn't taught you what we're up against, Captain, then I have no idea what will." There was an uncomfortable silence for a moment as he brought up new information on screen — a photograph of the girl who had shot her. "Ashley Foster drifted between part-time jobs after leaving school, but nine months ago she began working at the newsagent. The business is registered to a Pakistani immigrant who's currently out of the country. His niece, Aziza Hamidi, is running things in his absence, but the address we found for her is old. Background checks we ran came up blank."

"So we need to know how Ashley Foster knows Dr Cartwright," said Howard. "Was she in therapy?"

"Not that I can tell," said Palu. "Her medical records are thin. There would be no reason to believe she is anything other than a healthy teenager, if not for today's events."

Sarah rankled. "The bitch was running and gunning like a Spetnaz with a death wish. Ashley Foster has serious issues, I promise you."

"Her actions warrant extreme caution," Bennett agreed, much to Sarah's surprise.

Palu nodded. "We need to find out what her motives are. We have the address of her parents. Let's pay them a visit and see if they know anything about their daughter's hobbies."

Sarah went to get up from the table, caught unawares by the new pain in her shoulder. Fortunately, no one seemed to notice her wincing.

"Where do you think you're going?" Howard asked her. "You still need rest."

"I'm fine. Maybe if you hadn't let yourself get taken hostage, I wouldn't have got shot."

Howard glowered at her across the table, but he didn't say anything. Perhaps he was too tired to argue. Sarah, however, was always in the mood to argue. She turned to Bradley. "You should've taken your shot earlier. We could have had her."

Bradley dropped his head in shame.

"Enough," said Palu. "Dr Bennett? Is Captain Stone fit to resume active duty?"

"Not even close. She's still partially sedated, and her body needs to replace the blood it lost."

"Am I in any danger?" asked Sarah. "Beyond passing out or accidentally farting?"

Dr Bennett folded her arms and gave a tiny shrug. "Your stitches could open up. You could go into shock if you lose more blood. But, I suppose, if you take it easy, you may get away with just feeling like you're eighty years old. Good enough reason for you to stay put if you ask me."

"I'm going," said Sarah. "I'm the one Ashley Foster shot, and I would like to know who raised her to be a cross between Norman Bates and Rambo. This girl has training. I don't think we should take her for granted."

"This is not a mission of force," said Palu. "We just need to speak with the family before we make any snap decisions. If you have a grudge, you should let Howard take this one alone. The family will feel threatened enough, without having a mob turn up on their doorstep in the middle of the night."

Sarah sighed, and slowly realised her mouth was writing cheques her body couldn't cash. It was difficult to stand, and she felt like she could sleep a week. But she couldn't sit this one out. A bullet in her shoulder had made it personal. "You're right, it's not the right call to go in heavy, but sending me in with Howard is the right call. Not only am I a woman, which has its own benefits, but I'm a trained interrogator. In the Army, I was a liaison for local tribes and villagers. I can get answers from people who don't want to give them, trust me."

"Are you saying you tortured people?" asked Bradley.

Sarah shook her head. "Not torture. I just have a built-in bullshit detector. If a person is hiding something, I can tell."

Howard glanced at Palu. "It's true. Part of the reason I brought her in was because of her interrogation background. None of us have that."

Sarah thought about how her skills weren't as great as her MOD file probably made out. It had only taken a woman and some watermelons to fool her.

Palu waved a hand. "Okay fine, go, but I want no violence. The parents are innocent civilians until we know differently. It's their daughter we're after. Show a little diplomacy where possible."

"Hey, diplomacy is my middle name," said Sarah.

"Follow me," said Howard "We need to make a few stops before we set off."

"We should make a move now. Ashley could be at her parent's house for all we know."

"If you want my advice, I think you should get back in bed, but if you're determined to come with me, I would rather you had a weapon this time. Especially if we run into Ashley Foster again."

Sarah grinned from ear to ear. "A weapon? Now you're talking."

Howard took her through the Earthworm until they reached the MCU's armoury — a small vault nestled inside the head section behind a steel door.

Sarah gawped at the equipment on endless benches and shelves, a veritable museum of assault rifles, handguns, and other tactical weapons. There were rows upon rows of Glock 9mms, Colt 45s, and many other side-arms. What surprised her most, though, was a nest of military assault rifles lined up against the far wall. "Is that a FAMAS?" she said, jaw agape.

"Yes."

"British forces don't use French assault rifles. How did you get it?"

Howard tapped a finger against his nose. "Special consignment.

The MCU can use whatever hardware it feels is right for the situation. Originally, we were going to operate internationally — similar to the CIA and MI6 — but things never progressed that far. We still have a mandate that allows us to use heavy force if necessary, but we have an armoury stocked for three hundred personnel."

Sarah let out a whistle, and she spotted an F2000 that impressed her even more. The weapon looked like something out of a sci-fi movie.

"Small arms only on this ride," Howard told her. "So grab yourself something comfortable."

Sarah went to the handgun rack and perused the choices. She saw Brownings, American Smith and Wessons, Walther PPKs, and various Glocks. In addition, there was a single Colt .45 and an M1911 (the 'Yankee Fist'), but her eyes were drawn to a SIG-Sauer P229. It was smaller and lighter than most of the other handguns, and similar to the side-arm she had used on her tours in Afghanistan. Seeing one now made her skin prickle, the heat of the Middle-Eastern sun suddenly on the back of her neck. The nostalgia soon went away though, and she placed her hand around the grip. Long ago, she had convinced herself that the bad guys had beaten her, but now she realised the war wasn't over. She was still a soldier with a job to do. A duty.

"The SIG?" said Howard, raising an eyebrow. "Not bad, but I prefer something a little more robust."

Sarah blew a raspberry out of her cheeks. "If you pick up a Desert Eagle, I'll assume you have a tiny penis."

Howard smirked, then picked up a two-tone, silver handgun that was not a great deal bigger than her SIG. Unlike the stainless steel of her weapon, Howard's gun was a mix of Aluminium and polymer. "Ruger P95 Double Action," he said. "Just feels right."

"I was the same way picking my vibrator. I liked the cocking action on the Bushmaster 3000."

Howard blushed, and Sarah betrayed herself by letting a chuckle slip out. It was too was too much fun rattling his cage. Somewhere deep inside, this guy with a jutting chin and perfectly shaved sideburns was just dying to let loose and enjoy himself. She knew it.

Howard put on his grey woollen jacket and immediately his phone began to ring. He pulled out the mob-sat and looked at the screen. "Palu just sent us the Foster's home address. You ready to head out?"

Sarah grabbed a waist holster and nodded. "We meeting Mandy up top?"

"Yeah. You'll rarely find him any place else."

Sarah thought about how Mandy had carried her through the Earthworm after her injury, and how concerned he had seemed. "You know," she said, "you'll have to tell me how he made that helicopter disappear yesterday. I don't imagine he left it in the middle of the field."

"And you'd be right," said Howard. "I'm sure Mandy will let you in on the secret if you ask him."

"He *does* talk then?"

"Sometimes."

"What's his story? I don't think he's ex RAF."

"He's not," said Howard. "He's never been in the forces. He's a civilian. Paid for flight lessons himself. He was married once, but you'll have to ask *him* about it."

Sarah said no more. They headed up the staircase that exited into the derelict farm. Night had long ago fallen, which made the abandoned sheds and agricultural equipment even more haunting. Gaps in the crumbling brickwork whistled as a breeze passed through them and owls hooted in the rotten eaves of the old buildings. Sarah hugged herself and shivered, despite not feeling cold.

They hurried to the warehouse where, sure enough, Mandy was waiting for them. The Range Rovers were parked near the front of the shed, one of them pockmarked with bullet holes. "Best take a saloon," said Howard. "If Ashley Foster warned her parents, they might be on the lookout for Range Rovers."

Mandy grunted at them and fumbled in the pockets of his cargo pants, pulling out the correct set of keys. They unlocked a 2010 Jaguar XFR. Nothing too flashy, but far more luxurious than what Sarah was used to. Before the MCU had fallen into disrepair, it'd clearly been given money to burn.

Mandy held open the Jaguar's rear door for Sarah. She considered asking to drive, but knew she couldn't shove Mandy aside like she had Bradley. Howard sat up front, which left Sarah dumped in the back. For once, she didn't complain. She needed the room to spread out and air her aches. While she still had her wits about her, it took a concerted effort not to collapse into sobs.

The address Palu had given them was back in Oxford, so Mandy started the engine and headed across the field. Every jolt from the saloon's suspension caused Sarah's shoulder to flare, but she gritted her teeth and hid it as best she could. "Do the parents know we're coming?" she asked.

"No," said Howard. "Unless Ashley warned them. We'll play things cautiously. Mattock will be in the area ready to provide backup if needed."

Sarah swallowed. "The SAS guy?"

"Yeah, Bradley told you about him? Mattock's a good bloke to have in a pinch. No nonsense kind of bloke. You should like him."

She doubted it. "What background do the Fosters have? Any extreme political views?"

"Both voted Conservative, but we'll try not to hold it against them."

Mandy snorted in the driver's seat.

Sarah frowned. "Don't you take orders from a Conservative Prime Minister?"

Howard looked back at her and shrugged. "Until the next politician comes to power. They're all the same, whatever party they represent."

"Something we can agree on," said Sarah.

It took ten minutes to enter the main roads because the Jaguar wasn't built for off-roading like the Range Rovers were. They had to take it slow. Sarah spent the time considering what she would do if she got hold of the people responsible for the attacks on the United Kingdom. The SIG holster at her hip suddenly felt heavier, and it worried her how much she liked the feel of it there, hidden beneath her blazer.

How much she wanted to pull the trigger.

13

JACKED IN

When they reached the Foster's home address, it was four in the morning. The sky had turned a light shade of blue as the sun prepared to make a return. A chill made Sarah wonder if it was the weather or the fact that she was a few pints short of blood. Howard and Mandy had kept silent the entire journey. Both seemed tired. She probably looked pretty rotten herself.

The houses in the area were a mixture of detached and semi-detached properties, with short lawns and well-kept bushes. Mandy pulled up in front of a detached home and blocked the driveway. A sleek, black Audi sat in front of a double garage next to a Mini Cooper. Both cars looked new.

Sarah pressed her forehead against the car window and squinted. "Doesn't look like Ashley had a troubled upbringing."

"Nobody knows what goes on behind closed doors," said Howard. He put a hand on the door release. "You ready?"

"Yeah. What's the plan? Do we have fake Police badges or something?"

"You've been watching too many movies. We don't have specific identification, but most people don't tend to ask. Just speak with authority and people will do what you say. If we need to, we can have Palu arrange for the local police to meet us, but that's not how we want to do this."

"Okay, I'll follow your lead." Sarah pulled open her door and stepped onto the driveway. They strolled up the driveway and approached the front door. A wall lantern switched on as they neared. Howard rang the bell twice more before the hallway light came on.

The front door opened and a bleary-eyed man in his fifties appeared, fully dressed despite the hour. "Have you found her?" he asked.

Howard frowned. "I'm sorry?"

The man looked at them like they were idiots. "My daughter, Ashley. Have you found her? You're the police, I take it?"

"No, we're not the police. We're special investigators for the Home Office."

Mr Foster nodded. "Oh, well, the police came by earlier. They said our daughter is involved in a kidnapping."

"That's right," said Howard. "A Dr Cartwright is also involved. Do you know him?"

Mr Foster shook his head and sighed.

"We'd like to come in for a chat, if that's okay," said Howard, pressing. "We'd very much like to locate your daughter, as I'm sure you would."

"Yes, please, of course." Mr Foster stood aside and allowed them into the hallway. His wife was coming down the stairs as they entered, wearing a dressing gown and rubbing at her eyes. Sarah noted the woman's eye make-up.

Howard nodded to the woman. "Ma'am."

"They've come about Ashley," said Mr Foster to his wife.

"Come into the kitchen. I'll put some tea on."

They headed down the hallway and entered a kitchen at the back of the house. The floor was a deep brown wood, and the units were solid oak. Granite work surfaces and an expansive centre island completed the extravagant look. Clearly the Foster family were doing all right for themselves.

"You have a lovely home," Sarah remarked.

"Thank you," said Mrs Foster, glancing at Sarah but then looking away.

"You're looking at my scars?"

"Um, yes, I'm sorry. It's rude."

"It's okay. I served in Afghanistan; left a part of me over there."

"That's horrible."

"It is, but I'm here to talk about your daughter, not my troubles."

"I hope you don't mind us waking you so early, Mr and Mrs Foster," said Howard.

Mrs Foster smiled. "Please, call us Leanne and Paul. We just want to know our daughter is safe."

Howard took a seat at the island. "Leanne, Paul, what do you know about what's happened? Are you certain you don't know Dr Cartwright?"

Leanne set two mugs of steaming tea on the counter and sat opposite Howard. "We don't know anything," she said. "Ashley went to work this morning as usual. Next thing we know, the police are contacting us and claiming our daughter is wanted in connection with kidnapping and possible shooting. They wouldn't tell us anything else. It's insane."

Paul hugged his wife. "I'm sure everything will work itself out, sweetheart. None of this makes any sense, but Ashley is a good girl. There has to be an explanation."

Howard smiled, then waited a moment until the couple composed themselves. "Can you tell us about your daughter? Does Ashley have any kind of problems that you know about?"

Leanne shook her head. "Ashley wouldn't hurt a fly."

"She hasn't been in therapy?" Howard enquired. "Or in trouble with the courts? Sorry for having to ask such questions."

Paul frowned. "She's had no problems at all like that. She's just a normal teenaged girl. What exactly do you think my daughter has done? She's just a girl. It's all a mistake!"

"You're right," said Sarah. "The police got it wrong when they said she was involved in a kidnapping. What I saw was your daughter helping a man escape questioning. A man connected to the recent bombings."

The faces of both parents dropped. It was Leanne who spoke. "Who are you people? If you're not the police..."

Howard sipped his tea and allowed a silence to settle over the room before he spoke. "We work for an agency committed to preventing terrorist attacks against our nation. Ashley is involved with a man linked to the recent bombings. We're trying to find out how."

Paul rubbed at his eyes. "Our daughter is innocent. I don't know what she's mixed up in, but she's a sweet girl."

"I believe you," said Howard warmly. "She's too young to have done anything so wrong. She's gotten mixed up in something she doesn't understand. All I want is to do is find her and help her. To do that though, I need to know all I can about her. Has she been acting strangely recently, or out of character?"

Paul shook his head, but Leanne nodded. "She's been out a lot. I assumed she was seeing somebody." Her eyes went wide as if something obviously occurred to her. "Maybe that's it. Maybe this psychiatrist, Dr Cartwright, has seduced our daughter and gotten her involved in something. Psychiatrists know all kinds of ways to manipulate young minds, don't they? It makes perfect sense."

Howard exchanged a glance with Sarah. "Perhaps you're right," he said. "Do you have any idea where Ashley could be? The slightest guess?"

"No," said Leanne.

"Me either," said Paul. "I don't know where Ashley likes to go other than work."

"Do you know her boss?" Howard asked.

Paul shook his head. "I've met the woman once or twice when I've stopped by the newsagent. Asian lady with a heavy accent. Whenever I see her, she's all covered up in those dresses they wear. You know what I mean?"

Howard nodded. "Does Aziza Hamidi sound familiar?"

"All I know is that my daughter refers to her boss as 'Zee.'"

"Thank you, that's useful. Is there anything else you can think of that might help us locate your daughter? Any friends she likes to visit, or someplace she might go if she were in trouble?"

"She'd come here," Leanne spluttered. "This is her home."

Howard looked at Sarah. "Anything you'd like to add?"

"Just two questions, really," she studied the married couple for a moment, leaving it long enough to make them fidget uncomfortably. "The first question I have for you both is, why have neither of you asked what we know about your daughter? The normal reaction to have when we arrived would be to ask if we knew anything at all about Ashley's wellbeing. Whether or not she's safe, if there's been any sighting of her, etc. A parent would want to know everything they could, but the two of you have hardly asked a thing. Your only concern has been telling us that your daughter is innocent. Neither of you has made much eye-contact with each other either. Usually, during a conversation, people glance at one another for visual cues, but you both seem to be on the same page about everything without any mutual confirmation. Also, Mrs Foster, your mascara is confusing me."

"M-My mascara. What?"

"It's not smudged. Haven't you been crying over what's happened today? Isn't Ashley your baby? You might have reapplied it, granted but it's the middle of the night."

"T-This is outrageous."

Paul slammed his fists on the counter. "How dare you?"

"Okay," Sarah said, holding up her palms in apology. "Maybe I'm wrong. If so, I apologise. The other question I wanted to ask, though, is how do you know Dr Cartwright's a psychiatrist? We never told you he was. We only told you he was a doctor."

"The police told us," said Paul.

Sarah frowned. "But your wife said the police gave no details other than that Ashley is wanted in connection with a kidnapping. When I asked if you'd heard the name Dr Cartwright, you initially said no."

Howard nodded. "The police wouldn't have shared any information about a suspect. They wouldn't have mentioned Dr Cartwright or his profession."

Paul had gone bright red. "The man works opposite our daughter in that clinic. It wasn't a massive assumption to make."

"No," said Sarah. "You specifically said he was a psychiatrist. The clinic across the road has half a dozen specialists and several GP offices. It might make sense for you to guess that Cartwright is a doctor, but not specifically that he's a psychiatrist."

Leanne shifted on her stool. "Perhaps I met Dr Cartwright before and just couldn't remember. Come to think of it, Ashley might have gone out for a drink with him one time."

Sarah smiled. "Oh, that explains it then. Well, I guess we should get going if we're going to find your daughter."

Leanne stood up from the breakfast bar. "Yes, well, let me give you some breakfast for the road. A banana or something."

Sarah frowned. She'd had the feeling the Fosters wanted her and Howard gone, but now they were suddenly being offered breakfast.

"That's quite alright," said Howard, waving a hand.

"Please, I insist," Leanne reached for the middle of the counter where a wooden bowl of apples and bananas sat.

"Stop," said Sarah. "We're okay."

"I won't hear of it." Leanne ignored her and kept on reaching. She picked up an apple, but then fumbled it to the floor. "Silly me, could one of you pick that up for me?"

Howard bent to pick the bruised apple up off the tiles.

"Howard, get down!" Sarah slid the SIG from its holster and pointed it at Leanne Foster.

Leanne delved into the fruit bowl just as Paul slipped from his stool and kneed Howard in the face.

Howard hit the floor, moaning.

Leanne pulled a gun from the bottom of the fruit bowl and pointed it.

Sarah fired first.

The first bullet struck Leanne in the shoulder, the following two in the chest. The woman cartwheeled backwards, dead before she hit the ground. Paul saw his dead wife and charged at Sarah, but she was ready for him. Forgetting how weak and weary she was, she leapt aside and kicked him in the knee. Paul stumbled, but then came at her again. Sarah smashed the butt of her SIG against his temple and dropped him to his knees.

"Lie down on the ground!" she shouted.

Paul Foster snarled. "You bitch."

Sarah snarled right back in his face. "The worst bitch you ever met, so don't even blink if you want to keep your teeth."

Howard clambered to his feet, clutching his right eyebrow. "Shit, I'm hurt."

Sarah rolled her eyes. "We can discuss facial injuries later, but trust me you'll lose."

Howard tittered and reached into his jacket to pull out his mob-sat. He dialled a number. "Mattock? I need an extraction at—"

Blam!

Sarah ducked as gunfire rang again in the kitchen. Coming at them from the back of the room was Ashley Foster, running and gunning like she had outside the clinic. Sarah narrowed her eyes, woozy from exertion yet energised with rage.

Howard leapt behind the breakfast bar and pulled out his Ruger. Sarah leapt up from behind the breakfast table and zeroed in on Ashley. It was time for a little payback. "Get down or I'll sh—"

Paul barrelled into her from the side, causing her to fire a round into the ceiling. He followed up the attack by almost breaking her jaw with a punch. She sprawled to ground as all of her injuries coalesced and left her a gelatinous mess. The pain in her shoulder made her vision spin.

"Not as big a bitch as you thought, huh?" Paul raised his foot to stamp on her skull, but Howard rose up and let off a shot. It missed, but was enough to send Paul running to join his daughter at the back of the kitchen. Howard tried to take a follow-up shot, but Ashley fired at him first and forced him back down behind the island.

Sarah tried to catch her breath as the Fosters escaped through a back door. They couldn't be allowed to get away.

Once the coast was clear, Howard scurried over to help her. "How did you know she had a gun hidden in the fruit bowl?"

Sarah blinked away the stars in her vision. "Fruit and I have a long history. Now, come on, let's get after them."

As if in reply, gunfire rang outside, preceding the sound of an engine starting up.

Sarah flinched. "Shit! Mandy!"

Howard took off, and Sarah staggered after him. She held her SIG in front of her, ready to take down anyone who even looked at her wrong. Howard yanked open the front door and they both ducked out onto the driveway. The sleek black Audi had rocketed away from the garage, shunting the MCU's Jaguar out of the way. Lights in the nearby houses flipped on like beacons, alerted by the gunfire and stock car antics.

"We really need to get a mechanic on staff," said Howard, shaking his head.

Sarah looked at the crumpled wing of the Jaguar and clucked. "Too bad we don't have the budget."

"It's 'we' now, is it?"

"Come on." She raced over to the Jaguar and found Mandy still sitting in the driver's seat. It was clear from the shattered front windows that Ashley and her father had fired at him as they made their escape. He looked none too happy about it. Sarah slid in beside the big man and Howard threw himself across the back seat.

Without word, Mandy slammed his foot on the accelerator and the Jaguar squealed away from the curb. The Foster's Audi was fast, and it roared through the neighbourhood like an angry wasp, but Mandy's Jaguar was quick too, deceptively so for such a big car. It wasn't long before they gained a few yards on their target. Sarah clocked the speedometer at seventy.

"It's a TT," said Howard from the back seat. "They have a few horsepower on us, but we have Mandy."

To prove a point, the TT careened around an upcoming corner while Mandy seemed to float around it. The Audi raced for the highway. They followed, two car distances behind.

But that distance started to grow larger.

"They're getting away!" Sarah yelled.

Howard grunted. "We can't keep up with them on the straight. Maybe we can cut them off at the exit." He pulled out his mob-sat and put another call through to Mattock. "We're in pursuit of target, heading north on A4114, Abingdon Road. Requesting backup at River Thames, south side." Howard listened for a second, then put the mob-sat back in his pocket. He leant forward between the front seats. "Mattock will be at the river in six."

Sarah hissed. "That will be too late. We'll be at the river any minute."

Howard's face went blank as he searched for an idea. Ahead, the TT continued pulling away. Sarah pulled out her SIG and took aim through the side window. She knew she shouldn't discharge her weapon on a public highway, but no way was she letting this bitch get away from her twice. She pulled the trigger and fired a shot. The discharge made no sound in the rushing wind and the bullet seemed to disappear. She fired several more times, but there was too much distance between the two cars to get a hit. "Damn it! They're getting away."

"No, they're not," said Howard. He turned around and rifled through the Jaguar's rear compartment behind the seats. What he came back with both shocked and delighted Sarah.

"Now you're turning me on," she said.

Howard held the L129A1 Sharpshooter against his shoulder and grinned. "A gift from our American cousins."

The morning roads were empty, so the Fosters were able to gain more and more distance every second. Nothing was in the way to force them to slow down. "You need to hurry," said Sarah. "They'll be out of range soon."

Howard rolled down his window and shoved his upper body out of the car, righting the rifle against his shoulder. A few seconds passed while he squinted into the scope. Then he let off an ear-piercing shot.

The TT continued speeding away. He'd missed.

Howard concentrated and then fired again. This time the TT jerked to the left. For a second, it looked like it would flip, but its safety systems kicked in and the tyres regained their grip on the road. A thick strip of rubber disconnected from the TT and whizzed by the Jaguar's windscreen. Sarah smiled as she realised Howard had hit the rear tyre. Despite the damage, the TT continued speeding along.

"They must have run flats," Sarah said.

"Doesn't matter," said Howard. "It'll slow them down."

Mandy leant forward behind the wheel, his eyes narrowing, shoulders stiffening. It wouldn't be long before they caught up to the TT.

Sarah waited with her SIG across her lap She'd already killed Leanne Foster tonight. Could she take more lives? Did she even care? The Fosters had given up their right to mercy when they'd gotten involved with Hesbani. There was no obvious link, but Sarah knew that *Shab Bekhier* was behind this. A shiver ran down her neck.

They were right behind the TT now.

Sarah checked her watch: 5:12AM.

"Get ready," said Howard. He'd placed the Sharpshooter down on the back seat and was holding his Ruger now. "Mandy, try to run them off the road as soon as it's safe. If they refuse to stop, Sarah and I will have to take them out."

Mandy brought the Jaguar up on the TT's rear bumper. The Audi's rear tyre had gone completely flat now, and the vehicle hitched from side to side as Paul obviously fought against the steering. Sarah could see Ashley sitting beside him, looking back at them through the rear windscreen. Sarah gave the girl the middle finger.

Ashley fired.

Sarah ducked as the Jaguar's windscreen cracked, but she was right back up to return fire through her window. The TT continued veering back and forth, still speeding at over fifty.

Sarah took another shot as a ricochet from Ashley's weapon bounced off the Jaguar's roof and almost took the other side of her face. Her ears were ringing, and in the distance she could hear the sirens of alerted police. She wondered what would happen if they were to get involved. The MCU was supposed to be secret, so what would the police have to say about the dead woman she'd just left in a middle-class neighbourhood? How much influence did MCU have?

Ashley let off another shot and forced Sarah to duck back inside the car. It was too dangerous to keep exchanging shots like this.

"River's coming up," Howard informed her. "Let's hope Mattock is there waiting for us."

Mandy yanked the steering wheel and brought the Jaguar up around the side of the slowing TT. As Sarah looked to her left, she saw Paul gripping the steering wheel and facing forward defiantly. Was he scared for himself, or his daughter?

Ashley leant over her father's lap and let off another pair of shot. The Jaguar's unprotected side windows shattered.

Mandy trod on the brake and pulled back before Ashley had chance to fire on them any more, but Sarah cried out when she saw him bleeding and half-conscious behind the wheel. His black clothing made the source of the blood hard to detect, but the splatter around his neck and face made it clear he'd been hit.

"Mandy!"

The Jaguar veered sideways. Sarah and Howard were powerless to do anything as the vehicle hopped the embankment and smashed head-first into a lorry parked in a lay-by. Sarah's body turned to jelly. Her bones rattled inside her skin. Her head bucked so hard that she thought it might fall off her shoulders. Then, suddenly, all she could see was white.

Something smothered her face, making her panic, and it took several anguished seconds before she realised it was the airbag. She pawed and swatted at the balloon until it deflated and got out of her way.

Mandy hung upside down from the driver's seat beside her, held in place by his seatbelt. He wasn't moving, and blood dripped down his forehead, pattering against the roof beneath them. Howard was lost in the back somewhere.

Sarah unclipped her seatbelt and eased herself the right way around. She shuffled towards the nearest sight of tarmac, kicking with her legs and pulling with her fingertips. Blood leaked from a gash on the back of her hand, which caused her to moan. She couldn't lose any more blood — already felt close to passing out.

Pulling herself into a shaft of sunlight, Sarah crawled through the hole left by the Jaguar's missing windscreen. It was a tight fit, but she made her way out of the car. It disturbed her she had done this before, but this time, instead of the scorching sands of Afghanistan, it was a coarse roadway in England.

Footsteps sounded nearby. Paul Foster appeared and pointed a gun in Sarah's face. Ashley stood beside her father, sneering. "Just kill the bitch, dad."

"I will, but you get out of here first."

"No way."

Paul looked at his daughter. "Don't you hear that? The police will be here any minute. Get out of here now while I deal with this. I'll be with you soon. You know where to go. There's still work to be done."

"Um, is everyone okay?"

Sarah glanced up to see a chubby man wandering towards them. He was rubbing his head and staggering. He'd obviously been asleep in the lorry.

"Is anybody hurt?"

Paul raised his gun and shot the man in the face. Then he turned back to his daughter. "Go!"

Ashley took off like lightning. The bitch had nine-lives, and Sarah didn't have the energy to take them all. She was finished. It was finally over.

"I'm sorry about this," said Paul, pointing the gun at her face again, "but you're part of the problem."

"W-What problem?" Sarah realised she needed to know why he was doing this. She didn't want to die in ignorance.

"The problem with the world," said Paul through a hate-filled sneer, "is that ninety-nine percent of us toil and suffer to make life better for the other one percent. Don't you think that's wrong? Don't you feel ashamed for being a part of that? For fighting to protect it?" Paul pressed the gun barrel against her forehead. "Well, I'm sorry, but no more one percent."

Something inside Sarah reacted, even if most of her had given up. She whacked Paul's gun aside just as he was about to pull the trigger. The sudden blow caught him off guard, and he stumbled. Sarah pushed up from the ground and struck him square in the sternum with the heel of her palm. The air went rushing out of him. His face puffed up like a balloon. She went to strike again, but Paul recovered and punched her in the ribs. She tried to shake the blow off, but before she could recover, the gun was back in her face.

"You just made this a whole lot easier," said Paul, and he pulled the trigger.

14

WEAKNESS

AFGHANISTAN, 2008

Sarah didn't know how long she'd been asleep for when they dragged her from the cell. They took Hamish too, who'd recovered enough from his beating to share some bread and water with Sarah. The soldier killed by the IED had been one of the privates, not Sarah's corporal as she'd feared. Hamish had been dragged out of the Snatch right after Sarah had been taken. He'd tried to put up a fight, but they'd beaten him bloody.

Now they were being manhandled and carried away. Every time Sarah stumbled or lost her footing, she received an elbow in the back or a sandal up her backside. She was subdued and pathetic, but Hamish was irate and defiant. He bellowed and cursed at their captors, even as the men slapped and punched him in the face.

"Shut up, Hamish. They'll kill you if you don't shut up."

"They're gunna kill me anyhow. Why make it easy for 'em?"

"They're going to let us go. Al Sharir told me so last night."

Hamish looked at her with his one eye that wasn't completely swollen shut. "Really?"

"Yes! So keep quiet."

Hamish caught another shove in his back, but this time he didn't react. They were taken in silence to a dusty yard, walled off on every side. A group of men had gathered there, with Al-Sharir and Wazir Hesbani among them. A boy knelt in the centre of the yard, crying and begging. He looked around fifteen, in jeans and a Ramones t-shirt. It was his fuzzy beard and cheap sandals that gave him away as a native Afghan.

Al-Sharir summoned Sarah and Hamish before him and had them lowered to their knees beside the boy. Sarah gritted her teeth at the pain in her wounded thigh. It was burning like nothing she'd ever felt before. The wound had been weeping and throbbing all night.

Al-Sharir gave her a thin smile. "Hello, Captain, how are you feeling today?"

Sarah looked him in the eye. "Looking forward to you keeping your word."

"I shall keep my word, do not fear."

Sarah let out a breath. She'd been anxious that Al-Sharir would change his mind, so it was a relief to hear that he had not. "Thank you," she said.

"But we have business to attend to first. We won't keep you longer than we need."

Sarah frowned. What business was there? She wanted to go back to Camp Bastion.

Hesbani scowled at her for a moment, then turned and pointed at the teenaged boy kneeling beside her. "This man has been found guilty of murder. Under Islamic law, he is to be put to death."

The boy wailed and prayed to Allah.

"He's just a child," Sarah said. "What could he have done?"

"He has been found guilty of slaughter, and must be held accountable before almighty Allah." Hesbani struck the boy and bloodied his mouth. A man standing in the crowd caught the boy and kept him upright on his knees. The boy begged for mercy.

Hamish growled. "Leave 'im be, you tossers."

Hesbani glanced curiously at Hamish. "What is *tosser*?"

"It's a fella what hits kids."

"Then I am indeed a *tosser*." Hesbani struck the boy again.

Sarah closed her eyes. "Please stop."

Al-Sharir raised a hand to stop the violence. He took a step towards Sarah and looked down upon her. "Would you like to know this boy's crimes? His actions have caused many deaths."

Sarah knew what the boy would be guilty of, it was clear from his clothing. The boy had probably grown up in a village controlled by NATO forces, lived on their handouts, and begged for Western clothing. "He's been helping the allied forces, informing on the Taliban. He's just a child doing what he thinks is *right*."

Al-Sharir shook his head as though he pitied her. "No, he is not reporting on Taliban. He *is* Taliban."

Sarah's jaw dropped. "No..."

Hesbani spat at the boy. "Confused by clothing, are you, Captain? He dress so to get close to Western troops, no? He spy on them from few feet away. IED that take you and your men is his creation. Clever boy, no?"

Sarah frowned. "That doesn't make any sense. The IED belongs to you. *You* set the trap."

Al-Sharir knelt in front of her. "No. Taliban left the IED. I just cleaned up mess. That is why the boy is here. He enjoys setting bombs. He is evil."

Sarah looked at the sobbing child and struggled to reconcile what she was hearing. "I don't believe you."

Hesbani laughed. "Why? Because he is boy? No, he is killer. Trained from birth to make bomb and kill your soldiers. He has killed many dozen. Your own men now. Murder is all he knows. Not just a boy."

"It is true," said Al-Sharir. "The boy is well known to us. He has a talent for death. The Taliban have trained many innocent children to be killers like him, but this boy truly excels. Once they reach a certain age, they are irredeemable. It is my duty to see their wicked lives ended."

Sarah didn't understand. "Why do you care if he kills Allied soldiers?"

"I care because every death he causes keeps your invading armies here longer. I believe in fighting for Afghanistan's freedom, but buried bombs and booby traps are not the way of Allah. There is no honour in creating something that can kill a child as easily as a soldier. Last week, one of this boy's bombs killed an innocent girl and her mother. The girl was five years old. Her father saw the whole thing. He brought their remains back to the village before taking his own life. Warriors should only kill other warriors. That is Allah's will."

Sarah swallowed. Part of her had already stopped caring about what happened to the boy after hearing all this, but another part reminded her it was not the boy's fault. He'd been raised by the Taliban. "Hand the boy over to Camp Bastion and we'll deal with him. You said you want the fighting to stop, so cooperate."

"Cooperate with foreign invaders?" Hesbani snarled at her. "We deal with own problems, enforce own laws. We want death to end, but can only happen if we unite against West."

"My friend is right," said Al-Sharir, easing Hesbani back a step. "Why should we hand the boy over when it is *our* laws he has broken? Muslim lives he has taken? You wish to imprison the boy, but Allah demands a greater punishment."

"Kill the bastard." Hamish shrugged. "If you don't, our lot will eventually." Sarah stared at her corporal and he shrugged again "What? We lost three young boys to that IED. The kid deserves an execution. He's Taliban."

"That's not who we are," said Sarah. "We're here to help these people, not execute them. We're soldiers not killers."

Hesbani was losing patience. "The boy has been found guilty under Islamic law. He will die."

Al-Sharir raised his hand to Hesbani. "Perhaps the Captain is right. Perhaps we can compromise. The boy does not have to die." He placed a hand against the boy's bruised cheek and smiled. "*Ta shaista starge lare.*" Then he gave Hesbani a nod and the boy was dragged to his feet.

"Your lucky day," said Hesbani, grabbing the boy by his throat and holding him on his feet. With his free hand he slid a rusty *peshkabz* from a scabbard on his belt. The ceremonial dagger was commonplace amongst the hill tribes of Afghanistan, but not so common in the South. The boy yelled in terror, kicking his legs so hard that both sandals flew off his feet. Hesbani controlled the boy with a single hand while waving the dagger in front of the boy's face with the other.

Hesbani shoved the dagger into the boy's left eye.

Then the right.

The boy slumped to the ground, howling in a way that wasn't human. He clutched his ruined eyes and convulsed in the dirt. Sarah lurched forward and threw up. Hamish moaned beside her.

"Your turn now," said Hesbani, grabbing Hamish by the back of his shirt and dragging him to his feet.

Hamish struggled until members of the crowd restrained him and Hesbani smashed him in the face with the dagger's handle. Tears blinded him, and all the fight left him.

Sarah cried out to Al-Sharir. "You said you would let us go."

"No, I said that I would let *you* go."

"Please. Please, don't kill him."

Al-Sharir tapped his chin with his forefinger and seemed to think for a few seconds. Eventually, he nodded and said, "Okay, I have idea. Wazir, take his eyes. We send them back with the captain as a gift."

"No!" Sarah screamed.

"Just kill me," Hamish moaned. "I'd rather die."

Hesbani kicked Hamish in the back of the legs and sent him onto his knees.

Sarah tried to get up, but a the crowd held her down. Al-Sharir stood in front of her, his face suddenly hard and violent. "Do not struggle, Captain. You have an innocent one inside of you, remember? It is the only reason you live."

Hamish looked at her with wide eyes, surprised by the revelation. No one besides Thomas had known she was pregnant.

"Just let us go," she begged. "You'll just make things worse if you execute a British soldier."

Al-Sharir raised an eyebrow. "Ah, but I save more than I kill. The boy killer will set no more bombs. Any debt I have to the British Army is paid, no? I tell you what, I shall allow you to decide your corporal's fate. I have already been fair to you, but still you ask for more. So, Captain, do I have Wazir kill your corporal, or should he just take his eyes?"

"Neither. Please, neither."

Al-Sharir nodded. "Okay, third choice. I let him go and blind *you* instead. Your child will be safe and your corporal shall live. Your face is badly hurt already. This way, you will not have to look in the mirror."

"Y-You're sick!"

"You offend me. I am being more kind than you deserve. Now make your choice."

Sarah caught Hamish's gaze as they looked at each other in complete horror. Neither of them made a sound.

"Make decision!" Al-Sharir bellowed.

Sarah sobbed. "I can't!"

Al-Sharir's face turned wicked, a mask dropping from the monster beneath. "Fine. Your choices are shrinking. Now the choice is whether to blind you or kill him. Your sight, Captain, or your man's life."

Sarah couldn't find her voice.

Al-Sharir folded his arms. "Fine. Wazir, take the Captain's eyes. We'll send her corporal back with her unharmed to tell everybody what a hero she is."

"No!" Sarah's gushed in floods of tears. "Don't hurt me. Don't! Not me."

Hamish stared at her with bloodshot, terror-filled eyes. His expression froze in place and he teetered back and forth in the dirt as if stunned.

Sarah stared down at the dirt.

Al-Sharir turned to face the crowd. "And there we have it. The British see themselves as noble and just, yet none of them are prepared to suffer for their convictions. They lack faith and courage. They would rather watch a friend die than lose something of their own." He turned back to Sarah, a shadow across his face. "Your greed, your selfishness... it shall be your downfall. Paradise does not open for men who think themselves kings. Wazir, get it over with. I tire of being around these soulless devils."

Sarah couldn't watch. She'd sentenced her corporal to death, and she couldn't even bring herself to watch. Al-Sharir was right, she lacked courage. In fact, she had none of it at all.

She heard the sound of sinewy meat being cut, followed by a desperate gargling sound as Hamish choked to death on his own blood. From the corner of her eye, she watched Hesbani wipe his knife clean on Hamish's chest before dragging his body away.

The crowd cheered and celebrated in Allah's name.

OXFORD, 2014

Paul Foster was dead before he pulled the trigger all the way. His head exploded in a cloud of mist and he slumped face down on top of Sarah. Sarah just lay there beneath his weight, wondering why she hadn't died. Somebody had saved her, but who?

Paul's body rolled aside, and Sarah's rescuer, a middle-aged man with a face cut from rock, revealed himself. A large scar sliced the top of his shaved head like the seam on a tennis ball. "You all right, luv?"

Sarah couldn't speak.

The man patted her down with harsh, all-business hands. His expression, as he looked at her, was oddly compassionate considering the harshness of his battle-hardened features. "Are you in pain?" he asked. "Can you move?"

Sarah nodded.

"Let's give it a go then."

Sarah took the man's rough hand and he yanked her to her feet. She dusted herself off and tried to regain her equilibrium before she fell back down. She tried to speak, but her rescuer bolted off toward the crumpled mess of the Jaguar XFR before she had the chance. There were other men already there, six in total, and they all wore urban combat suits covered in pouches. In the middle of the road was the Foster's Audi TT. Its flat tyre had brought it to a stop.

Sarah watched the chaos for a moment, then snapped back to reality. "Howard!" she yelled. "Mandy!"

Both men were still inside the wrecked Jaguar. The response team were already forcing the wrecked vehicle's frame apart with the Jaws of Life.

"Stay back, Captain," said the man who had shot Paul. "We have this under control."

"You're Mattock," she said.

"I am, and you're Captain Stone. What the bleedin' hell happened here, luv?"

"I don't know." It was the truth. Sarah's mind was a blur. "We were trying to run them off the road. Mandy got shot."

Mattock grimaced. "Mandy took a bullet?"

Sarah swallowed. She'd never exchanged two words with the silent giant, but she hated knowing he was hurt. "I don't know how bad it was," was all she could say.

"How about Howard? Is he okay?"

"I don't know. He was in the back."

"We'll have 'em out soon enough, Captain, but we need to get you out of here. Old Bill is coming."

To prove his point, a fleet of police cars skidded to a stop in the middle of the road.

"What will you tell them?" Sarah asked.

"I can get this squared away, but with Mandy and Howard incapacitated, we can't afford to have you retained for questioning. We need to get you out of here and back to the Earthworm, pronto."

"I'm not leaving Howard and Mandy."

"I'm not giving you a choice, luv. You look like shit, and you're the only witness to this entire fuck fest. If the Old Bill get 'old of you, you'll be answering questions until the Queen farts. All the while, there are bad guys out there plotting their next move."

Sarah gave in. Even if she wanted to stay, Mattock looked like he would crush her in his fist until she changed her mind. "Okay," she said. "What should I do?"

"Take this." He handed her a slim, electronic device. "It's an MCU mob-sat. Take off now, find someplace safe, and then call Palu. He'll have you extracted. Don't let the plods catch you until I have this all squared away, understand?"

"Yes."

"Then get your arse in gear, girl."

The police were getting out of their cars and heading toward the scene. Sarah wanted to run, but she couldn't take her eyes off the upturned Jaguar. Howard and Mandy were still inside. It felt wrong to leave them. She'd made a habit of leaving people behind, and she hated herself for it.

But what else could she do?

She could catch the sons of bitches responsible, that's what.

"Get moving," Mattock shouted at her.

Sarah bolted, disappearing through the overgrown verge and onto a grassy embankment. Ashley Foster had escaped again, but maybe if Sarah was lucky, they would run into each other again.

15

STRENGTH

It was half-seven when Sarah stopped running. She reached a bus stop and keeled over on the bench, dangling her head between her legs. Maybe she could lie low there for a while, pretending she was waiting for a bus. Hiding in plain sight. Covered in cuts and bruises.

She pulled the mob-sat from her blazer and switched it on, then hit the icon marked CONTACTS. A long list of names appeared, including Prime Minister Breslow. Impressive.

A bus stopped at the side of the road, but Sarah remained seated until it closed its doors and drove away. When it did, she searched the contacts list and found DIRECTOR PALU.

Palu picked up right away, but said nothing. Not knowing what else to do, Sarah stated her name.

"Sarah, are you all right? Mattock just reported in. He told me what happened."

"I'm a total mess, but that was true when you hired me. I need... rescuing."

"Where are you?"

Sarah looked around until she spotted a bus timetable and read out the address. "I'm sitting in a bus shelter in Botley. Bus stop 12, Raleigh Park Road."

"Lie low. Bradley's on his way."

"Roger that."

"Are you hurt?"

"Only emotionally. I... killed Leanne Foster. Mattock killed Paul Foster. Ashley got away. The whole family is involved in this somehow."

Palu exhaled. "Dr Bennett and I are looking into every lead we have. We'll figure it out. Just sit tight, okay?"

"Will do. I'll report in if I need to move."

"Roger that."

Sarah slumped on the bench and watched the morning traffic. Whatever pain killers Bennet had given her had now worn off, and the pain was all she could focus on.

Forty minutes later, Bradley parked in front of the bus stop in the remaining Jaguar from MCU. By that time, the shelter was full of commuters, and they eyed Sarah suspiciously as she got into the car. Bradley was a sight for sore eyes, and he looked glad to see her too. "Are you okay, Captain?"

"I'm not a captain so stop calling me that. Just get me back to the Earthworm."

Bradley said nothing for a moment, then he gave her good news. "Howard's going to be okay."

Sarah stared at him. "Really?"

"He has a broken arm and a concussion, but nothing that won't heal."

"What about Mandy?"

Bradley went quiet.

"Bradley!"

"We don't know yet. He took a slug in his lung. Mattock took him to John Radcliffe Hospital, and he'll update us as soon as he learns anything. Things went pretty bad, huh?"

Sarah let her head drop. Her shoulder was throbbing. "What do we have on Ashley Foster? We can't let her get away with this."

"We won't," said Bradley. "Bennett and Palu are finding everything they can. There has to be a reason the Fosters are involved in whatever's going on. We'll link them to Hesbani, and then it's just a matter of time."

Sarah rubbed at her scars and tried to figure things out. Paul Foster had been concerned about his daughter getting to safety, the same way any father would be, but something must have happened to make a middle-class family man militant. Discovering Paul Foster's trigger could be the key to figuring everything out.

"Is Howard back at the Earthworm?" she asked.

Bradley looked away from the road. "One of Mattock's men took him there. I heard he reached you in the nick of time."

Sarah pictured Paul Foster kneeling over her about to pull the trigger. "He saved my life. Just like you did back at the clinic."

Bradley blushed. "I'm improving."

Sarah didn't allow him to make light of the matter. Too much was at stake. "But you need to do a lot better. You could have ended the situation sooner. We would have Dr Cartwright in custody and Ashley dead or wounded. Everything that's happened this morning is because you didn't pull the trigger when you were supposed to." Sarah remembered how quickly she had pulled the trigger on Leanne. No hesitation. Had she been born with that, or had she learned it? "Soon as you're sure, Bradley, you act. I know you were thinking about whether or not you could take a human life, but trust me, more people die if you don't pull the trigger."

Bradley looked like he was about to erupt into tears.

Sarah softened. "Look, I'm not one to give anybody a lecture. Since Howard brought me in, I've been nothing but a liability, but unlike me you're going to be sticking around. You need to get better at this."

Bradley suddenly seemed determined. He gripped the steering wheel harder. "I will."

"So you're not going to quit?"

"Not while there are people like Hesbani in the world. I'll get better, I promise."

"Don't promise me. Promise yourself. You're too young and sweet to get killed in the line of duty."

Bradley chuckled. "Thank you, Captain."

"It's Sarah."

"Sorry. Thank you, Sarah."

She cleared her throat. "Now, get me back to Dr Bennett so she can give me more of the good stuff. My shoulder is killing me. I think my stitches opened."

Bradley pulled onto the highway and picked up speed. "What were you doing all the way over in Botley?"

"I headed in the same direction Ashley went and kept on going. I was hoping to get another shot at her, but she was gone. Eventually my legs gave up, and when I stopped I was in Botley."

"It's a nice village," said Bradley, glancing out his window. "The kind of place where they probably still keep budgies in cages."

"Knutsford was a nice little village, too. So were Studley, Arborfield, and Dartmouth. That's what at stake here."

Bradley looked at her. "You don't think Botley could be a target, do you?"

"Probably not. Even if Ashley headed here, it doesn't mean the village is a target. All the same, let's get Palu on the radio. Maybe we can pick up Ashley if we're lucky."

Bradley thumbed a button on the steering wheel and the audible sound of dialling took over the car's interior.

"Bradley?"

"Palu, it's Sarah."

"Sarah. Are you with Bradley?"

"Yes, we're together. We think we might have a lead on Ashley Foster. She might have ended up in Botley, same as me.."

Silence.

Bradley tapped the dashboard with his finger. "Sir, you there?"

Palu came back on. "Dr Bennett has just found something; a reason the Fosters might have had a grudge."

"Go on," said Sarah.

"The HS2 link."

Sarah and Bradley exchanged confused glances. Sarah leant forwards into the intercom. "The train line the Government is building? What the hell does that have to do with anything?"

"Paul Foster and his family were forced to sell their previous home to make way for the proposed route. Paul built the home himself twenty-five years ago and raised his family there for two decades. He and his wife had a son who died of Leukaemia last year. They buried him on the property."

"They forced them to sell? That's horrible," said Bradley.

"But not illegal," said Palu. "When the Government forced the sale of land, they also relocated the boy's body."

"Kicked them out of their own home," said Bradley, tutting.

"They were compensated generously, of course," Palu added, "but it still might be why the family has a grudge against the Government." There was a short pause before Palu spoke again. "There's also another lead. Paul Foster ran a construction company. Part of his services included demolition. We believe he may have been the one supplying explosives for the attacks, maybe even designed the suicide vests himself — he has a background in engineering."

Sarah punched the dashboard. "All *this* because he was forced to sell his mansion? There has to be more to it than that."

"Perhaps," said Palu. "We're still working on it, but you should know that Paul Fosters's construction company is based in Botley. If you think Ashley might have ended up in Botley, that could be where she heads."

Sarah's eyes narrowed. "What's the address?"

Palu gave it to them.

"You need to send Mattock there right now."

"Negative. Mattock is taking care of Agent Dobbs. You and Bradley are our only available assets. Are you able to respond?"

Sarah swallowed. "Palu, I'm not the right woman for this job. I can barely stand, and every time I try to help, I end up on my knees with a gun in my face."

"You don't have a choice, Sarah. You're all we have right now. We dragged you into this and I'm sorry, but that's the way it is."

Sarah said nothing. For the first time since she'd lost Thomas and their baby, she felt real, icy fear. Hesbani had been the man responsible for destroying her entire life. Did she have it in her to face him again? She couldn't even close her eyes at night without seeing his snarling face and whimpering.

"We're on it," said Bradley. "Rebrief when we arrive at destination."

"Roger that," said Palu.

The line went dead.

Sarah felt her heart pounding in her chest. Her body was wracked with agony. The only place that didn't hurt, ironically, was her face. For once, her scars were numb.

Bradley started back towards Botley when he noticed Sarah staring out the window. "Hey, come back to me. I can't do this without you."

"I'm here," she said.

"We can deal with this. Ashley Foster is alone and desperate. We can take her in, but I need you with me." When Sarah hesitated, Bradley said, "You're the one always telling me not to freeze up, so now I need you to follow your own advice and man up."

Sarah glared at him. "Man up? Does it look like I have a dick?"

Bradley shrugged. "Sometimes. You're kind of intimidating."

"Intimidating?"

"Yeah, I don't know if you know, but you're kind of snarly. You remind me of an abused Jack Russell Terrier my nan adopted. It bit anyone who tried to pet it. The only reason it was like that, though, was because it was mistreated and abandoned. It loved my nan though, and as soon as it realised it could trust her, it became the most loyal pet in the world. That's kind of like you, Captain. You've had some bad experiences, but I know there's a good, loyal person underneath all the snarling. I just want you to know that you can trust me."

Sarah bristled, softened, then bristled again. "I can only trust you if you pull the trigger when you're supposed to."

"I promise to pull the trigger when it's needed, but only if you get your head back in the game."

The past was pulling Sarah down, dragging her into a vacuous pit of despair, but there was suddenly a chance dangling in front of her — a chance to change the path she was on. She couldn't live with the anger inside anymore, it was eating her up. She had to take back her life and her self-respect. Afghanistan had taken more than just her face, it had taken part of who she had been. Perhaps there was still time to get it back.

"Okay, Bradley, step on it. That psychopathic little bitch is not going to get away again. This time, she's mine."

Fifteen minutes later, they were back in Botley. They entered onto a high street, passing by a Roman-style market hall nestled between Tudor cottages and other mid-century buildings. They found Foster Homes & Construction at the far end of the village, hidden down a side-street beside a small builder's merchant. The lights were off, but there were men at work in the adjacent business.

Bradley parked the Jaguar up on the curb. "You ready?"

Sarah breathed. She felt like shit. "I'm ready."

They headed to the unlit offices of Foster's construction company. Sarah crept up to the window and peered inside. There was nothing except the flashing LED of an answering phone. Bradley gave the front door a shove, and they were both surprised when it opened. They took out their guns and clicked off the safeties.

Bradley slid inside first, Sarah close behind him. Instinctively, they moved to opposite sides of the room.

"I don't think anyone's here," whispered Bradley. "We must've missed her."

Sarah didn't respond. Her focus was on the blinking answering machine on the reception desk in front of her. She stepped over to the machine and pressed 'PLAY.'

Bradley lowered his weapon and came to listen. They were both disappointed when they heard an automated message for PPI insurance claims, so Sarah used the barrel of her SIG to jab the machine's buttons.

"What are you doing?" Bradley asked her.

"Checking for old messages."

Another voicemail played. Sarah knew the voice well from the previous two tapes she'd viewed at MCU — and from her nightmares. It was Hesbani.

"*Two Syrian freedom fighters killed by British Peacekeepers. Balance the scales.*" That was the whole message.

"Is that Hesbani?" Bradely asked. "What do you think it means?"

"I don't know. Come on, we need to comb this place and see if we can—"

A noise caught their attention, making them turn their guns towards the back of the room. Ashley Foster was standing in the doorway of one of the offices, staring at them in shock. She didn't draw a weapon of her own, which let Sarah know that she no longer had a gun.

"Don't fucking move," Sarah growled. "I'm just dying to take your head off."

Ashley recovered from her shock and snickered. "You've already had your chance. Don't think you have what it takes."

Sarah stepped forward and aimed at Ashley's forehead. "Let's test that theory."

Some of the defiance left Ashley's eyes, and for the first time since Sarah had set eyes on the girl, she was just a bratty, unsure teenager. Bradley took a step towards the girl while Sarah sought to keep her talking. "What's this all about, Ashley? Your mum and dad are both dead. For what?"

Ashley recoiled. Of course, she hadn't known her father was dead.

There were tears in her eyes, but she growled like a pit bull. "I'm going to fucking kill you."

"Not if I kill you first."

"Stop this, Ashley," said Bradley, having approached several steps. "Nobody else has to get hurt. Let us take you in so we can hear your side of the story. I promise we'll listen."

"Yeah," said Sarah, deciding the soft approach might be their best option. "You look like shit, Ashley. You're pale, sweaty... it looks like you're in a lot of pain. Let us take care of you."

Ashley wavered. She could have bolted, but instead she seemed to gravitate towards Bradley. His offer to help had got through to her, and it suddenly seemed like she had got in this over her head. All the same, Sarah was still poised to blow her head off.

Bradley took another step towards Ashley, lowering his gun to his side. "Let us help you."

Ashley held up a bandaged hand. Blood leaked down her wrist from where Bradley had shot her earlier. "You've already helped enough."

"You gave me no choice. Don't force me to shoot you again. This can all end right now. You just have to come with me."

Sarah kept her gun trained on Ashley. This girl had tried to gun them down like a commando earlier. They shouldn't take her lightly, even though she was clearly close to exhaustion. "Ashley, put your hands behind your head and get down on your knees. Cooperate and I'll be gentle."

Ashley's lower lip quivered. "Please. I just want to see my dad."

"It's okay," said Bradley. "We'll get you what you need."

"Bradley, step back." Sarah didn't like how close he was getting to Ashley. Just because she appeared unarmed didn't mean she was harmless. But instead of attacking, Ashley broke down in tears. She turned away and hugged herself, shaking as she wept. Bradley moved towards her, his free hand out in front of him, gun pointed at the floor.

Sarah raised her voice. "Ashley, get down on your knees right now before I blow your goddamn brains all over the wall."

Ashley span around, a flash of metal gliding through the air towards Bradley's throat. Sarah cried out, unable to let a shot off for risk of hitting her partner. But the bitch was about to stab him.

Bradley ducked under the blade and buried a left hook into Ashley's ribcage. She folded up in pain, gasping desperately. Then Bradley raised his gun and pulled the trigger. The dark room flashed white as the gunshot echoed off the walls. Ashley screamed, hopping on one leg as blood gushed out of her mangled foot.

Sarah closed the distance between them and was just in time to catch Ashley in her arms. The girl stared at her, a mixture of agony and rage on her face. "The bastard shot me in the foot."

Sarah sneered. "I'd have shot you in the face."

Sarah shoved Ashley down to the ground face first and waited while Bradley cuffed her. The girl fought them the whole time until Sarah lost her patience. She grabbed the girl's hair and slammed her nose into the floorboards, knocking her out cold. Sarah cricked her neck and sighed. "God, I've been dying to do that. Let's take this bitch in."

16

RUIN

Getting Ashley back to MCU had been an ordeal. She woke from unconsciousness not five minutes later, screaming and yelling and alerting some of the men working at the builder's yard next door. Sarah was already weak without having to wrestle an adrenaline-fuelled teenagers or battle with concerned citizens, so they bundled her into the car as quickly as possible. Bradley secured her in the back, but he seemed upset about shooting her. Sarah told him several times he had done the right thing. Bradley could've killed Ashley Foster, and it still would've been the right thing. He'd done a good job by taking her alive.

Palu met them at the abandoned farm and helped take custody of the prisoner. Ashley was silent and sullen, which Sarah assumed was because of the beating, but when they led her from the car to the Earthworm's concealed entrance, she keeled over and vomited. The girl was unwell, and Sarah feared she'd given Ashley a concussion. Would she get in trouble for that?

They carried her gently down into the Earthworm, heading straight for Dr Bennett's infirmary. "Once she's been treated, she'll be taken to the holding cells in the middle section of the Earthworm," Palu explained en route. Sarah needed treatment too. Her own gunshot wound was burning fiercely and she felt like she might have to stop and throw up.

Dr Bennett dealt with Ashley for little over an hour before coming out to talk with them. She handed Sarah some painkillers and a glass of water, which she took greedily. "Are you done with her, doctor?" she asked after downing the pills. "I need to talk to her."

Bennett sniffed. "The girl's a mess — wounds all over. I'm not sure how much she'll be able to give you, so why don't you let her rest for a while?"

"You do know that Ashley Foster and her family might be responsible for four suicide attacks?"

"She's just a girl. We don't know *what* she's guilty of yet."

Sarah couldn't believe what she was hearing. "She's guilty of shooting me. You should know, you patched me up."

"If you need to talk to her, fine, but I think we should let Director Palu decide the best course of action. He's the one in charge here, not you."

"Let Sarah in," Palu ordered. "She's earned the right to question this girl."

Sarah smirked.

Dr Bennett folded her arms and appeared to have just chewed a lemon. "Very well. I have the patient on painkillers, so she's a little drowsy. Go easy on her."

"The girl's a psychopath," said Sarah. "She tried to slice Bradley's throat."

"Until I pulled the trigger," Bradley commented.

Sarah patted him on the back. "That's a hand and a foot you have on the resume now. It's a start."

Dr Bennett opened the door to the infirmary and let them through. From on the bed, Ashley scowled at as if a foul smell had descended upon her. Sarah was surprised to see Howard in the infirmary too, his left arm in a cast. "You look like you've been in a car accident," Sarah said to him.

Howard was sat up, his legs dangling over the side of the bed. "I should have been wearing a seatbelt. Do you have any news on Mandy?"

Sarah shook her head.

"Mandy was still in surgery last time I spoke with Mattock," said Palu. "As soon as I hear more, I'll tell you."

Everybody was silent for a moment.

Ashley grabbed their attention. "I'm glad your man is suffering. I'm just sorry I didn't kill him. Where the hell am I, anyway? You people aren't police."

Sarah clenched her fists. "Keep talking and you'll wish you were dead."

Ashley laughed. Despite her petulance, she still looked ill. Her breathing was irregular, and her skin was moist and translucent.

"Is she going to be okay?" Bradley asked the doctor. "She looks dreadful."

Dr Bennett shrugged. "She's missing two toes and her hand is already infected. Despite that, her injuries aren't life-threatening."

"So why does she look like a bag of shit warmed up in an oven?"

"Fever from the infection. Shock from the pain."

Sarah pouted. "Poor thing."

"We'll have to get her a card," said Howard from the next bed.

"Screw you!" Ashley spat at them.

Palu walked to the foot of Ashley's bed and studied her quietly. Ashley pulled the blanket aside and stuck her tongue out obscenely. "Want to climb in, big boy? I've never had *mocha* before."

Palu tilted his head. "What on earth happened to you, child? Has this world chewed you up so badly? If so, I want you to know that I understand. Life can be cruel. It can turn our hearts to stone before we even reach puberty. I know."

Ashley rolled her eyes. "You have no idea what you're talking about. You work for the Government. You make me sick."

"Perhaps you and I are not so different," Palu continued. "I'd like to tell you a story, Ashley. Would that be okay?"

Ashley rolled her eyes again. "Knock yourself out."

Palu sat down on the bed. "When I was a young boy, I lived in the Punjab. My family were *Jat*, a proud people of Sikh heritage. During British rule, we were considered a martial race, but my father was just a farmer. He tended the fields and kept goats. Some would say he was a man of peace, yet deep in his blood was the fighting spirit of the *Jat*. The year was 1984, and a woman I hadn't even heard of had just been assassinated in New Delhi by her Sikh bodyguards. The woman's name was Indira Gandhi, and she was Prime Minister of India. I was just a boy. I knew nothing of events outside my home or the small school I attended in the village."

Ashley feigned boredom. "When are you going to get to the car chase?"

"After Indira Gandhi was murdered, there were many troubles in India. Because the perpetrators were Sikh, the Hindus of India felt the assassination had been a conspiracy by our people. In the towns and cities, Sikh men and women were attacked in the streets and beaten to death by angry mobs. I could see the anxiety on my father's face growing every day as he continued to work in the fields. He assured us the violence would not reach our quiet little farm, but he was wrong. My father's farm was large, you see, and one of only few in the region. Some of our Hindu neighbours found opportunity in the crisis by stirring up hatred in the village towards the Sikhs. Soon, fingers pointed at my family and a mob arrived at our door. My father locked my mother and me inside and went to talk sense to our neighbours and friends who had known us for years. I do not know what my father said to them, but they beat him into a coma and set fire to our farm. I saw it all from my bedroom window. Later that night, they beat me as well, and took my mother to the fields. She screamed all night."

Sarah swallowed. Her stomach hurt hearing Palu's tale of misery and woe. It was even worse than her own retched past.

Palu finished up his story, seemingly unmoved, as if he had replayed it a hundred times in his head and it was now just a numb recital. "My father died in hospital a week later. Our farm was purchased by our neighbours for practically nothing. I was sent to

Britain to live with my uncle. Two years later, I was due to return to India, but I received news that my mother had killed herself. I never saw her again after the night the mob came for us. So, Ashley, you are not the only one who feels betrayed and angry. I watched my neighbours destroy my home and family while the Government did nothing to stop it. The men responsible were never punished. My blood boiled for many years at the mere thought of it, but I did not repeat the cycle of violence. I have not allowed my anger to manifest and spread. I chose a different path. Ashley, you need to choose a different path too. Help us ensure there are no more attacks on innocent people. No one else has to get hurt. Do you understand?"

"I can't help you. I-It's too late."

Palu patted her knee under the covers. He stared at her intently. "What do you mean, Ashley?"

Ashley cleared her throat and looked at them like they were idiots. "Don't you get it? This is more than just a few suicide-vests. This entire country is about to come crumbling down. There'll be no United Kingdom left."

"Please explain it to us, Ashley," said Palu. "Is this because of a man named Wazir Hesbani? Do you know where he is? How do you know Dr Cartwright?"

"Cartwright? My dad went to see him for grief counselling after my brother died. Hesbani reached out to us through the clinic. Him and the doc went to Oxford together or something. Cartwright thinks he and Hesbani are old buddies with dreams of changing the world, but Hesbani just uses him like a puppet. For a doctor, he's a complete moron."

Sarah licked her lips. So it was true. Hesbani really was behind all this. "Where is Hesbani now?"

Ashley grunted. "He's everywhere. Don't you feel him? His shadow is looming over this country like an axe about to fall. Before this is all over, people will be too afraid to leave their homes. They'll forget about their cars, their jobs, their gluttonous shopping sprees. People will be reminded of what really matters, what is truly valuable. Life.

People need to respect life before we have any hope of changing as a species."

The girl sounded just like Al-Sharir, but his hands didn't seem to be involved in any of this. It was too messy. Had Hesbani taken the old man's teachings and applied them in his own barbaric way?

"And you think the way to make people respect life is through violence?" said Sarah incredulously. "Don't you find that a little hypocritical? Your entire argument falls apart once you get to the indiscriminate killing."

"Sometimes death is the only way to ensure life. What time is it?"

Sarah sneered in disgust. "Why are you involved in this, Ashley? What did your mother and father die for? This can't all be because the Government bulldozed your house and moved your brother's body."

Ashley's face crinkled up in anger. "You're damn right, it's not! Taking the home where I grew up, where my little brother played before he died, was just the first thing they did to us. I asked what time it is."

Sarah checked her watch. "It's twelve-thirty, and what do you mean? What did the Government do to you?"

Ashley shook her head irritably. "When my dad put up a fight and started a petition to stop the HS2 link, the government blacklisted his construction company. Suddenly my father lost all his civil contracts. No more new-builds, no more municipal structures, no more maintenance contracts. The taxman wanted to investigate his every movement too, grinding the business into the ground with red tape. The company my dad spent his entire life building was destroyed overnight out of bureaucratic spite. If the Government is willing to do that to a hardworking, law-abiding family man, they've lost their right to be in charge."

"Looked like you were doing all right to me," said Howard from the next bed. "Your new gaff wasn't exactly a hovel. Did you buy it with the fair settlement you got from the Government?"

"Fair settlement? Are you kidding? We got *half* what the house was worth, and the house we moved to is rented. They took everything from us just so people can get to London a few minutes faster on the train. That's what my family's entire life was destroyed for."

Ashley's sob story didn't excuse what she'd done, but it was a disgraceful tale of corruption. Whatever the reasoning though, the innocent people of the UK hadn't done anything to deserve being blown up.

"Where's Hesbani?" Sarah demanded again. "I heard his goddamn voice on your dad's answering machine. Where do I find him?"

"What you all need to worry about is the next suicide bomb. There's going to be an explosion in less than two hours."

Palu jerked upright, still perched on the bed. "Ashley, this is important. This is your chance to undo some of what you've done. We can only help you if you help us. Where's the next attack going to be?"

Ashley looked like she was about to cry, like the weight of it all was suddenly too much, but then she surprised them all by cackling. "I don't want to help you people. I want you all to burn."

Palu stood from the bed and turned his back on Ashley. He took a slow breath inwards, straightened his tie, and then spun back around and smashed his fist into Ashley's wounded foot beneath the sheets.

Ashley yowled.

Palu ripped off the sheets and grabbed the girl's wounded hand and squeezed. "Tell me where the next target is!"

Ashley screamed.

Dr Bennett gasped. "Director Palu!"

"Where is the next target? Tell me or I'll start biting off fingers."

Sarah stumbled into Bradley, shocked by the sudden fury of the man who was supposedly in charge here. She had no problem with violence, but it had been a surprise.

Ashley wailed in agony as Palu slapped her face. "T-The answering machine. I-It's orders for the next target. Stop!"

Palu stopped his assault, readjusted his tie again, and then turned to the others. "Sarah, what did you say about an answering machine message?"

"It was Hesbani. He said two freedom fighters had been killed in Syria."

"It's going to be an eye for an eye," said Bradley. "In the second videotape, Hesbani warned that for every life taken on foreign soil, we would lose the same in return."

"What does that tell us?" asked Howard, standing from the bed. "Two freedom fighters will be killed in the UK?"

"Law enforcement," said Sarah. "They're going to hit our police officers."

Ashley grinned at them. "Tick tock, bitches."

Sarah struck Ashely with a backhanded blow causing blood to trickled from the corner of the girl's mouth. It didn't stop her grinning though. Sarah pulled the SIG from her waistband and pressed it against Ashley's forehead. "Tick tock, bitch. Three seconds until I smear your brains on the pillow. Where's the bomb?"

Ashley closed her eyes and pressed her lips together. Three seconds passed, but Sarah didn't pull the trigger. The bluff hadn't worked. Ashley was prepared to die. Sarah lowered the SIG and sighed. "There's nothing left in you but hate, is there?"

Ashley opened her eyes. "You want to kill me, do it. I'll never help you. I set the latest bomb myself. You'll never find it."

Sarah reholstered her gun and wiped the sweat from her forehead. The group moved far enough away from Ashley so that they could speak in private. Dr Bennett helped Howard over to join the conversation. "We need to go back to the Foster's residence," said Sarah. "If Ashley made the bomb herself, that might be where she did it."

Bradley agreed. "Especially if it was recent. That's where you found her hiding out this morning, right?"

Sarah nodded. "Hiding out with crazy mum and dad."

"Let's go back to the house," said Howard. "The police have only processed the scene of Leanne Foster's death, so who knows what's still there to be found."

Sarah frowned. "You sure you can manage with your arm?"

Howard held up his cast. "You can sign it once we stop Hesbani. Anyway, you have a gunshot wound and seem to be doing fine."

"I'm barely standing, but point taken."

Palu grunted. "Both of you need to get going. I'll have Mattock clear away the police team and meet you there. At this rate, I won't have any uninjured agents left. Bradley, you and Dr Bennet stay here and get what you can from her." He pointed at Ashley with a sneer on his face.

Everyone agreed the plan and got going. Before Sarah left the room though, Ashley got her attention by grinning. "Tick tock," she warned again. "Tick tock."

17

JACK IN THE BOX

Despite Sarah breaking every speed limit on the way to the Foster's home, Mattock still arrived before she and Howard did. His Range Rover, identical to the ones back at MCU, was parked up on the curb out front.

Mattock got out and joined them on the driveway. "The neighbours have eyes on us," he told them.

"I'm not surprised," said Howard.

Sarah nodded at the police tape across the property's front door. "Are the police still here?"

Mattock sniffed. "Nah, I gave them their marching orders."

Sarah raised an eyebrow. "We can do that?"

"Not often, but we have some clout when we need it. I got authorisation from the Home Office directly. Leanne Foster's body has been moved to the morgue, and forensics have catalogued the scene of the crime, but I don't think they got around to investigating the rest of the house. They don't rush these things, for obvious reasons, but right now caution isn't going to do us any favours."

"No joke," said Sarah. "We need to find answers in this house or we could be looking at a lot more dead bodies."

"Let's get started then," said Mattock, and he led them inside the house. While Leanne Foster's body had been removed, her blood still stained the tiles and spattered the kitchen cupboards. Sarah was sickened by the sight of it, so she concentrated on the little tickets placed around the house — markers for whatever evidence had been found by the police forensics.

"What are we searching for?" asked Mattock. He picked up a chipped coffee mug and examined it as though it might reveal something.

Sarah opened the kitchen drawers, seeking out paperwork, IDs, anything that might tell her something about what Hesbani was planning. "There's another suicide bomb and the attack is due to happen soon. Ashley Foster isn't talking, so we need to find answers. We have one shot at this."

Mattock clenched his jaw. "Bleeding nutcases, the lot of 'em. Ain't seen nothing like this — normal families turning to terrorism."

"We can figure out the whys later," said Howard. "We need to turn this place over quickly."

Mattock nodded. "I'll check upstairs."

Sarah and Howard took the back of the house first. The kitchen and study were a bust. That left the lounge and dining room at the front of the house.

Howard checked the dining room while Sarah took the lounge. On each of its wall were multiple pictures of the Foster family holding hands, hugging, and otherwise posing for the camera. They looked happy. A picture on a side table showed a quaint, extended cottage with timber beams and white walls. It had a double garage and a giant front lawn. On the front lawn was a bouncy castle with a grinning infant who must have been Ashley's brother.

Other than the photographs, the living room was bare and fashionable, with few knickknacks or surfaces to accumulate dust. An LCD television hung on the wall in front of a leather sofa that had two small tables on either side. A chest of drawers sat against the back wall, but before Sarah got a chance to search it, Mattock rushed into the room and startled her. "You need to see this," he said.

Sarah grabbed Howard and they went upstairs with Mattock. "I think it's the girl's room," Mattock said. "It's a mess. I can't believe the police missed it."

Sarah walked into Ashley's bedroom and the coppery smell of blood hit her. There was too much for it to have belonged to Dr Cartwright, who was slumped against the far wall beside a bed. A bullet hole marked his temple. When had this happened?

Howard knelt in front of the body. "The police like to work from one room to the next. They obviously never made it upstairs. Why do you think the Fosters took out the doc after going to the trouble of rescuing him?"

"To keep him from talking," said Sarah. "He seemed to have doubts about what they were doing. Maybe his conscience was kicking in."

Mattock nodded to the bed. "Or maybe Ashley had one last job for Cartwright before he became expendable."

Dried blood caked Ashley's bed, and crumpled towels and bowls of bloody water sat on the large, square bedside table. At the foot of the bed was an open medical kit.

"He must have fixed Ashley's wounds after the shootout," said Howard.

Sarah shook her head. "No, this is more than that. There's too much blood."

Mattock nodded as if he thought the same thing. "What are you thinking?"

"I'm not sure yet." She knelt over the medical kit and rooted through its contents. There were bandages and gauze, and a bloody scalpel and sutures. There was also an empty vial of iodine. The strangest thing inside the bag, though, was an empty box of condoms.

"What have you got?" Howard asked.

Sarah sighed and tried to make sense of what she was seeing. "I think... I think Cartwright cut Ashley open."

Howard frowned. "Why?"

Mattock saw something on the windowsill and picked it up. It was a coil of bloodstained electrical wire. "Maybe this has something to do with it."

Sarah's stomach ached as things suddenly pieced together. "There's a bomb inside Ashley Foster. After Dr Cartwright escaped his office, he cut Ashley open and placed a goddamn bomb inside of her while her parents watched."

"No way," said Howard. "No one is that crazy."

"Sounds a bit far-fetched, luv," said Mattock. "You sure you're not jumping to conclusions?"

But Sarah was sure. She knew what anger and a need for revenge could do to a person. "Ashley Foster is willing to die. They rescued Dr Cartwright so that he could place a bomb inside her, then, once he'd served his purpose, they took him out. They must have used something compact like C4. They wrapped it in condoms and Cartwright inserted it inside her. Ashley is the suicide bomber, I'm certain."

Howard got on the mob-sat. "Palu? Ashley Foster is the next suicide bomber. It's possible that the bomb is inside her. You need to—"

Howard flinched and the mob-sat slipped from his grasp and landed amongst the bloody bandages on the floor.

Sarah stared at him. "What? What is it?"

Howard face turned white. "I think we're too late."

18

SPINNING TOP

Howard called MCU a dozen times on the frantic trip back to the Earthworm. Sarah and Mattock both drove 120mph down the dual carriageway, his Range Rover following her Jaguar. Several times Sarah thought she might crash, but she couldn't slow down. Not until she reached the Earthworm and saw it for herself.

As soon as they reached the derelict farm, it became clear the worst had happened. A plume of black smoke billowed from the middle of the open field, venting from some burning structure beneath. Howard opened the concealed entrance, and they beat it down the steps as fast as they could. Nobody spoke. The horror was too much to put into words.

As they reached the lower steps, they heard a blood-curdling siren. "It's the evacuation alarm," Howard shouted over the din as he entered the entry code for the hatch into the tail section. Then he moved to a panel on the wall and deactivated the siren. Inside, the only light came from red strobe lights overhead, and parallel strips that illuminated the floor. They sprinted through the large, unused tail section and made it over to the other end, fearful of what they would find.

As soon as Howard opened the next hatch, the epicentre of

destruction presented itself. Smoke billowed out at them in angry clouds and he had to cover his mouth to keep from choking. Mattock unclipped something from his belt and threw it into the hallway. It was a glow stick and, as it snapped to life, it bathed everything in a soft green glow.

Howard shouted into the smoke and a weak reply came from somewhere down the hallway. Sarah didn't hang around; she took off into the black haze at once. She had to grope her way blindly along the walls, using the pleading voice as a beacon. "Palu? I-Is that you? Where are you?"

"I'm here. Keep moving forward."

Sarah found him slumped in the hallway, caked in soot and breathing into his scrunched up tie. Blood poured from a thick gash on his bald head, but otherwise he seemed okay — alert. Maybe things weren't as bad as they seemed.

Sarah knelt beside him. "Are you okay?"

"I don't know what happened."

"The bomb was inside Ashley Foster. She was the next suicide bomber, and we were the freedom fighters she intended to hit."

"They planned this all along."

Sarah nodded. "Yeah, they planned this all along — or at least something like this. Paul Foster told his daughter to run, so perhaps we weren't the original target, but I think she went back to her dad's construction company because she knew she would get picked up there. Dr Cartwright sewed the bomb inside her right after he escaped. He's dead."

Palu dragged himself up off the floor. "Then we have nothing. All our leads are gone."

Sarah put an arm around the man's waist and helped steady him. Howard and Mattock joined them, and they headed back into the tail section so that they could dump Palu into one of the dusty seats away from all the smoke.

"Palu?" said Howard. "Where are Bradley and Dr Bennett?"

"They were in the infirmary with Ashley."

"We need to go back and get them," said Sarah.

Palu shook his head. "You need to wait for the smoke to clear. The sprinklers kicked in and dealt with the fire, but it'll take a while for the extractors to clear the air."

Sarah flopped on a chair and let her chin fall to her chest. "This just keeps getting worse."

They waited as long as they could, but it wasn't long before they were all sprinting back down the hallway towards the infirmary. Palu stayed behind, still catching his breath.

The infirmary was nothing but a black smudge now. Its tiles had cracked from the heat, and its furniture was smashed against the walls. In the middle of the floor was a wet, lumpy mess that must once have been Ashley Foster.

Movement caught Sarah's eye, and she spotted Dr Bennett on the floor — still alive.

"Jessica?" she said. "Jessica, it's okay."

Bennett was on her knees in the corner, hunched over somebody and performing CPR. She was moaning and sobbing as she did so. Sarah hurried towards her.

Bradley was dead. Even with Bennett performing CPR, it was obvious he wasn't coming back. His face was an unrecognisable mess, but his bright blue eyes gave away that it was him. One of his ribs jutted out of his torso.

Sarah placed a hand on Dr Bennett's shoulder. It made her flinch, but she continued performing CPR. Sarah gave her a little shake. "He's gone. There's nothing you can do."

Bennett stopped pumping and looked up at Sarah, tears in her eyes. "He shielded me. Somehow, he managed to stand in front of me when it... when everything happened."

Dr Bennett allowed Sarah to walk her out of the ruined infirmary, but Mattock and Howard stayed behind with Bradley's body. Both of the tough, confident men were clearly distraught.

In the corridor, Dr Bennett produced a handkerchief and wiped soot from her face. "I don't understand it. How did Ashley get a bomb down here?"

"It was inside her," Sarah explained. "Did she have any recently stitched wounds when you examined her?"

"The girl was covered in wounds, head to toe. I had no reason to think..."

Sarah patted her shoulder. "None of us knew. This whole thing has been impossible to predict from the start."

"No, it hasn't!" Bennett snapped at her. "Bradley getting hurt was very easy to predict. He was going to leave the MCU yesterday because he *knew* this was too much for him. *You* stopped him from leaving, Sarah. His death is on your goddamn hands."

Sarah wanted to argue, but Bennett was right in a way. Bradley was dead because she had made him stay. The kid had never been cut out for this. And yet, she didn't feel that was true. Bradley had been a good soldier. He had wanted to fight the good fight.

Sarah swallowed. "I'm sorry, Jessica."

Bennett shook her head, fought off another wave of tears, and then marched down the hallway on her own.

"Are you okay?" Palu asked Sarah when he arrived from the empty tail section. He moved stiffly, but seemed to be okay.

Sarah shook her head. "Not at all."

She went back into the infirmary where Mattock and Howard were now sitting on the floor with Bradley. The smoke had cleared, and the scene would have looked a little less like a nightmare if not for the blood and bodies. Sarah thought about how Bradley had compared her to a Jack Russell Terrier. He'd been right about her, and had stuck up for her all the way. She'd almost made a friend, but nothing had changed in the end. She was still the same person she'd always been. She should never have let herself give a damn. This was her reward for caring. Trusting people was never worth the risk.

She was done.

AFGHANISTAN, 2008

Sarah sat, staring out the window as the banged-up Corolla bounced across the rocky flats. The doors rattled in their rusty fixtures, and grit coated the loose edges. Every time she bit down, she was met with a jarring crunch of sand between her teeth.

They told her they were taking her back to camp as promised but she doubted it. This didn't look like the desert. Al-Sharir was upfront with Hesbani while two other men guarded Sarah in the back with AK47s across their laps. After they slaughtered Hamish, Sarah had given up any hope of getting home alive. Her hand moved to her belly and she tried not to weep as she thought about how she'd failed her unborn child. It had been her job to protect it. It had been her job to protect Hamish and the men too, but she'd failed at every turn. She was going to Hell.

They drove for two hours in the banged-up Corolla, only managing 40mph on the uneven, treacherous terrain. Sarah tried to spot landmarks, but there were none — just hills and crags and the occasional pack of goats. Camp Bastion was isolated in the desert, which was why Sarah knew she wasn't being taken there. If the Corolla came within five miles of the camp, Al-Sharir and his men would be seized. They were just looking for a good spot to bury her.

The Corolla's gears crunched as the car slowed down, and Al-Sharir and Hesbani exchanged heated words. Sarah couldn't translate them quickly enough to get the gist, but they were discussing her. They were disagreeing.

The car came to a stop and the two men with AK47s dragged Sarah outside. She fell weakly onto her hands and knees. Hesbani appeared and kicked her away from the car while the men aimed their AKs at her. Sarah didn't put her hands up or beg. There was nothing she could do that would make a difference.

"You're a bunch of monsters," she muttered, spitting into the sand.

Al-Sharir got out and stood over her, calm as always. "I guarantee, Captain, if our countries were to count bodies, yours would win. You judge us by standards your own people fail to uphold."

Sarah didn't respond. Al-Sharir was probably right, but that didn't make what he was doing now acceptable. He spoke about ending violence, yet he exercised it as freely as the Taliban. "You gave me your word you would let me go," she said, looking him in the eye.

"Words mean nothing to the West," Hesbani snarled. "You English shake hands in friendship with left while picking our pocket with right, all while hiding missile behind back. I will not rest until I see your people in ruins as you seek to see ours."

"We want to help you!" Sarah cried out, tired of saying it. "Say what you want about my country, but you don't speak for me, you son-of-a-bitch. I wanted to do some good, but now you can all just suck my dick."

Hesbani seemed confused by the insult, but Al-Sharir chuckled. "You are a warrior, Captain. True of heart and ignorant of fear. Allah protects those who are true to their beliefs. May he keep you safe now."

Sarah waited for the bullet.

The AKs stayed pointed at her, but Al-Sharir didn't give the kill order. Instead, he smiled at her and said, "You may leave now, Captain. Your Camp Bastion is ten miles in that direction," he pointed. "It is hot, and you are tired and injured. It is more likely you will die, but if you are with child, as you say, Allah will watch over you and guide you home. Do not take up arms against my people again, or there will be great consequences. I could have killed you, so you owe your life to me, and all that you do with it."

Sarah couldn't believe it. She stared across the empty desert at an unreachable horizon. If she could keep walking in a straight line, maybe she could find Camp Bastion, but if she veered even slightly off course she'd miss it by a mile and die in the dirt.

"Teach your child to respect Allah," Hesbani shouted after her as she walked away. "Or I'll cut its throat the same way I cut your Corporal's throat."

Sarah almost ran to claw out Hesbani's eyes then, but she was too beaten. She hated herself for walking away from the man who'd killed her squad and scarred her face, but she wanted to live. She was a coward.

Sarah managed a dozen steps before she looked back. Not only were the men not following her, but they were climbing back inside the Corolla. It really did seem like they were letting her go. When they sped off in the opposite direction, she let out a deep sigh of relief and crumpled to the ground. She cried for an hour before getting up and beginning her long walk.

Her legs gave out shortly after nightfall. She might have walked twenty miles, but in the rocky wilderness it was impossible to tell. When she finally stopped for a rest, crumpling to her hands and knees, the scorching rock had turned frigid.

She needed to keep moving, but her entire body ached. She was numb from the head down. Getting up was too difficult, so she crawled until even that was too much. Her father would have gloated, seeing her give up like this. She was exactly what he said all women were: weak and delicate.

I'm sorry, she told her unborn child. *I'm sorry,* she told her husband Thomas. *I can't do it.*

When a routine patrol from Camp Bastion passed by, she heard the rumbling engine of their Snatch-2, but she couldn't lift her head to search for the vehicle. She couldn't call out or wave. She could only lie there, dying.

If not for the thermal imaging goggles, the patrol might have driven right by her. Instead, four British soldiers found Sarah close to death and took her back to Camp Bastion. She held her tummy on the way back and thanked God.

19

DIABLO

Sarah's eyes had focused on Bradley's body for so long that they felt crusty when she turned them upwards to see Palu hobbling into the ruined infirmary.

Mattock was leant up against the blackened wall, and he raised a scarred eyebrow curiously. "What is it, Boss?"

Palu's face sagged. Despite having cleaned himself up, he appeared to have aged ten years. "There's been another video," he said.

Howard climbed to his feet awkwardly as he forgot his one arm was in a cast. "Shab Bekhier?"

"Yes, the same three men as before, with Hesbani as the mouth-piece again. I have it ready to view in the conference room. Fortunately, our systems are all still operational and the main power is back on. The damage was confined to the infirmary, so we need to move out of here before the ceiling comes down on us."

Mattock started walking. "We need to find this Hesbani and put an end to this fucking circus."

Howard offered Sarah his good hand to help her up off the floor. "You coming?"

"No, I'm out."

He frowned. "What do you mean, *you're out?*"

"I'm not cut out for this. All I've done is screw up, and now Bradley is dead."

"That isn't your fault, Captain," Mattock told her.

"Isn't it? Seems all I've ever done is guide people to their deaths. I can't take it anymore."

"I don't have time for this," said Palu. "I'll be waiting in the conference room, everybody ready to go in five minutes."

"You're wasting time," Sarah said. "Just go."

Howard shook his head. "You're a part of this, Sarah. You've bled with us, and you need to see this through to the end."

"Bradley died because of me."

"Bradley died because you made him believe in himself. You're the only one who did. We need you on this team."

"What team? There's not enough of us to play five-a-side football."

"Exactly," said Mattock. "So the last thing we need is you scarpering. If you think people have died because of you, the only way you'll ever get the blood off your hands is by stopping people like Hesbani. Bradley died for this team. Don't piss on his memory by quitting. He had the balls to stay when it got hard. Do you?"

Sarah stared at Bradley. He had barely been a man, and perhaps in some way that was what had brought out something maternal in Sarah, feelings that she thought she'd lost long ago.

No, not lost, taken. Taken by Hesbani.

Sarah remembered lying face down in the desert after Hesbani had crushed her spirits in the heat of Afghanistan. It was time to find her way out of the desert and stop being afraid. She took Howard's hand. "I'll stay in this thing until Hesbani is stopped, but then I'm gone."

Howard heaved her up. "You help us find Hesbani, I'll personally drive you to your doorstep and never bother you again."

"Sounds perfect. Come on, we've got another video to watch."

"I'll bring the popcorn," said Mattock.

They set off to the conference room where they found Dr Bennet and Palu already waiting for them. Bennett looked upset at Sarah's presence, but she didn't kick up a fuss. Instead, she nodded and said, "Glad we're all here."

Sarah nodded and sat down at the table.

Palu wasted no time. "This was posted on Clip Share ten minutes ago. Hesbani must have known about Ashley Foster's plan to blow herself up."

"How?" Howard asked. "Nobody knows the MCU exists."

"I don't think we were the target," Palu told them. "The plan was to hit whoever took Ashley into custody. We weren't the specific target, the whole of law enforcement was. We weren't the only ones hurt today."

Sarah folded her arms, causing the pain in her shoulder to flare up. "What do you mean? Who else was hit?"

Palu pressed play without another word.

Hesbani and two other men appeared on screen again. Sarah was becoming surer that one of the three men was white. Like everything else, it made little sense. Hesbani would never work with a non-Muslim. The third person stayed near the back, slightly built with only their dark eyes on display. Their shorter height suggested they could be female. It was impossible to tell whether the video had been taken at night or during the day, but the ceiling's light source was rocking to-and-fro like it had in both the previous videos.

"United Kingdom, you have been warned, yet you continue on your wicked path. Two freedom fighters in Islamic Syria were killed by British soldiers. Shab Bakhier pledged to you that blood would be met with blood. In response to your wanton murder of these innocent Syrians, we have struck at your own warriors. More deaths shall occur if Prime Minister Breslow does not recall the UK's troops from foreign soil. Today saw the death of more of Allah's martyrs. Paul, Leanne, and Ashley Foster died today, trying to save you from yourselves. They are by Allah's side now, reaping their eternal reward. These are your final moments, Britain. Have your Prime Minister seek forgiveness now, or watch your crooked empire burn to the ground."

There was silence for a moment as the video ended.

"Four police officers were killed outside Scotland Yard this morning," explained Palu. "Hit by a sniper. Early reports suggest a van pulled up at the end of the road and the shooter fired through an open window. The attack took less than five-seconds."

"Only a pro could hit four targets on a horizontal plane in five-seconds," said Mattock. "Does Hesbani have any military connections?"

Palu shook his head. "Only with the Taliban, and they aren't known for their marksmanship."

"With Ashley Foster dead," said Howard, "where do we have to go from here?"

"I'm not sure," Palu admitted. "Thames Valley Police are going through the Foster's home and business right now. Police Commissioner Howe will keep me updated. Home Office have briefed him fully on our operation."

"And until then?" Sarah asked. "We just wait? After what they did to Bradley and Mandy?"

"Did you see anything in the video that could help us, Sarah?" Dr Bennett asked, staying on task.

Sarah thought about it. "It was the same location as before. No window, no landmarks. Just a table, a lamp, and a swinging light bulb above them."

"What about the men in the video?" Howard asked.

"I'm still certain the speaker is Hesbani, although his English is far better than it was when I knew him. Maybe he's been over here for a while. Also, I'm more convinced the ever that one of the people in the video is a westerner."

"Perhaps he's the sniper," Mattock suggested. "Maybe they have a British soldier in their ranks. Wouldn't be the first time somebody has flipped."

Sarah wondered what could make a person terrorise their own country. She couldn't understand it. The hate and anger made sense, but not the willingness to take it out on innocent strangers.

Bennett leaned against the table and sighed. "What about Bradley?"

"What about him?" said Howard.

"Before he went to pick up Sarah, he was working on a lead. Did he get anything?"

Palu nodded to Bradley's laptop, still sitting open on the table. "I'm not sure. He was tracking the owner of the newsagent, the Pakistani immigrant. I don't know if he found anything."

Dr Bennett moved in front of Bradley's laptop and began typing. "Looks like he was researching land registry and property records for a Mr Hamil Hamidi."

Palu nodded. "That's the owner of the newsagent."

"Maybe it's Hesbani's alias," suggested Howard. "The name he's been using in this country."

"What about the niece?" Sarah asked. "Didn't we find out that the newsagent is run by a niece?"

Bennett nodded. "Aziza Hamidi. There's nothing on her except employment records at the newsagent. It doesn't look like Bradley managed to... no, wait."

Palu leant forward. "What is it?"

"One second." Bennett zipped a file onto the large television screen.

"What we looking at?" Mattock asked.

"Bradley compiled a list of all the properties registered to Hamil Hamidi."

They took a moment to examine the list. Sarah spotted the Oxfordshire newsagent and multiple other businesses ranging from a florist to a halal slaughterhouse. Whoever Hamil Hamidi was, he was well-heeled with a seemingly endless range of investments. One item on the list in particular caught Sarah's attention. It was a listed building described as derelict. The address was what had interested her: Thornton Cross Station House (Derelict, Class 2 listed building), 1 Station Road, Redditch. "He owns a property next to a train station. The videos all had an unstable light source, like a bulb swinging."

Howard's brow furrowed. "Possibly caused by the vibrations of incoming and outgoing trains?"

Sarah nodded. "It's a long shot, but it could be where where Hesbani has been making the videos."

"Then that's where we'll look for him," said Mattock. "Hopefully we find him there and we can finally kick his bloody arse."

"That's going to be all me," said Sarah. "And God help anybody who gets in my way." She was scared shitless, but she knew the only way she would ever get any peace was by facing Hesbani and taking the son-of-a-bitch down.

Palu folded his arms and eased back in his chair. "So you're back with us then, Captain?"

"You're damn right I am — and it's Sarah."

"Glad to have you with us, Sarah."

"Well," said Mattock, "guess that's the team talk over. Shall we make a move?"

Sarah stood up. "I'm driving."

20

NEW HOPE

Despite the town of Redditch being close to her flat in Moseley, Sarah hadn't visited it before. It was just another Birmingham satellite town, with patches of parkland shoved up against industrial sections, and residential estates centred around small shopping hubs. Despite the annoying amount of roundabouts and ring roads, the town was quite pretty. Sarah spotted signs for both a lake and an abbey, and they passed several playing fields full of children. Did Hesbani have this place on his hit list as well?

It was Wednesday morning, and Sarah couldn't believe how little sleep she could operate on. It was like having cotton wool inside her skull, but somehow she felt more alert and focused than ever. She pulled off the highway and onto the ring road that would take them into the town centre. Signs indicated a rail station ahead, so Sarah reported in, fiddling with the steering wheel's controls to reach Palu. "We're in Redditch," she told him. "Just heading to the station now."

"I've put the local police on alert," Palu informed her. "They've been told you're an anti-terrorist task force working under the purview of the Met. They'll back you up if needed."

"Roger that," Howard said from the passenger seat. "Permission to use force if necessary?"

"Lethal force granted, but know that you will be operating in a civilian centre. There can be absolutely no collateral damage. I want every bullet accounted for."

"I'll beat Hesbani to death with my shoes if I have to," said Sarah. "No need for bullets."

"Keep me updated." Palu signed off.

Mattock was chuckling to himself. "You know, Sarah, you have quite the dry sense of humour. Reminds me of someone I know."

Sarah clenched the wheel. "If you mean my father, I don't want to hear it."

"Fair enough."

Howard looked at her, but she refused to make eye-contact. "You okay?"

"I'm fine. I just can't go into... that."

They came up by a courthouse and a glass-fronted college, and continued following signs until they reached the rail station. They found it opposite an open-air bus depot.

"That must be it," said Mattock, pointing to a large Georgian house right next to the station. "It's a derelict building, right? That place looks pretty derelict."

Sarah pulled into the station's car park and they got out. The platform was almost deserted, no doubt because of the terrorism alert. Sarah, Mattock, and Howard were wearing luminous yellow jackets to look like workmen, because people paid workmen no mind, especially when it came to derelict buildings.

The new rail station had been placed directly in front of the old one, but they couldn't enter the fenced-off area around the derelict station without crossing over the tracks. The front of the building had been blocked in by an elevated bus lane. The entire plot was a no man's land.

Howard cleared his throat. "Any ideas on how we get inside?"

Sarah looked around. "If Hesbani is using this place, there must be a way in and out. He wouldn't climb a fence in front of a station full of people."

"What about there?" Mattock pointed to an office block adjacent to the rear of the derelict station house.

Sarah nodded. "Let's check it out."

They found a footpath and headed around the new train station towards the old. They came out around the opposite side and headed towards the office block. When they got there, they found it abandoned as well. Not derelict, but vacant. FOR RENT signs covered the ground-floor windows. The office block was empty. Private.

"This must be it," said Sarah. "Let's keep our heads low and find a way through."

They crept up to the office building, looking out for the slightest movement. There were people working in other offices further down the road, and there was a driving test centre nearby, but nobody was paying attention to them. The yellow workmen jackets were doing their job.

"What about here?" said Mattock. He was pointing to a gated alleyway at the side of the vacant office building.

"Is the gate unlocked?" asked Sarah.

Mattock grabbed the lock and twisted it. The metal gate creaked open. "Yep."

Sarah and Howard looked at one another as Mattock slipped into the alleyway and disappeared. Things were going smoother than expected, but they kept their heads down as they followed the pathway into a yard. A chain-link fence separated the office plot from the derelict station house, but there was a wide tear in the bottom of the steel mesh.

"Okay," said Sarah, "let's get our dicks out."

Mattock pulled out his weapon and took point. His gun was big — a long-barrelled revolver. He stepped through the gap in the fence and moved into the grounds of the old station house. Sarah went after him, followed by Howard, and they all kept an eye on the boarded-up windows, wary of anything lurking behind them. Was Hesbani inside?

Sarah wasn't sure how she would react if he was. The man had haunted her dreams for six years. The thought of meeting him face to face was like meeting the bogeyman.

The derelict station's doorframe was rotten, and when Mattock shoved, it swung aside easily on crooked hinges. There was nothing inside the old station house but darkness.

Sarah stepped inside first, and flinched as fallen masonry crunched underfoot. There were old fare tickets and route maps fading against the stone floor like carpeting.

"Looks like it's ready to crumble any minute," Howard whispered. "Why haven't they demolished it already?"

"Because somebody owns it," said Sarah. "Whoever this Hamil Hamidi is, he obviously wants the place left standing."

They checked out all the side rooms, but found nothing of interest. Now they needed to check the upper floors. They congregated in front of the house's grand staircase and looked upwards. "I'm not sure trying to climb that thing is a sound idea," said Mattock. "Bloody thing's falling apart."

Sarah shrugged. "It's just a bit of peeling paint."

She took the first step, her SIG pointed up the stairs. Howard and Mattock followed carefully behind her. Dust puffed out beneath their boots as they disturbed thick piles of rubbish. It looked like nobody had come through here in years, but there were telltale signs that it was an illusion. There were a few places on each step where the stone showed through the dust — recent footsteps.

Open-fronted rooms took up the upstairs landing, their interiors gutted and leaving no way to tell what had once been there. Probably retail units.

Mattock tutted. "This floor is a bust too by the looks of it."

Sarah ground her teeth. They couldn't afford not to find anything. It was the only solid lead they had. The only chance they had to stop further attacks. She made for the next set of stairs and started upwards, causing Howard and Mattock to hiss at her to be cautious. She ignored them, and left them with no option but to follow.

When they reached the third and final floor, Sarah grinned. "Found you!"

The entire third floor was open-plan, and completely clear of debris. A line of desks and wall-mounted cork boards had been erected. The cork boards were covered with detailed drawings of bombs, inked maps, and creased letters. In the centre of the room was a video camera perched atop a tripod, its lens pointing at a bare desk with a single lamp plugged into a double power outlet. As a train departed the nearby station, Sarah looked up and saw a bare bulb swinging back and forth. They had found Hesbani's lair.

"You were right," said Howard, coming up behind her. "This is the place. We've got him."

Sarah went to the nearest desk and plucked a photograph from on of the cork boards. It was a psychiatric report on Caroline Pugh with Dr Cartwright's signature on the bottom. Paper-clipped to the back was a flyer for the pub she had blown up. Sarah found similar files for Jeffrey Blanchfield and the people responsible for blowing up Dart-mouth and Arborfield. There were several other files concerning people yet to become involved. Were they preparing to blow them-selves up too?

Howard examined the files. "We should get these to the local police right away. This is exactly what we needed to find."

Sarah was about to speak, but then her eyes settled on the far end of the cork board. She ripped four pages off the board and held them up for Howard and Mattock to see. "These are the other targets." She leafed through the papers and found photocopies of maps and local newspapers. Four more villages. Three towns. And a city — London. Millions were in danger.

"I'll call Palu," said Howard. "We need to move on this."

Blam!

Everyone hit the ground as a gunshot rang out. Sarah ducked beneath the desk and aimed her SIG, but she couldn't find a target.

Another gunshot. *Blam!*

The desk above Sarah's head splintered and a man in a balaclava emerged from an alcove, clutching pistols in each hand. He zeroed in on Sarah and took another shot.

Mattock and Howard leapt from cover and fired, forcing the stranger to duck and make a run for it. He headed for the stairs, leaping down the steps three at a time. Sarah took off after him, and while the stranger was fast, something had possessed Sarah. Blood pulsed in her temples, and her entire body shuddered as her boots pounded the steps. Howard and Mattock gave chase behind her, but they had no chance of keeping up with the chase. Ahead, the balaclava man sped across the first floor towards the next set of steps. Sarah was gaining on him, but he turned and let off a couple of shots, forcing her to duck inside one of the gutted shop fronts. She fired back three times.

The balaclava man grunted

Sarah's last round had hit home, catching the target in the leg. The man clutched at his thigh and cursed out loud, but before Sarah could line up another shot, he turned and let rip with both guns. Howard and Mattock caught up to her, but were forced to retreat back up the stairs. Sarah hid inside the empty shop front and waited.

Blam Blam Blam Clink!

One of pistols ran dry. The shooter threw it to the floor. He still had ammunition in his other weapon though, so Sarah followed after the limping man cautiously. She slipped out of the shop front and stalked him down the final flight of stairs. In his desperation, the wounded assailant was still able to keep up a decent pace. He made it out into the yard.

"There's nowhere to go," Sarah shouted as she exited the old train station after him. He fired off another shot, but it went nowhere near her. Panicked screaming came from the nearby train platform as the handful of people waiting there heard the gunshots.

Finally, the balaclava man stopped running. He turned and put his hands in the air, his gun pointed up at the sky. "All right, you got me."

"Get on your knees," she ordered.

"On a first date, lass?"

Sarah growled. "Do it!"

The man got down on his knees, hands still lofted above his head.

"Now drop the gun."

"But then I would'na have anything to shoot you with?"

Sarah glared. Mattock and Howard came up behind her and pointed their guns. Mattock bellowed. "Drop the gun or I'll make you eat it arse-first."

The balaclava man huffed. "Aye, all right, I hear you." He dropped his gun and Sarah kicked it away. Then she stood in front of the man, staring. For some reason, he gave her an odd feeling. Was it his accent?

"Who are you?" she demanded.

The man shrugged. "See for yoursen."

Sarah grabbed the top of the balaclava and tore it away. The face that looked back at her was a ghost.

"Good to see you again, Captain. It's been a wee while."

Sarah was so shocked to see her ex-corporal that she didn't see it coming when he leapt up and clocked her in the jaw. Her vision was still spinning when Hamish snatched away her SIG and turned it on her.

21

RETURN OF THE JEDI

Howard shoved Sarah to the ground just as Hamish took a single, wayward shot and then escaped into the alley. Mattock helped them both to their feet, but she couldn't remain standing of her own accord. She wasn't stunned because of the blow to her jaw, but because of the horror of what she had just witnessed. It *couldn't* have been Hamish. Sarah had watched him die. She'd *let* him die.

Howard grabbed her by the shoulders and shook her. "Sarah, are you okay?"

She stared blankly and tried to speak, but couldn't. Then Mattock slapped her. "Wake up! The wanker's getting away."

Sarah snapped back into focus, and they took off into the alleyway. They were just in time to watch Hamish jump into the side of a black van with a rear spoiler. Sarah could see a woman inside wearing a burka. She was kneeling behind something mounted inside of the van.

Oh shit!

"Get down!" Sarah dived back into the alley, dragging Howard and Mattock with her. The woman in the burka fired a mounted PK machine gun at them, releasing a torrent of bullets so rapidly that the noise became an incessant drone.

"Bleeding 'ell," Mattock yelled over the din. "They've got a goddamn bullet chucker."

Sarah peeked around the corner and tried to make out who the woman was, but the burka hid her identity. When the woman spotted Sarah, she pivoted the machine gun and the brickwork next to Sarah's head exploded.

"Unidentified woman. Belt-loaded PK."

"She could fire a thousand rounds before she runs out," Mattock yelled.

"We're pinned down," said Howard.

The PK was a heavy piece of machinery from the soviet era, and pivoting it from one side to side was a slow, arduous affair. If Sarah could somehow draw the woman's aim, she might create an opportunity for Mattock and Howard to return fire.

"I'm going to break cover," she told them. "Soon as I start running, you'll have a couple seconds to take her out."

Howard grabbed her arm. "Don't be insane. You'll get cut to ribbons."

"Not if you do your jobs." She shrugged free of his grasp and sprinted out of the alleyway. There was no cover, no place to go, and so she had to keep moving. Immediately, Machine gun fire hit the ground at her heels, a rainfall of lead. If Howard and Mattock weren't quick enough, the death stream would catch her and tear her to pieces.

Small arms fire sounded behind her, Howard and Mattock breaking cover.

The machine gun stopped.

Sarah turned and saw the woman in the burka dive for cover inside the van. Then she saw Hamish appear behind her and slide the panel door shut. The van rolled backwards, tyres bucking over the curb, and then the unknown driver shifted into gear and swung the vehicle around. Hamish was about to escape.

Sarah ran after the van.

Howard and Mattock fired continuously until they needed to

reload. Mattock started thumbing bullets into the chamber of his revolver while Howard slapped another clip into his grip.

Sarah put everything she had into her legs, sprinting right at the vehicle as it circled around to face the road. It would speed away any second, and she couldn't let that happen. She altered her run to place her between the van and its escape.

Sarah spotted the driver. Her jaw clenched. Her eyes narrowed. *Hesbani.*

Hesbani glared right back at her, picking up speed and steering the van towards where she was standing. His face held a mixture of anger and surprise, as he was clearly shocked to see her. Sarah continued to stand her ground, even as the van sped towards her. She raised her right hand and extended her middle finger, then, just in time to avoid getting run over, she leapt aside and landed on her stomach, forced to watch as the van squealed away into the road.

She was going to destroy Hesbani if it was the last thing she ever did.

Hesbani probably thought he'd not been identified by the authorities — he'd been using a false name after all — but he would know now that his number was up. There was to be no more clandestine plotting, no more hiding in the shadows, and no more self-indulgent videos. His face would be on the desks of every law enforcement agency in the UK. That would make him desperate. And even more dangerous.

Sarah leapt to her feet and shouted to Mattock and Howard. "We need to get back inside that building and rip it apart for evidence. Hesbani's on the run now. We only have a small window of time before he disappears."

The sound of police sirens filled the air. "You and Howard get back inside the station house," said Mattock. "I'll clear things with the Old Bill as best I can, but they ain't gunna like this. That PK made a right sodding mess."

Sarah patted Mattock on the shoulder and hurried back toward the bullet-riddled station house.

Howard stopped in the alleyway and glanced around. "Do you hear that?"

Sarah frowned, but then her eyes went wide as she heard the forceful hissing of escaping air. "I don't—"

The third floor of the station house exploded.

Wooden boards flew from the windows as flames burst through the openings. Bricks and stones rained down on Sarah and Howard, and a fist-sized piece of debris struck her injured shoulder and almost sent her spiralling into a pain-induced coma. Everything they needed had just gone up in flames.

Howard hit the deck and took cover, but Sarah fought to stay on her feet. She dodged towards the burning station house and made it to the entrance. Howard shouted at her to get back, but there was no way. Burning rubble continued to rain down on her, but all she could think about was the fact that every clue to stopping Hesbani was inside this building on the third floor.

Her mind made up, Sarah sprinted into the building, even as clouds of smoke blinded her. It reminded her of the infirmary where Bradley's body was probably getting cold, and it only made her more determined. She covered her mouth with the sleeve of her workman's jacket and made her way to the staircase as quickly as she could.

Every step she took became more difficult, but she wouldn't let it stop her. She reached the next set of steps and felt heat from above. Fires raged, consuming the rotten wood and pockmarked masonry. The right side of Sarah's face started to sweat. The left side was incapable of doing so. Howard's voice echoed from outside, pleading for her to come back.

Sarah forced herself up the steps, battling heat and smoke. She thought she might collapse several times, but willed herself to keep going.

The entire third floor was aflame. Embers fell from the ceiling timbers and filled the air like firebugs. Sarah flinched as a burning splinter sizzled on her neck. The desks and cork boards were being consumed by flames, but one desk was only smouldering, so she raced towards it. It wasn't everything, but it could be *something*.

Sarah cried out as something struck her back and knocked her onto her belly. A chunk of masonry had pinned her to the floor, pressing down on her lungs. She choked and spluttered as she tried to grab a breath. Her arms and legs tingled, and it took a concerted effort to move them.

The building burned all around her.

Sarah clawed her way out from underneath the chunk of masonry, but she couldn't make it to her feet. She felt like she was swimming, and any attempt to get up only made her sink lower, so she crawled instead, dragging herself towards the smouldering desk. A sheet of paper floated to the floor, blown free by the explosion. She snatched at it and was able to shove the paper into her trouser pocket, grinning at her small victory.

But that was all she had. She was done. As much as she wanted to stand up and make it to the table, it was turning to ash right before her eyes. She tried to cry out in anguish, but could only manage a weak cough. Her vision was beginning to blur.

"Sarah!"

She couldn't see Howard, but his voice was close by.

"Sarah, hold on."

She waited, listening to the crackling of flames. Then she felt herself hoisted upwards and dragged backwards through the smoke.

AFGHANISTAN, 2008

As soon as Camp Bastion's patrol found Sarah, they had rushed her back to base. There, a pair of Army surgeons rehydrated her and stitched up the festering wound in her thigh. They could do very little about her facial wounds though. When she came around, they told her she'd been out for twenty-four hours. When she asked about her baby, they told her there was no baby. She had miscarried during surgery and they had been forced to perform a hysterectomy. She hadn't cried upon hearing the news, despite feeling more pain than she ever had in her entire life. That had always bothered her.

At 0600 hours, Major Burke had come by to see her. He told her he was sorry, and that if she'd told him she was pregnant, he would never have sent her out. Sarah said it was okay and that it had been her decision not to tell him.

Then Major Burke had got down to business. "Sergeant Miller?"

Sarah closed her eyes. "Dead."

"Private Owen?"

"Dead."

"Privates Murs and McElderry?"

"Dead."

"Corporal Hamish Barnes?"

Sarah swallowed a lump in her throat. "D-Dead."

Burke sighed. "Christ, what a cluster fuck. We've blanketed the area in troops, but the village has been abandoned. Seems like the Taliban had a stranglehold on the place the whole time and we didn't even know it. We'll find these men, don't you worry, Captain."

But Sarah knew they wouldn't. Al-Sharir had eluded the West long enough to know what he was doing. He wouldn't be caught sleeping, and his right-hand man, Hesbani, was a rabid dog born for war. He would never be captured alive, and killing him would only make him the martyr he dreamed of.

She needed to talk to Thomas. He needed to know about their baby. He needed to know how sorry she was. "I need to speak to my husband. Please, Major. I need to see Thomas."

Major Burke's face fell. He knew Thomas well, had even attended their wedding, but he looked at Sarah now as if she'd asked for something he couldn't make sense of. "Sarah, I'm sorry. I tried to reach Thomas as soon as you came in. American Command told me he was carrying out a spec op in the area, leading a team of local insurgents in an unmarked minibus."

"O-Okay, when will the op be over?"

"That's the thing," said Burke, his lips thinning. "One of our Apache patrols came across a bus in that area this morning. After what happened to your squad, we mistook it for hostile."

Sarah wanted to throw up. "I-Is Thomas okay?"

"The Apache fired on the bus. There were no survivors. I'm so sorry, Sarah. The bus was unmarked. I gave the order myself."

Sarah threw up over the side of the bed. One week ago, she had been leaving the Army to start a family in sunny Florida with a man she adored. Now she had nothing. Not even her face.

Burke stood at the foot of her bed, staring at her with a mixture of concern and shame. He was a good man, but right now she hated him. "Sarah, do you understand what I've just told you?" he asked.

"Yes, I understand, sir. Now get out of my fucking sight."

Sarah was discharged from the Army a week later.

22

THE PHANTOM MENACE

Firemen gave Sarah oxygen while Howard barked into his mob sat. If he hadn't gone back into the building after her, she would have never made it out again. The Fire Service were still dealing with the inferno even now, damping it down in places while it reignited in others. The nearby rail station had been closed off, but gawping spectators surrounded it like ants around a biscuit. Another bomb had gone off in a small town, and the public's fear was tangible, yet so was their utter disbelief. British towns were going up like fireworks and nobody knew where the devastation would hit next.

Sarah was still dealing with the fact that Hamish was alive — and working with Hesbani.

"You could have died going in there," Howard chided her. "What were you thinking?"

"If we don't catch Hesbani, there'll be more attacks."

"We'll get him, Sarah, but we can do it without you killing yourself."

"What the hell do you know about anything?" she snarled. "Hesbani ruined my life a long time ago, and now he's planning to ruin thousands more. The guy lives for this. He's a monster. If you don't have the stomach to get the job done, maybe you should go home."

"I'm just saying be careful. There's a difference between risk and stupidity."

"This isn't a goddamn university classroom, Howard. Theory goes out the window on the battlefield. You do what needs to be done or you lose. And I won't lose again. I can't."

Howard huffed. "Well, guess what? You *did* lose. Hesbani got away. The lone wolf routine isn't working for you, is it? As for my time in the classroom, I used to think predicting and preventing a terrorist's actions was better than dealing with the aftermath when people were already dead. But then one of my colleagues was arrested for poisoning a tea urn at a Christian fundraiser, and I realised you can't predict terrorism. It can't be studied or formulated. After thousands of years of human history, we still don't understand evil. My uncle was at that Christian fundraiser." He swallowed. "Stop convincing yourself that being a bitch is okay just because you've lost something. You're not the only one who's suffered at the hands of evil. You're not special."

"Look, I'm... I'm sorry. You're right."

Howard was still fuming. "You know, the reason I brought you to MCU in the first place was because I thought we had something in common. Now I know that we don't. I do this because I want to save innocent lives, but you're doing this because you want to kill bad guys — and if you can't do that, you're happy to kill *yourself*. It's not courage, acting the way you do, it's cowardice. Face yourself in the mirror and decide you want to be someone again. Do that and you'll have my respect. Until then, you're just a bitch."

Howard marched off before Sarah could respond, but even if he'd given her time, she wasn't sure she could've said anything. After everything that had happened, Sarah's head was a mess. She felt responsible for Bradley's death, but was angry that they had ever brought her into this goddamn situation. She was scared. Scared of trusting. Scared of finding out she made it out of Afghanistan alive while everyone around her hadn't. If she allowed herself a life again, would guilt overwhelm her? Would the faces of Miller, Thomas, and her baby haunt her? Or would they come back from the dead like Hamish? Even if she wanted to let go of the past, what future could she ever hope to have? She was a damaged freak.

Like a wild animal, Sarah let out a yowl. She lost all control and she screamed, kicked, and thrashed at anything within reach. She wanted to explode, to claw out her own eyes so she wouldn't have to look at herself ever again, but then, after her energy was all gone, all she could do was flop to the floor in defeat as a flood of tears took over her.

"Bloody hell, girl. If your old man could see you now."

Sarah glared up at Mattock. "He'd laugh at me and then walk away in shame, right? Don't you think I fucking know that? You can tell my dad all about this at your next poker night. Have a laugh on me."

Mattock snickered. "You're right, he would leave his daughter lying on the ground in tears, because that's the kind of bloke he is. No wonder you're such a mess, luv. My old man was a bus driver, lovely man. Would've given his right arm if I'd needed it. Your old man is a cold-hearted killer and not much of anything else. Luck of the draw, I suppose."

Sarah choked on a sob. "I thought all SAS loved my father. He's a hero."

"You're damn right he's a hero. Don't mean he's not a total prick though. There're many things I miss about the forces, but Major Stone ain't one of 'em."

Sarah laughed, so unexpectedly that she ended up drooling. She wiped the spittle away with the back of her hand and laughed again. "That makes two of us," she said. "He never forgave me for not having a cock between my legs."

Mattock offered Sarah his hand. "Believe me, any decent father would be proud to have a daughter like you." Sarah didn't take his hand because she was too overwhelmed, so Mattock frowned at her. "Bloody hell, luv, will you get your arse up? I'm a trained killer, not a bleedin' nanny." He grabbed her under the arms and yanked her to her feet.

"Man up, soldier. There're still arses to be kicked, and from what I can see, you still have both legs. Stop your bawling."

Sarah nodded and wiped her eyes. "I think we're long overdue a big fucking win."

"Amen to that, Captain."

"My friends call me Sarah."

"Sarah it is, then."

23

DADDY'S GIRL

Mattock talked with the police again while Sarah rejoined Howard. He looked like he was ready for a fight again as she approached him, but Sarah raised her hands to show she was coming in peace. "I admit I may have a slight attitude problem."

Howard raised an eyebrow. "A *slight* problem?"

"Okay, fine, I'm a bitch, but I'm ready to play nice. I know you've got my back. I've got yours too."

"I know you do."

"Okay, so Hallmark moment aside, Hesbani has more attacks planned, and we have no leads."

"Yes, we do." Howard pulled a wedge of papers from his jacket pocket. "I held onto these after you handed them to me. It's the files on the suicide bombers. We've got them!"

Sarah grabbed Howard and kissed him hard on the mouth. "You beauty. We need to get these sent out right now."

Howard's cheeks reddened. "Already done. I photographed the documents and sent them to Palu. He and Bennett are sending the info to every agency in the country. Prime Minister Breslow herself has commended the MCU for its efforts, although publicly she'll probably decry us for our failures. Either way, Hesbani's remaining bombers will be swept up within the hour."

Sarah was so relieved that they'd finally done some good. No matter what Hesbani did from here, they had foiled at least part of his plan. If they could capture some of his suicide bombers alive, they would have suspects to interview, information to gather.

"We'll get Hesbani," said Howard. "Once we have his people, it's only a matter of time."

Sarah nodded. "I just hope we find him fast. He still has people with him."

"You're right. We have no idea who the man in the balaclava was, or the woman in the van."

Sarah considered telling him about Hamish, but didn't quite know how to explain it. How could she admit that she had allowed one of her men to die in Afghanistan, but that he was back from the grave and in league with the man who had supposedly killed him?

Howard glanced at his sleeve and wiped off a layer of soot, then tugged at his cuffs to straightened up his workman's jacket. "Pity Hesbani's hideout went up in flames. It might have shed light on who his accomplices were. We still don't know if Al-Sharir is behind this."

Sarah's eyes went wide. "Balls, I forgot!"

Howard looked confused. "Huh?"

She pulled out the piece of paper she'd grabbed inside the burning building and started reading it. When she finished, she looked at Howard and swallowed. "This isn't good."

"What is it?"

She handed him the piece of paper. "It's Hesbani's script for the final videotape."

Howard read it and his expression grew grim. "We have to get back to MCU. We can't let this happen."

"No shit."

They left Mattock with the police and headed for the car. It had turned late, the sun disappearing, so Sarah put her foot down as she reached the M5 motorway heading south towards London. If Hesbani's plan was still in place, London was where they needed to be. Within half an hour, they met up with Palu and Dr Bennett in the Earthworm's conference room. Howard scanned Hesbani's script with his mob-sat and brought it up on the television screen.

People of Britain. Today your empire burns. Your capital is in ruins and your figurehead is dead. Such is the will of Allah. Shab Bekhier has carried out its mission as promised. You might try to stop us, you might try to kill us, but what we have done today will serve as a stark warning to future generations. My name is Al Al-Sharir, and all I have done, I have done for the glory of Allah.

"Why is Hesbani still claiming to be Al-Sharir?" Bennett asked. "Unless we're assuming that Al-Sharir might still be involved."

Sarah thought about Hamish, and how Al-Sharir had ordered Hesbani to slit his throat in the middle of the desert. "I don't know," she admitted. "Perhaps everything I thought about Al-Sharir is wrong. I thought he lived by a certain set of rules. Now, I'm not so sure."

Howard drummed his fingertips on the desk. "Have we brought in any of the documented suicide bombers yet?"

Palu answered. "Scotland Yard is carrying out a raid as we speak. As soon as they have them in custody, gaining information on Hesbani's whereabouts will be their top priority."

"We need to warn them that Hesbani's planning to take out Prime Minister Breslow," said Bennett.

"Are we sure about that?" asked Howard.

Bennett shrugged. "*Your figurehead is dead.* Who else could it be?"

"I suppose you're right," agreed Howard, "but how? The Prime Minister is the most protected woman in the country."

Bennett shook her head. "I disagree. In America there's a small army protecting our President, but your Prime Minister is relatively defenceless. There's no Secret Service to take a bullet for Breslow, or armed convoys taking her from one place to the next. Your Prime Minister is a soft target."

"She's right," said Sarah. "We don't plan for assassination attempts like other nations. With our political system, the ramifications of executing a Prime Minister isn't worth the risk. The party in power would just place someone else in charge and all current policies would continue. The only reason to kill our Prime Minister is to make a statement. This whole thing has been about an eye-for-an-eye. We helped take out Saddam, Bin Laden, Gaddafi... now Hesbani wants to take out one of ours."

Palu stood. "I'll put through a call to Breslow. We have a prerogative to warn her."

Sarah leaned back and tried to think like Hesbani. Killing Breslow would be prime time news all over the world, but somehow it didn't quite fit. Breslow had only been in power for two years and had been behind a concerted effort to pull troops out of the Middle East. Her recent tax hikes and cutbacks on education had made her an unpopular leader, unlikely to get a second term. Killing her wouldn't crush the people of Great Britain's spirits. It wasn't grand enough. Hesbani wanted to be immortalised, but killing Breslow wouldn't gain him that everlasting notoriety that Bin Laden had achieved on 9/11. He would be a footnote in history, a buried headline.

Howard's mob-sat rang, and after a brief call, he looked relieved. "Mandy's okay," he told them. "His surgery was a success, and he's awake. Mattock is on his way to check on him."

Sarah smiled. "Thank God. Mandy promised to be lead singer in my band."

Howard smirked.

The sudden good news, however, made Sarah think of things less fortunate. "What have we done with Bradley?"

"He's comfortable," said Bennett. "I wrapped him in blankets and laid him inside his dorm until the coroner collects him."

"He had a room here at the Earthworm?"

Bennett nodded. "There are dorm rooms in the rear of the head section. I can take you to him if you'd like."

Sarah nodded. "Please."

Bennett took her on a five-minute walk to the dorms and then said, "I'll leave you alone."

"No, I'd like you to stay, please, Dr Bennett."

"I... um, well, okay."

Bradley's body was wrapped in a bundle of white sheets on a small cot bed, a bible placed on his chest. "He was a Christian?"

"It seemed like the right thing to do, but I don't know whether he believed or not. Seems like he was only around for a short while."

Sarah looked around the room, finding it cluttered. Bradley had tried to make it a home. A large black and white print of Trafalgar Square hung on one wall, and on the other was an image of the royal crown hanging above the inscription: *Keep Calm and Carry On.* Bradley clearly hadn't yet found himself beyond knowing his love of country.

Sarah sighed. "What did you know about him? What was he like?"

Bennett shrugged. "A sweet boy. Smart. Smarter than he realised. Loved his country, loved his queen; just wanted to do some good. I'm ashamed to say I underestimated how brave he was. In the end, he proved he was more than just a sweet boy."

"He loved the Queen?" Sarah tittered. She remembered when she had pledged allegiance in front of Elizabeth II's portrait. She couldn't imagine doing so now.

"He loved everything about this country. Tell you the truth, I was never that happy about being posted here from the States, but Bradley's enthusiasm was infectious. Brits can be rude and vulgar, and your roads make no sense at all, but deep down, y'all are about the most accommodating people on the planet. This country tries to please everybody all the time, and it probably comes about as close as any country has. America always prides itself on being free, but I've never been anywhere freer than Britain. You can be poor, sick, uneducated, or even from an enemy nation, and this country will take care of you. That's why I'm happy to be here now. I think the United Kingdom is a place worth fighting for."

Sarah nodded ruefully. "Somehow I lost sight of that."

"You weren't fighting for your nation before, Sarah, you were fighting for your government. It's not the same. MCU is fighting the good fight, for no other agenda than saving lives. We don't care about oil, political favours, or international sanctions. The only thing we care about is stopping the bad guys. I think that's what you care about too, Sarah. Perhaps it's the only thing left you care about."

Sarah looked at the doctor, and for the first time admired her. "Let me guess, you threw in a couple of psychology courses when you studied for your medical degree?"

Bennett smiled. "Most doctors do. How else are we supposed to screw with y'all's heads?"

Sarah offered a hand. "Thanks for not being the bitch I thought you were, Dr Bennett."

"Likewise."

The two women shook hands, and Sarah heaved a sigh. "I need to say goodbye to Bradley. Could I have a minute?"

"Of course." Jessica left the room while Sarah knelt beside Bradley. "Hey kid, it's Sarah. I wanted to let you know you were right. The problem wasn't with how other people saw me; it was about how I saw myself. If I hadn't met you, I might never have learned that lesson. I promise I'll get Hesbani for this. I'll make him pay. God save the Queen, Bradley. See you in the next fight."

24

INDEPENDANT WOMAN

"I informed Prime Minister Breslow," Palu told them. "She was scheduled to attend the VE Day river parade today, but she's cancelled."

"She should have cancelled the whole parade," said Sarah. "We're in the midst of a terrorist attack, and people are packing their sandwiches to go stand by the river."

Palu shrugged. "I believe the expected attendance has more than halved, but most people don't think anything bad will ever happen to them. Others refuse to be cowed."

"All are idiots," said Sarah.

Howard was frowning. "Hesbani has this all wrong. He'd know the Prime Minister would remain at Downing Street after all these attacks, so why would he not assassinate her first? All he's done is send her into hiding."

"You're right," said Sarah. "Something about this doesn't add up. I still don't think Breslow is a big enough target for Hesbani. He wants to become a hero to the terrorist community. Breslow isn't important enough."

"I dare say I agree," said Bennett. "No disrespect, but your Prime Minister is a fairly benign figure in world events."

"So what are we thinking then?" asked Palu. "Who's a bigger target than the Prime Minister? Who's the 'figurehead' Hesbani was talking about?"

"The Queen," said Sarah, knowing it was true. Bradley's unashamed love for the royal family was indicative of a large portion of the country. The Queen was the embodiment of British pride and a symbol of the British Empire. "Hesbani wants to punish us for our imperialistic past. What person represents Britain's heritage more than the Queen?"

"There's no way of knowing for certain," said Howard, "but I buy that. The Queen would be the jewel in a terrorist's crown, excuse the pun."

Bennett pulled a face. "How could Hesbani hope to assassinate the Queen? She's hardly ever in public."

"Except for today," said Howard. "It's May eighth, VE Day. The Queen is scheduled to travel via barge down the Thames. She'll be awarding veteran medals on the stretch in front of Westminster."

Sarah shook her head and tutted. "How the hell can we be having a parade when half-a-dozen villages have been bombed?"

"That's exactly why," Palu snapped at her. "The Queen has already spoken out against the terrorists, clarifying that her plans will not be altered by fear. Today is about remembering the men and woman who fight for our freedom, and it would be a great disservice to not do so because of monsters like Hesbani."

"I can see why Bradley loved the old dear," Sarah commented. "She's got balls."

"We should warn Her Majesty," said Bennett.

Sarah shook her head. "We do that and Hesbani might disappear. This is our best chance of catching him out in the open. He doesn't know what we found at the station house. As long as he remains in the dark, we have the upper hand."

Bennett folded her arms. "It's unethical not to warn her. Negligent also."

"So is letting Hesbani escape to kill more people."

Palu motioned for silence. "We'll hold off on warning the royal household for now as we don't know for sure that the threat is arrayed against the Queen. Hesbani's script mentioned the capital in ruins. I believe there are more targets we don't yet know about."

Howard bashed his fist on the desk. "Christ! Where does this end?"

"I think he'll be focused on hitting Westminster," said Sarah. "Hesbani will want something iconic. What would be a more lasting image than the Houses of Parliament burning?"

Palu nodded. "We need to get bodies on the ground. Howard and Sarah, get to Westminster and find Hesbani. Dr Bennett and I will coordinate from here. The Scotland Yard sweep is in progress as we speak. Soon as I hear anything, I'll let you know what we have."

Sarah acknowledged with a grunt. "What about Mattock's team? We need every body we put out."

"Agreed. As soon as Mandy is here, I'll send Mattock to assist you. Get yourselves armed. I want you on the road in ten."

"Good work, partner," Howard told Sarah as they left the conference room.

"We're not partners yet."

Howard frowned.

She patted him on the back. "I still need to earn that honour."

Howard took her to the armoury again where she replaced her the SIG she had lost to Hamish with another identical model. They both strapped on Kevlar vests beneath their clothes and then left. Sarah knew her way around the Earthworm well enough by now that she made it out into the derelict farm only a few minutes later. The MCU was starting to feel like home.

She and Howard got in the remaining Jag and took off. By the time they reached the highway, the lunchtime rush had started. Despite all the devastation, people still had to earn a living.

Once upon a time, the people of Britain would have banded together in a crisis, lining the streets in solidarity. Nowadays, people acted like nothing had happened. They lived life as individuals, where once they had been a community. Sarah wondered if the country would ever get back to those days of unified spirit.

The lunchtime rush hour resulted in the drive taking more than an hour, and by the time they parked on Great College Street — opposite Big Ben — it was one-thirty. The Queen was due to appear at three.

Howard rummaged in the Jag's boot while Sarah surveyed the area. Westminster seemed ancient in the soft sunlight, and Parliament's sharp spikes caught the light and sparkled like a castle out of Camelot. The nearby river added to the fantasy. What ruined it, however, was the endless lines of beeping traffic and photo-snapping tourists. People already lined the banks of the Thames, investing hours of their time to get a decent spot for the short-lived festivities. Sarah hoped they didn't end up getting a show they weren't expecting. If the Queen was shot, the entire world would see it live. Even now, there were news choppers hovering overhead. Their cameras wouldn't miss a thing. Westminster was the grandest place in the city, making it the grandest place to assassinate a monarch.

"Where do we start?" Howard asked as he slammed the boot closed. He handed her a small radio which she attached to the lapel of her jacket.

"The officers killed in front of Scotland Yard were hit by a sniper, right? My guess would be that Hesbani is planning to hit Her Majesty as she comes down the river." Nearby, a gentleman smoking a cigarette gave her an astonished glance, obviously having heard her. "Hey," Sarah shouted at the guy. "Go smoke somewhere else before I stub it out in your eye."

The man saw her scars and hurried away.

Howard frowned. "I thought you were going with a different attitude from now on."

"I am. Did you hear me use any bad language?"

"Yeah, right, well done."

"Thank you. Now, if I were a sniper, where would I be?"

Howard looked up at Big Ben. "How about up there?"

Sarah considered the bell tower behind the giant clock and knew it looked right out over the Thames. If nothing else, it would make a good place for Sarah and Howard to survey the area. "Okay, make a call or something and get us inside."

Howard called Palu, who got them clearance right away. A security guard met them at the front entrance and they were shown inside. Sarah glanced at the guard's name badge. "How easy is it to access Big Ben, Dave?"

The guard looked very serious, like he thought this was his moment to truly fulfil his role. "Technically, Big Ben is the name of the bell. The tower itself is named the Elizabeth Tower. To answer your question, there are sporadic tours, usually arranged by local MPs trying to impress their constituents, but during special occasions like today the tower is off-limits. Bomb threats are the greatest concern. What are you two then? MI5, Special Branch? I was going to apply to join the Met, but got myself a dodgy knee, you see. So what are you looking for? You can tell me, I've signed all the confidentiality forms."

"What about snipers?" asked Howard, ignoring Dave's babble.

Dave shrugged. His shoulders were wide but his belly was fat. It didn't look like the guy had ever made the trip to the top of the tower himself. "It's a good spot, I suppose, but this place is never empty. I think a sniper probably wants to be hidden, right?"

Sarah nodded with disappointment. A sniper would have no chance of staying hidden here. She wondered if Hesbani was the sniper himself, or was it Hamish, or maybe the woman in the burka? She didn't remember Hamish having any particular skill with a rifle, and Hesbani's fondness for knives suggested he wouldn't be found detached from the kill behind a sniper's scope. That left the women in the burka. Who the hell was she?

"Can we go to the bell tower?" Sarah asked the guard.

Dave nodded and directed them to the top. "I'll join you up there in a few minutes," he said. "You need anything in the meantime, just holler."

From inside the tower, Sarah could see the sunshine gleaming off the river and bathing the city in an orange halo. From up so high, the city noise disappeared and it was peaceful.

"Don't suppose you can see anything?" Howard asked.

Sarah shook her head. "It's like an ant farm down there. We'll never spot anything from up here without a telescope."

"Try these." Howard handed her a small, sleek set of binoculars.

"Where did you get these?"

"Out of the boot. You didn't think I'd come on a surveillance mission with nothing to *survey* with, did you?"

Sarah snatched the binoculars. "Knew you would come in handy some day."

"Hey, you're the one who has to keep being rescued."

"Those days are over, and as I remember it, you've been a damsel in distress yourself since we met too."

"Maybe our odds would be better if we stuck together."

Sarah frowned. Howard stood like a boy asking a girl out on a first date. "If you're asking me to be your partner," she said, "I'm afraid I already promised myself to one of Dr Bennett's cats."

Howard punched the air. "Those damned cats, always in on my action."

Sarah giggled and then remembered why they were there. She looked through the binoculars and London came back to life. The ants had become people and cars again. "There are civilians everywhere," she said. "I don't even know what to look for."

"The parade is set to begin soon," said Howard. "We need to look out for anybody acting outside of expected parameters. Commuters should be moving. Tourists should be spectating and taking pictures. Is there anybody doing something different?"

Sarah scanned below. Just as Howard had predicted, there were several lines of suited business people trying to get where they were going as quickly as possible. Their main obstacle was the dawdling groups of tourists taking photographs. It was like watching a river flowing around boulders. Various boats, mostly small outboard vessels, lined the width of the Thames, most of them emblazoned with Union

Jacks and other patriotic symbols. There were also Nepalese, Cypriote, and several other national emblems for those who had aided Britain during the Second World War. To Sarah's left was the *London Eye*. The city's giant Ferris Wheel might make a good spot for a sniper, but while it was moving, it would require a lot of on-the-fly adjustments. It couldn't be ruled out as a possible location, but it wasn't ideal. There were many other buildings on the opposite side of the river, but none were particularly tall. They would also be extremely busy during a working day which made the likelihood of discovery high.

Where would she want to be if she was going to set up a rifle? Somewhere high with a nice long approach, target coming towards, not across. She would want to be invisible.

Sarah scanned with the binoculars but kept coming up empty. The best place to snipe a boat coming down the river was from atop Westminster Bridge, but the road was flat and low. There were no elevations or interior spaces in which to hide like there was in Tower Bridge. Sarah hated to admit it, but she didn't think they would find the sniper at this section of the Thames.

Howard was silent behind her, sensing her frustration. If they didn't find a clue, they'd be forced to warn the Queen's security. The parade would be cancelled, and even more panic would descend upon the country. Hesbani would disappear into the woodwork.

Sarah took one last look, wishing with all her damaged heart to find something. She checked out the ferry boats departing from Westminster Pier, the buses crossing the bridge, the carriages on the London Eye, and the office buildings on the opposite bank. She was just about to give up when she spotted something on the other side of the river. "Howard, what's that building across the river with the big green tower?"

"Er... County Hall. There's a *Sea Life* centre there and some restaurants."

Sarah nodded and kept the binoculars to her eyes. "Well, right now there's a black van with a rear spoiler broken in front of it."

Howard blanched. "You're kidding me? The same one we saw at the station house in Redditch?"

Sarah studied the van and was certain. Its hazard lights were blinking, and one of its tyres was flat. "Come on," she said. "We've got the bastards."

They raced down Elizabeth Tower and bumped into Dave at the bottom.

"Everything good?" he asked.

"Ask me in ten minutes," Sarah told him. "If it looks like I just kicked the shit out of someone, then yes, everything is absolutely dandy."

25

FAMILY

Sarah's heart was thumping. Every second it took them to reach the van was a second Hesbani might be getting away — or putting his plan into action. When they reached the Jag, Sarah threw herself into the driver's seat, ignoring the agony of her multiple wounds, and reversed before Howard even got fully in the car. Crossing over Westminster Bridge, she had to fight the urge to hammer on the horn as the traffic crawled between the pedestrian-covered pavements, but the last thing she could afford to do was to alert Hesbani they were coming.

Howard got on the radio. "Palu, we have a possible target sighting. North Bank, outside County Hall. Black transit van with rear, roof-mounted spoiler. Alert authorities. Back-up needed."

"Roger that. Will alert local authorities. Mattock en route to provide back-up."

"Tell him to hurry his arse up," said Sarah. "I could really use him about now. He's the only one without a gunshot wound slowing them down."

"Roger that. Engage target if necessary, but be careful. You don't know what to expect."

"Don't worry," said Sarah. "The only people dying today are terrorists."

The radio clicked off, and Sarah put her foot down as the traffic opened up ahead. She glanced at Howard beside her. "You ready, partner?"

He held up his Ruger with one hand, his other still in a cast. "Hell yes. Time to beat Hesbani's arse."

"You sound like me."

"Not necessarily a bad thing."

"Don't get soppy on me."

"Wouldn't dream of it, Captain."

"It's Sarah. Now, let's do this." They reached the end of the bridge and raced into oncoming traffic, crossing the lanes and heading for the parked-up van on the other side. There was a cacophony of blaring horns and swerving tyres, but it was too late for Hesbani to get an early warning now. The Jag skidded to a halt right in front of the van.

"Police," Sarah shouted as she leapt out of the car, "or something." She pulled out her SIG and nearby pedestrians scattered. Mobile phones appeared out of pockets and went up in the air. Some dialled 999 while others captured video footage.

Howard and Sarah approached opposite sides of the van. Sarah took the passenger side with the sliding door. The windows were blacked out, but she could see that there was nobody in the front seat. "I'm opening the side door," she shouted to Howard. "I'm going in after three."

"Roger that."

"One..." Sarah threw the door open, trying to catch the occupants unaware. The plan didn't work, and she was the one taken by surprise. Hamish leapt out of the van and smashed his meaty forehead into Sarah's face.

Sarah staggered backwards as she felt her nose break. Blood came thick and fast, but she was too determined to let it stop her. She blinked away tears and growled. Rather than attack again, Hamish took off in a stumbling limp. The wound where she had shot him was now wrapped in a thick white bandage. As he ran, he fired wildly behind him, causing chaos in the streets.

Sarah was going to go after him, ready to chase him to the ends of the earth, but Howard stood in her way and kept her from running off. He pointed to the van's interior, his face stark white.

"What? What is it?" Sarah glanced around quickly. "Holy shit! Is that what I think it is?"

The van's rear compartment was chock-full of plastic explosives. Bricks of the stuff had been piled on top of a wooden pallet. At either end of the pallet were dozens of glass containers filled with amber liquid. Whatever it was, there were enough explosives inside the van to wipe Westminster off the map.

Sarah looked towards the bridge. Hamish was getting away. "There's nothing I can do here," she told Howard. "Call this in. I'm going after Hamish."

Howard shook his head, confused. "Who?"

Sarah realised she hadn't yet explained about Hamish, but there was no time to get into it now. "Just call it in," she said, and then sprinted towards the bridge. Already, she was losing sight of her ex-corporal, but she wouldn't let him get away. Not this time.

Sarah sprinted, reaching a speed she'd not managed since her days in the army — before her thigh had been torn up by IED shrapnel. It felt good to have her muscles moving in sync again, her entire body focused on the single goal of momentum. The tiredness and pain of the last few days ebbed away, and she felt strong and powerful, fully awake for the first time in years. It was rebirth.

Sarah caught sight of Hamish and gained on him. He wasn't in the shape he'd been in six years ago, and the wound in his leg was slowing him down. Several times, he glanced over his shoulder and saw she was closing the distance between them. He was halfway across the bridge when he realised he wouldn't escape. He stopped and pointed his gun at her. The SIG he had taken from Sarah. Sarah raised her own identical weapon.

"Dinae come a step closer, Captain," he yelled at her. "Not another wee step, you hear me?"

Sarah slowed right down, but still strolled towards him. "You're done Hamish. We know all about Hesbani's plan. We've got your van full of explosives. We'll find your stashed rifle. It was a stupid plan, you were never a marksman."

Hamish grinned. "Aye, you're right there. I never was much cop with a rifle, was I? You know, I only joined the Army to avoid the dole queues, but I was a loyal soldier all the same. Straight as an arrow, for all the good it did me."

Sarah wasn't about to get dragged into the past, not when she was finally ready to let it go. "You're going to have much more to worry about than the unemployment line when this is all over, Corporal. What the hell are you thinking, working with Hesbani? He slit your throat, Hamish. I watched him do it."

"Aye, he did, but it wasn't him what killed me. It was you, remember? You made the choice." He lifted his head to show a chubby pink scar across his throat that almost put Sarah's own wounds to shame. It was a thick slug, slithering from ear to ear.

"I'm sorry," said Sarah, and she meant it. "I made the wrong decision. I was afraid and it made me selfish. It still doesn't explain all this though. Killing innocent people makes nothing better. It makes nothing right." The sound of sirens came from both sides of the river as Police arrived in squad cars to block both ends of the bridge. Sarah raised her SIG, pointing it at Hamish's chest. "You're finished, Corporal. Stand down."

Hamish laughed. "A captain is supposed to protect their men. You chose your own well-being over mine. You turned your back on me, and then guess what?"

"What?"

"The goddamn Government refused to pay my daughter any money because I wasn't confirmed dead."

Sarah hadn't even known Hamish had had a daughter. "I told them you were dead. I said I saw you die."

"Aye, I'm sure you did. Didn't stop 'em welching on their obligation, though. Fucking crooks."

"But you're not dead," said Sarah, reaffirming her grip on her SIG. "So they don't owe you a thing."

Hamish growled, hatred seething from his pores. "I was *left* for dead and abandoned by my bloody captain, not to mention being kept prisoner for a year. Believe me, that's as good as dead. They owe me alright."

"So what changed? When did you go from prisoner to terrorist?"

"I'm nae the terrorist! The UK government is the terrorist, do you nae see it? I realised it the day one of their bloody bombs hit a school in the village they were holding me at. Do you know what it's like to see wee children on fire? It changes you, Captain, I dinae need to tell you. After that day, I begged Hesbani to let me help him get revenge. Six months later, he finally trusted me enough to let me go back home, as a member of Shab Bekhier."

Sarah sighed. Her gun lowered. "Mistakes happen in war."

"I'll nae accept that. Not if it means seeing innocent children burn."

"Your suicide bombs have killed children in this country. You're a hypocrite."

Hamish sneered. "Our children aren't innocent. They're brats bred on consumption. They'll grow up to be bankers and bureaucrats. Their sacrifice will help save the truly innocent."

Sarah shook her head. "What happened to the man I served with? You were never like this, Hamish. You wanted to help the people of Afghanistan."

"That man was left to die in the desert."

"What could I have done?"

Hamish swallowed and looked like he might combust with his hatred for her. "You could have done your job and protected your men. You could have saved me, but you chose yourself and that fucking baby inside of you."

Sarah swallowed. "You understand nothing, Hamish. You think I got away scot free? I died in that desert just the same as you did."

"We should nae have been there! Do you nae realise that? Look what they did to you. Did they treat you like a hero for all that you gave? Did they apologise for what happened to your face?"

Sarah thought about how she'd been discarded after her blow-up at Major Burke in her hospital bed. The Army liked to make out that an injured soldier only had themselves to blame. The report had said: 'Captain Stone breached protocol by assisting an unidentified civilian,' then went on to blame her for the death of her squad. The woman with the watermelons had ended Sarah's life, but it was her own government who put the dirt on her coffin. "No, they didn't treat me like a hero," she admitted, "because I wasn't one."

"Then what are you doing here, Captain? Why are you fighting for a country that dinae give a wee shit about you?"

"I'm not doing it for my country. I'm doing it for twenty-nine dead children killed by Hesbani's bombs."

"Well, I suppose we have something in common then."

"I suppose we do." Sarah raised her SIG and let off a shot. She hit Hamish in the shoulder, knocking her original SIG from his hand and rocking him against the railings. As his sleeve rolled up, Sarah spotted a dagger tattoo on his wrist.

Hamish gritted his teeth and started to sag. He spat blood. "You dinae even know what you're fighting for."

"You're finished, Corporal. Stand down before I put you down."

Hamish grunted. "I may be finished, but Hesbani ain't. You really think I'm the shooter? I couldn't hit a barn door with a rocket launcher. You have the right game, but the wrong player."

Sarah took a step forward, lowering her SIG. "Who's the shooter?"

Hamish just grinned.

Sarah fired off a shot into his knee. The sound of more gunfire brought armed police hurrying up each end of the bridge. They approached cautiously, shouting warnings to stand down. Hamish slumped to the ground, clutching his knee and gritting his teeth. He wouldn't give voice to the pain.

Sarah pointed the gun at his head. "I'll give you credit, you're a lot tougher than I remember."

"Conviction does that to a man. Do what you want. My conscience is clean. How about yours?"

Sarah pressed the barrel against his forehead. "Might as well send you on your merry way then. I'm sure there won't be any virgins waiting for you."

"If you kill me, the police will take you down. Whoever you're working with, you don't have the authority to kill people in the middle of a London street with cameras filming."

Sarah saw spiralling helicopters converge above Westminster Bridge as police surrounded the area. Hamish was right. If she fired another shot, the police would likely shoot her.

The radio on her lapel squawked and Howard's voice came though. "Sarah, the bomb squad is on its way. The Met have called off the parade. The Queen is already onboard her royal barge, but she's being returned to HMS *Britannia* under heavy guard. She'll remain onboard until the threat has passed. It's over, Sarah. Let the police take things from here."

Sarah switched the radio off, then removed the muzzle of her gun from Hamish's forehead. "You see? You've lost. The Queen is safe. They're taking her to safety right now."

Hamish spat blood on the pavement. "Way I see it, Her Majesty is still out in the open. Doesn't sound like she's safe to me."

Sarah frowned. "Where's the sniper? Where's Hesbani?"

"You'll never reach him. Don't matter where the Queen is, he'll get her."

The choppers buzzed over the bridge, whipping up a gale. Sarah suddenly had an idea where to find Hesbani, but before she could confirm it, Hamish leapt up on his good leg and shoved himself against the railing. At first, Sarah thought he would make a grab for her gun, but instead he threw himself over the railing. By the time she reacted,

204 IAIN ROB WRIGHT

he was gone, only frothing water beneath the bridge where he had landed.

He had taken her only chance of confirming her theory. If she was wrong...

With the situation defused, police officers started up either end of the bridge. They pointed their assault rifles at Sarah and shouted at her to drop her weapon and hit the ground, but she held onto her SIG for now. It was the only thing keeping the police from rushing her. She opened up her radio so that the MCU could hear her, and spoke loudly enough that the police would hear her too. It didn't matter who was listening so long as somebody was. "There's still a terrorist threat," she said. "The Queen is in danger. I think there's a sniper in a news chopper."

"DROP YOUR WEAPON!"

She carried on. "There's going to be an attempt on the Queen's life any minute."

"DROP YOUR WEAPON OR WE WILL FIRE."

Sarah eased her grip on the SIG, but couldn't bring herself to drop it. As soon as she did that, the police would rush her and take her out of the game. And this was her game.

"THREE SECONDS. THREE..."

Sarah swallowed.

"TWO..."

A voice came over Sarah's radio. "Sarah, I hear you loud and clear, mate. Looks like you could do with a lift out of there, sharpish."

It was Mattock, and Sarah gushed when she heard his calm cockney voice. "Mattock. Shit, I could really do with a way out of this."

"Roger that. I'll pull your arse out of the fire, luv."

Sarah glanced around the bridge. "Where are you?"

"Right behind you."

Sarah was blown sideways as a Griffin helicopter swooped beside the bridge. The police were taken by surprise too and leapt into cover behind railings, not knowing whether to open fire. Sarah grabbed her hair to stop it blinding her.

"Stop pissing around and hop onboard," yelled Mattock.

Sarah glanced at the police squads. They were already breaking cover and coming back towards her. She had to move now. *Screw it!*

She stepped back to give herself a run up, then sprinted towards the railing. She leapt into the air, spiking her foot on top of the steel railing and launching herself off the bridge. For a moment, it felt like she was flying. Voices of the police shouting at her faded away as she fell. The river flowed beneath her.

Mattock grabbed a hold of her wrist in mid-air and dragged her onboard. She ended up on her face, ankles dangling out the doorway.

"You okay, Sarah?" Mattock shouted over the din of the engines.

She pulled herself fully inside the chopper. "Just glad to see you."

"Where's Hesbani?"

"I don't know for sure, but I think he might be in a news chopper. Hamish seemed pretty sure Hesbani can get a shot at the Queen wherever she is on the river. A helicopter is the only thing that makes sense."

Mattock helped her to her feet as the chopper tilted and made a getaway. "The Queen is en route east to the HMS *Britannia* who will pick her up."

"Then that's where we head. Wait, who's piloting this thing?"

Mattock nodded to the cockpit. "Best pilot there is, even with a gunshot wound."

Sarah clambered into the co-pilot's seat and grinned at Mandy. There was a bulge beneath his shirt where a heavy bandage no doubt covered his injuries. Dr Bennett sure was generous with those painkillers.

"You okay?" she asked him.

He turned to her, a blank expression on his face, then said, "Just a flesh wound. Glad you're still with us, Captain."

Sarah couldn't help but feel like she was among family.

26

KICK OFF

Sarah joined Mattock at the rear of the chopper where he was adjusting the sights on an AR-15. "I didn't bring anything bigger," he apologised, "but Mandy can loose a couple of Hellfires if need be."

Sarah hated hellfire missiles. They were too indiscriminate. Like the one that had hit the bus her husband had been sitting in. "There are too many boats on the water. There'll be casualties."

"What's the plan then? How do we stop Hesbani if he's airborne?"

Sarah shrugged. "When the time comes, we'll do whatever we have to, but we need to find him first."

The HMS *Britannia* floated ahead, not as large as its name implied. The Queen's barge sailed towards it, easy to identify by its lavish red and gold accoutrements.

"There's a dozen choppers in the air," said Mandy. "How do we know which one we're looking for?"

"Can we hail them?" Sarah asked.

Mandy nodded and fiddled with the dashboard knobs. "Be advised, all aircraft in the vicinity of HMS *Britannia*, please identify. Possible threat, please be advised."

The radio squawked back with replies from other pilots. Some expressed concern and broke away while others were news hounds unwilling to lose sight of the Queen. By the time Mandy got off the radio, only three helicopters remained unidentified.

"Who do we have left?" asked Mattock.

Sarah peered out the side hatch and tried to make out the decals on the other helicopters. "Never Stop News, BBC World, and... the third is too far away."

"Get us up closer, Mandy," Mattock ordered.

The Griffin tilted forward and picked up speed. They passed the Never Stop News chopper first and Sarah tried to see who was inside, and could just about make out the shape of a man in the pilot's seat. He waved as they passed. Seeing inside the BBC chopper was easier, and there was a crew of three; none of them Hesbani.

"It has to be the last chopper," said Sarah.

"If they have a high-powered rifle," Mattock said with a hint of panic, "they can take a shot at the Queen at any time."

Sarah watched the slow-moving barge with the royal regalia. Any sniper worth his salt would be setting up their shot right now.

The radio squawked. "Unidentified civilian aircraft, this is HMS *Britannia*. You are not cleared for this airspace. Please vacate the area immediately."

Sarah climbed into the co-pilot's seat and grabbed a headset. "HMS *Britannia*, this is... *Agent* Stone of the MCU. We are in pursuit of a suspected terrorist. Please be advised, there is an imminent threat to Her Majesty. Repeat: imminent threat to Her Majesty. Oh, and if you're hearing this, Hesbani, they're going to have to fish you out of the Thames when this is done."

"Stand down, MCU 3402" came a gruff voice. "You are in restricted airspace. Leave the area or face hostile response."

Sarah switched the radio off and turned to Mattock. "Call Palu and see if he can buy us some time. I don't fancy getting shot down by the goddamn Navy."

Mattock was already on his mob-sat. "Me either."

As they got closer to the final helicopter, Sarah saw that it belonged to one of Rupert Murdoch's rags. Mandy edged up alongside it and Sarah prepared to fire her SIG — not the best weapon to take on a helicopter, but it was better than making hand gestures. They were met with dumbfounded expressions from the people inside: three middle-aged men in turtle-necks. Sarah recognised one from the evening news.

"Shit, it's not them! It's not the right chopper."

As if to prove her point, there was an ear-piercing *ping* as something hit the Griffin's hull.

Ping!

"Some cheeky bugger's shooting at us," Mattock growled. "Mandy, take us up. It must be the *Britannia*."

"No," said Mandy, "we're being fired on from the rear." He pulled back on the yoke and Sarah and Mattock tumbled to the back of the cabin. The wind howled through the open side hatch as the helicopter spun around.

"They must be in the first chopper," Sarah shouted over the bellow of the engines. "Never Stop News. Get us on their six, Mandy."

Mandy didn't reply, but the helicopter zipped back and forth, making the Griffin a hard target for any further sniper fire. Mattock grabbed hold of a seat and grimaced. "I'm gonna chuck my bloody guts up in a minute."

"Grow some balls," Sarah grabbed hold of the nylon rigging bolted to the roof. "There's worse than this at Disney World."

"I never pegged you for a *Mouseketeer*."

The cabin tilted left and right and Sarah swung from the nylon handholds like a rag doll, her feet flailing in the air.

Ping!

"Shit, we're in the line of fire again," said Mattock. "Mandy, get us out of their sights already."

The chopper zipped sideways at 90-degrees. Sarah's legs swung around in a circle as she held on for dear life.

Snap!

Sarah hit the floor of the cabin and moaned in pain. The nylon rigging was still wrapped around her wrist but it had come loose from its rivets.

Mandy righted the chopper while Mattock helped Sarah to her feet. "You went a bit of a pisser there, luv."

Sarah shrugged free of him and strapped herself in beside Mandy up front. She turned to him and saw the glint in his eyes. "You're enjoying this, aren't you?"

Mandy stared back at her with his typical poker face, but this time she was sure there was a grin at the corners of his mouth

They hurtled through the air, heading for the Never Stop News chopper. It was a game of chicken now, but they were playing against a suicide bomber. In a game of chicken, a suicide bomber always won.

It was a relief when Mandy dived underneath the other chopper just as they were about to collide, and the Griffin swooped through the air in a long arc, eventually coming up behind its target.

They'd found their sniper.

Hanging out of the side door with a long, scoped rifle was the woman in the burka. Something about the woman was familiar. Covered from head to toe, only her hands and eyes were visibly. Sarah realised she knew the woman.

The woman in the burka had the sniper rifle propped over a left wrist that was missing a hand.

Sarah's mouth dropped. "It can't be."

"What?" Mattock still looked like he might vomit.

"I know the shooter. She was responsible for the death of my squad in Afghanistan."

"You mean the woman with the watermelons?"

"You know about that?"

"It's in your file." He placed a hand on her shoulder. "Think you owe that mad tart some payback, don't you?"

Sarah nodded. Boy did she! Mattock's hand on her shoulder felt nice, and for the first time in a long time, she felt like part of a team. Instead of blaming her for her past mistakes, Mattock wanted to help her make things right. Sarah held her up her SIG. One well-placed shot could put an end to this.

The Never Stop News chopper was just ahead of the Griffin now, so Sarah leaned out of the side hatch and brought up her aim.

PING!

She flinched back inside. The bullet had hit the hull a mere inch from her skull.

She leaned back out and tried to get a shot off again.

PING!

"Damn it," she said. "I won't be able to get a shot off while the bitch is zeroed in on me. She's too good."

Mattock went up to the side door and blindly fired his AR-15. It was more a show of support than anything else.

PING!

"Shit!" Mattock dropped the assault rifle out of the hatch and fell backwards into the cabin, clutching his bleeding hand. "Bugger it," he said. "That was my Monopoly-playing hand."

"Now we've all been shot," said Sarah, then helped Mattock onto the rear bench seat. A moment later, the cockpit window shattered and the Griffin's interior became a wind tunnel. Mandy cursed from the pilot's seat and quickly gained altitude.

PING!

The shot came from beneath them this time, hitting the underside of the hull. Mandy tilted the chopper sideways to evade.

"We can't get near them," said Mattock. "We'll end up in the Thames if we keep taking fire like this."

Sarah clenched her fingers around her SIG's grip. "As soon as she gets some distance, she'll line up a shot on the Queen."

Mattock growled. "The old bird must be under cover by now surely. How is the shooter planning on getting a line on her?"

"I don't know," admitted Sarah, "but if I know Hesbani, he won't accept failure. The threat isn't over until he's stopped."

"Then what the hell do we do, luv?"

Sarah stood up and looked around the cabin before scrambling back into the cockpit. "Mandy, is it safe to get directly above the other chopper?"

Mandy nodded. "It'll keep us out of the line of sight, but they'll also be out of ours. We won't be able to do anything but stay with them."

Sarah had suspected that. It would be okay. "Take us right above the other chopper. Then, when I give the word, bring us out ten feet on their right. Understand?"

Mandy didn't question her, he just nodded.

Sarah headed back into the cabin and knelt.

"What you doing?" Mattock asked her.

"Ever see Tarzan?"

Sarah picked up the nylon rigging that had pulled loose from the ceiling and straightened it out. There was about twelve feet of rope. She went to Mattock's seat and reached underneath him.

"Aye up, luv. I'm married."

Sarah rolled her eyes. She looped the nylon rope around the fixings beneath Mattock's seat and yanked it tight. It only had to be strong enough to hold her for a second.

Mattock gave her the strangest look then. "You're not about to do what I think you are, are you?"

Sarah smirked. "I always wanted to join the circus."

She wrapped the other end of the nylon rope around her waist and made sure it was secure. Then she stood in the open hatch and stared down at the whirling propeller blades of the other chopper. "Mandy," she shouted, "take us to the right, just like I said."

The chopper moved. The whirling blades beneath Sarah shifted away until there was an opening gap between the two helicopters. The one-handed woman was unaware that Sarah was looking right down on her. She was too busy setting up her shot at the Queen, not with the high-powered rifle she had been firing at the Griffin, but with a Javelin Missile launcher. She was planning to take out the entire barge.

And time was about to run out.

"Okay. Oh, bloody hell. Damn it, here goes nothing. Mandy start moving back over the top of them. Move left." The Griffin started swinging back the other way. Sarah took a deep breath and then jumped out of the helicopter.

She immediately regretted it, kicking at thin air in terror, as the wind, and whirling propellers of the other chopper, rushed up to meet her. She fell within mere inches of the deadly blades, but carried on falling. The nylon rope caught and went taut. Sarah's body jolted. As Mandy continued moving the Griffin back over, the rope hit the propellers and snapped in two. Suddenly, she was flying again, held in place by nothing but gravity and momentum. The sideways momentum of the Griffin threw her towards the other chopper. She landed right inside the side hatch. Right on top of the woman in the burka. The Javelin launcher clattered to the floor and Sarah kicked out a leg and booted it out of the cabin and into the Thames.

God save the Queen.

A fist hit Sarah's jaw and sent her sprawling across the floor. The woman in the burka was a wild animal, clawing and hissing, and punching at Sarah's face with her right fist and her left stump. Sarah saw stars as she tried to find an opening in the fight, but the attack was too vicious. With no choice left but to fight dirty, Sarah grabbed the woman's headdress and yanked it free. Then Sarah was face to face with the woman who had blown her friend, Sergeant Miller, to pieces.

The woman glared at Sarah, teeth bared like a wolf. Her eyes were a deep brown, and small scars criss-crossed the weathered skin of her nose and cheeks.

"Fucking hell," said Sarah. "You're uglier than I am." She whipped her SIG out of its holster and smashed the butt against the woman's nose, breaking it with ease. The woman sprawled away from Sarah, hitting the bench on the far side of the cabin. Sarah prepared to fire her weapon, but the sound of a gun cocking halted her.

Sarah turned to find Hesbani in the cockpit, aiming a gun right at her face. "I believe you and my sister have met before. What a reunion this is. Aziza, are you okay?"

The woman clutched her broken nose but grunted in affirmation. Sarah kept her SIG aimed at the woman's head. "You have a lovely family, Hesbani. I didn't know inbreeding was so prevalent in Afghanistan."

"I have very little family," Hesbani replied. "Thanks to the immoral West."

Sarah rolled her eyes. "God, you terrorists are boring. Always the same doom and gloom, end-of-the-world bullshit. Don't you people ever crack a joke? I must admit, your English is better."

"I have been here many years, plotting the United Kingdom's demise" He started to squeeze the trigger. She saw it in his eyes.

"Don't do something you'll regret, Hesbani. You pull your trigger and I pull mine. It's bye bye, sis."

Hesbani released the pressure on his trigger, but seemed no less angry. His upper lip curled. "Allah's influence has turned your people against you. Jeffrey Blanchfield, Caroline Pugh. Your own citizens are realising their own wickedness and repenting. Things are changing. What I have done will matter always."

"I remember when Madonna mattered. Things change, buddy, so don't get over-excited."

"Your empire will crumble. Your monarch will bleed."

"Hate to tell you this, but sis dropped her rocket launcher. You didn't have a spare, did you?"

"The mission has only just begun. I am just one man. Allah's will is infinite."

"Your dagger tattoo is backwards." Sarah noted the henna on his exposed wrist. She was stalling for time while she considered her next move. If she lost her aim on Aziza, Hesbani would shoot her. Luckily, she knew how much the man liked to spout his hatred.

Hesbani sneered. "Al-Sharir wished to die for Allah. I wish to kill *for* him. Only death—"

"Can ensure life. Yeah, yeah, I've heard it before. Stick it on a T-shirt already. God, no wonder Al-Sharir kicked you out of his club."

Hesbani glanced ahead for a moment and adjusted the chopper's trajectory. Mandy was swooping in and out of view, trying to unnerve him, but when Hesbani turned back to Sarah, his expression was cold and inhuman. "Al-Sharir is a short-sighted fool. He treats war like a tea party."

"So why use his name?"

"Because his name means more than mine. The Muslim nations will rally behind Al-Sharir. He has become a false idol, but one that can be used to achieve Allah's goals."

"Perhaps," said Sarah, "but we have one advantage you don't."

"What is that?"

"We can change. You might hurt us, but we'll always get back on our feet and do whatever we have to do to beat you. If we can't win now, we'll win later. You're not fighting infidels. You're fighting the future, battling progress. Change frightens small men like you. I'm sorry, Hesbani, but you will lose. No one can stop the human race evolving."

Aziza started for Sarah, but Sarah took one look at her and shook her head. "If you want to keep the hand you have left, you'll stay the fuck where you are."

Aziza looked to her brother who nodded almost imperceptibly. She sat back against the bench.

"So..." said Sarah. "Where do we go from here? You shoot me, I shoot your sister. I shoot your sister, you shoot me. Maybe we can all head for the beach and make a day of it."

Hesbani chuckled. "We've been in a similar position once before, remember? Who lives and who dies? I believe you chose yourself last time."

Sarah nodded. "I did, but that didn't work out so well for me. Maybe this time, I'll try something different. And it's *Captain* to you, dickhead."

Sarah pulled the trigger and executed Hesbani's sister.

27

PENALTIES

"Nooooo!" Hesbani screamed and let off a shot, but Sarah had already leapt behind the bench. Aziza clutched her chest in shock, bleeding out fast. Pulling the trigger had felt good.

Hesbani fired again and again, filling the cabin with ricochets. *Ping, ping, ping!* Sarah closed her eyes and prayed for Hesbani's firearm to empty before he managed to put a round in her. It didn't take long until she heard that familiar and reassuring sound.

Kik Kik!

Hesbani's gun ran empty. He threw it to the ground in a rage. Sarah rose over the back of the bench and was just about to shoot when she realised she'd dropped her own weapon while diving for cover. Damn it. Hesbani glared at her, but he softened when he glanced at his sister. Aziza was not yet dead, and with her final breaths she spoke. "Brother... finish our mission. I will see you at... Allah's side."

He nodded and whispered back to her. "Allahu Akbar."

Aziza did not respond.

"The bitch is dead," said Sarah, "and I have to say, she had it coming."

Hesbani rushed back into the cockpit and shoved forward on the yoke. The helicopter's nose dipped and they picked up speed. Sarah hit the floor and held on to whatever she could. "H-Hesbani, it's... it's over. Just give up."

"Nothing is over. I wanted to kill you in Afghanistan — Al-Sharir should have let me — but now your death will serve a greater purpose. Are you ready to become a martyr?"

Sarah realised what Hesbani was doing, and her whole body shook with despair. It spread through her like wildfire. He was going to dive bomb them into royal barge. This was the final suicide bomb, and Sarah was part of it.

"Don't do this," Sarah pleaded. "Your mission is a lie. No god wishes for innocent blood to be spilt. Allah doesn't want this!"

Hesbani cackled. "You know nothing of Allah's will. You are a woman, a whore. So is your Queen."

Sarah lunged into the cockpit and threw herself against Hesbani. He snarled at her, but she silenced him with a swift head butt. Then she was on top of him, straddling him with her thighs. She remembered when he had done the same to her, right before he had burned her face.

She head butted him again, then shouted in his face while his eyes rolled about in their sockets. "Here's your choice, dickhead. Either I snap your neck or I gouge out your eyes. Your choice."

Hesbani glared at her. "Fuck... you... whore."

"All right, both it is then." Sarah drove her thumbnails into Hesbani's eyes, ignoring the sickening feel of yielding flesh and blood vessels rupturing. Hesbani wailed, bucking in his seat like he was having a fit. His panic strengthened him, and he freed one of his arms to fight her.

Sarah wrapped her hands around his head and jaw and twisted as hard as she could.

SNAP!

Hesbani went still.

Sarah sat there on his lap for a second as all the pain from her past — all the regrets, death, and bloodshed — came gushing to the surface. Then she let out a gut-wrenching scream. It felt like her insides would explode. It was only Mattock's voice coming through the radio that snapped her out of it.

"Sarah, are you there? Speak to me."

Sarah glanced out the cockpit window and saw the Thames rushing up to meet her. Directly in front of her was the royal barge. "Shit!"

"Sarah, are you okay? What's the situation?"

Sarah grabbed the yoke and yanked it towards her. She had no idea how to pilot a helicopter, but she prayed to mother fucking Allah that she could pull it out of the nosedive it was in. The yoke resisted her, and the entire cockpit vibrated. The helicopter continued plummeting towards the water. Sarah kept a hold of the stick as best she could, and slowly, bit by bit, more and more of the horizon appeared through the cockpit window. The city of London tilted back and forth, moving around her. She closed her eyes and hoped for the best.

The console fizzed and sparked. Sarah opened her eyes and saw that the helicopter had come out of its nosedive and levelled out, but now someone was firing at her from below.

Tatter tatter tatter.

The helicopter rocked back and forth. Its interior lights flickered. The sounds of the engine grew weaker, coughing and spluttering. The steering became heavy in her hands. The chopper was dying. She thumbed the button on her lapel radio. "Mattock. Shit, Mattock, the goddamn *Britannia* is firing at me. I can't fly this thing and it's falling to pieces."

"Sarah!" It was Mandy on the line. "Keep a firm but loose grip on the yoke. Let it move freely, but keep it under your control. Guide it where you want it to go."

Sarah did as she was told. "Okay. Okay, it's working. Now what?"

"Try to level off. Keep her steady and facing forward."

"Okay, I have her steady. Now what? I can't land this thing."

"No, you can't," Mandy agreed. "You've lost your landing skids, and your petrol tank is leaking. You're going to fall out of the sky no matter what."

Sarah felt her heart sink. "So what the hell do I do?"

"Jump! Get the chopper lined up to go down in the river and then jump."

Sarah didn't bother responding. She knew the helicopter was falling apart — it might even explode — and there was only one way out. She tumbled into the rear cabin and searched desperately beneath the bench for an orange life jacket. She found one and put it on. The chopper was losing altitude fast, and she was confident it would end up in a clear stretch of the river. Nothing sailed close to the *Britannia*. If there was going to be casualties, it would only be her. That was enough to bring her some peace in her possibly final moments.

"We've got you, luv," came Mattock's voice across the radio. "Soon as you hit the water, we'll be down to get you. You're not on your own."

"I know," said Sarah. "Thank you."

And then she jumped.

28

FINAL RESULT

The slap of the river was like getting hit by God. It knocked Sarah's senses sideways and clacked her teeth together. Her body gave up as she sank beneath the Thames, and her empty lungs yearned for oxygen. She felt no pain, only rising pressure, and as that pressure mounted, she knew blessed relief would soon follow.

But sinking to her death shouldn't be the reward for all the heartbreak in her life. She deserved better than this.

And she would get it.

Sarah flailed every limb and swam upwards towards the light. There was a chance she wouldn't make it, having sunk so low, but when she broke the surface of the water, she knew she had made it. The sounds of the city returned, wild and panicked.

Sarah gasped for air.

The Navy surrounded her in small crafts sent forth from the HMS *Britannia*. Sailors pointed rifles at her and bellowed commands that were nothing but an audible blur. In the distance, the Never Stop News helicopter sank beneath the river, its tail boom pointing up into the air. It was comforting to know Hesbani would sink along with it.

Sarah flinched as something hit the water beside her. At first, she thought she was being shot at again, but then she turned to see it was the bottom rungs of a rope ladder. "Told you we'd get you," Mattock shouted from the hovering Griffin.

Sarah grabbed hold of the ladder, and this time she didn't mind being rescued. In fact, if Mattock wanted to carry her in his arms like a baby all the way home, that would be just fine.

Mandy hovered close enough to the water that it was easy for Sarah to drag herself up the ladder and inside, but Mattock still helped her climb the last few rungs before easing her onto the bench. "That was one hell of an ending," he said. "They should make a movie about this."

"Long as I don't have to play myself, they can do whatever the hell they like."

And then there was nothing but darkness.

Sarah woke two days later in the Earthworm's infirmary with Dr Bennett leaning over her attentively. "You had quite a week, sweetheart. You've been out like a light for a long while. How are you feeling?"

Sarah stretched and felt pain all over her body. "I feel like I went a few rounds with a rhino," she said, "but you should see the rhino."

Then she fell asleep again for a few hours.

Later, she got herself up and onto a pair of crutches. Palu asked her to stay at the Earthworm until she was better, and then for as long as she wished. The MCU was granted additional funding after its success, and soon the Earthworm would be buzzing again. They were going to need as many experienced officers as they could get.

It was then that Sarah knew. Howard, Palu, Mattock, and Bennett would never stop trying to protect the country against a threat that would never cease. This work was their life, and all they had was each other. Sarah might have been able to join them if the scars of her past weren't so deep. Stopping Hesbani had put a lot of her regrets to bed, but she still had a long way to go if she was to find peace. She wasn't ready to embrace a future in the MCU. Not until she knew herself better. She couldn't afford to have people relying on her.

"You sure you won't stay?" Howard asked her a few days later as she headed up top to meet Mandy. He was waiting to take her home to her flat.

"I'm sure I *can't* stay. I wish it were different, but I'm not a hero like the rest of you. I'm an emotional rollercoaster, and I don't want anyone getting caught in my wreckage. But it was good meeting you, Howard. I had fun."

"Fun isn't the word I'd use."

"I jumped out of a helicopter... twice. If I didn't call it fun, I'd have to call it lunacy."

"Fun it is then. I'll miss you, Sarah. Your bite isn't as bad as your bark... once one gets to know you."

"Tell that to Hesbani," she said, smiling. "See you, Howard. Take care of yourself, okay?"

"You too, Sarah. Stay in touch."

"Maybe."

Then Sarah left the Earthworm forever. Mandy took her to her flat in Mosely, not saying a word the whole way. It wasn't awkward though. Mandy didn't get things done with words, he got things done with actions.

It had been a week since the last attack, and the country was slipping out of panic and into outrage. The hostilities in the Middle East would intensify. The Americans were back onboard, and it looked like Afghanistan would be occupied for another ten years at least. The Taliban had been reinvigorated by Hesbani's actions, and the entire terrorist community had rallied behind the misused name of Al-Sharir. The man himself had not yet emerged to shed light on the truth, and for all anyone knew, Hesbani could have killed his old mentor. There was trouble ahead, for sure, but Sarah wasn't the one to deal with it.

She had only one last obligation.

A few days later, Sarah found herself at the periphery of Bradley's funeral, sitting at the back of the church and watching his family and friends grieve. They shared stories about a boy who was kind, a young man who wanted to change the world. Sarah couldn't help but shed a tear from the duct that still worked.

By the time Bradley's casket was laid to rest, Sarah felt more in touch with herself than she had since she'd felt a baby growing inside her. She owed it to Bradley to show kindness wherever she could because the world had been deprived of someone wonderful. She had to fill that void as much as possible She would come up short, but she would do her best.

Sarah edged behind a willow tree as the funeral finished. Howard, Palu, Mattock, and Bennett were there, but they didn't spot her. Their grief was deep and real, their focus entirely on Bradley. That was the way Sarah wanted it. She needed to put the past behind her, and holding a reunion was not conducive to that.

It was time to go. Bradley was gone, and now she needed to leave too. She stepped backwards, remaining concealed behind the willow tree. There was a bus stop nearby that would take her home. She headed for churchyard's exit.

But something was tugging at her. After what she'd been through with the members of the MCU, it almost felt like she'd been part of a family again. Despite the horror of everything she'd been through, the gaping hole inside of her had felt a little fuller. Perhaps she was doing the wrong thing by walking away from them. Maybe she was still running from herself.

"What am I doing? I have a chance to do something good with my life. There's a place for me here and I'm too scared to take it." Sarah suddenly realised that it was time to put the fear and pain behind her, to finally take a chance on something. She belonged with the MCU.

She turned around, ready to head back to the funeral and ask Palu and the others for a second chance, but when she turned, she bumped into someone else standing in her way.

Her eyes went wide. "You!"

"Yes... me."

Sarah's world went dark as a thick bag went over her head and something hard struck the base of her skull. She tried to call out to her friends, but as she faded, she realised she had none.

GET THE NEXT MCU BOOK 'HOT ZONE' RIGHT NOW ON AMAZON.

HOT ZONE: SUMMARY

Sarah Stone is missing.

The terrorism threat in the UK is growing. MCU agent, Howard Hopkins, has been called to hospital. Not because he is sick, but because there has been an outbreak. Somebody has intentionally infected hundreds of people with Ebola Virus. It's time for the Major Crimes Unit to act.

Sarah Stone hasn't seen home for 4 months. Someone is keeping her captive. She intends to find out who and why. Then make them pay.

Soon Sarah and Howard's paths will cross, and they may not be on the same side when it happens. They are both looking for the same man, a psychotic doctor with a grudge against Western society and a mission to inflict upon the world the biological terrors of impoverished Africa. He won't be happy until Ebola, HIV, and Malaria are as much a threat in the United Kingdom and Europe as they are in the 3rd World.

How do you fight an enemy you can't see?

Dedicated to my fans
you rule!

NOTE FROM THE AUTHOR

Thanks for picking up book number 2 in the Major Crime Unit series. I hope that means you read book 1 (Soft Target) and enjoyed it. If not you can get it here. This latest adventure for Sarah Stone and the MCU gang was a lot of fun to write and focuses on some of the threats that we face right now in the world, but please do not be afraid. This is just a work of fiction. You are quite safe. Before you begin, I just need to quickly tell you that I could not have written this book without the following two people.

Jack Millis – the greatest fan and friend a guy could ask for. He helped me with a lot of the character work and if my characters jump off the page, it's because of him.

Nev Murray – a great guy and a constant supporter of my work. He helped me whip this book into shape so that you can enjoy it. He runs a fantastic blog dedicated to reading at the following address. Check it out:

http://confessionsofareviewer.blogspot.co.uk/

And without further ado, please turn the page, keep your hands inside the cart at all times, and get ready to take that plunge.

"Lord have mercy upon mankind. Deliver and save the world from the dreadful Ebola Virus."
   – Lailah Gifty Akita

"It's one billionth our size and it's beating us."
   – Sam Daniels, Outbreak (1995), Warner Bros.

CHAPTER TWENTY-NINE

"**D**r Krenshaw, are you busy? Mrs Drayton hasn't been seen in almost two hours and she's becoming difficult. Could you spare a minute to see her?"

Dr Alistair Krenshaw, an epidemiologist by specialisation, but willing to help out however he could, noticed the young brunette and smiled. Not even thirty-years-old, he suspected, and an attractive young thing for sure, yet he couldn't, for the life of him, remember her name.

"Of course," he said. "Would you like to fill me in on her condition, Nurse...? I'm sorry, you seem to have forgotten your name badge."

The nurse looked down at the bare patch on her tunic and blushed. "Oh, no, I had it earlier, but one of the patients on the night shift got a little...*grabby*. I must have lost it then. My name is Suzanne."

"My word, are you okay, Suzanne?"

"Nothing I'm not used to at 3 AM on a Friday night, Doctor."

Krenshaw patted Suzanne softly on the shoulder, admiring her ability to deflect an incident others might have made into an issue. "So," he said, "what seems to be the problem with Mrs Drayton?"

"She's been complaining of stomach cramps, can't keep anything down. We have her on a drip, but she's demanding that we give her something for the pain. It's a simple case of gastroenteritis but she's making a meal of it. We really need to free up her bed, though. We're inundated with new admissions since they closed St Elizabeth. These spending cuts are going to put us all in early graves."

Krenshaw knew patients like Mrs Drayton well. Most patients were subservient, looking upon doctors with complete reverence, while those like Mrs Drayton thought they knew exactly what was wrong with them and exactly how they should be treated. Gastric conditions made patients feel like their lives were hurtling to a painful end, but it would always pass within 24 hours or so; trying to make someone with stomach-flu understand that was always a challenge.

Doctor and nurse entered the A&E ward and visited Mrs Drayton in her cubicle. Lying on the bed, the old woman was a picture of misery, with grey hair matted against her sweating forehead and horn rimmed spectacles as crooked as her nose.

"Are you the doctor?" Mrs Drayton demanded, before clutching her stomach and moaning.

Krenshaw smiled without warmth of any kind. It was a skill he had learned, just as he had learned how to take blood and administer a suppository. "I am a consultant," he explained, "but your nurse, Suzanne, summoned me to come speak with you. I understand you are in some discomfort."

"I'm on death's door," the woman said, clutching her stomach again. "I need summin' for the pain."

"I suspect you have a virus, Mrs Drayton. Uncomfortable and painful it may be, but very little that can be done about it unfortunately, other than allowing it to run its course."

The old woman's face puckered, not from pain but anger. "Bleedin' NHS. Useless. You don't wanna help nobody. I had to wait twenny-minutes for an ambulance because you lot closed the St Elizabeth. It's all about saving money for your fat bonuses, ain't it?"

Krenshaw glanced at the comely Nurse Suzanne, who was rolling her eyes and huffing. He gave the girl a subtle grin before turning back to the disgruntled patient. "Okay, Mrs Drayton. If you insist you cannot cope with the pain, we will do what we can." He plucked out his prescription pad, scribbled something on it, and handed it to Suzanne. "Nurse, could you fill this for Mrs Drayton and get her some pain relief, please? I will take a brief look at her charts while you're gone. Anything I can do to earn that fat bonus, no?"

"Of course, Doctor." Suzanne left the cubicle.

"Thank you, Doctor," said Mrs Drayton, sounding like a completely different person now she'd got her way. "I hate to be a bother, but I'm in absolute agony. I feel like I'm dyin'."

Krenshaw smiled at the patient, showing his teeth in something not far removed from a snarl. "Mrs Drayton, I have worked in places as far flung as the Congo, Sudan, and even Malaysia. I have seen men and women bleed from their eyeballs and cough up tissue from their lungs. I have seen the destruction wrought by evils such as Ebola, HIV, and Dengue Fever. What you have, Mrs Drayton, is a tummy bug. Now, I have sworn an oath to help you and help you I will, but please refrain from the hyperbole because it hurts my ears."

Mrs Drayton looked at him like he'd just broken wind, so revolted was the expression on her face. For a moment she merely trembled, but then finally exploded. "How dare you speak to me that way. I pay your wages. Bleedin' NHS. Where do they get you people from? I remember when doctors used to have manners. The way you just spoke to me is disgusting."

Krenshaw ceased paying attention to the vitriolic harridan and instead checked upon her readings. All of Mrs Drayton's vitals were fine, as expected. Her salt levels had come back low, but the saline drip would remedy that. He went over to the drip stand and examined the contents. The saline bag was full, recently changed by the lovely Nurse Suzanne.

With his back still to the ranting Mrs Drayton, Krenshaw reached in and removed something from the breast pocket of his doctor's coat.

The ampule was attached to a syringe he had fashioned himself and filled with a liquid he had brought all the way from Liberia several years before. He had been keeping it for just such an occasion. Removing the barrier from the needle's tip, Krenshaw pierced the top of the saline bag just above the fill-line, then pressed down gently on the syringe, not needing to use much of the contents to get the desired result. Mrs Drayton continued howling indignities at his back, oblivious to the fact he was killing her.

Suzanne returned just as he was recapping the syringe and plopping it back inside his breast pocket. He gave her a quizzical look. "That was quick."

She smiled, but it became more of a smirk. "I didn't want Mrs Drayton to be in pain any longer."

Mrs Drayton noticed Suzanne had returned and so changed the focus of her tirade. "Give me them blasted pills and lemme out of 'ere, right now. I can't believe the way your colleague just spoke to me. I'm gunna lodge a serious complaint, you just see if I don't. Disgusting. You should both be sacked. Bleedin' NHS."

Krenshaw stepped out of the cubicle and waited for the nurse to finish her duties and follow him. When Suzanne eventually stepped out to join him, he raised a dark eyebrow and chuckled. "I believe I've freed up that bed for you, Nurse. That is, unless you've persuaded Mrs Drayton to prolong her stay."

Suzanne tilted her head as she looked at him strangely. "Whatever did you say to her?"

"Nothing that was not true." Krenshaw told her. "When does your shift end, Nurse?"

"In an hour. Do you need me to do something?"

"Only come have breakfast with me. It's been a retched night shift, wouldn't you agree?"

Suzanne blushed. Ten years younger than Krenshaw, at least, but he had seen the attraction every time she looked at him. Eventually she managed to answer. "I would love to, Doctor."

"Excellent. And, please, call me *Alistair*."

"Okay... *Alistair*. I will meet you out front in an hour."

"I look forward to it. I will carry on with my rounds until then. You know how it is: always more people to treat." He patted the ampule of liquid in his breast pocket and began to laugh.

Nurse Suzanne did not understand the joke. She would soon.

CHAPTER THIRTY

Howard was alone when he arrived at Reading's Whiteknight Hospital. It was a hive of activity, more so than normal for a hospital. Doctors and nurses buzzed around inside as well as out, and a great white tent had been established in the grounds. A cadre of police officers kept back anyone without proper business in a way that made the place seem more like a crime scene than a centre of healing.

Howard pulled into the parking lot and headed towards a cordoned area reserved for officials. He flashed his badge at the attending steward and pulled up beside a shiny red Audi. The steward came over and greeted Howard as he got out of his car.

"The quarantine has been set up on the lawns," he said, "but the response team is operating inside the hospital. There's a triage operating in the A&E and you'll probably find someone in charge there." A brief silence ensued while the steward stared at Howard with a strange grin on his face. Then the man said, "So they've called the MCU in on this, have they? Congratulations on saving the Queen last year. I saw it all on the news."

Howard nodded. "Thanks."

He didn't have time for conversation, so he politely dismissed the steward and headed off towards the hospital. The walk was short, thanks to the prioritised parking, but the closer Howard got the slower he walked. Something about hospitals scared him far worse than any member of Al-Qaeda or deranged lunatic. Disease tore a man apart secretly from the inside and waged war with no other agenda than to win.

When Howard passed by the monolithic tent on the hospital's lawn, he took a quick glance at the entrance flap. The men and women inside the tent all wore white 'spacesuits,' which made them look more alien than human. Their appearance was enough to send another wave of panic through him, as it likely did any other member of the public, which was why none of the space suited personnel lingered outside the privacy of the giant tent for more than a handful of seconds. Nor had anyone in authority yet spoken the word, *Ebola*. As much as the media was trying to incite fear, the government was trying to play things down. Howard knew the truth, though; that over four hundred cases of Ebola had been reported and that over two-thirds of them were currently at Whiteknight hospital being treated. Somehow the bogeyman of West Africa had made its way to the United Kingdom, and had done so with vigour.

Wanting to find someone in charge, Howard headed towards the A&E entrance, stepping around the back of an ambulance with flashing lights and passing through the open glass doors. Chaos reigned inside. The hallways teemed with the sick and injured, while nary a nurse or doctor remained in sight. With the major health crisis confined to the tent outside on the lawn, only a skeleton crew remained inside the hospital proper, and that didn't help the old man moaning on an unattended gurney or the young man with his nose dripping blood down his shirt. The injured and infirm stumbled around like zombies, seeking help from whoever would listen.

Howard managed to flag down a solitary nurse. She hurried over to him, but seemed like she had a hundred other places to be.

"May I help you?" she asked wearily. Her name badge read: Suzanne.

"Hello, Suzanne. I'm with the MCU. I need to speak to whoever is in charge of the quarantine outside."

"They're set up in maternity ward 1. You want Mr Cotta."

"Thank you." Howard hurried away, eager to exit the pandemonium of the A&E ward. He left the atmosphere of coughs, sniffles, and moans, and entered into the eerie silence of the maternity ward. The large space was mostly empty except for the rear of the ward where a dozen beds would typically be lined up, but were now probably being used inside the big white tent. Now the ward contained only a single, long desk with a large projector screen set up at one end and a dozen chairs around it. A handful of men and women looked over at Howard as he entered.

"May I help you?" Howard was asked for the second time in as many minutes.

"I'm Agent Howard Hopkins of the MCU. I'm here to investigate the possible terrorist implications of this current health crisis. I believe you are expecting me."

"Indeed we are," said a middle aged woman in a doctor's coat. She trotted over to him and offered her hand. "My name is Doctor Hart. I'm the hospital's senior pathologist. Mr Cotta here is in charge. He's been loaned to us by the World Health Organisation."

A tall, razor-cheeked gentleman with hard grey eyes nodded and spoke in what, to Howard's ears at least, sounded like an Italian accent. "Pleased to meet you, Agent Hopkins. I am afraid our most pressing concern is treating and containing this outbreak, not helping law enforcement find out what caused it. Surely that can come afterwards?"

Howard saw the awkward expressions on everyone's faces and realised that Mr Cotta was no friend to anybody there. He was a problem solver, sent in to take charge; similar to Howard in some respects. "I understand your priorities perfectly well, Mr Cotta. They are not dissimilar to my own. If terrorism is responsible, there could be further outbreaks. Therefore, finding those responsible is the best way of keeping this situation contained, wouldn't you agree?"

Mr Cotta stared at Howard for a moment, statuesque in his stillness. Then he spoke, "Very well, Agent Hopkins, you may have a seat at the table, but please do not impede our work."

"The last thing I wish to do, as I am sure you would not wish to impede mine." Howard took a seat, despite everyone else electing to stand. It would make it easier for them to forget he was there.

"I don't understand how the outbreak is so staggered," one of the doctors said. "The most mature cases are almost three weeks old, the newest less than one week. If the virus had spread organically then it would have been more systematic. This is almost like a dozen outbreaks spread out over time."

"As if someone were infecting people purposefully?" asked Howard.

Dr Hart nodded affirmatively. Her hair was quite strikingly blonde. "Quite possibly. If somebody has a strain of Ebola virus they could potentially infect people by injecting them or finding some other way of compromising their system. Typical infection is through contact with bodily fluids but a pure form of the virus would be even easier to catch."

Howard leant an elbow on the table. "Has anybody asked the patients whether they came into contact with syringes recently? We need to canvass them for common similarities."

"It's very hard to quiz somebody suffering with Ebola," said Cotta. "What with all the agony and dying they are doing. Do you see?"

Howard frowned. "I thought Ebola was relatively treatable in the early stages."

"Perhaps you are thinking of rabies, Agent Hopkins."

"It's not so," explained Dr Hart. "There is little we can do for Ebola sufferers other than keep them hydrated and try to steer them through. The death rate for Ebola in areas with good health care is usually around 40%, but this current outbreak has been far worse. We have lost more than 70% of the initial victims. It appears the traditional *ebolavirus* we are used to seeing has mutated, possibly tampered with."

"We are calling it *Ebola Reading*," said Cotta. "There were previously five different species of *ebolavirus*, only four known to affect humans. This is the sixth."

Howard felt his stomach juices crash against his insides. "How is this species of the virus different?"

"It is just worse," said Cotta bluntly. "Perhaps you should go and see for yourself, Agent Hopkins. Trust me, it will intensify your efforts to stop this virus from spreading."

"I'll take you," said Dr Hart. "Mr Cotta is right. If you are involved in stopping the outbreak, then you should see it first-hand."

Howard wanted to get out of his chair and run screaming to an isolated cave where nobody could ever so much as sneeze near him, but he was an agent of the Major Crimes Unit and his job was to find out who was behind the Ebola outbreak and bring them to justice. His fear was secondary to the task at hand, so he got up gingerly from his seat and nodded. "Thank you, Dr Hart. Let's get it out of the way so we can get back to business."

Cotta snickered. "Try not to look so unwell, agent Hopkins. It would be embarrassing if you were to faint."

As soon as Dr Hart signed Howard into the entry register and led him inside the giant white tent, he was grabbed by a gang of chaperones and bundled into one of the spacesuits. They taped up his wrists, sprayed him with a fine mist of something he imagined to be bleach, and went through the safety protocols with him.

"Do not touch the patients. Do not touch any bodily fluids of the patient. If you do come into contact with bodily fluids, remain where you are and alert your nearest colleague. Do not remove your safety equipment. If your safety equipment develops a tear or rip, remain where you are and alert your nearest colleague. Dispose of all needles and sharps in puncture-proof sealed containers. When you wish to exit the quarantine area, you must do so through the decontamination area and wait for clearance."

"It's not as scary as it sounds," came Dr Hart's voice inside Howard's helmet. The slight crackling nature of it let him know that there was a cheap radio system installed into the suits.

"Really?" he said back. "Because this is about as nervous as I've ever been — and I've been shot by a serial killer before."

"Ebola is harder to catch than you think. Most people who have caught it in the past, mostly in the 3rd World, have been friends, relatives, and health care workers in regular, prolonged contact with the infected. You are quite safe inside your suit."

"How is this thing spreading if it's not easy to catch?"

"That's what I thought you were here to find out, Agent Hopkins. It shouldn't be so easy to catch, which is why your concerns about terrorism hold water. If somebody is responsible for what you are about to see, then I hope you catch them and throw them in a very dark cell."

Dr Hart led Howard through a plastic flap and into the first section of the vast tent. Each bed was partitioned from the next by a curtain and there were even portable toilets with pull-around privacy drapes. The people here looked more terrified than ill. They had puffy eyes, sweaty foreheads, and didn't seem entirely comfortable in their beds, but most of them seemed okay for the most part. One woman was even reading a trashy magazine and chuckling to herself periodically. The front cover held the headline: **Tom Cruise Worships Aliens**, followed by the smaller by-line of: **Meet the Zombie Boy Who Likes Turtles.**

"The early stages resemble influenza," Dr Hart explained through the radio. Fever, headaches, joint and muscle pain. Patients are bedridden and weak, but they are able to cope. Some extremely rare cases get better after this stage. They are the lucky ones."

Howard glanced at the woman with the magazine and wondered if she was one of the 'lucky ones.' Then he decided that no one with Ebola was 'lucky,' even if they got well. Dr Hart led him over to the next flap of plastic, which sectioned off the next area.

"Are you ready?" she asked him. "We are about to see patients in the later stages of the disease. It will be distressing."

Howard took a few deep breaths, embarrassed when he realised that they would be echoing though the radio in Dr Hart's suit. "Okay," he said. "I'm ready."

They passed beneath the flap into the next room. This area took up the majority of the tent and was approximately the size of a narrow football field. Rows upon rows of beds were filled with the sickest people Howard had ever seen. A teenaged girl to his left lay beneath bloodstained sheets, a trickle of blood leaking from her ear and staining the pillow. Her entire face had gone an angry shade of purple and there was no expression on it other than pain and delirium. Another woman, a decade older, lay trembling and muttering as fever took her senses. From elsewhere in the room, a person wretched and vomited in the most painful-sounding fashion. Tears filled Howard's eyes. It was like standing in the pits of hell, agony and fear intoxicating the very air itself. A dozen spacesuits milled about casually, unable to do anything but provide comfort and care. They were more caretakers of the dead than curers of the sick.

The teenaged girl spotted Howard standing at the foot of her bed and reached out a frail arm to him. She tried to speak, but all that came from her lips was a gargled choke followed by spitting blood. She slumped back on her pillows, eyes staring at the ceiling. An alarm sounded. Two spacesuits came rushing over, while a third pulled over a crash cart and started uncoiling a defibrillator.

"I want to leave," said Howard.

Dr Hart didn't argue. "Okay."

The three spacesuits started giving the young girl electric shocks, trying to jumpstart her heart. Her body leapt from the bed each time.

"Get me the hell out of here now," shouted Howard. "I need to leave. I need... I need... I can't breathe."

Dr Hart grabbed Howard by the helmet and pulled his visor up against her own. Through the plastic windows they made eye contact. "You're panicking," she said. "That's okay. Everybody panics. Just concentrate on your breathing and remind yourself that you are healthy. You are okay. You are not infected. These people are dying, though, and they need our help. We are going to help them. We are going to walk out of this tent and find a way to stop this. Okay?"

Howard couldn't nod because she still held his helmet, so he said, "Okay. I'm okay. I'm okay."

"Good. Follow me."

Dr Hart took him to the decontamination area where they showered in their suits before once again getting sprayed with the fine mist of bleach. Then they passed through into another area where they removed the suits and washed their hands, face, and necks thoroughly beneath scalding showers. They were then signed out and back in the fresh air a minute later. Howard took the longest breaths of his life.

Dr Hart patted him on the back. "Are you okay, Agent Hopkins?"

Howard managed to straighten up. "You just saw me almost wet myself. I think you can start calling me Howard."

"Then you can call me Stevie."

"Stevie?"

"Stephanie," she explained. "But my friends call me Stevie."

"Okay, Stevie. Thank you for keeping me calm back there. Please don't tell Mr Cotta. I think he knew this would happen."

"I won't mention it, and it's nothing to be embarrassed about. There's something instinctively terrifying about diseases. They send our inner caveman into a tizzy."

Howard frowned. "A tizzy?"

"That's about the best way to explain it. We're biologically conditioned to fear disease in the same way we would fear swimming with a crocodile. Our fear responses kick in and make us panic. It takes a while to overcome that. No reason to be embarrassed, I assure you."

"You're kind," Howard told her. "And brave."

"Ha! A member of the MCU calling me *brave*. I couldn't do what you people do. The way you stopped that terrorist last year. Were you involved in that, by the way?"

Howard thought about the events Stevie was referring to and

nodded his head slowly. "I was involved, yes, but the real hero was a woman who was working with me. She was only with the MCU temporarily but was as brave as you are."

"Perhaps you should invite her back then."

"Yeah," said Howard, thinking: If only anyone knew where she was.

CHAPTER THIRTY-ONE

Sarah got out of bed and switched on the television, switching to the news as she always did this time in the morning. The old flat screen flickered persistently and the colours were odd at the corners, but it got her through the endless days. At first she'd hoped to see news of her imminent rescue, but other than some early reports of her initial disappearance, there had been nothing. The world did not seem to care very much that Sarah Stone was gone from the world. Her scarred, mangled face would not be missed, nor perhaps even remembered.

For a while, she had almost been able to conjure up the face of the man who had abducted her. The glaring eyes and straight teeth were a fuzzy image at the back of her mind, but it wasn't clear enough to make an ID. The blow to her head had cleaned her clock and wiped any memories she had of the events away.

Now she sat on her bed, staring at a familiar face onscreen.

MCU Director Palu seemed to have aged in the last year. The hair on either side of his head had gone a frosty white and he'd grown a moustache of the same colour. His medium-brown skin seemed a little paler too. Yet, when the man spoke he demanded authority, each word as confident as the last.

"The current outbreak has indeed been attributed to Ebola Virus," said Palu to a microphone, "as the press has indeed been speculating for days. The majority of cases have been contained to a temporary treatment site at Reading's Whiteknight Hospital. Everything that can be done for the patients and their families is being done. Everything that can be done to contain the current outbreak is being done. Everything that can be done to find a vaccine is being done. We, as yet, do not know what allowed this disease to enter our shores, but we have no reason at all to believe it will expand beyond our control. The National Health Service is doing all that it can to educate people on preventative measures and are confident that they can deal with the additional strain on resources this outbreak has caused. Thank you." He took no questions.

The news report switched back to the studio where the grim face of news anchor Jack Millis filled the screen. Sarah recognised the man, knew he'd made his name by reporting on the Dartmouth bombing she herself had been involved with. Now, Jack Millis spoke in the foreboding tones of a man who loved to make a crisis worse. The more people were afraid, the more they would look to him for guidance. How, Sarah would like to give the simpering fool a good hard kick in the nuts.

"A message of hope," he said. "Yet one has to ask themselves why the director of the MCU is involved in this crisis at all. Isn't the domain of the MCU terrorism and serious crime? Is their involvement a "sign" that this outbreak may not be the work of unfortunate happenstance, but instead the maniacal plotting of a deranged criminal? If terrorism is indeed behind this outbreak of one of the most deadly of diseases, then should we be preparing ourselves for further attacks, further outbreaks? Sobering thoughts, Britain. Sobering indeed. Thank you for joining me this morning. I'm Jack Millis and you've been watching *Morning with JM.*"

Sarah grunted, switched off the television, and remained sitting on the bed. The MCU had been on the brink of closure when she'd helped them catch a terrorist named Hesbani. Now the organisation seemed to be going from strength to strength, and even expanding beyond the scope of terrorism. Last week she had seen on the news that the MCU had helped to apprehend an escaped serial killer, Richard Heinz. It appeared they were going from success to success, and she was glad. She looked back on her time with the MCU fondly, despite not doing so at the time. She'd been a broken mess when MCU agent, Howard Hopkins, had come to ask for her help. By the end of her association with MCU she'd actually started to look towards the future. Things didn't seem quite so bleak. Aside from the ones on the left side of her face, her scars had finally begun to heal.

Then someone had abducted her and any thoughts of the future became muddy and dark. She didn't even know if her captors intended to let her live, yet four months they had held her hostage without so much as questioning her. She'd been treated well and never tortured, yet any attempt she made to leave was met with immediate force. She hadn't been able to walk for a week the last time she'd attempted to attack one of her guards, so she had relented and resigned herself to her fate, watching the news each day to try and see if she could gain any clue into who was keeping her and if anybody was looking for her.

Her initial suspicion was that Hesbani's men were taking revenge on her for her interference in the terrorist plot last year, but they were savages who would want her blood. They would have tortured and beaten her, before executing her to provide a message to those who interfered with their agendas. Hesbani's supporters, however, had not even appeared in the news once. The man's operations had died with him; and his former boss, Al Al-Sharir, had not been heard from in almost a decade. The *Shab Bakhair* cell was finished.

So who the hell was keeping her and what did they want?

The door to her en suite room — for it was no cell by anyone's standards — opened and in stepped one of her regular guards. The short, stubby man was named Rat by his colleagues and he had likely got the name from his two sharp front teeth. He was friendly enough, yet there was no mistaking the violent nature of the man bubbling away beneath the surface. Sarah recognised it because she was the same. Yet, in her current predicament, her violent impulses were shackled and impotent. She had no outlet for her anger other than by trying once again to escape, but her body had not yet recovered from the last time.

Trying to figure a way out consumed most of Sarah's day, as it should have. A prisoner had a duty to think about attaining freedom and she was no different. While she suspected she might die soon, she also knew that she would do all she could to try and avoid that happening. Her next escape attempt would be her seventh and she hoped against hope that it would be the last.

"Brought you breakfast, sweetheart" said Rat, wrinkling his nose at her like the creature he was named after.

Sarah glanced at the watch they had let her keep and frowned. "It's almost afternoon."

Rat placed the tray of cereal and coffee on the bedside table and shrugged. "The lads were up late last night with business. We have other priorities than looking after you."

"I thought I heard something last night. What were you up to? Kidnapping children, or just molesting them?"

Rat didn't get angry. He was too used to Sarah's attempts to rile him. Instead he just flashed his rodent smile at her. "Only molesting that'll get done is on you if you don't keep a lid on that smart mouth."

"You'd need to find a dick first. I get the impression you're sadly lacking."

Rat chuckled. "When are you going to give up the attitude? I'll never take anything you say personally, so stop trying to get a rise out of me. You're my prisoner and have cause to hate me, so why would I be offended to find out that you do?"

"A very coherent statement for a degenerate like you, Rat."

"You'd be surprised how smart degenerates can be. In fact this country is run by degenerates, and where would we be without them?"

Sarah rolled her eyes. "Oh, here we go. Country of infidels and degenerates, huh? You're going to destroy us for the glory of Allah?"

"I don't fight for Allah, luv. Don't even like the fella."

"Then whom?"

"Certainly not for no god."

"Then what are you keeping me for? What agenda do you have?"

"I have no agenda. I take orders. Orders are simpler than agendas. They pay better, too."

Sarah was beginning to unravel the man without him knowing it. After months of getting nothing but silent treatment from Rat, she had got him to open up and start bantering insults with her. Now he had forgotten himself enough that he was dropping information without even realising it."

"You're a mercenary," she spat. "At least I can respect a fundamentalist. At least they're fighting for something worthier than money. They have a cause."

Rat back snapped at her. "I have a cause."

"To get rich? How very honourable."

"No, not just to get rich. I'm going to change things, make things better. I'm going to liberate the people of this country from the oppression of an unfair system."

"Sure you're not the first terrorist to think his cause is noble. You're misguided, same as the rest of them."

Rat let his calm slip a little and snarled at her. "I'm not a terrorist. I'm fighting *for* this country not against it."

Sarah eyeballed the man closely. "You're fighting for this country? How?"

"Just shut your goddamn mouth or I'll break your jaw again."

Sarah still felt the pain of the last beating, so decided to keep quiet. Rat might think himself a freedom fighter or hero of some kind, but he was not averse to giving a woman — and a prisoner no less — a good kicking. He left her room and locked the door behind him, leaving Sarah alone once again. She got off the bed and went over to the television. Her captors had screwed the set down onto the cabinet, but they had paid no mind to the back of television, where she had removed six delicate screws from the rear panel using the steel clasp of her watch. She was now able to slide the back off the unit with ease, and inside was her ticket to freedom.

The television's various circuit boards were pressed from copper, extremely sharp at the edges. Sarah had spent enough time examining the different pieces of electronics to understand that the PCBs were the closest thing she would find to a weapon. There was one attached to the television's inputs that was slim and about fifteen centimetres long, similar in size to the rulers children kept inside their pencil cases. She'd already unscrewed the PCB ahead of time, but had left it connected for the time being. Yanking it free would eliminate her use of the television for good, the only solace in her confinement, but it was the only thing she had managed to find in four months of confinement that was sharp enough to cut a man's throat.

She yanked the circuit board free and pulled out the wires, feeling its sharpness immediately. Its edges cut into her fingers as she clutched it tightly. She took it over to her bed and used a corner to slice a hole in her pillow case, and less than a minute later she had cut a strip of cotton and fashioned a makeshift grip around one end of the circuit board. Next she forced one of the sharp corners against the wall until it snapped, leaving behind a jagged, deadly edge. She did the same on the opposite corner and eventually managed to fashion a point. She had a knife. A flimsy, yet wickedly sharp copper knife.

All she needed to do now was wait for Rat's next visit.

CHAPTER THIRTY-TWO

Back in the makeshift office on maternity ward 1, Howard sat and listened to the experts once again. Currently, they were discussing the possibilities of what could have caused the outbreak of Ebola Reading. "It's very much the same virus," one of the doctors explained, pointing out a squiggly, knotted, worm-like creature on the projector screen. "The proteins are unaltered. The only changes seem to be within the binding cells, impacting the rate of infection on the host. If the virus has been tampered with, it has been tweaked in only a minor way, but even doing that much would take a genius-level knowledge of genetics."

"Is it possible that the virus changed on its own?" asked Howard.

"Absolutely," said Cotta. "Viruses mutate constantly to survive."

"Could it go airborne?"

Cotta shook his head. "Don't let the media fool you, Agent Hopkins. The Ebola Virus is too far removed from the ability to transmit that way. It would take millennia for an organism to evolve in such a way."

"But there's a possibility that the virus is being modified manually? Is it possible to make it airborne through engineering?"

Cotta shook his head again, even more adamantly. "It would be a profound achievement to even come close. If this is a case of genetic engineering, then I wholly suspect that this slight alteration is the sum total of whoever is responsible's ability. More important is how the virus got started. We need to find out why so many ex-patients of this hospital have come down with a rare 3rd World disease."

Howard sat forward and put his elbows on the table. "You just said *ex*-patients. What do you mean?"

Cotta looked at him and frowned. The man had a way of looking at the rest of the room like he were surrounded by children. "You don't know? Almost every patient in quarantine has visited this hospital within the last month or so. The first patients came in the longest time ago, several weeks. The newest cases were in this hospital as recently as 6 days ago. That is why all of the cases are local to the town of Reading. It seems that Whiteknight is the commonality in all these cases."

Howard chewed at the inside of his cheek. This was sounding more and more like something deliberate. "Then the source of infection is the hospital itself," he said.

Cotta nodded. "So it would appear."

Dr Hart added, "We have checked the blood bank, intravenous medicines, water supply, the cafeteria. All have been cleared of the virus. All in-patients have been relocated to the Royal Berkshire. We will be closing A&E within the next few hours and redirecting ambulances there as well. Then medical forensics will scour Whiteknight from top to bottom."

Howard pushed a strand of hair out of his eyes. "You said this thing passes via infected bodily fluids. Is there an area in the hospital that all the patients would have visited? An area where they may have all passed through?"

"We don't know," admitted Dr Hart. "There are many places where patients congregate, but the ones we have checked have been clear and there is one thing that doesn't fit about it being the hospital itself that is causing the infection."

Howard frowned. "Oh?"

"No employees of the hospital have been infected. Not a single one. Doctors, nurses, and porters are all healthy. It is only ex-patients who have been infected. If the reservoir was the cafeteria, for instance, then the infection rate would be the same amongst staff. There is nowhere that patients visit that staff do not."

"Which," said Cotta, "makes it highly likely that it is medical supplies or equipment that is at fault."

"Does this hospital have a strain of Ebola on site?" asked Howard.

Dr Hart shook her head. "Of course not. We have a pathology lab, but we use it only for testing patient samples. The nearest place that has Ebola on ice is probably Porton Down, and that's military."

"So how do you think this thing started?" Howard wasn't the expert here and he didn't intend to act like one. He was getting lost in the possibilities.

"We are checking the patient backgrounds," said Cotta. "Usually these things start after a patient travels to a 'hot zone,' a place where natural reservoirs of the virus exist. One of the early patients, deceased now, has family in Sierra Leone. Possibly he was the one who brought the Ebola Virus into the UK."

Howard nodded, but there were things that still did not add up. "That doesn't explain why this is a new strain, does it? Ebola Reading is different. People are dying in unnatural patterns. No doctors or nurses have been infected. Mother Nature is predictable, whereas man is quite the opposite. If this virus isn't conforming to typical behaviours, then it seems highly likely that someone is behind this."

Dr Hart agreed. "I don't doubt what you are saying, Agent Hopkins. The reason you are here is because there are certain elements of pre-meditation about this."

"We are not detectives," snapped Cotta. "We are here to study and contain the virus. We are wasting time trying to help agent Hopkins with his investigations. We have already dwelled on it far too long."

Howard didn't react. Cotta was making it more and more obvious that he resented MCU's involvement. Howard could even understand why. He was there to snoop and pry, to ask question after question, casting an ever wider net until he found answers. Cotta was concerned with exact opposite methods, working in ever decreasing circles until he had the virus trapped, understood, and contained.

"I would like nothing more than to get out of your way, Mr Cotta," said Howard, "but you experts, here, are the only ones who can answer my questions."

"I agree," said Cotta. "Which is why I will give you Dr Hart. Leave the rest of us in peace and direct your questions only to her from now on."

Howard looked at Dr Hart who seemed a little put out by her services being offered on her behalf but not upset or angry. She smiled at Howard and tucked a strand of blonde hair behind her ear. "Okay, I suppose that makes sense. Where would you like to begin?"

"With the staff. I want to know who saw to these patients."

Dr Hart frowned. "You think it was a healthcare worker?"

"I think somebody did this, somebody who knew what they were doing. A member of the public would be too ignorant of a virus like Ebola, not to mention incapable of getting a live strain of it. Anyone outside of the health industry would be terrified to be in the same room as Ebola Virus. No, I think whoever did this was somebody comfortable being around deadly diseases. I think a doctor did this."

Cotta chuckled. "You have your theory, Lieutenant Columbo, now go investigate it somewhere else."

Howard smiled. "I will, but only after I interview everybody in this room."

Of course, Cotta had been furious at the indignity of having Howard disrupt his work, even though he himself was exempt from questioning. Cotta was from the WHO and had not even been in the country at the time of the initial outbreak. Several other members of his task force were also of no interest, for they had been loaned out from other institutions. Only a handful of the doctors and experts present worked at Whiteknight hospital fulltime and Howard gained very little from them to help his investigation. They all seemed like well-adjusted individuals, full of compassion and distress at the number of people sick on their watch. Howard took as much info as he could from them before deciding to take his investigation elsewhere — much to the delight of Cotta.

Dr Hart led him to a secure office that was piled with stacks and stacks of files and paperwork. "These are all of the patient records for the infected patients," she said. "Cotta has had them all placed into a digital database, but we'll have to do things the old fashioned way."

Howard moved over to the largest pile on the office's cheap pine desk and picked up the top file. "Sometimes it's easier to lay out the facts when you can hold them in your hands. Is there anything the patients have in common, other than having visited Whiteknight previously? They're all ex-patients, but what were they in for?"

"Absolutely everything," said Dr Hart, flapping her arms. "The first case was an old lady called Eleanor Drayton. She came in with a stomach bug but returned less than a week later with debilitating flu-like symptoms. We gave her a bed but didn't realise the severity of her condition until she started coughing up blood. The next cases came nonstop for days, ranging from people staying in the cancer wards to a group of outpatients who had only come in for minor procedures. One young man, who has thankfully shown signs of recuperation, came into A&E to have his pinkie reattached after cutting it off with a hedge trimmer. He went to surgery. There is no commonality, no department they all went to."

"Maybe they didn't go to the virus, maybe the virus came to them. Do doctors move around departments?"

"Not really. Some of the more senior doctors and consultants may have wide ranging expertise and help other departments when they are busy."

"Second opinions, you mean?"

Dr Hart nodded. "Or just picking up the slack for undermanned departments. Sometimes doctors may go on rounds, if they're free. It's something the directors of the trust promote in order to cut waiting times. If a heart surgeon is free, which is rare, granted, he might go down to A&E to deal with minor wounds, discharge those already seen to, or just fill in paperwork. It's not a popular scheme, especially with the more specialised doctors, but it has helped us rise slightly above our peers, which comes in handy when those same heart surgeons and oncologists want government hand-outs for expensive new equipment."

Howard opened up the folder in his hand and glanced at it. "Let's start at the beginning. Who dealt with Mrs Drayton?"

"Let me see," Dr Hart looked through the file for a few moments, checking over the squiggles and signatures that meant nothing to him. "Suzanne Mitchell was the attending nurse. Dr Chris Casey, the attending doctor. I know them well. Neither would have anything to do with this."

Howard said nothing, unwilling to rule anybody out.

"Wait, what's this?" Dr Hart pulled a handwritten page from the file and examined it. "It's a letter of complaint about Dr Krenshaw. He's an area consultant, one of the most senior doctors in the trust."

"Why did Mrs Drayton complain about him?"

"The usual. He was rude to her, allegedly. Krenshaw can be quite abrupt with patients. He spent a decade in Africa, treating AIDS, malaria…"

"Ebola?" Howard enquired.

"I don't know. He did a lot of humanitarian work, so I suppose he would have come up against it at some point. He is an epidemiologist with a PHD in infectious diseases."

Howard raised his eyebrow. "You mean the most qualified, most suspicious person in this hospital? Wow, you think you might have suggested his name earlier?"

"Look, Agent Hopkins. These are my colleagues, people I trust, people who have dedicated their lives to healing. While everybody might scream out 'guilty' to you, to me they are friends. I suspect none of them, but I am helping you because I know you have an investigation to do. Dr Krenshaw is a humanitarian, above reproach."

Howard gave no reply. He was verging on anger for not being informed immediately of Dr Krenshaw's suspect credentials immediately, but the longer the tense silence went on, the more he understood that Dr Hart and her colleagues were not conditioned to view each other with suspicion. They relied on one another too much.

"Okay," said Howard gently. "Where is Dr Krenshaw now? I need to speak with him."

"He isn't here. He moves between hospitals in the trust."

Howard folded his arms and thought. Did that make the man more or less suspect? There had been no confirmed outbreaks at other hospitals, so perhaps Krenshaw wasn't the source of the outbreak. There had also been no confirmed infections within the last few days — did that correspond with Krenshaw's absence?

"We need to cross-reference Krenshaw with the infected patients," Howard said.

Dr Hart exhaled and put her hands on her hips. "Okay, I'll get started."

Howard got started too. He leafed through a stack of files and was frustrated to find a dozen different doctor signatures. It seemed that no member of staff was exclusive to the infected patients, so that was his leading theory shot.

"I think I've found something," said Dr Hart.

Howard went over to the doctor where she sat cross-legged and barefoot on the floor. "What is it?"

"I've cross-checked the patient's original hospital visits — when they likely became infected — with the days Dr Krenshaw was at Whiteknight. He was in the hospital the same times as every single patient infected with Ebola Virus. That might be true of other doctors, of course, but..."

"It certainly makes Krenshaw a person of interest, and with his specialisation in infectious diseases, I have to speak to him right away. Where can I find him?"

"I'll be right back," said Dr Hart, exiting suddenly and leaving her shoes behind.

Howard tapped his foot, anxious to get going. Everything added up to the culprit being this epidemiologist, Krenshaw, and if it was him, then the man could be planning another biological attack right that very second.

Dr Hart returned five minutes later, her lips thin, her nostrils flared. "I found out where Dr Krenshaw is," she said. "He's at Reading Children's Hospital."

Howard headed towards the door. "We need to move."

CHAPTER THIRTY-THREE

The door opened and Sarah readied herself. She was sitting on the bed, pretending to read a book she'd been given. Her heart was beating like a drum and she hoped the trepidation didn't show on her face.

It was Rat who finally entered, her most regular tormentor and the one she had expected to see. It was strange, but she had started to look forward to seeing his bucktoothed grin and dark, staring eyes. Rat's was the only face she saw for days at a time and it was sickeningly welcome against the loneliness and isolation she'd had to endure. But tonight, Sarah intended it to be the last time she was forced to look upon Rat's face with appreciation.

Rat was carrying a tray of what looked like Chinese food and it smelt delicious. Her captors would often bring her takeaway and snack foods rather than anything homemade. That suggested they were, at the very least, within a town or village, maybe even a city. If she were to escape, there would be places to go, people to plead to for help. She wouldn't need to get far, just out.

"I read that one," said Rat, pointing to her book. "The one where all the animals escape the zoo and attack people, yeah?"

Sarah eyed the cover of the novel and shrugged. "Only just started reading it. We can start a book club when I finish. You can bring the biscuits."

Rat smirked. "You haven't lost your wit, have you? Most people are morose by now."

"Most people don't know what the word 'morose' means. You're not as dumb as you look, which is pretty bloody dumb."

"As I've repeatedly told you, there's more to me than meets the eye."

"There's more teeth to you than meets the mouth."

That one seemed to hurt Rat a little. As much as he claimed indifference to her, he was starting to care. Stockholm syndrome worked both ways. As it was documented that hostages could start to enjoy the company of their captors, so too could captors begin to like the company of their wards. Rat was starting to think they were odd friends. She was about to wipe that foolish notion from his head.

"Who is keeping me captive, Rat? Tell me or I'll kill you." She made one last attempt to prise a name out of Rat and to give him a chance to do the right thing.

"Pope Francis," he replied dryly.

"Then you can tell the Pope that I gave you fair warning."

"Huh?"

Sarah leapt off the bed, sliding the shiv out from beneath her pillow and swinging it towards Rat's neck. His eyes opened wide as he realised what was happening. She'd caught him too far off guard for him to avoid the blade swiping through the air towards him. He snatched out at her but was wrong-footed and couldn't move fast enough.

He was going to die.

At the last moment, Sarah flinched and altered the direction of her swing. She buried the shiv deep in the hollow beneath Rat's collarbone instead of her original target of his jugular. Much as she hated her captor, she couldn't say for sure that he deserved to die. His screams of agony did enough to satiate her need for revenge, but she was forced to wrestle with the man as he gritted his teeth and tried to grab her throat.

Sarah grunted and strained, trying to fight the man off, but even wounded he was stronger.

"Bitch!"

Sarah growled. "Say that again."

"Bitch."

Sarah loosed rat's arm and grabbed the handle of the shiv, yanking it down like a lever. The wound opened up wider and Rat mewled like a kitten and slumped to the ground.

The shiv was narrow and thin, so came away easy as Sarah pulled it back from Rat's collarbone, leaving him to hiss and curse at her feebly. She stepped over him and headed to the unlocked door, the shiv dripping blood behind her. Before opening the door, she ran her hand over the blade and used the blood to cover her face. She would be up against dangerous men, and the best way to beat men in a fight was making them piss themselves before the first punch ever got thrown. A snarling woman covered in blood was enough to unnerve the bravest warrior.

Sarah left the room and entered a corridor. Despite the homely adornments of her incarceration, she now found herself inside the utilitarian hallways of some kind of factory or office building. It was the type of place where miserable employees marched around from nine-till-five. Currently it lay deserted. That boded well, for it meant her escape might not yet have announced itself. Rat's screams were loud, but they seemed to fade the further she went down the corridor. Around the next bend she was forced to stop. A tough-looking guy with a shaved brown pate was leaning up against the wall and taking drags on a cigar. Against the backdrop of his black combat fatigues, the civilised gesture seemed out of place. Sarah smeared some more blood from her hands onto her face and put her theory into action. She staggered around the corner, hiding the shiv behind her back while glancing around erratically and chattering her teeth. The blood was still wet on her face.

"Paper pictures," she muttered. "Bits of string."

The confused guard threw his cigar down on the floor and stood on it, then just looked at Sarah. His dark complexion went almost white as he tried to comprehend what he was looking at.

Sarah made it even more confusing for him. She swung her one arm around like a jellyfish and hopped towards him. The other arm, with the shiv, she kept tucked behind her back. "The doctor in the house isn't dead," she muttered. "The teeth were not his."

"The hell is wrong with you? W-where's Rat?"

Sarah did a quick squat thrust then threw herself into the wall, bashing her forehead and kicking out like a wingless fly. "Boom goes the dynamite."

The guard seemed to realise that he had to do something. She wasn't just an insane woman, she was a prisoner on the loose. He stepped towards her and, as soon as he did, Sarah spun around and slashed his cheek with the shiv. As he recoiled, she booted him in the nuts and followed it up with a knee to the face as he doubled over. He was out cold.

Two down, Sarah told herself. *How many more?*

She raced down the corridor, passing through the only door at the end and hoping it led to salvation. When she opened it and passed through into what appeared to be a large warehouse, she was faced by a gang of glaring men. They seemed undeterred by the blood on her face and immediately sprinted towards her.

Sarah bolted left, heading for the nearest side of the warehouse that had windows. Maybe she could throw herself clear through the glass and get to safety.

The men chased after her, three of them in total.

There was a bench up ahead, piled high with what looked like engine parts. Sarah slipped past it, waving her arms and shoving a bunch of metal debris into the path of her pursuers. She heard a man curse as he no doubt stumbled over one of the obstacles, but all three men continued to chase her. As she got closer to the windows, she saw that she wouldn't be able to throw herself through the glass or scream for help. The frames started a good four-feet above the ground and did not lead outside; they merely separated one warehouse floor from the next.

There was nowhere to run.

Sarah spun around, swinging the bloody shiv.

"Put the blade down," one of the men growled at her, an older gentleman who had brought her food on occasion when Rat was busy, "and we'll be gentle."

"Or don't," said a younger man with bad skin. "And we'll make you fucking eat it."

Sarah wasn't going back to her room. She was done being a prisoner. They would have to beat her to death before she allowed them to recapture her. Perhaps four months in captivity should have tamed her like a canary, but it had only made her desperate like a trapped dog, and now she felt rabid.

"You can take me down," she said in a snarl, "but the first one to try loses an eye. Or a testicle. That's if you pussies have any."

A man she had not seen before, possessing a rough beard and scraggly grey ponytail, leapt for her then. She sent him back with a slice in his forehead the width of a pencil.

"Damn it!"

"Who's next?" Sarah waved the shiv menacingly.

Nobody else came at her.

She glanced around, trying to find an exit, but there were a dozen doors leading off from the warehouse and no telling where any of them led. Then she saw it. A fire exit. It seemed to sparkle at her like a beacon. If she could only reach it, if she could make it outside...

Sarah broke into a sprint, taking advantage of the men's reluctance to grab her and their surprise at her sudden bolt. They gave chase, but Sarah had bought herself enough of a head start to stay ahead of them. She raced across the warehouse toward the fire door, panting and moaning in excitement. The closer she got, the more certain she was that she was going to make it. She was going to escape. The men at her back were bellowing at her to stop, making her even more confident that she was going to get away. The rabbit was escaping the yapping dogs.

Sarah threw herself against the release bar of the fire exit and exited out into the glorious afternoon sunshine. She had hoped to find a street full of people, but instead found herself standing in a paved courtyard inhabited by a pair of black vans and a car she was sure she recognised. The sleek red Jaguar e-type caught her attention long enough to stop her in her tracks. It was a relic of her past.

From the corner of her vision Sarah saw someone step out behind her. When she turned around to face the stranger, something struck her hard beneath the chin. Her legs folded, vision tilted, and when she finally managed to see straight again, she was lying on the ground looking up at a face she knew well. A face she both loved and hated.

The stern green eyes glared down at her disapprovingly while Sarah shook her head in disbelief.

Only one word escaped her lips. "Daddy?"

CHAPTER THIRTY-FOUR

"Daddy!" Sarah wanted to say other words but she couldn't. "Daddy..."

Her father looked down at her with an expression of irritation that had defined her childhood. "Most men manage to break out within three months," he said, "but then...you're not a man, are you?"

Sarah wanted to stand, but she couldn't move from her spot on the floor. "W-what?"

Her father offered his hand and yanked her up to her feet. "I'll explain everything, but get yourself cleaned up first. You look like a savage. I heard your scars were bad, but I had no idea they were so unsightly, especially with all that blood on your face. Come on, stop dawdling."

Sarah followed her father and allowed herself to be ushered back inside the warehouse, the place she had just fought so desperately to escape. Suddenly the torment of her four-month incarceration was forgotten and all that remained were burning questions. Had her father been keeping her locked up? Why?

She was directed to a toilet block and told to clean herself up and get the blood off her face. She did as she was told, feeling like a little girl, and came back out again as quickly as she could.

"I don't understand," she said as her father walked her to their next destination. The group of men who had chased her now strolled casually behind her. The grey haired man with the thick gouge across his forehead was chatting away merrily to one of his colleagues even as his face dripped blood. These were hard men, the type of men her father was used to working with. Major Stone was renowned throughout the British military as one of the SAS's most distinguished of distinguished men. He had seen action in every British conflict from the Iranian embassy siege right through to the most recent turmoil in Syria. He had spent a good portion of his life overseas or, at the very least, encamped somewhere ready to go overseas. Truth be told, Sarah barely knew the man.

A man staggered into the warehouse on the opposite side, getting everyone's attention. It was Rat, battered and bloody. He clutched the wound on his shoulder and walked in a stoop like Quasimodo. "Bitch stabbed me," he shouted, slumping over one of the floor's many tables.

Nobody seemed to care.

"Then perhaps you should have paid better attention," said Sarah's father flatly.

Rat said nothing else. He remained slumped in pain until his colleagues took him under the arms and led him away. That left Sarah alone with her father as they continued walking through the oily warehouse.

"Who are all these men," she asked him. "And what is this place?"

"They are *my* men, and this place is just an old assembly plant. I think they used to make elevator parts. What some men are willing to call a living baffles me."

"Don't you care that I stabbed one of your men?"

"Of course I care. Rat should've done better than to let you get the jump on him. I'll deal with him later."

"I meant, don't you care that he's injured?"

"He'll live, but I'm sure you intended that."

She nodded. "I don't kill a man unless I know he deserves it."

"Those feminine sensibilities will get you nowhere," he grunted. "The man was keeping you prisoner. He didn't deserve your mercy."

"He wasn't keeping me prisoner, you were. Why?"

"I'll get to that," he motioned towards an open office door and led her inside the dim, windowless room. She took a seat on one side of a gnarled wooden desk while her father sat on the other. One of his men appeared and handed him a glass of brandy before disappearing quickly. Sarah's father had not changed a bit in the years since she'd last seen him.

"Why am I here?" she demanded, regaining a slither of her courage now that she knew who was responsible for her capture. Despite her fear of her father, she no longer felt in danger. What harm could a man mean to his own daughter?

"Because you inserted yourself into things which did not concern you."

"What are you talking about? Why have you been keeping me prisoner? Why didn't you come see me yourself, instead of hiding behind Rat?"

"Because I needed to see how you operate under stress. I must say I am a little disappointed it took you so long to escape. Still, you are a woman, I suppose."

The comment from anybody else would have summoned Sarah's anger, but from her father it was crippling. "I thought I was going to die," she said meekly. "Is that what you wanted, me to be scared for my life? You're supposed to be my father."

"I *am* your father, and you are my daughter. I needed to see if you were capable of being anything more."

Sarah leant forward and placed her clenched fist on the table between them. She tried to maintain eye contact with her father but failed. She was twelve-years old again, pleading with him not to vanish for another year, but as much as she wanted to hate him right now, she did not want to make him mad, or make him disappear on her.

"I want answers," she said.

"Hesbani. There's your answer."

Sarah flopped back in her chair, both eyebrows raising of their own accord. "Hesbani? What about Hesbani?"

"You killed him."

Sarah said nothing. She wasn't sure what question to ask or what her father was getting at.

Her father accepted the silence as permission to continue. "Hesbani was my target. I had been tasked with bringing him home."

Sarah bolted forwards again. "You were helping a terrorist?"

"No, you stupid girl. I was helping the Pakistani government apprehend him. They wanted Hesbani for acts of terror he'd committed within their borders in protest against their cooperation with the British and American government. I had a man already embedded in Hesbani's operation, a man you knew..."

Sarah's eyes stretched wide as she realised. "Hamish?"

Her father nodded gravely. "A good man. Risked his life getting close to Hesbani. Pity you took him out."

"Only after he tried to take out me!"

Her father laughed, a rare gesture. "I admit he had issues, many of them aimed at you, but I wasn't very much interested at the time. Never did I think the two of you would cross paths. Regardless, Hamish is gone and so is Hesbani, along with my men's paycheque. Keeping you captive gave them some small restitution, but not enough by far."

Sarah shook her head in disbelief. "This was revenge?"

"Don't flatter yourself, Sarah. My men are not a bunch of simpering schoolgirls. We do not concern ourselves with things as petty as revenge. You have been held captive as a test. I wanted to see if you could escape. I was always against you joining the army, but you did it anyway and became a captain. I had resigned myself to almost accepting your bad decisions, especially when I heard you were unexpectedly married, but then the poor chap died, didn't he?"

Sarah thought about Thomas and almost let out a sob. She had gotten so good at not thinking about him that having him brought up unexpectedly got through her barriers and pricked at her heart.

"Then," her father went on, "you had your own accident and all but disappeared of the face of the earth. Licking your wounds, I assumed, but then, lo and behold, you pop up on the ten-o-clock news, hero of the hour. You even managed to make that ridiculous outfit, MCU, look respectable. Your victory saved them from the brink, you know? If you'd stayed on with them, I probably would've left you alone."

Sarah was still at a loss. Every couple of seconds she would remind herself that she was sitting in front of her father, the esteemed Major Stone, and would find it utterly surreal. Then she would remember that he had kidnapped her and held her hostage for four months and would get extremely angry. "Why didn't you leave me alone? You've been pretty good at that for most of my life."

Her father rolled his eyes. "Save the melodramatics. Some men are meant for more than raising ungrateful children into ungrateful adults. You have no idea the freedoms you have because of men like me. I have done more for you away then I ever would have at home. You had your mother, so don't act hard done by."

"Mum died when I was seventeen."

"Your childhood was already over, so why would you have needed her any longer? Anyway, I do not have you here to discuss family. You are here because you escaped, *finally*. As much as you interfering with Hesbani caused me great irritation, I was also impressed. It appears you do have a certain aptitude to our line of work, and to end up working within clandestine services, like your father, speaks of a certain family predilection, don't you agree? I wanted to see for myself how much of a man you are. You certainly wear your scars well. If you cut your hair short, I wouldn't even know you lacked a cock."

Sarah shifted in her seat. The thought of being anything like her father was akin to having bugs crawl beneath her skin. "Your men aren't SAS, are they?" she said. "They look more like mercenaries."

"And mercenaries is what they are. I am no longer in the employ of the British Army. I was tired of murdering civilians and bombing weddings based on the merest whiff of semi-accurate Intel. Do you know how many woman and children I have killed at the bequest of so-called Right Honourable gentlemen? One Prime Minister after another, sending hired thugs to murder and devastate their enemies, and for what? This woman we have in charge, Breslow, is worst of all. Her foreign war policy is going to double the amount of young men endangering their lives for worthless causes. All she cares about is getting her fingers in as many pies as she can. Thought people would have learned their lesson about putting women in charge with Thatcher. One thing I can assure you, sweet daughter of mine, is that no war I have ever fought in was waged for any other reason than to take what the other man has. I am a murderer, Sarah, I cannot change that, but I can change the reasons why. My days of taking orders from Westminster have stopped, and if I get my wish, I'll see the place crumble with Breslow buried beneath the rubble."

"So now you kill for money?" said Sarah, blinking. "Is that what you call honour?"

"It is more honourable to kill for money than the false flag of liberation. The British Empire hasn't liberated a single country in its entire existence — in fact it has only ever achieved the opposite. Now the Empire has crumbled and the Star Spangled Banner has replaced it with intentions even less noble and greedier. I am tired of the hypocrisy, Sarah. I fight for reasons of my own choosing now. As do my men."

"You didn't seem too concerned about Rat," she said. "You speak a good game, but you don't seem any more caring than you ever have."

"Rat is merely wounded. I do not weep for wounds. I am no woman."

"I don't know what you are, father. Tell you the truth, I'm tired of trying to figure it out. Am I allowed to leave here, or are you going to lock me back up?"

"You are free to leave," he said and she almost wept with joy. She kept her emotions contained, though, and gave only an imperceptible nod.

"Then I am going home." She got up out of her seat.

"You have no home, Sarah," Her father almost shouted it at her. "The Army did to you what it does to every soldier. It used you up and left you to die under the weight of your own nightmares. It sent you to war against people guilty of no crimes other than daring to have self-interest. Britain sends men like us to kill hundreds, in order to punish a scant few who actually deserve it. You, Sarah, are nothing more than a worn-down cog in a machine designed to trample poorer nations into the mud while blaming them for trying to claw their way out of it. Don't you want to do things on your own terms? Don't you ever wish you could put your skills, your experience, to a truly good cause?"

Sarah sat back down. "What are you talking about?"

"I am talking about recruiting you. A woman can be useful in certain situations and, as far as women go, you seem to be among the best."

"Better than most men," she grunted.

"Perhaps. I'm offering you a place on my team, Sarah. We fight for causes we believe in. We pay ourselves and fund our own operations. We do not take orders, we take jobs. If you are happy with your old life, daughter, then leave. Go back to whatever life you think you can have with that grotesque face of yours. Or join me and do what you're good at."

"And what is that?" she asked curiously.

"Killing bad guys."

CHAPTER THIRTY-FIVE

Howard pulled the Range Rover up in a skid, leaving it in a disabled bay right outside the main doors of the hospital. His 'Official' plates would take care of any complainers.

"Where will we find Krenshaw?" he asked Dr Hart in the seat beside him.

"He oversees a training scheme for interns wanting to specialise in childhood diseases. His experience with the African orphanages makes him a key expert in the field. Many doctors have studied under him."

"Then I hope he is innocent," said Howard. "He sounds like a saint."

They headed through into the calm reception area and caught the attention of a receptionist, who seemed surprised then flustered by their urgency.

"C-Can I help you?"

Howard flashed his MCU badge. "Dr Krenshaw, where is he?"

The receptionist didn't need to check her computer. She knew off the top of her head. "He's on the 1st floor. Seminar Room 2."

Howard took Dr Hart by the arm and got her moving again. "I may need you to point him out to me. I don't want to announce my presence, in case he runs."

"This is crazy."

"I do crazy for a living," he said.

They took the stairs up, dodging past sick children still well enough to play ball in the corridors. Upstairs was quieter; deserted, in fact. From the signs on the walls and doors, it seemed that the 1st floor was dedicated to training and research. It had only one ward and that was a cancer ward. No doubt the sickest children were placed upstairs because it was more peaceful. Howard hoped that apprehending Krenshaw would be a calm affair. He was carrying a gun inside his jacket but had no intention of using it unless he had to, yet he followed protocol and unpopped the holster.

Dr Hart moved a little ahead of him and stopped just short of the door into Seminar Room 2. She turned to him and said, "You're not going to hurt anyone, are you?"

"I will do whatever the situation requires, Dr Hart. I understand you have divided loyalties here, but someone is responsible for infecting hundreds of people with Ebola. What do you expect to happen? If Krenshaw is our man, do you expect him to shrug and say, 'Oh dear, you caught me?' That's not how these things go."

Dr Hart looked like a sad kitten and Howard felt bad about being stern with her, yet he had a job to do and couldn't let her distract him. "You should stay here," he said. "I know I wanted you to point him out, but I would rather have you out of the way unless necessary. There's no other way out of this room, is there?"

"I don't think so. I'll stay right here."

Howard approached the door and carefully opened it. Inside he found a small classroom of a dozen desks and twice as many seats filled with scribbling students. They all looked up at Howard as he entered, but Howard's focus went to the front of the room where a large whiteboard lay unattended. The classic teaching position at the front of the classroom was unmanned.

"Where is Dr Krenshaw?" Howard asked the students.

A young brunette in spectacles answered his question. "He was unable to take the class today. He's helping the Paediatric Haematology department. It's on the ground floor."

Howard flew out of the classroom and grabbed a startled Dr Hart. "He's in the Haematology department. That's blood, right?"

Dr Hart nodded as they hurried. "Yes. This hospital specialises in malignant blood borne infections. They perform tests on children from all over the area to help study and diagnose Leukaemia and various lymphomas."

"I don't like the sound of this," said Howard.

"You don't think he's going to harm a bunch of children, do you?"

Howard took the stairs three at a time, shouting out to Dr Hart running behind him. "Whoever is behind the outbreak at Whiteknight is capable of doing anything."

"But Dr Krenshaw spent a decade *helping* children in Africa."

Howard saw the sign for MALIGNANT HAEMATOLOGY and headed in its direction. "I don't have the answers," he said. "Dr Krenshaw does and I intend to get them."

"You don't know he did anything. You don't know anything for sure."

Howard burst through the double doors at the end of the corridor and was met with the sight of a dozen sick children and their worried parents. Their heavy-lidded, dark-eyed stares made him shudder. Once again he felt like the very air itself was toxic and he forced himself to slow down.

"Are you okay?" Dr Hart asked him as he wobbled on his feet.

"I-I'm fine. I just...don't like hospitals. My father had three strokes before he died and my family seemed to be in and out of hospitals for years. I think it's the smell that brings back the memories."

Dr Hart nodded. "They're not meant to be fun places, but I'm sorry you had such a bad experience."

"Thank you. Let's get this over with."

Dr Hart pointed suddenly. "That's Dr Krenshaw, over there."

Howard followed her pointing finger to a tall, bony-faced man in a white doctor's coat. Krenshaw didn't see Howard marching towards him at first, but then he looked up from his clipboard and gave an expression of curiosity, followed by something else — was it concern?

"Dr Krenshaw?" asked Howard.

"Yes?" The man noticed Dr Hart standing beside Howard and nodded. "Stevie, always a pleasure to see you."

Dr Hart shuffled her feet and averted her eyes. "Thank you, Alistair. You too."

Howard took charge of the conversation, not wanting to give the doctor time to put his thoughts in order. "Dr Krenshaw, I am Agent Hopkins with MCU. Is there somewhere we can talk privately?"

Dr Krenshaw flashed a smile and said, "Of course, please, right this way."

He led Howard and Dr Hart though the ward towards a staff area at the back. All of the nurses seemed baffled by what was going on, but all of them smiled and nodded at Dr Krenshaw, obviously a man they liked and respected. Howard wavered momentarily from his certainty that Krenshaw was the man responsible for the outbreak. Perhaps he wasn't. All the same, questions needed answering.

"Just through here." Dr Krenshaw directed them.

Howard and Dr Hart moved past Krenshaw into a private office, but, as they did so, Krenshaw snatched out at Dr Hart and wrapped his arm around her throat, placing himself behind her. Howard spun around, ready to act, but stopped when he saw that Krenshaw had produced a syringe and placed it against Dr Hart's neck.

"HIV," Krenshaw stated calmly. "That is what is inside this syringe. Not quite as elegant as Ebola, granted, but just as incurable."

Dr Hart was frozen in unblinking terror. Her eyes were stretched wide and focused on Howard.

Howard backed off, kept his hands where everybody could see them. "Let's not do anything unnecessary, Doctor."

"Everything I have done is necessary."

"I don't understand. Explain it to me. Why Ebola? Why this?"

"Because people need to care." Krenshaw's lips moved into a snarl.

"We cosy up in front of our televisions or sit on our air-conditioned trains listening to our iPods while half the world suffers in poverty. People in China toil in factories so that we can have cheap goods. Families in the Middle East live in dirt because any wealth their countries have either goes to us or the puppet governments we have left to rule over them. Africa is full of starving and sick children because we would rather spend our money growing fat and gluttonous than sharing with the 3rd World what we have. Maybe if the children of Britain start dying from Ebola, HIV, and malaria, we might just get down off our pedestals long enough to notice those begging at our feet. This country makes me sick. Now it is my turn to make *it* sick."

Howard nodded as if he understood, although he didn't. It was a worldview far too simplistic for him to accept "You're doing this to teach a lesson?"

"Yes. The only lesson this country will ever listen to. We are content to watch little black children and little Asian children dying on our television screens — it's no different to any other form of entertainment — but I wonder how indifferent this nation will be when it joins the 3rd World in its suffering and little white children begin to die. I'm sure it will be only too happy to fund all the cures the world needs then."

"I understand," said Howard. "It makes sense. I have seen the sick and the dying, too, thanks to what you have done, and I definitely see things differently now. Your plan has worked. I'm sure extra money is being spent on Ebola as we speak. You can stop all this. It doesn't need to go further."

Krenshaw shook his head with a grimace. "Eradicating Ebola won't even make a dent in the world's ills. There are a hundred more diseases that need attention, like the one inside this syringe."

Dr Hart spoke up, her voice aquiver. "Don't do this, Alistair. HIV is being cured. We're almost there."

"Then let me help speed things along."

Howard watched in horror as Krenshaw pumped the contents of the syringe into Dr Hart's neck, before shoving the wailing women away. The smart move would have been for Howard to leave Dr Hart and pursue Krenshaw, but rationality took no part in his decision as he wrapped his arms around the sobbing woman and helped her to the ground as she clawed desperately at her neck.

Krenshaw was out the door before Howard even had time to glance up. He didn't want to imagine what the murderous doctor would do next.

CHAPTER THIRTY-SIX

Sarah was sat eating a sandwich when her father came barging back into the office where he had left her to think. And think she had.

In a way her father seemed proud of her. She'd followed in his footsteps, after a fashion, and managed to take down a man he himself had been after. She'd also prematurely finished her military career at a rank only one below his own, although her regiment in no way compared to the inimitable SAS. The Special Air Service were so tough that they often went overseas to train other nation's Special Forces. The only ones anywhere near as brutally efficient were the Russian Alpha Group and the US Navy Seals. Sarah herself had passed the entry tests for the SAS but was denied on the basis of her gender. Women did not belong in the Special Forces.

But then she had joined MCU, a joint enterprise between the USA and UK that had promised to be the epitome of counter-terrorism and intelligence. It had initially fallen short, but Sarah's actions helped elevate it to its intended position. Over the last few months, she had watched the various news reports discussing the increased funding and prestige of the organisation and she could not help but feel satisfied.

She knew the men and women who worked at MCU were hard-working and dedicated, and it pleased her to hear of their increased prosperity.

"We have a new mission," her father said. "Are you in or out?"

Sarah put down her sandwich and cleared her throat. "I finally stop being a hostage and now you want me to take a job with you?"

"I want nothing, Sarah. You are my daughter and duty demands I offer you a chance to do something with your life. With that face you have no chance of finding a man, so at least I can no longer blame you for failing to settle down. If military is your chosen path, I promise you will find no greater vocation than the one I am offering you."

"What's the job?" she asked.

"A manhunt. We are to apprehend a doctor and return him to the South African government who want him for biological attacks on the border towns of their country."

"This doctor has killed people?"

"Many."

Sarah stood up, brushed bread crumbs off her lap. "Okay, I'm in."

The famously morose Major Stone actually managed a slight smile. "Then let's get you into something suitable. We leave on the hour."

Sarah was hustled into an old locker room that had probably once belonged to the staff of whatever business once operated inside the warehouse. She was given a set of combat fatigues to change into and then, once she was dressed, was led back out into the middle of the warehouse's main floor. A trail of blood snaked a path to wherever Rat had scurried off to.

The grey haired, ponytailed man, whose forehead she had sliced, motioned for her to join him at a bench in the centre of the room. He beamed at her, despite the thick bandage taped to his forehead.

"Sorry about that," she said, pointing to his bandage.

"Hey, I was about to do far worse to you, so forget about it."

Sarah shrugged. "Fair enough. I'm Sarah."

"Of course you are. I'm Ollie."

Sarah frowned.

"What's wrong?"

"Nothing, you just don't seem like an Ollie."

"Call me what you like. I don't mind."

"No, Ollie is fine."

Ollie yanked a tarpaulin off the bench and Sarah whistled at what she saw.

"Top of the line stuff," he explained, running an appreciative hand over the assortment of firearms and ammunition.

Sarah spotted a familiar 9mm SIG and picked it up. "Mind if I take this one?"

"Sure. The boys are too manly to go for the P226, they prefer something bigger like a .45, but I always stock it because it's a nice shooter and easy to conceal. I've used it a time or two myself, so it's well looked after."

Sarah could see the truth of it. The small, black pistol gleamed with a thin layer of oil and the cocking action was the smoothest she'd ever felt. There was even a delicate laser sight attached to the bottom of the muzzle.

Ollie picked up a sheath with the handle of a Ka-Bar knife sticking out the top. "Back-up," he said, handing it to her. "US Marines swear by 'em."

Sarah took the sheath and fastened it to her utility belt. All of a sudden she felt like she was acting in some play. Only hours before she had been a prisoner and now she was suited and booted like a GI Joe. It was all a bit surreal.

Her father came up from the far end of the warehouse, followed by the rest of his men, all suited up in the same combat uniforms as Sarah; even Rat, who now walked as if uninjured. Whatever painkiller they had given him was stronger than anything over the counter. The weasely man glared when he saw her.

Sarah's father took the floor, his men standing to attention. "Alright, men," he barked. "We have a new team member and, while she may be a woman, she is my daughter also, with a set of balls almost as big as my own."

There was sprinkling of laughter from everybody except Rat.

"Now," Major Stone continued. "Sarah took a few lumps out of a couple of you, but remember that you all went through similar trials of initiation once upon a time. All is fair. There will be no grudges." He shot a quick glance to Rat, who recoiled. "Our next target is a doctor by the name of Alistair Krenshaw. He is wanted for using human test subjects on the borders of South Africa. He is a suspected terrorist with designs on biological warfare. It is believed the atrocities he committed in South Africa were trial experiments for something much bigger. He has been back, working in the UK for two years now, an expert in his field. The South African government has not forgotten or forgiven his crimes, though. We have a sighting on him nearby and we are going to pick him up in a nice quick 'stop and grab.' No casualties. No unnecessary attention."

Sarah swallowed. Never having served under her father before, this was the first time she'd witnessed him in action. The complete respect and attention of his men was something she could never hope to emulate. He was one of them, yet above them in every way.

Major Stone marched over to the weapons bench and picked up a Colt Commander with a walnut grip, then cocked it with ease. "We have fought and beaten men of all kinds," he said. "We have fought entire armies and won. We have killed kings and sultans, men who thought themselves Gods, yet were forced to weep as we brought them crashing down to earth. We are peerless. Superior to marines, paratroopers, and even the SAS itself. We are better than them all. We are without equal and charged with the simple tasks of running down a little doctor in a white coat. The poor bastard is going to piss himself."

Everybody laughed, except Sarah who was trying to comprehend how this small band of mercenaries could compare themselves to the likes of the SAS.

Major Stone also remained deadly serious and barked an order. "Let's move out, men."

Sarah tried to speak with her father, but he turned and marched away before she had chance. Ollie stood beside her instead, smiling kindly. "Don't worry," he said. "I got your back."

Sarah didn't reply. She followed after the other men, still utterly confused by how she'd suddenly been inducted into her absent father's private army. Somehow it felt like things were only going to get more confusing.

CHAPTER THIRTY-SEVEN

Dr Hart was still sobbing in Howard's arms when help finally arrived. It was only a couple of nurses, but Howard was still glad to see them, for they would be far more useful in dealing with the situation than he. Did Dr Hart have AIDS now, or was HIV different? He cursed himself for being so ignorant as not to know. Dr Krenshaw had a point about the West caring little about maladies which did not affect them. The public knew more about the top ten pop chart than it did the top ten deadliest diseases.

"The syringe could have been full of water," he said soothingly to Dr Hart, who continued to cling to him desperately. "It was probably a bluff. A good one because it worked. There didn't even need to be anything dangerous inside the syringe for him to make me back off. I'm sure you're fine. It's okay. It's..." His mouth kept moving but he had idea what words to say.

Dr Hart tried to get a hold of herself, turning her sobs into choking shudders. "G-G-Go...go after him."

Howard took a moment but then understood. He couldn't help Dr Hart, but he could sure as hell go after Dr Krenshaw and bring him to justice. If the syringe had been a bluff, the quickest way to find out would be to put Krenshaw's balls in a vice and ask him. He placed the doctor into the concerned care of the two nurses and clenched his fists. "Dr Krenshaw. Where did he go?"

"Towards the car park out back," one of the nurses replied. "He stopped by the staffroom to grab his briefcase but then went out the fire exit. You may still catch him."

Howard took off like a horse out of the gates. He spotted a sign for the staff car park and careened around the corridors towards it. Even before he made it outside he spotted Krenshaw through the wide glass doors. The doctor was running for his life but was skinny and unfit, carrying what looked like a heavy briefcase. He was beating it across the car park, but Howard was right out the door after him. This time, he had no qualms about pulling out his gun and firing it. He aimed a round into the air.

Krenshaw froze in his tracks, crouching down and turning slowly to face Howard. A couple of bystanders leapt for cover behind their cars.

"Give yourself up, Doctor. Or I'll be forced to shoot you."

Krenshaw didn't look afraid. In fact he seemed amused. In his free hand he held a small glass cylinder.

Howard stayed where he was but kept his gun levelled. "What do you have in your hand, Doctor?"

Krenshaw's lips drew back like a curtain into the delighted grimace of a corpse. "Just a concoction I whipped up. Weaponised Dengue Fever, if you must know. Symptoms start with fever, headaches, nausea and vomiting, before progressing to a rash and fluid in the chest. The beauty of this particular strain is that it is highly symptomatic. You see, the more typical strain affects less than one-quarter of infected patients. This will infect over 90% with the most severe case. I carry it with me everywhere. Call it an insurance policy. You try to stop me and I smash the phial, which contains a highly concentrated dose of the disease. It may not cause an epidemic, but it will, at the very least, infect you and me, and perhaps a few dozen sick children inside this hospital."

"Have you not already infected them with something nasty?" asked

Howard. He dared not take another step forward and was forced to stall for time. Maybe he could shoot the doctor without the phial smashing, but the fear of what was inside escaping made his blood run too cold to try.

"Alas, no," said Krenshaw. "I was just about to begin my rounds. You see, I like to do my most important work at night and evening is nearly upon us. Morning and afternoon seem like queer times to give people death sentences, don't you agree?"

Howard felt sick. "You were going to infect a bunch of children. You're mad."

"I am very sane, I assure you. In fact it takes a huge level of sanity to make the sacrifices I am making. I want to change the world for the better. Infecting a bunch of sickly white children with HIV is a means to an end. They would get the best care, maybe even live full lives, but the fear would be enough to get this country to pay attention."

"Your mission is over, Doctor. Just hand the phial over and give yourself up."

"Hand it over? Are you so sure you want to take this from me? You have gone quite a striking shade of alabaster."

Howard tried to swallow, but there was a lump in his throat. He spoke in a squawk. "Nobody else is getting sick today, Doctor. This isn't the way."

"It is the only way." Krenshaw tossed the phial into the air.

Howard felt his eyes almost fall out of his head as he watched the small glass bottle arc towards him. His legs tried to carry him away, to run, but he knew it was wrong thing to do, so, with a diving lunge, he threw himself forwards instead. The phial was tiny, but as it tumbled it caught the dimming sunlight and glinted. It gave Howard something to focus on. He hit the pavement hard, chin striking the ground and sending him dizzy. For a few seconds, he forgot himself and lay there in a daze. When he got his wits back he panicked and looked around urgently. He opened up his hands and almost wept when he saw the intact phial clutched in his right fist. His relief turned to fury, though, when he saw the word INSULIN printed on the label. It had been a bluff.

Howard clambered back to his feet, ignoring the spike of pain in his left kneecap where it had struck the pavement. Krenshaw had already made a run for it and had gained a good lead. A parked car up ahead blinked and beeped as the doctor unlocked it with his key fob. There was too much distance between them now for Howard to get to Krenshaw before the doctor hopped in his car and drove away.

Howard brought up his gun, drew a bead, and fired. His round struck the bumper of a car and ricocheted. There were still bystanders hiding in cover and they yelled out in fright now. Howard couldn't risk them getting hit. He lowered his gun and sprinted, hoping against hope that Krenshaw would fail to escape in time. But Krenshaw was almost at his car and seemed to realise he was home-free. He turned around to smirk at Howard.

"Until next time," the doctor gloated, clutching the briefcase to his chest like it was a prize.

There was the sudden screech of skidding tyres.

Two jet-black vans pulled up behind Krenshaw, making the doctor spin around in fright and stumble on his heels. Two burly men in balaclavas hopped out of one of the vans and grabbed Krenshaw before he even knew what was happening, then they bundled him inside the van and held him down on the floor as he struggled. A third person hopped out the front of the other van and ran around to close the side door of the other. This person wasn't wearing a balaclava and was, in fact, a woman.

Howard tripped and stumbled, before stopping completely. In front of him was a woman who'd gone missing more than four months ago and not been heard from since. A former colleague.

Sarah noticed Howard standing there and froze with the same shocked expression that he no doubt wore on his own face. The driver of the van shouted at her and she got moving again, slamming the side door shut of the first van before hopping back into the front passenger seat of the other. Then both vans took off, tyres squealing as they took off around the corner and disappeared.

Howard stood rooted to the spot for so long that he began to shiver from the cold. He couldn't believe who he had just seen: Captain Sarah Stone.

CHAPTER THIRTY-EIGHT

Howard found Dr Hart sitting inside a small waiting room with a sofa and coffee machine. There was a nurse beside her, rubbing her back as she prodded anxiously at the red spot on her neck. The nurse left when Howard entered.

"Are you okay?" Howard asked Dr Hart. She was a pretty woman, not much over forty, but right now she was haggard and grey and her blonde hair seemed almost white. She didn't say anything in reply to him, just stared at a spot on the wall, barely blinking.

"Krenshaw was bluffing," said Howard enthusiastically. He plucked the insulin phial from his pocket and showed it to her. "He convinced me this was Dengue Fever but it's just plain old Insulin. The syringe he stabbed you with was probably nothing."

"They've pried open his locker," she eventually said, a detached numbness to her voice. "You should go take a look."

Howard took her advice and left her alone. On his way to find a nurse to direct him, he took out his mobsat and placed a call through to the Earthworm, MCU's base of operations. He went straight through to Director Palu.

"Howard. Update me."

Howard cleared his throat and began. "My investigation at Whiteknight seemed to confirm the epidemic was engineered and led me to a suspect named Dr Alistair Krenshaw. I tracked him down to Reading Children's Hospital where he was planning to carry out a second act of terror. This time a mass infection of the HIV virus on already sick children."

"You stopped it?"

"I did, but Krenshaw managed to escape. He was...abducted."

There was a brief pause before Palu spoke. "Abducted?"

"Two black vans pulled up right behind Krenshaw and two men leapt out and dragged him into the back. Palu... Sarah was with them. Sarah Stone."

The next pause was even longer.

"I know," said Howard. "It doesn't make any sense, but it was her, I swear. There's no doubt in my mind."

"Then, where the hell has she been? And who is she working with?"

Howard stopped in the middle of the corridor and leaned up against the wall, groaning. "I have no idea, but whoever she is with has the doctor and I am positive Krenshaw is our man. What is Sarah involved in?"

"Do you have a description of the men she was with?"

"No. They were wearing balaclavas."

"I'll have Jessica check CCTV for the area. I'm sure the hospital will have something."

"Check the rear car park," said Howard. "That's where the black vans arrived."

"Do you have any other leads?"

Howard sighed. "Not yet. I'm about to search Krenshaw's locker and see what I find. Can you have someone gather everything we have on the doctor?"

"Of course. Good work, Howard. We'll catch Krenshaw; only a matter of time."

"I'll keep you updated." Howard ended the call, found a nurse, and asked to be taken to Krenshaw's locker. Inside the staff changing area, there was another nurse already there waiting for him.

"This is the doctor's locker," the woman told him, indicating which one she meant.

The locker was hanging slightly ajar, so Howard fondled the edge and swung it open wider. Inside was not a comforting sight. The top metal shelf was stacked with phials of clear liquid. A bundle of unsealed syringes right beside them.

"Do we know what's inside them?" asked Howard of the nurse.

"We'll need to get them to a lab, but I can tell you they aren't legally endorsed."

"What do you mean?"

"I mean that these didn't come from an approved pharmaceutical supplier. They're either black market or, worse, homemade. There're no labels, no serial numbers. Even the bottles aren't NHS issue. Whatever is in these phials didn't come through the system."

Howard thanked the nurse and asked her to bring Dr Hart to him. She would still be understandably distraught, but he needed answers.

She appeared five minutes later, back in charge of her emotions, yet slightly timid in voice. "What can I do for you, Agent Hopkins?"

"Is there any way of finding out what is inside these phials?"

"They can be tested for HIV fairly quickly, if that's what you mean? I'll contact the lab and fast track it myself."

Howard nodded grimly. "What are you going to do about yourself?"

She shrugged, almost as if she didn't care. Howard thought it more likely the numbness of shock, or maybe she just knew there was little she could do. "I'll have to start on anti-retroviral immediately," she explained, "whether I am infected or not. It will take three months or so before any blood tests will be reliable."

Howard put himself in the doctor's shoes and felt quite sick. It was going to be a long three months of hell while she was forced to wait for results on whether or not she was gravely ill. "Krenshaw admitted he never managed to infect any of the children," he said, hoping it would give her some solace.

"You let him get away, though?"

Howard didn't take it personally. If anyone had the right to apportion blame, it was Dr Hart. "I'm sorry. I have all my people working on it. We'll get him, I promise." He chose not to complicate matters by explaining about the black vans and his former colleague appearing to snatch Krenshaw away just as he was about to get away.

"I need to go back to Whiteknight," she said, looking away from him. "I can get treatment there and I need to get back to trying to deal with the Ebola epidemic."

Howard nodded. Any friendliness that had existed between them was now gone, extinguished the moment Krenshaw plunged a syringe into her neck. Howard had failed the woman, and could tell that Dr Hart regretted ever having met him. He regretted it, too, but for different reasons.

"If you need anything..."

Dr Hart nodded, turned around, and left.

For a while, Howard stood alone in the locker room, staring at the collection of unlabelled liquids in the locker and shuddering. Eventually a nurse came in and started loading everything into a padded yellow crate. "I'll get this sent straight to the pathology lab in Slough," she told him. "If you leave me your details, I'll have them call you with the results."

"Thank you." Howard left her his details and thanked her, then exited the hospital as quickly as he could and stood out in the fresh air of the newly arrived night. It felt good to be in the open, out of the claustrophobic confines of the hospital. His breaths were longer, steadier, and, as he walked over to the curb where his MCU Range Rover was parked, he began to feel better. He wondered where Dr Hart had gone and how she was getting back to Whiteknight. Running, probably, if it got her away from him. The thought of her alone and scared brought tears to Howard's eyes as he finally allowed himself to acknowledge how much today's ordeal had upset him. He'd been relentlessly afraid the entire time, but it was Dr Hart who had been hurt.

A shrill ring caused Howard to flinch from his thoughts and pull his mobsat from his coat. He answered the call and placed it to his ear. "Hopkins."

"Howard!" It was Jessica Bennett, a Georgia gal transferred from MCU America and currently his closest colleague, as well as probably the smartest person he knew. She, too, was a doctor but specialised in the mind rather than the body. "I checked the hospital CCTV and got a good look at the black vans. I saw the men you saw. Was that really Sarah?"

"I'm certain of it. I looked her right in the eye. Not like she could be mistaken for anyone else with those scars of hers."

"I thought she was dead."

"Me too. Looks like everything we assumed was wrong. She's working with someone and they have Krenshaw."

"It's her daddy," Jessica blurted out, her southern state accent more prevalent when she wasn't speaking slowly.

Howard unlocked the Range Rover and got in behind the wheel where it was warmer and quieter. He adjusted the mobsat against his ear and then continued the conversation. "Her father? How do you know?"

Jessica told him. "The men in the back of the vans were wearing balaclavas, but I got a clear view at the driver who wasn't wearing a mask of any kind. I ran his face through the Interpol and military databases and it came up as a wanted war criminal, Major Jonathan Stone."

Howard flopped back against the leather driver's seat. "That makes no sense. Sarah's father is a Major in the Army. Isn't he SAS?"

"He was," said Jessica, "but he went AWOL with a group of his men almost a year ago. He was last seen in Syria, taking out an ISIS leader."

"Well, that's good. He's still on our side by the sound of it."

"No. He killed the ISIS leader on behalf of a Saudi Prince who lost a cousin in a rebel attack. He was paid to do it."

"He's a mercenary."

"Looks like it. He's been off the radar since he assassinated that ISIS leader, and Interpol had assumed he'd gone into hiding."

Howard rubbed at his eyes, feeling exhauster. "What has Sarah got herself into?"

"I don't know, but if her daddy has Krenshaw, it's because somebody else is paying for him."

"Any background on Krenshaw yet?"

"Not much. I've requested his work records from World Health Alliance who employed him during his time in Africa. They haven't gotten back to me yet. He's been back in the country for two years and has held senior posts in the NHS the entire time. There's nothing to suggest he's dangerous."

Howard huffed. "Believe me, he's dangerous. I stood there and watched him inject an innocent woman with HIV."

"My Lord."

"Yeah," said Howard. "We need to get this guy, Jessica."

"I have Mandy and Mattock checking out Krenshaw's home and his office at Whiteknight, to see if we can find any clue as to what his next move might have been. I'll keep working on Sarah's daddy, see if I can figure out where he might be operating out of. I ran the plates on one of the black vans, but it came back as a stolen Nissan. They'll probably shed the plates as soon as they get chance."

Howard cursed. "I swear, if I get a hold of Sarah..."

"Don't assume she's on the wrong side of this. We don't have the facts yet."

Howard sighed. "No, you're right. At least Krenshaw is out of action for now. I would hate to think he was still at large with a dirty syringe full of whatever he planned on unleashing next. Whiteknight hospital is a nightmare, Jessica. Two hundred people dying in agony, dozens already dead. Krenshaw planned on infecting a children's hospital with HIV. The man is capable of anything when it comes to his mission. He wants the UK to see the suffering of Africa first-hand. He thinks his work will result in money and effort being diverted to finding a cure for all of these diseases."

Jessica moaned. "He's a martyr. There's no worse kind of madman."

"I know. He doesn't want anything but to carry out his mission. If he manages to get free, there's no limit to what he might do."

"Then let's just hope that whatever Sarah is doing works out for the best."

Howard thought about Sarah for a moment. He had worked with her for less than a month, but he knew that as much as she was aggressive and unhelpful, she was a good person deep at heart. She had a strong instinct to protect the innocent, but she also hated the United Kingdom for what it did to her. If she was with her father there was no way of knowing what she was involved in or what she was thinking. If they were both carrying a grudge towards their country, there was no telling what they might do.

Howard had an idea. "Jessica, don't focus your efforts on Sarah's father, focus it on Sarah herself. If we can work out what happened to her — how she disappeared — we might be able to figure out how and why she ended up with her father."

"But we already searched high and low for her," said Jessica. "We couldn't find anything. You, yourself, followed every lead you could find."

"We assumed then that a remnant of Hesbani's crew was involved with her disappearance. Now we know different. Look at known associates of Major Stone, particularly the men who deserted with him. If we can find anything on them we might be able to link it to Sarah and find out where she is."

"Okay, Howard. I'm on it. You stay safe, okay?"

"I'll do my best. Just get back to me as soon as you have something. I want to put a stop to this before Sarah ends up doing something she'll regret."

"Sarah never struck me as a woman who regretted anything."

"Then you don't know Sarah at all. The woman I knew was nothing but a list of regrets. Let's not give her any chance to add to it."

CHAPTER THIRTY-NINE

That had been Howard, she was sure of it. He'd been standing there only twenty-metres away from Sarah, watching while she helped kidnap a man. A man he, too, had been after. What did the MCU want with Krenshaw? Was she impeding a government operation by intervening and getting to the doctor first? Did she even care?

Sarah sat up front with her father in the first of the two black vans, staring at the back streets as they slunk away from the main roads.

"Did you get a look at that man in the car park," her father asked. "He saw your face. You should never got out of the van without a mask. What the Hell were you doing?"

"I didn't think. I was just trying to help. Your men were making a scene, and excuse me if my wits aren't that sharp. I've been locked up with nothing to do for four months."

"There are no excuses for mistakes. You've compromised this entire unit. That man looked like a police officer."

"He's MCU," Sarah said. "I know him. He knows me."

Her father punched the top of the steering wheel. "Damn it, Sarah. My unit can only exist if it fades in and out of the shadows. If you've been recognised then your MCU boyfriend has something to work with. It's not like it would be hard to get a positive ID on a face like yours, even if he hadn't known you already."

Sarah looked away, out of her window, anything to avoid the burning glare of her father. "He isn't my boyfriend. I worked with him for a couple of weeks at most."

Her father glanced at her for a moment, then stopped the van at the edge of a side street. Before he spoke he let out a disappointed grunt. "If you've been ID'd then we need to get this mission done quickly and disappear. There's no going back for you now, Sarah. You can't change your mind because you know too much now about me and my men. If I let you leave, they can use you to get to me."

Sarah frowned. "Who exactly would be trying to get to you? What have you done?"

"My duty," he said. "A grievous crime in this day and age. I'm serious, Sarah. You're in this now. This is your life. The choice has been taken away from you. Do you understand? You can't go back to your old life."

Sarah grunted. "I don't have an old life to go back to. This isn't about my choice being made for me, though, is it? It's about your choice being made. You're stuck with me now. You can't get rid of me, even if you want to."

Major Stone glared at her so hard that she shrank in her seat. "Sarah, there's always a way to get rid of someone, even a daughter. Don't forget that."

Sarah opened her mouth to speak but dared not. She felt like she was sitting beside a great venomous lizard ready to strike at the slightest movement. Was there any love her father held for her at all?

He pulled away from the curb and headed back out onto the main road. Twenty-minutes later, they were back at the warehouse's courtyard, where they parked up next to the bright red e-type Jaguar. The courtyard was enclosed and hidden from the roadside, which made the warehouse an excellent hideout — for that, Sarah realised, was what it was. Everybody got out of the vans and Dr Krenshaw, clutching a briefcase tightly to his chest, was bundled into the warehouse. There he was taken away by her father and a pair of men she had yet to speak to.

"He's getting your old room," said Ollie.

"Then I hope he doesn't fancy watching the telly."

Ollie didn't understand her comment — how could he? — so he just smiled and headed off.

Rat came up to her a minute later, the expression on his face far less kind. "I hear you're with us for the duration. Good. Gives me time to get a little payback."

Sarah rolled her eyes like he was nothing but a mere irritation. "You should be thanking me. I was going to kill you."

"I'm not as easy to kill as you think, sweetheart."

"All men die the same when you cut their throats. Maybe next time I won't aim for your shoulder."

Rat sneered and walked away.

Sarah milled around the warehouse, glad to be alone for a while. From all of the oily workbenches, she assumed the warehouse had once been concerned with some kind of assembly. The odd scrap of metal here and there further suggested that this place once housed bored employees fitting things together. Now it was a staging area for a team of ex-SAS. How things changed. Six months ago, she had almost had her life on track. Now she felt utterly directionless. Her father's orders were the only thing steering her, and that was not necessarily something she was comfortable with. She held no great love for her father, had not known him well enough to have such depth of emotion, yet there was a yearning inside of her, a deep desire to gain the respect — if not love — of Major Stone. It was fantasy, most likely, but the little girl inside of her couldn't let it go. After all that had happened, a hug from her daddy could mend so much, yet the thought of it happening felt childishly naive. Her father was a brutal killer, not a hugger.

It was a while before the others began filtering back to the main floor of the warehouse. Sarah took the opportunity to make the acquaintance of the rest of the group. The black man she'd beaten up upon her escape was named Rupert, of all things. He was embarrassed about the incident more than angry and admitted that her ruse of insanity had utterly bewildered him. For a hired killer, he was friendly, but there was an air of regimentality to him that suggested he was an institutionalised military man. Men like Rupert could not go back to ordinary life. There were two other men. Graves, a man who was older than her father by at least a decade, but his wiry frame and leather skin only added to his aura of lethality – like a wizened cobra. Spots was a much younger man, with the worst acne Sarah had ever seen. He smiled more than Graves did but not by much. Both men oozed with the coiled menace of warriors-on-standby, ready to strike out and kill at a moment's notice, just waiting for their next order. They were brutal soldiers; elite grunts.

Sarah made her way over to Ollie, who she deemed the least likely to suddenly attack her. The man seemed out of place amongst the others, less a soldier and less a killer. He smiled at her warmly when she approached him. "Hey, Sarah. You doing okay?"

"Just a bit Alice in Wonderland, you know?"

"Curiouser and curiouser," he replied.

"Exactly. So what are we going to do with the doctor now that we have him?"

"Ask your father. He tells us what to do when he needs us to do it. We don't ask questions."

Sarah frowned. "You don't ask questions? Why would you not want to know what you're fighting for?"

"I know what I'm fighting for," he said. "Your father. I'm not ex-SAS like the other guys, never even served, but I'm just as willing to jump into the flames for what I believe in."

"If you never served, then how do you know my father?"

Ollie smiled at her as if he admired her questioning nature. "I'm an old friend of his, but I was never in the forces. I was a teacher."

Sarah almost barked at him, so unexpected were his words. "You were a teacher?"

Ollie chuckled. "Yes, I was a teacher. I went to teach in Sri Lanka in my early twenties, married a local woman, Darla. She was a teacher, too. There was a long civil war going on in Sri Lanka, back then. The insurgents were the Tamil Tigers. One day they decided to take our school hostage in order to make demands of the Government. The government refused to even negotiate and a firefight ensued. The Tamil Tigers, used the children as human shields and barricaded the windows. We were trapped there as hostages for three days. Even when they cut off the water and electricity, turning the building into a sweating furnace, the Tigers did not submit. They were prepared to die before giving themselves up. Eventually the school burned. My wife didn't make it out of her classroom. I was trapped in another part of the building but managed to get out. When I finally got to her, she was already dead."

Sarah felt her left eye twitch, setting off a flare of pain in her scarred eyelid. "I'm sorry," she said quietly. "Seems like everywhere you turn these days there are terrorists wrecking lives."

"It wasn't the Tamil Tigers who killed my wife," Ollie told her. "It was the government retaliation. They firebombed the entire school and let it burn. They wanted to kill the rebels more than they valued the life of their children. About half of us made it out alive, but the rest were left to burn. Nowadays, the Sri Lankan government boasts about how they are the only modern nation to entirely oust its terrorists. But the truth is, the terrorists are the ones in charge."

"I'm sorry," said Sarah.

"Anyway," Ollie continued cheerily, despite the sadness in my eyes. "I moved back home and resumed contact with your father. He gave me purpose; a chance to eliminate the types of men who killed my lovely Darla. I'm not a born killer, Sarah, but I've turned my hand to it pretty well. In fact, I quite enjoy it. I don't know what that means for my soul."

Sarah understood the quenching pleasure of revenge and patted him on the shoulder. "Our soul isn't in jeopardy when we kill bad people. It's in jeopardy when we stop protecting the good ones."

"Alright, men," Major Stone barked, marching onto the warehouse floor. "Gather up."

Everyone stopped talking and assembled.

"Well done on another successful mission," he said. "We have the doctor safe and secure and I've just gotten the clearances we need to get him — and us — out of the country."

"We're leaving?" said Rat unhappily, now favouring his shoulder again and letting the pain show in his voice. "We only just came back home."

Major Stone shot him a stony glance. "Your home is this unit, Rat. You gave up any entitlement to a home when you defected, as did I. Unfortunately, my daughter has been ID'd, which means we need to disappear for a while. Once we complete our mission and get out of the country, the heat will die off and we will come back."

Sarah looked down at the floor as angry glances shot her way.

"So, where are we going, Major?" asked Ollie in a tone that suggested he had little problem with having to leave.

"We're heading to Libya. We'll land in Tripoli and head along the coast to Tunisia where we can pose as tourists and soak up the sun for a while."

There was a quick cheer and suddenly Sarah didn't feel so bad anymore. In fact, a bit of sunbathing sounded pretty good to her, although she wasn't so sure her face and gender would make life easy in the more rural parts of the country. There was one other thing on her mind. "I thought Dr Krenshaw was wanted by the South African government. So why are we heading to Tripoli?"

Her father turned his glare to her and once again made her feel tiny. "Which is why they are having their people collect the doctor in Libya. South Africa doesn't want to advertise their involvement in an unsanctioned manhunt. It's a lot easier to conduct ourselves quietly in a place like Libya."

Sarah was quiet.

Her father straightened up and lifted his chin. "Right, clear off, you lot. Our flights are at 0600 from Heathrow, so get your socks on by 0400."

Everyone dispersed.

Her father marched away and Sarah went after him, asking, "What do we do once we get to Libya?"

Major Stone turned on her and bore into her with his emerald eyes. "I need for you to understand something for me, Sarah. You do not ask questions. I give orders and you follow them. You are a soldier now, not my daughter, so when I dismiss you, do not chase after me and start demanding to know things I have elected not to tell you."

Sarah growled. "Are you capable of being anything other than an arsehole?"

"I'll let you have that one, because you're new. You don't want to see what happens next time. Now get out of my sight."

Sarah clenched her fists as her father — her superior — marched away into one of the offices. When she finally calmed down enough to walk away, Rat was laughing at her. He was too far away to have made out the words, but he could obviously tell she had just received a dressing down.

"You won't get any special treatment around here," he said.

"I don't need any," she said.

"I would've been the first to help you settle in if you'd been a little nicer to me. Then you went and stabbed me, you bitch."

Sarah marched up to Rat and stood right in his face. He wasn't afraid of her. In fact, he was snickering with delight.

"Say that word again," she said.

"You think you're something really hot, don't you? Don't forget I watched you rot in a cell for four months. I know you're nothing but a weak, ordinary woman. You won't last with us. We're men."

Sarah grinned, repressing a sudden urge to bite the man's face and listen to him squeal. "And don't forget I saw how weak and stupid you are. You were the guard who let me escape. I played you like a fucking flute."

"Shut up, you ugly bitch."

Sarah smashed her elbow into Rat's collarbone, right where she had stabbed him earlier. He hit the floor, bellowing as she kicked him in the stomach.

"I did warn you," she said, looking down at him. "I always warn you."

Ollie came up beside and moved her away. "You're not making any friends," he said to her privately. "Rat doesn't look like much, but he holds grudges and follows them through. Be careful."

Sarah shrugged. "What's the worst he can do?"

Ollie wasn't joking when he spoke. "He can put a bullet in your back the next time he's supposed to be watching it, and I would hate to see that."

Sarah looked over at Rat, who had gotten back to his feet and was glaring at her. If he wasn't an enemy before, he was now.

"Why do you even care?"

Ollie became flustered before he managed to answer. "Guess it's just nice having someone new around. Gets a bit tiring being surrounded by vicious killers night and day."

"I'm a vicious killer," she said.

Ollie nodded. "Less vicious, and that makes you a saint around here."

Sarah chuckled. "What have I got myself into?"

"A dysfunctional family."

"Yeah," she said. "The Manson family."

CHAPTER FORTY

The Earthworm was abuzz despite the late hour. Since the MCU had its funding renewed, a major recruitment operation had been put into place. The tail section of the facility was now fully manned by twenty-eight data analysts who used the very latest in technology. Their surveillance capabilities were on par with America's NSA and the hardware it ran on was newer than anything NASA owned. In less than a year it would be obsolete, such was the nature of surveillance technology.

The Earthworm's middle section housed the infirmary, the dorms, and a host of offices and training rooms. Any member of MCU could access this area, but Howard kept on going until he was at the head section, where only Level 1 operatives could enter. He pressed his thumb against the scanner and went inside. It was like entering the belly of a great beast. Soft lighting merged with the blinking switches of whirring computers and all four walls were lined with monitors displaying graphs, charts, and various other readouts. In the centre of the electric grotto was the MCU's senior team: Director Palu, Strike Team Leader Mattock, and Dr Jessica Bennett. Howard, too, was part of that leadership team.

Jessica got up and hugged him, not unusual since they'd worked closely together over the last few months. "I'm glad you're okay," she told him. "You sounded bad on the phone."

Howard gave her an affectionate pat on the arm. "It's not pretty at Whiteknight. I prefer traditional terrorists who just blow things up. At least that's quick and final. The people I saw at Whiteknight are suffering, not knowing if they're going to live or die. Krenshaw was going to give an even more protracted death sentence to a bunch of children. He was going to infect them all with HIV."

"Have we confirmed that yet?" Palu asked him, looking grim yet indefatigable as ever.

Howard nodded. "I got the call from the lab ten minutes ago. The tests were positive, which means Dr Hart, who was trying to help me, might be infected."

Jessica obviously saw how devastating that fact was to him, because she ushered him down onto a chair as though he were an invalid. "HIV is very treatable these days," she told him, "and there's no guarantee Dr Hart will be infected anyway. Early treatment might prevent the virus taking hold."

Howard nodded. "I hope so. Let's just catch Krenshaw, then I'll feel better."

"That's the plan," said Palu. "And we have leads to that effect."

"Is it true you saw Sarah?" Mattock asked Howard.

"Yes."

"Blimey. I was sure the lass was dead. Glad she's not."

Howard was glad to see Sarah alive, too, but not under such circumstances. "We don't know what she's involved in. She helped kidnap Krenshaw."

"If she's really with her father," said Palu. "Then it can't be anything good. We've received some unofficial reports from local Intel that Major Stone hasn't just gone rogue, but has allied himself with our enemies. Our Iranian ambassador was assassinated eight months ago at a time when Sarah's father was rumoured to be in the country. A local resistance group swears Stone did it. The resulting turmoil led to the embassy being abandoned and our people ousted, something the Iranian government no doubt enjoyed immensely."

"I know Major Stone," said Mattock. "Served under him in Afghanistan and Iraq. He's an unlovable sod with barely a care for anyone, but he lives by his honour. If he's gone rogue, then it's for a reason he deems valid. If he's helping foreign governments, it's because he thinks it's for the greater good. His men will be following him because they believe in whatever cause he has sold them."

"Sarah, too?" said Jessica.

Mattock nodded. "It's her father. As much as he's a cold-hearted sonofabitch, it's obvious the poor girl loves him."

Jessica frowned. "Don't think 'poor girl' is an appropriate way to describe Sarah Stone. She has bigger chestnuts than you do."

Mattock grinned. "Bloody right she does, but she's a good egg deep down, I know it. Whatever monkey business her father's into, she's probably just been dragged along for the ride. Especially after what one of the analysts showed me."

"What?" Howard quickly asked.

Mattock nodded at Jessica. "Show him."

Jessica tapped a command into the laptop in front of her and one of the wall-mounted monitors started playing a video.

"We did what you told us to do," Mattock explained. "We ran checks on all of Major Stone's men who went AWOL with him. We got a hit on an active mobile phone at the time Sarah went missing. It was unregistered, but we ran voice analysis against all of Major Stone's men and managed to match a phone call from Corporal Patrick Rattiger. His military record reads more like a rap sheet. At the time of his desertion he was up for court martial, accused of slaughtering unarmed prisoners taken from the ranks of a Taliban outshoot. He cut off both their hands and left them to bleed to death from the stumps. The mobile phone we traced is dead now so we can't track it, but on the day Sarah went missing, Rattiger made a call outside Forest Glade Cemetery."

Howard recognised the name immediately. "That's where Bradley was buried."

Bradley was a former colleague who had died during a previous mission when the Earthworm was attacked. He had been intending to quit but never got the chance.

Mattock pointed. "This is a CCTV feed from an office building across the road. Look at the top left of the picture."

Howard leaned forward. "That's Sarah! She was at Bradley's funeral?"

"Looks like it," said Jessica. "I don't know why she didn't come join the rest of us."

"Maybe she was planning to," said Mattock. "But watch what happens."

Howard was agog as he watched Sarah's father appear, flanked by two brutish men. Sarah didn't see them until it was too late. She was struck on the head and bundled into the back of a familiar-looking black van, gone before she even knew what was happening."

"Her father abducted her? But why?"

"We don't know," said Palu. "Nobody currently knows what is going on with Major Stone. He is a completely unknown entity since he went rogue. Sarah, however, is still one of us, until we know otherwise. I don't care how brief her time on this team was, she helped us, and without her efforts the MCU would be no more. We owe her."

Jessica sat back in her chair and folded her arms. "I agree. I did everything I could to find her, but this is the first chance we've gotten to find out what really happened to her."

"I'd like to bring the lass back into the fold," said Mattock. "She'd be much better off with us than her old shite of a dad."

"Then what's our next move?" asked Howard.

It was at this point that Palu smiled. From his laptop he brought up some info on one of the monitors. "The phone that led us to the cemetery stayed in use for another three days. Listed here are the location that calls were made from. Many are from within Greater London."

Howard scanned the list and looked for something to jump out at him. "Are any of these rural areas, or maybe even industrial parks?"

Palu went back to his laptop and spent a few minutes without saying anything. Eventually, he spoke. "There are none rural, but there were six calls made from an area named Leeson on the outskirts of Watford. It's listed as having several warehouses and factories in the vicinity."

"Any of them abandoned?"

Palu tapped in some more commands then looked up with an eyebrow raised. "Yes. M.Hickman Springs has been listed as untenanted for over eighteen-months."

Mattock looked at Howard. "You thinking it's some sort of hideout?"

"If Major Stone is a wanted man he needs somewhere to lay low. This warehouse might be where he's going to ground between missions."

Mattock put his hands on the desk, went to stand up. "I'll get a team together."

Howard waved him back down. "No. I don't think we should go in hard. I don't want to risk Sarah being a casualty. I'll go in alone."

"No, you bloody won't," said Jessica, more partial nowadays to British slang than her own American. "You don't know how many men Major Stone has with him. It's a foolish idea."

"If Sarah is there, I can get to her in private and try to find out what's going on. If Krenshaw is there, going in quiet is far better than provoking a firefight. If he unleashes another of his diseases then at least only I run the risk of being exposed."

"You're assuming Krenshaw is free to act. He is a captive of Major Stone."

Howard grunted. "I'm not assuming anything after what I've been through today."

Mattock still looked ready to get up and leave, but he waited for Palu to speak. "Your call, guvnor."

Palu let out a deep sigh and knitted his fingers together. "This has been a very long day for you, Howard. Are you sure you wouldn't like to sit this one out?"

"I'm fine. I'll rest after I speak with Sarah." He took a deep breath and let it out in a long, drawn out sigh. "Look, I brought Sarah into the MCU, and if she's in trouble then it's my fault. I need to get to her."

Director Palu shook his head. "You're not going alone. Take Jessica with you as back up and stay in radio contact with Mattock's team who will remain close by. The moment things even look like they're turning sour, Mattock moves in."

"Jessica doesn't have the experience for this," said Howard.

Jessica didn't react because she probably agreed with him. She'd only been on a handful of missions, and none had gone flawlessly, although she had handled herself well in all.

"I know Jessica is a little green," agreed Palu, "but if you're having to watch out for her, you're less likely to take risks. That's why she's going with you."

Jessica spoke up now. "I want to see Sarah safe and sound as much as you, Howard. You need backup."

"Okay, fine, but I'm leaving now, so get ready."

"I'd suggest wearing a vest," said Mattock. "Major Stone's men are trained warriors and I wouldn't be the least bit surprised if they're well-armed."

"Yes," said Palu. "I expect you all back here alive, so prepare for the worst."

Howard got up and went over to the door. "One thing you can never prepare for is the worst."

"Then prepare for lots of highly trained psychopaths trying to kill you," said Mattock.

Howard smirked. "Now *that* I can prepare for."

He left, taking Jessica with him.

CHAPTER FORTY-ONE

Sarah lay on a cot bed in an oily room full of sharp edges. Perversely, she missed the comfort of the mock bedroom her father had held her in for the four months prior. Originally, the cot bed had been side-by-side with several others in another room, but Ollie had dragged it into a separate room for her to get some privacy away from the men. She didn't know if it was a condescending gesture or one of kindness, but she couldn't deny that she would not have enjoyed sleeping next to the likes of Rat. Not that she could sleep particularly well on her own either. In the windowless darkness, she couldn't even make out her own arm in front of her. It was cold and her skin was grimy, both things non-conducive to sleep, yet she had managed a few hours during the early hours of morning and was fading off again.

Before she had chance to sleep more, she was eventually snapped awake from the gruff holler of her father's voice. She sat up on the bed, disorientated and groggy. The back of her throat and nose seemed fused together and her eyes wept with tiredness, but she was a solider, and as any soldier was trained to do, she shook the cobwebs free and got her head in the game. She pulled on her boots and slipped out into the warehouse's main floor, where she realised that she was the last to arrive. The other men noticed her tardiness but said nothing. Her father, however, glared. The group were all dressed in their civvies, ready to blend in with the crowds.

Dr Krenshaw had been brought before them and looked remarkably well for a prisoner. Despite his ordeal, he was smartly dressed and still had his briefcase. The man's colourless eyes were unmoving above the bony crags of his cheeks and for a moment he took on that familiar corpse-like appearance. This was the man MCU wanted, which meant he was dangerous. She had helped a fugitive escape custody and was now about to smuggle him out of the country.

Rupert nodded to Sarah and handed her a bottle of water, which she swigged from gladly. Spots and Graves blanked her, standing to attention already as they eagerly awaited instruction. Rat, as always, shot daggers at her. His shoulder was patched up beneath his shirt, causing a bulge, but he no longer favoured it. The glazed look to his eye was probably due to whatever strong painkiller he had also taken yesterday.

"We won't be coming back here," said Major Stone. "So if you want it, bring it. Ollie has our exit packages. Get your papers and be ready to leave in ten."

Sarah hung back while the men gathered around Ollie. The last time she had served alongside men like these, she had been their captain. Now she attempted to remain unnoticed, feeling completely out of her depth. When the group dispersed, Ollie nodded at her to come over. He held out a bundle of papers, which she took, surprised to see that it was a passport with her face and first name but a different last name — *Reid*.

"It's fool proof," Ollie told her.

"How did you get these so quickly?"

"One of your father's contacts in the city. I went out and got them while the rest of you slept."

"You must be knackered?"

Ollie smiled. It wasn't just his hair that was grey but his entire face, yet he seemed to beam bright whenever he smiled, and he had the same glinting emerald eyes of her father. "I haven't had a good night's sleep in ten years."

Sarah ran a finger over her scars. "Yeah, I get that."

Banded together with the passport was a one-way ticket to Libya and a credit card in the name of Sarah Reid. Whoever her father's contact was possessed impressive speed and skill.

Dr Krenshaw headed after her father as he marched towards the warehouse's exit and Sarah frowned, thinking the so-called prisoner should be tied up or under guard. Her father was walking with Krenshaw casually like an old friend. They even seemed to be chatting.

"What did Krenshaw do?" Sarah asked Ollie.

"Made a bunch of people sick. Did you catch the news about the Ebola outbreak in Reading? That was him. I hear your mates at the MCU are after him."

Sarah nodded. "I ran into one of them. Krenshaw must be pretty bad if MCU are hunting him down."

"He's just about the worst," said Ollie. "The type of coward who relies on viruses and diseases to do his dirty work deserves to be put down."

"So what the hell are we doing with him? Why are we getting in the way of his capture and punishment?"

Ollie laughed and patted her on the shoulder, leaving his hand there and saying, "For the money."

Sarah screwed her face up. "There has to be more to this than money."

"Not really. Money allows us to be choosier with our next mission. We can't always fight the good fight, Sarah."

"There *is* no good fight if we help men like Krenshaw evade capture."

"Life isn't black and white. I wish it was because then I would know if I was one of the good guys or one of the bad. Tell you the truth,

I think I might be a little bit of both, but my intentions lean in the right direction. I'm sure you understand that."

Sarah hated to admit it but she did. "I guess we should just try to be more good than bad."

Ollie headed off in the direction her father had gone. Sarah realised she was the only one left in the warehouse now and considered the prospect of staying behind. Sure, Howard had seen her and she had impeded his operation, but she knew the man. Howard would listen if she went to him, but doing so would betray her father. If she did that, she wasn't so sure she would get to carry on living. She was under no illusion that her father lacked the ability to show affection, but she had begun to feel that he could at least grow to respect her. Betraying him now would undo all she had accomplished in the last twenty-four hours.

She just couldn't do it. Her father had served his country a lifetime longer than she had and it would be wrong to second-guess his motives. He said he was doing what was right, and she had no reason to doubt him. Killing bad guys had been her father's entire life, placed ever above his own personal desires. Major Stone deserved trust, not just from her but from anybody who ever served under him.

Sarah swallowed her doubts and hurried out of the warehouse, where everyone else was gathered in the floodlit courtyard. The sky overhead was black and the wind whistled through the battered drain-pipes of the building. Krenshaw climbed inside the back of one of the jet black vans of his own volition, a leather briefcase clutched tightly against his chest. Rat and Graves hopped in beside him. Ollie took the driver's seat of the second van while Spots and Rupert jumped in the back and pulled closed the sliding door.

Sarah's father came up beside her and motioned to the long-snouted e-type Jaguar. "You're riding with me," he said.

"Wow, okay." As a child, Sarah had not even been allowed to look at her father's prized classic, so to be getting inside of it was an honour, yet she couldn't help but bring something up. "A little conspicuous, don't you think? Aren't we about to flee the country?"

"Plates are false and the car is registered to a ghost. It's more conspicuous to be driving around in a pair of black vans that have already been spotted by the MCU, which is why the men can go ahead and we'll follow behind."

"I'm honoured to be in the non-expendable car," she said.

Her father grunted. "Don't be. I know that if my men get captured they won't speak. I want you with me."

Sarah rolled her eyes. "God, you can't consider me as anything but a liability, can you? Is it just because I'm a woman, or is there more to it?"

"It's just because you're a woman."

Sarah's mouth dropped open, but anything she was about to say was cut off by the roar of the Jaguar's engine. The two black vans headed out of the courtyard and her father began to follow. They were just about to head out onto the main road, when they were forced to slam on the brakes.

Three black Range Rovers skidded in front of the courtyard's exit, blocking any escape.

Major Stone gripped the steering wheel tightly. "Damn it! It's your friends from the MCU. Did you contact them?"

Sarah growled. "No, I didn't."

Sergeant Mattock and a group of men she didn't recognise leapt out of the Range Rovers and immediately aimed their assault rifles. The sides of the two black vans opened up and Sarah's father's men leapt out and opened fire. Krenshaw scurried into cover near the warehouse but couldn't get inside since the door had locked behind them. Under the harsh glare of the floodlights, he looked once again like a grimacing corpse.

Sarah ducked down beneath the dashboard. Her father opened his door and slid out into cover behind it, pulling out his Colt Commander and letting off a series of eardrum-busting shots.

"I'm not armed," Sarah said, flinching as more gunfire rattled the very air around her.

"Why the hell not?" her father demanded.

"We're heading to the airport," she said. "I didn't think guns were appropriate."

"In the glove compartment."

Sarah flinched as the windscreen shattered and rained glass on her. "What?"

Her father bellowed at her. "In the goddamn glove compartment."

Sarah fiddled with the catch and yanked the glove compartment open. Inside was a Mac-10 and two magazines. An unwieldy and unsophisticated weapon, but perhaps the ideal thing to keep hidden inside a glove compartment. She punched one of the magazines into the handle of the snub nosed machine pistol and crawled out into cover. Bullets pinged the classic Jaguar and she could almost hear her father wince every time it was hit. The MCU were raining down Hell on them. Major Stone's men gave the same in return, letting off round after whizzing round from their own pistols and revolvers.

Sarah snuck a peek over the car door she was kneeling behind and saw Sergeant Mattock. He was aiming shots carefully, not, as yet, lining up kill shots, seemingly more interested in suppressing the enemy than killing him. It was a stupid tactic and not something Mattock would not do ignorantly. Ollie was blind-firing around the back of one of the vans, squeezing his eyes shut in fear as he pulled the trigger on a shiny revolver. He might not have been the solider the rest of the men were, but he was keeping his ground all the same. Rat was an entirely different animal. He was smiling gleefully as he unloaded round upon round into one of the MCU's black Range Rovers. Spots and the older man, Graves, had similar expressions on their faces, but her father's final man, Rupert, was completely blank, returning fire like a robot and showing no emotion of any kind. Sarah had seen men like him before, the ones who entered a daze under fire and let their training take complete charge of their actions. A pure soldier — not good, not evil, just thoroughly trained to do a job.

"Sarah, take the blighters out," her father shouted at her from the other side of the car, bellowing through the open interior.

Sarah looked at the Mac-10 in her hands and realised she was in a firefight. She couldn't stay in cover while her comrades took heavy fire. She was going to have to get involved. It was time to commit herself to her new family. She leapt up and pulled the trigger.

Mattock didn't see her until it was too late.

CHAPTER 14

"Sarah, dinner in one hour."

Eight-year-old Sarah ran through the living room and into the kitchen where her mother stood in front of the stove. The air was hot, from both the bright sunlight coming through the window and from the heat coming from the cottage's Aga. They had lived there less than a year, after having decided to lay down roots, instead of moving all over the world with her daddy. Sarah loved her new home and had even made a friend at school. Her name was Holly and her parents were farmers. Sometimes, Sarah even got to spend time with her daddy, who was home at the moment for two whole weeks. Her daddy was a brave soldier.

"Can I go out and play until it's ready?" Sarah asked her mother.

"Of course, but don't wander off into the road. Stay by the house."

"Can I have a biscuit to take out with me?"

Her mother turned away from the bubbling pot on the stove and looked at her daughter. She rolled her eyes. "Go on, then. But only one."

Sarah hopped up in the air and then ran over to the biscuit tin, taking out her favourite chocolate digestive. She took a bite immediately but took the rest out into the sunshine with her. She decided to play beside the house, in the pebbled driveway that was flat enough for her to kick her football around. Her father was always on at her about how little girls should not be interested in playing football, but she loved running around and kicking it far more than playing with her dolls or the plastic kitchen she had got for Christmas.

Her daddy was in the garage, where she was not to disturb him. She often heard him talking in there on the phone he had at the back, inside a little office, but she never understood what he was saying. He spoke lots about places with funny names and about men that sounded scary. She always stayed away from the garage.

Her daddy's car was parked out on the drive, where it always was when he was home. When he was gone it would sit under a big blanket in the garage. It was really long and a shiny red and looked lots of fun to drive in, but she had never been allowed to go with her father when he drove it. Sometimes her mother was allowed to sit in the passenger seat, but never Sarah. Sometimes, when her father wasn't looking, she would run her hands over it and enjoy the feel of the cold metal.

The lure of the car called to Sarah now and she crept towards it, marvelling at the shafts of light that bounced of its long, round nose. It was a Jagwa and worth lots of money. One day, when she was grown, Sarah was going to own a Jagwa, too. She took another bite of her biscuit and then placed her hands along the bonnet, slowly sliding her fingertips along the bodywork. The hood was made of fabric and could be pulled down in the sunshine, but right now it was up. She ran her fingers along the rough material and found it extremely soft and supple compared to the stiffness of the bodywork. She wondered what it would be like to ride along with the top down, visiting the seaside and seeing the seagulls overhead.

"Sarah!"

Sarah flinched so badly that she tripped and fell backwards. A shard of pebble bit into her palm and made her cry out. Her father appeared, towering over her, and dragged her back up to her feet.

"Look what you've done," he shouted while shoving her head in the direction of the car.

She was already in tears, but she was able to see what she had done. On the roof of her daddy's Jagwa was a chocolaty handprint. Her whole body shook in fear, and she wet herself when she realised what was to come.

"Look at you, you stupid girl. You've pissed yourself." Her daddy's hand struck the back of her legs, making her scream. He hit her two more times before he let her go. By that time, her mother had exited the cottage and was standing on the drive.

"What's happened?" she said meekly.

Sarah's father growled. "The little brat covered my car in chocolate."

"Don't be so hard on her. She's a child."

"Get her out of my sight. If I see her again tonight I'm leaving. Do you know how little time I get to myself? Do you know what I do for this country and this family?"

Sarah's mother said nothing, as she rarely did. She just shot her husband a hateful stare and pulled her sobbing daughter in close. A year later she divorced Sarah's father and they went to live in a cramped flat in the city by themselves. Sarah never missed that old cottage even once. And she missed her father even less.

CHAPTER FORTY-TWO

Mattock took the bullet without fuss, as was his manner. Howard had watched in horror when Sarah leapt up out of cover and fired off a spray of bullets, sending Mattock reeling to the ground, hit and bleeding.

"We have to get out there and help," said Howard. He and Jessica were sitting inside the rearmost of the three black Range Rovers, doing nothing. Mattock had insisted that he and his team secure the perimeter before Howard and Jessica went in to retrieve Krenshaw and Sarah, but when they arrived in the area, the scout team observed Major Stone and his men gearing up to leave. Going in quiet was no longer an option. They had eyes on Krenshaw, out in the open, and he was attempting to flee. Palu gave Mattock the okay and Howard and Jessica were demoted to spectators. Now, Mattock was down, shot by a woman who less than six months ago had fought side-by-side with him.

Howard didn't need to wait for Jessica to agree with him. She was already out of the car and firing off shots across the bonnet, sending a rodent-featured man into hiding. Howard slid across the seats and exited out on the same side, using the long vehicle as sufficient, though imperfect, cover. Major Stone and his men were well-armed, but with handguns and machine pistols. Mattock's team carried recent-issue L85A2 British assault rifles. It was a one-sided affair until Sarah blind-sided Mattock.

A leather-skinned, older man popped up from behind the door of one of the black vans and Howard aimed and shot. A spray of red mist erupted from the back of the man's skull and he fell down in a lifeless heap. At the same time, Jessica emptied her magazine and managed to wing a stocky black man in the neck, sending him face first into the open where bullets whizzed over his head. The wounded man screamed for help, begged for it in fact, but was soon shut up. Major Stone leapt out of cover and fired a shot from his hefty pistol, reducing his own man's skull to mush. He was back down in cover before anyone could take a shot at him.

"Give up, Major Stone," shouted Howard. "Two of your men are down and we have you pinned. You'll die here if you don't give yourself up."

The gunfire stopped. Although Mattock was down, his men still numbered seven and were more than happy to keep shooting at fish in barrels, yet they waited now to see if a ceasefire ensued. It didn't appear that Major Stone was going to come out with his hands up, but Howard's words had apparently made the man pause to think.

Howard decided to push the situation. "Do you want your daughter to die, Major Stone? Sarah, I know you can hear me. Mattock's dead. I watched you shoot him when he wasn't looking. Do you really want any more bloodshed? Do you want to shoot me next, or how about Jessica? We were on the same team not so long ago, Sarah. What happened to you?"

There was no answer, so Howard placed his gun down on the bonnet of the Range Rover and stood out from cover, his hands raised above his head.

Jessica grabbed at him but missed. "Howard, what the hell are you doing?"

"Major Stone, I am unarmed, and you are an honourable man. I know you won't shoot me. Come out and talk. Or send your daughter.

I'd like to ask her why she just murdered a man who thought very highly of her."

There was more silence and for a moment Howard worried that Major Stone and his people had managed to scurry away someplace, but then he saw the shifting shadows of someone moving behind the torn-up Jaguar. Dr Krenshaw was also still cowering in the background, trying to hide behind a steel wheelie bin.

"Just stop this, Major Stone. It's Dr Krenshaw we want. You needn't have got involved in this."

"Too late now," someone barked in a deep voice that Howard assumed belonged to Major Stone. He hoped he could appeal to the man's honour, or to his daughter's loyalties, but it seemed neither were about to listen.

There was a flash of movement beneath the floodlights.

Something arced into the air, a small black shadow against the glare of the flood lamps. It was followed by three more shadows. Each of them began falling to the ground, right towards Howard and the MCU strike team.

Howard turned and ran, screaming, "Grenades."

CHAPTER FORTY-THREE

As the MCU strike team leapt for cover, and a series of hellish bangs rocked the air, Major Stone grabbed Dr Krenshaw roughly by the arm and re-opened the warehouse door. Rat and Spots were both uninjured and quickly hurried into the warehouse behind Major Stone. Sarah stood, not knowing which way to go. Did she give herself up to MCU, and face what she had done? Or go after her father and get herself in deeper?

For a moment it seemed like the frightened part of her was going to win out and surrender, but then she thought about her time in the army, the death of her husband and unborn child, and of course the loss of her face. She thought about all the men sent to their deaths on missions they barely understood, and thought about all of the success the MCU had gained off the back of her efforts. She was tired of being used by others, only to be spat out. Her father would be no different, but at least he could get her out of the country. Choosing to follow her father offered the chance at a new life. Giving herself up to the MCU offered a return to her old one.

What made up her mind was Ollie. He'd stopped to wait for her by the door, looking afraid, yet determined. Sarah bolted inside the warehouse with him and caught up with the other men. Her father glanced at her and seemed like he was about to smile, but he quickly killed the expression before it had chance to take on life. Rat was less happy to see her and snarled and bared his teeth. "Shouldn't you be back there with your boyfriend? He seemed to know you pretty good."

"Yeah," said Spots, speaking to her for the first time that day. "If you've set us up I'll gut you."

"Agent Hopkins doesn't know me at all," she spat back at them. "If he *did* then he would be running the other way, same as the both of you should do."

Rat smirked and resumed his hurried march forward.

Spots, however, gave her a brief smirk and seemed to reconsider his position. "Just like your father."

Ollie came up on her back, grabbed her elbow lightly. Their running had turned into a determined march. "What a mess. How the hell did the MCU know how to find us?"

Sarah looked at him in surprise. "You mean you don't think *I* had anything to do with it?"

"If you sold us out to the MCU you would be with them now, wouldn't you? Instead you took a shot at one of them and escaped."

Sarah thought about how she had opened fire on Mattock and quickly shook the image from her mind. She liked the cockney hard man a lot and was ashamed at what she'd done. But done it she had and there was no chance to change it now. She needed to get the hell out of there.

Her father led them through to the opposite side of the warehouse, and once there he opened up what would once have been the public entrance to the street. A solitary vehicle sat in the small car park outside: a banged-up, 90s era BMW. He unlocked the vehicle and told them all to get in. Rat sat up front, while Ollie, Sarah, Spots, and Krenshaw wedged themselves uncomfortably into the back. The interior stunk of sweat and cigarettes and the roof cloth was ripped and hanging.

Spots had Krenshaw on his lap, still clutching his briefcase like a life preserver. Ollie sat on one side, while Sarah sat on the other. Major Stone started the engine and they took off, pretty powerfully for such an old car.

"Always good to have a few old bangers in reserve around the city," her father said as though he were trying to teach a lesson. "Never know when you're going to need an alternative escape plan."

Rat was hooting with laughter in the front seat and checking the magazine on his cumbrous Desert Eagle. A gun as powerful as his cock was probably small, Sarah assumed. Spots sat almost sideways on the seat in order to keep hold of Krenshaw and it made it hard for Sarah to see Ollie on the opposite side of the car. Sarah managed to glance over at him through the tangle of limbs and heads. "You okay, Ollie?"

He smiled at her. "I'm fine, just not a natural when it comes to the nasty stuff. I'll be okay."

"You look like you're about to shit yourself," Spots muttered.

"It's just adrenaline," said Krenshaw, a little calmer now as time passed. "It will wear off."

Sarah sneered. "Wow, did you learn that at medical school? Or at nursery when the teacher told you not to get over-excited?"

Krenshaw looked at her like one of his diseases, something to be studied and handled carefully, yet that did not stop him from talking to her with a voice dripping with disdain. "I find that stating the obvious to a patient is more comforting than explaining the complex. I was merely trying to be help calm your colleague down. You're rather rude."

"Compassion, huh? That's an odd emotion for a terrorist. Did you show compassion for the people you infected in Reading? Or South Africa?"

The doctor seemed confused. "I'm sorry, South Africa?"

"Heads down," shouted Major Stone. "Plods up ahead."

They all ducked down until they were told they had the all clear again. When Sarah looked out of the window, she saw that they were leaving Shepard's Bush, most of the way, already, to Heathrow.

"How will we get through airport security?" she asked her father. "MCU will have posted an alert to every airport in the country."

"Of course they will, but we're not going to be travelling as ourselves. Our false passports will get us out of the country without issue."

Sarah couldn't see how it was possible for a group of fugitives to move through an airport unmolested, but she had no option but to follow her father's lead. She glanced sideways at Krenshaw and felt revolted.

"How can you be so calm?" she asked the doctor. "You're wanted for the death of dozens of people."

He grinned. "Oh, I assure you that the number will exceed mere dozens when my virus takes its full course. Did you get to see my work in Reading? It was quite beautiful, don't you think? The West is slow to appreciate the rest of the world's suffering, but I did them the favour of speeding up the virus's infection rate and lethality. Whiteknight Hospital will be littered with the dead before the week's end. Maybe then, Westminster and the rest of Europe will actually start taking notice of what the 3rd World has had to endure for decades. Perhaps some of the money this country spends on mind-numbing television, to forget the World's suffering, will go where it is actually needed. Do you know that the NHS spends three-million-pounds per year on unnecessary plastic surgery? This country would rather throw money at plastic tits than a Congolese orphanage full of dying children. It spends sixteen-million a year on obesity. Can you believe it? All that money going to gluttons while nearly eight-hundred-and-seventy million people starve worldwide. It is time they took notice. Unfortunately, they will not do that until their charmed lives are endangered."

Sarah shook her head in disbelief. "You actually think you're one of the good guys, don't you?"

"History is full of martyrs. Even Jesus was hated in his time."

Ollie chuckled. "Talk about a deity complex. I suppose you think you'll live forever?"

"Alas, no. My AIDS is quite severe and I doubt I'll make another year."

Sarah flinched. "You have AIDS?"

"Get the fuck away from me," said Spots, trying to shove the doctor off his lap.

Krenshaw's demeanour changed and he spat his next words with venom. "You see? The way you all flinch proves my point about the stigma and disregard the West holds for Africa's suffering. I am, in actual fact, not infected with AIDS but dying of throat cancer — something you can't catch, so calm yourselves. My mission was decided upon, however, not for my own health concerns but for the poor people of Sub-Saharan Africa and beyond. When I watched a child of five die of untreated bronchitis, I decided that the human race was failing. No one mourned this five-year old girl, you see, for her parents had both already died of other untreated conditions. Her body lay in the dirt for hours, passers-by looking through her as though she did not even exist, until I took her in my arms and buried her in a field. I never knew her name and no one will ever know where she was buried. Her life was deemed no more important than that of a mayfly, and so I deemed the life of those who failed to help her no more significant than a mayfly. My revenge is a revenge you have wrought upon yourselves, and when I am no more, buried in some field the same way that nameless girl was, there will be hope and promise in the world again. Nothing unites humanity like fear. Let the whole world fear AIDS, Ebola, and every other 3rd World bogeyman. Perhaps then, we can find compassion that reaches beyond our own selfish borders."

The sun was coming up and Sarah blinked her eyes. She had nothing else to say to Krenshaw, for as much as she found him abhorrent, she understood the power of violence and intimidation to attain one's goals. What the doctor was suggesting might just have worked, too, if he'd been able to continue, but there was no part of what he was doing that was in any way right. As much as the world was off-kilter, there *were* people who cared about the plight of the 3rd World and Sarah was sure the number would grow of its own accord, without having to be beaten into compassion. Better to give willingly, she thought, than to have one's charitable arm thrust out forcefully.

They pulled into Heathrow airport ten-minutes later and finally got out of the cramped BMW. They straightened their backs and moaned with relief. Her father went around to the boot and put on a smart woollen overcoat and pulled up the collar. The rest of them had to face the cold morning in what they were wearing. When they got going, her father didn't bother locking the car, for they would not be going back to it, he told them.

"You did well," her father said to her as they walked towards the terminal.

"You killed Rupert," was all she said in reply, having wanted to bring it up the whole time in the car. "Your own man."

"He was dying. Even if he wasn't, he wouldn't have wanted to be captured."

Sarah huffed. "Captured. You speak like we're at war."

"We are. Maybe if you had continued to serve, you would have seen it more clearly. Was the needless bloodshed not clear to you when a British missile killed your husband? Thomas, wasn't it? What a crime he committed, being in the wrong place at the wrong time. I'm sure our government owned up to their crimes profusely. Made amends?"

Sarah shook her head. "They swept it under the rug."

"Of course they did, as they have with uncountable other vile acts before and after. If only you'd seen the things my men have seen, Sarah. Believe me, Graves and Rupert were ready to die for the mission. I did only what I would ask for myself. I would rather die than be brought in by this government's vipers."

"MCU aren't like that," she said. "They're good people trying to help. I know."

"Then perhaps you shouldn't have shot one of them. They might have had you back. Nice shot, by the way."

Sarah frowned. "What do you mean?"

"You winged my old sergeant. Barely even touched him to be

honest. The Sergeant Mattock I knew would have carried on fighting, but perhaps he's not quite as tough as he used to be."

Sarah had deliberately aimed at Mattock's hip, not wanting to deliver a kill wound and not wanting to risk a ricocheting round in his centre mass. She had spread her shots wide, yet grazed Mattock a little deeper than she'd meant to. The shock had turned his lights out and left him looking dead. When Howard had spoken out to her, he obviously thought as much, but there was no way she was going to kill Mattock. He was a good man. But shooting him was bad enough for her not to want to remain in the UK a moment longer than she had to.

Major Stone had them all spread out as they entered Terminal 1. They would be suspicious as a group, so were ordered to check in separately, before gathering back as strangers at the departure gate. Their guns were all left back in the car, a treasure trove for a would-be thief and impossible to get through security. Sarah and her father took charge of Krenshaw and headed off, while Rat, Spots and Ollie split off. As most major airports usually were, Heathrow was teeming with people. It was a place without circadian rhythms — no day, no night, always busy. Airports held a lot in common with Casinos in that respect and they both had the same depressing air of exhaustion and weariness.

Sarah stood beneath the passenger information screens and scanned for her flight details. Her father nudged her and told her not to bother. "We three aren't checking in as civilians. This way."

Sarah followed after her father, making sure Krenshaw stayed close by. She was still surprised by the doctor's compliance and astounded that he seemed in no way concerned. In fact, he seemed a little excited as they headed towards a security checkpoint at the far end of the check-in desks.

Her father pulled a small pouch the size of an old VHS tape and a shiny document from his coat pocket and handed it over to the unsmiling gate officer. Sarah noticed that the small pouch was stamped with the words: DIPLOMATIC BAG. The same thing was printed on Krenshaw's briefcase, she noticed.

Sarah was impressed when the three of them were ushered through without so much as a cursory inspection, and even Krenshaw's briefcase passed without scrutiny. The only think that got even the slightest look were the grotesque scars on her face, but that she was used to.

"We're all travelling under diplomatic papers," her father explained a moment later. "Our official business states we are in charge of a doctor and dangerous samples needed immediately by the World Health Organisation."

"In Libya?" asked Sarah.

Her father shrugged. "It won't need to pass deeper inspection. We're already through."

"How did you get diplomatic designation?"

"High friends in high places. The people I am working for have a great deal of clout."

"So why do they need someone like you? You're just a thug."

The comment earned a scolding glance and her father's emerald eyes drilled into her as he spoke. "Great minds don't always have great stomachs. A driver might steer a car, but he will go nowhere without tyres on the ground. I am a tyre. I carry the drivers of this world where they need to go, and if anything gets in my way, I roll right over it."

"I thought you were done taking orders?"

"I'm done being expendable and I'm done following orders I don't agree with."

"You still sound expendable to me," she said, not sure why she was so intent on harassing her father. "Tyres get replaced. I would much rather be the driver. The driver is in control of the tyres and they go wherever he wants them to, until they wear out or burst."

Her father's ruddy cheeks quivered.

"I think," Krenshaw interrupted, "that Major Stone merely used a flawed analogy. Truthfully, he is more like a syringe; surgically precise with the ability to penetrate while barely being noticed. While doctors may think themselves gods, it is the unassuming syringe that makes things happen."

Major Stone nodded at Krenshaw in what seemed to be thanks.

Sarah cursed. "What the hell is going on here? Why is our hostage jumping to your defence? And why does he seem so perfectly content to be in our custody?"

"Because he knows what's good for him," said her father flatly.

"How? South Africa will be far less gentle than we are."

"Trust me, daughter. I know what I am doing and Krenshaw understands his role. Everything is going as intended."

Sarah glanced at Krenshaw who seemed to be smiling, if a little confused by the conversation. Her father was looking at her now in a way far softer than she was used to, and it crumbled her resolve. He seemed to be asking her to trust him, which was something he never would have cared about in the past.

She grunted, flapped her arms in defeat. "Not like I can turn back now, is it?"

"Good. Let's go and get eyes on Rat and the others, then we can kick our heels for an hour until the flight."

They headed into a wide eating area and sat down at an open plan cafe, ordering some drinks and snacks from the tired-looking waitress. There, they were eventually joined by Ollie, Spots, and Rat. Rat, as usual, sneered at her on sight. Ollie was far gentler and gave her a pat on the back where she was sitting alone in the corner.

"Everything go okay?" he asked her.

She nodded. "Yeah. Too easy, in fact."

"That's what's so great about your father; he makes tough work seem like nothing."

Sarah studied Ollie as he sat down opposite her. There was something very comforting about his face, maybe even something familiar. He was a soft man doing hard work, and he didn't wear it well. "I don't get you," she said. "How did a man like you ever end up with a man like my father?"

"Obligation."

"Why are you obligated to my father?"

Ollie seemed put off for a second, as if he had spoken without thinking. It became obvious when he tried to backtrack. "He's... allowing me to make amends for what happened. My wife."

Sarah nodded. "I don't believe that's all of it. You're not a violent man — not by choice, anyway. My father rallied you to his cause, made you take up arms, but how did he do it? How did he even find you?"

Ollie sighed. "I've known your father a long time, Sarah, although he pretty much disappeared off the face of the earth when he joined the army. We grew up together as kids, me a few years older. Even back then, your father was tough. At school he would keep the bullies off me, even though he was younger, even when they towered over him. He was my little bodyguard. It wasn't because he loved me — I'm not sure he's ever loved anyone." He looked at her then and realised what he's said. "Sorry. It was because of his sense of duty that he protected me, and his sense of duty is unbreakable."

"Why did my father feel a sense of duty to you?" she urged.

Ollie began fiddling with his fingers and looking down at the wedding ring he still wore. "Your father never met my wife. We had already lost touch long before then, but when he found out she had died, he came immediately to visit me in Sri Lanka — again, probably because he felt a duty to do so. I found out that he had been in Sri Lanka a few times before, helping the government fight the Tamil Tigers, and he told me that he had once even looked in on me. He had seen how happy I was and felt his duty to me was complete, which was why he never reached out to me. His life and my life were too different to gel comfortably, so he stayed away. But when Darla was killed he had to come and make sure I was okay."

"I still don't understand," said Sarah. "I never heard him speak about you once. Who are you to my father?"

Ollie shook his head and exhaled slowly, before looking at her and saying, "I'm your father's brother, Sarah; your uncle. My wife was your auntie and the four-year-old son I had snatched away in the attack on my school was your cousin."

Sarah reeled back in her chair. As a young woman she'd had no one. Her mother died young and her father had shown no interest, yet all this time she had had a kindly uncle, a man who had now been turned to killing upon her father's influence. She floundered for a moment. "I...why didn't you ever...I..."

Ollie shrugged. "I didn't know you existed until six months ago. Your father and I had gone so long without contact that I grew old in the time since you were born. I'm sorry I kept it from you, but your father..."

Sarah nodded. She understood very well how her father had a way of making people dance to his tune, even if he was playing nothing but wrong notes. "It's okay," she said. "I'm glad I know."

"Okay, men," said her father almost half-an-hour later. "The plane is boarding, so let's move."

Everyone finished their drinks and got up. When they began heading towards the gate, Sarah noticed that Krenshaw had forgotten his briefcase. He'd left it beneath one of the tables. She headed back to get it.

"Leave it, Sarah," her father shouted.

Sarah pulled her hand away from the briefcase and frowned. "Why?"

"Because it's set to go off."

CHAPTER FORTY-FOUR

When Mattock sat up minutes after the attack, swearing and shouting, Howard almost wept. The man was part of his family and, while they may not always agree, there was a mutual respect between the two of them, as there was between all members of the MCU, which was what made Sarah's actions extra sickening.

"She'll pay for this," Howard growled as he knelt beside Mattock. The grenades had made short work of the three MCU Range Rovers and Major Stone and his people had got away; but no one was seriously hurt and that was the important thing. The only people to die were two of Major Stone's men. Men they were currently in the process of IDing.

Mattock gritted his teeth, pulled up his shirt and protective vest, and examined the damage. Blood was everywhere and Howard felt himself growing ever more furious at what his former colleague had down, but Mattock just ended up chuckling.

"Just a flesh wound," he said. His hands were covered in fresh red blood but he seemed entirely composed. "I'm bloody embarrassed for passing out like some pansy. She barely hit me."

"We have a team on the way," said Jessica. "We'll get you back to the Earthworm where I can take a proper look at you."

"I'm fine, luv." Mattock managed to climb to his feet, barely wincing. "Just point me in the right direction and I'm dandy."

Howard placed a hand on the man's shoulder. "I've got this now. Wherever Sarah and her father have gone with Krenshaw, I'll be the one to find them."

"Go easy on Sarah," said Mattock.

"Why? She shot you."

"If that bird had wanted me dead, I would be, mate. She shot to wound — barely at that. She's not too far gone. Reach out to her."

Howard thought about things for a minute. He'd seen Sarah shoot a gun before and it was true she knew what she was doing. There was little chance she would've missed the mark with a full magazine from a machine pistol. Perhaps she *had* intended merely to graze Mattock, but she still helped Krenshaw escape. After what he had witnessed at Whiteknight Hospital, that was unforgivable.

"Hey, I've got something over here."

Howard looked around to see one of the strike team members, a young blond guy called Wilder, shouting him over. At the man's feet was the body of an elderly gentleman, looking much frailer in death than he had in life only an hour before.

"What do you have?" Howard asked the young officer.

"I found these." Wilder handed over what he had, then said, "Oh, that I had wings like a dove! I would fly away and be at rest."

"I'm sorry, what?"

"It's from the bible. Seems like Major Stone and his people are planning on flying."

Howard frowned, then took the passport and ticket from the strange young man and ran his eyes over them. The name on the documents would probably be false, but the destination was Libya. It was pretty obvious Major Stone planned on getting out of the country.

"Can I leave you with this?" he asked Jessica, meaning the mess that was the three disabled Range Rovers and a handful of disorientated MCU agents.

"Yes, of course, but where are you going?"

Howard showed her the tickets. "There's no way I'm letting Krenshaw leave this country. I'll shoot him if I have to. They could still be heading for Heathrow."

Jessica sighed. "Wait for backup, Howard."

"Backup is here, licking its wounds." Mattock glared but Howard continued. "Major Stone's flight leaves in less than an hour. Someone needs to go, right now. It will take too long to assemble another team and make a plan."

"Then have Palu ground all flights to buy us time."

"We do that and Major Stone goes to ground. Our best chance is to pin him down at the airport where he can't escape, but I need to move now."

Jessica nodded slowly, knowing him well enough not to bother arguing. "Then go," she said. "But bloody be careful."

Howard put a call in to Mandy, MCU's most skilled driver, and told him he needed to get to the airport quickly. Ten minutes later, he was picked up by a sleek black Jaguar. Mandy spoke little, so Howard stated his destination. "Get me to Heathrow."

CHAPTER FORTY-FIVE

Mandy dropped Howard right outside the entrance to Terminal 1. Howard wasted no time rushing inside. He flashed his badge at airport security and was let through the check-in barriers without question. Palu had called ahead and airport security were ready and waiting to help in whatever ways it could. The leader of the security force was a short man named Tariq Riaz.

"What do you need from my team?" asked Tariq obligingly.

Howard told him. "I need a radio that I can reach you on. We are looking for a small group of men, and a woman with a badly scarred face."

"Should be easy enough to find. Here, take my radio. Set it to 'wide' and you'll broadcast to every member of the team. There are over a hundred of us in total, more than enough to handle whatever you need."

"Good. I don't want anyone getting hurt, so I'm going to try and get a view of the targets before deciding how to proceed. I'll head to the gate and see if I can get eyes on, but if your men spot the targets first I want to know right away."

Tariq nodded. "Of course. Is it true that one of the men you're after is responsible for the Ebola epidemic in Reading?"

"How did you know that?"

"The news. I just got an update about a firefight in Watford involving MCU and a man suspected for the Reading outbreak. Now, here you are, another MCU agent, chasing down a group of dangerous men."

The local police must have arrived on scene after Howard had left Mattock, Jessica, and the others. Once the local police got wind of anything, it went straight to the attention of the press.

Howard smiled. "You're smart. That's good. And you're correct, one of the men is responsible for Ebola Reading. He is extremely dangerous, so help me catch the sonofabitch."

"I'll do whatever you need me to," said Tariq.

Howard rushed off towards the appropriate departure gate, staying close to the walls and trying to merge with the various groups travelling. It was difficult to blend in with the various families, businessmen, and lovers en route to exotic destinations. He was the only one not wearing sandals and t-shirt, or formal business attire; not to mention that those travelling to Libya specifically wore the traditional gowns of that country. Howard stuck out like a sore thumb in his cheap suit and tie. He decided to roll up his sleeves, ditch the tie, and unbutton his collar. He also took the time to quickly purchase a baseball cap from one of the stores. It wasn't a perfect disguise, but it didn't need to be.

A ringing sound made him flinch and he realised it was his mobsat. He answered the call and it was Palu.

"Howard, the remainder of Mattock's team are finishing up with the local police and will be on your location in twenty. Can you hold things that long?"

"No. The flight to Libya leaves in twenty minutes. I have airport security helping me, so I will have to bring the targets in myself."

Palu breathed down the phone. "Okay. Are you armed?"

"Yes."

"I suspect Major Stone will be also."

"How would he get a gun through check-in?"

"Diplomatic papers. The entire team here at the Earthworm is working the Intel, and as part of that we ran every single check-in confirmed through Heathrow in the last hour. Three people were passed through as diplomats. Two men and a woman. When one of the analysts called up to confirm details, the officer in charge described the female in the group as 'a freak'. Upon elaboration he said that her face was badly scarred."

Howard exhaled. "Sarah. Pretty hard to hide with wounds like hers."

"If they got through with diplomatic bags they could be in possession of anything. Be careful. We've been getting more Intel that tells us Major Stone has been behind several recent attacks against UK assets abroad. I'm not sure he's simply gone rogue. I think he's turned against us entirely."

"Is there anyway Sarah doesn't know what her father is doing?"

Palu breathed down the phone again. "I don't see how. She engaged in a firefight with Mattock's men and helped Dr Krenshaw escape. We both know that Sarah has a grudge against this country. Her father might have convinced her to join his cause under the mutual flag of disenchantment."

"I still don't know what Major Stone's cause even is."

"I think it has something to do with Syria," said Palu. "I still have analysts working the angles, but Major Stone went rogue during a mission in Syria to take out an ISIS arms cache. He successfully found the site and lased it for an airstrike but never returned radio communication after the bombs dropped. Command assumed he and his team were lost, but they popped up a month later and assassinated that ISIS leader. Just be careful, Howard. Major Stone is one of the deadliest men this country has ever had at its disposal, and somehow we pissed him off."

"His daughter, too," said Howard. "I'll call in when I have something."

"Roger that."

Howard got moving again. He was approaching an eating area, surrounded by cafes and fast food chains on both sides. It was then that he saw Sarah sitting and drinking coffee. He had to suppress the urge to draw his gun right then and there, but it would have been the wrong move. With Krenshaw, Major Stone, and the other men, Sarah's group equalled six — all of them deadly.

Howard grabbed the radio Tariq had given him and called it in. "All targets located in," he looked around for a landmark, "area between Lorraine's Bistro and Lanier's Italian Cafe."

"Sending a team to you now," came Tariq's reply. "Over."

"Roger that." Howard moved into the doorway of a small amusement arcade and peered around the edge of the wall next to a fruit machine. There were people all around and the last thing he wanted to do was test the theory that Major Stone was carrying a weapon. The targets were all finishing their drinks and preparing to get up, though. The call had been made for their flight and they were able to board. That could not happen. If Major Stone made it onto the plane, he had the option of taking the pilot hostage and forcing a take-off. A man of Major Stone's abilities could drop himself down in the middle of the Sahara and disappear with the winds.

While Howard was still deciding what to do, Sarah broke off from the departing group and travelled back towards the cafe. For a moment, Howard thought she had spotted him, but he soon realised that she had forgotten something. Sarah bent down to pick up a briefcase from beneath one of the tables but recoiled when he farther shouted at her.

Howard heard the words exactly as Major Stone said them: "It's set to go off."

Howard had no choice anymore. He stepped out from cover and pointed his gun. "MCU, freeze!"

CHAPTER FORTY-SIX

"**M**CU, freeze!"

Sarah dove down behind the coffee counter while her father and his men dropped down into cover behind various upturned tables. Meanwhile, several hundred innocent travellers started a stampede at the sight of Howard's gun. Like frightened antelope they ran and leapt for cover and filled the air with their terrified screams. Sarah stood amongst the flowing river of people and felt lost, confused. The fact that Howard had managed to relocate her and her father was a shock, but it was probably inevitable since they'd been forced to flee so suddenly from the warehouse. Carefully laid plans were the ones that left most clues when gone awry.

"Sarah, get down on the floor," shouted Howard. "There's only two ways out of this airport, dead or alive, and unlike you I don't enjoy shooting former colleagues."

Sarah scurried from her hiding place over to where her father was hiding behind a table. Howard could probably have drawn a bead on her then, but she had counted on him not wanting to pull the trigger just yet and she was right. He didn't fire and she made it over to her father in one piece. Major Stone was unzipping the diplomatic pouch he'd been carrying in his coat pocket. Sarah was flabbergasted when he pulled out two pieces of a handgun, as well as a loaded magazine. He slid the detached barrel onto the handgun's frame and slapped the magazine into the bottom of the grip. It was a small gun, a bright silver Ruger.

"This is madness," Sarah told her father.

"This is war," he said. "There's no distinction between madness and sanity, only what's necessary. We need to get that briefcase."

"Why, what's in it?"

"Krenshaw's lifework, and it's going to go off right in our faces if we don't get it and reset the timer."

Howard shouted at them again. "Major Stone, Sarah, give yourselves up. None of you are getting away."

Sarah glanced around between the upturned tables and spotted Ollie — her Uncle — crouching next to Rat and Spots. Ollie gave her a sad look that suggested he regretted the situation as much as she did. They had crossed a line and neither could see a way back.

Krenshaw made a break for it. The skinny doctor raced across the cafe floor, heading for his briefcase, but stopped short and spun as a bullet struck his chest. He collapsed onto one of the tables and lay still.

There was more panic as the innocent bystanders abandoned their hiding places and broke for greater safety. The gun shot had been like a starting pistol and now they were all off their lines and running for their lives.

"This is the final warning," Howard bellowed in a voice more commanding than Sarah remembered. "Come out, hands up and empty. This ends now."

Major Stone leapt up and took a shot at Howard, missing the target by a hairsbreadth. The bullet lodged in the concrete of the wall and sent Howard leaping back into cover.

It was then that Airport security guards surrounded the area. Each carried a Heckler & Koch MP5. Enough firepower to rip a man to confetti.

Sarah went to put her hands in the air and surrender, but her father grabbed her shoulder and yanked her back down. "Don't disappoint me," he said to her, with a pulsing rage in his emerald eyes.

"We're done for," she said. "This is a colossal screw-up. I don't know what I'm even doing here with you. You never gave a damn about me and I followed you into Hell anyway. I'm an idiot."

"You are my daughter," he said. "And we will make it out of this, I promise you. You're one of my men now and I don't intend on seeing you die until you're ready."

Sarah shook her head. "You never made a single promise to me that you kept. You've been helping Krenshaw all along, haven't you? We didn't capture him, we rescued him."

"Krenshaw is a means to an end. His work is what matters. My mission is to make sure that what is inside that briefcase serves its purpose."

"What purpose?"

There was more gunfire and Sarah flinched, before carefully peering over an upturned table. To her utter surprise, Rat had managed to get the jump on one of the airport security guards and had taken his weapon, which he quickly turned on the rightful owner and two of his colleagues. Spots was quick to scurry over and grab one of the dead men's fallen MP5s and join the firefight.

The air filled with the sound of a dozen jackhammers.

Sarah's father beamed, the first time she'd ever seen such an expression from him. "See?" he said. "There is no situation my men can't handle."

"We're outnumbered five to one," she said.

"Exactly, they won't know what hit them."

Sarah's father leapt up and expended what was left of his handgun's ammo and sent a handful of guards into cover. It bought enough time for Spots to pick up another fallen MP5 and toss it to him. He caught the weapon easily and fired off a stream of rounds in one smooth motion, taking out another guard. The rest of the airport's vanguard visibly shrank as they realised they were losing men fast. Rat's assault had been quick and brutal, rocking their confidence and keeping them from advancing. Now, barely a single one of them dared to break cover.

Sarah stayed where she was. Things had got completely out of hand. She had just wanted to flee the country, start again. She had never wanted this, never wanted to fight her own country. As much as she hated what her government represented, she bore no malice to the people who fought under its banner. They were innocent cogs, like she had once been.

Finally, she broke cover, but not to fight. Instead, she hurried towards the briefcase, intending to stop whatever was inside of it from getting out. Was it Ebola, or something worse? The thought of something invisible yet deadly made her skin crawl. She wasn't trained to fight something she couldn't see. Put a man in front of her and she could pull the trigger, but a virus...

Whistling, snapping gunfire continued overhead as Sarah crawled along on her belly. She heard wounded men cry out in pain but was sure none of them were her father's men. Rat, Spots, and Major Stone were ex-SAS and could eat airport security guards for breakfast, as they were doing now — but they couldn't fight forever. This was a suicide mission. How had her father changed so much? What had happened to him to make him disregard his life?

She was just about to grab the briefcase, and could even hear something inside ticking, when a hefty boot caught her in the ribs.

"What are you doing, sweetheart?" Rat appeared in her view and kicked her hard again in the stomach. He fired off a few rounds from the two MP5s he was now holding akimbo, before ducking down into cover beside Sarah and grinning in her face.

Sarah tried to catch her breath but Rat punched her in the mouth and sent her into a daze.

"Told you I was going to get some payback, you ugly bitch," he said in the raspy tones of a predator.

"My...my father will kill you."

"Maybe, or maybe he won't give two shits. Way I see it, we're all dead anyway. The only thing that makes our lives mean anything is what's inside that briefcase. What do you plan on doing with it?"

Sarah winced and tried to catch her breath. "I plan on stopping it going off."

Rat laughed. "Good luck with that. I don't think it has an 'off' switch. *You* do, though." He prodded her mouth with the muzzle of one of the MP5s. The hot metal burned her lips, and then her tongue as Rat forced it between her teeth. "Say goodnight, sweetheart."

"Goodnight."

Rat's head exploded and Sarah yelled out in horror as his body toppled sideways.

Ollie looked down at Sarah with that same regretful smile he'd had on his face earlier. "I told you he'd stab you in the back as soon as he was supposed to be watching it. Come on, we have to give ourselves u-"

Ollie flew backwards and landed hard on his back. The colour red immediately began to bloom on his chest.

Sarah slid over to him on her belly. "Shit! Ollie. Ollie, no."

Ollie shook his head, gasped, then managed to talk in a groan. Blood appeared at the corners of his slowly moving mouth. "I knew about...the briefcase. I know and it's...wrong. You need to stop your father, Sarah. Darla, she would be...s-s-so ashamed."

"Shush," said Sarah, but Ollie was already dead. She didn't kiss him or weep, she had barely known the man; perhaps that was the biggest tragedy of all. There was still time to make it right, though. If Sarah had never got involved in any of this, then her father and Kren-shaw would have carried out their plan without a hiccup. Her involve-ment, however, had screwed everything up, and there was still time for her to put a stop to her father's mission.

Sarah turned away from Ollie and went to go back and grab the briefcase. She had to stop this.

But her father reached it first. Major Stone held the briefcase to his chest and stood up. "Everybody, cease your fire."

His voice was so booming that all of the remaining guards stopped firing immediately. They had lost so many men that they were probably eager for the bullets to stop flying.

Major Stone continued speaking. "I hold in my hands the most deadly disease known to man, engineered by the man responsible for this country's recent Ebola epidemic. My hand is on the release button. If I fall or sleep or get bored, this briefcase will open and the world's most deadly disease will escape. It will kill everybody here, as well as anyone who takes a breath of whatever air escapes into the vents above our heads. It has been engineered to survive almost indefinitely and to multiply quickly within its host. It has been set on a timer, which I have just extended and will continue to do so as long as I am alive. My men-" he looked around and saw Spots was the only one still standing, but he was bleeding badly from a wound in his stomach. His face was pale from massive blood loss. Major Stone exhaled, threw up an arm and casually shot Spots between the eyes with machine gun fire. His body slumped to the floor and Major Stone turned back to his audience. "Correction: my *daughter* and I are going to leave this airport through whatever back door is closest. Then we will enter a car and drive to safety. Once there, I will arrange for safe disposal of this virus. Do not doubt me, gentlemen, for I am entirely willing to watch this wretched world burn."

Howard stepped out from behind a cracked and crumbling pillar with his gun held up and ready. He was sweating badly. "We can't let you walk out of here, Major Stone. Not going to happen."

Major Stone nodded. "Of course. I understand. Then I suppose none of us will be walking out of here." He raised his MP5 and aimed it at Howard. It should have been enough to provoke a shot from one of the airport's security guards, but they obviously feared the virus too much to pull the trigger. "Would you prefer a bullet, Agent? Or would you like to lose your skin once the virus takes you? I offer you the courtesy of choice because you were once a friend of my daughter."

Howard put a hand up, just to reassert that no one should pull the trigger. "All flights have been grounded, Major. This airport is very easy to contain once it's on lockdown, which it now is. Your super-virus will wither and die right here where we stand."

Major Stone grunted. "Enough deaths to make the news, I assure you — and that is the point, after all. There are powerful men in this world who wish to send a message; and I am their messenger. The death of you and a handful of upstanding airport personnel will suffice, as Pyrrhic a victory as it may be. I am not a man who fails, upon my honour."

Howard lowered his gun and sighed. "What happened, Major? I saw what Krenshaw did to the people at Whiteknight hospital. Why do you want to follow a coward? Why do you want to be associated with a man like him?"

"He and I are not the same, Agent. Count the dead around you. Do I look like a coward?"

Howard looked around at all the dead bodies, men from both sides. "That's how people will remember you if you do this, Major."

"I'm SAS. Men in the SAS don't get to leave legacies. Make of me what you will once I am dead. I couldn't care less."

Sarah saw her father's finger twitch on the trigger, the MP5 still pointed at Howard. If he fired, Howard would die and the security guards would open fire. Then Major Stone's hand would fall from the briefcase and God-knows-what would be released into the confined atmosphere of the airport. She had to do something.

"Stop this, daddy. You're not going to achieve anything, don't you see? I don't want to die."

Her father looked down at her with sadness. "You are pitiful, daughter. Don't you want to die for something important?"

"No," she said. "I want to live for something important."

Major Stone shook his head. He scooped his foot around one of the MP5s that Rat had dropped when he died and kicked it towards her. "Shoot me, then," he said. "You want this to end, then be a man and finish it. Show me you have a cock."

Sarah looked down at the weapon by her leg and went to grab it but couldn't. She couldn't make her hand move towards the MP5, even though she knew that she could end this right now. She had killed men before, but she couldn't kill this one. She couldn't shoot her father.

Major Stone rolled his eyes and looked like he wanted to spit on her. "I wish I'd had a son. To think that Ollie lost a boy of four while you continue to live."

Sarah growled. "I'm not a fucking man, daddy; get over it already. But you're right, I can't shoot you." She leapt up and tackled her father around the legs, lifting him up and throwing him backwards. He fell onto his shoulders, the briefcase flailing in his hand, his MP5 firing at the ceiling. They hit the ground together and Sarah immediately started pummelling her father in the face, smashing his stern cheeks and grizzled chin, glaring into his emerald eyes that matched her own. She beamed and cackled as the blood began to escape Major Stone's mouth. "Doesn't mean I won't kick your arse, though," she screamed at him.

But it was a triumph all too short.

Her father shoved both thumbs into her eyes so hard that Sarah thought he'd blinded her. Then, he brought his legs up and kicked her so hard in the stomach that she felt a rib crack. She fell onto her face, struggling desperately for a breath. Men shouted all around her, but no shots were fired. Though she could barely see, she made out the shape of her father snatching up the briefcase and his MP5 before running away unmolested.

The next thing Sarah knew, men all around her were dragging her harshly to her feet. When her vision finally came back to her in full, she realised that the roughest hands of all belonged to her former partner, Howard. He looked at her like a hated enemy and it made her want to cry.

CHAPTER FORTY-SEVEN

Sarah didn't fight back as she was manhandled. Her arms were wrenched behind her back and she was dragged unceremoniously away from the bullet-ridden seating area to a place inside a small amusement arcade. Half of the remaining guards had chased after her father, but the rest stayed behind to clear up the mess Major Stone and his men had left behind.

"I want to speak with her alone," Howard said, marching up to Sarah until his sweating face was right up against hers. He grabbed her roughly by the arm and yanked her away from the two men guarding her.

Sarah couldn't bring herself to look her former colleague in the eye, so she stared down at the floor instead, then, when she spotted a blood-stain on the carpet, she looked at her shoes.

Howard shoved her back against the wall. "What the hell happened to you, Sarah? How did you get involved in all this?"

Sarah couldn't find her voice.

"Talk, Sarah. Believe me, I'm the last person who will be willing to listen."

Sarah forced herself to look up at Howard and felt tears run down the good side of her face. The other side lacked feeling and the ducts rarely opened beneath her left eye. "I didn't know," she said. "I...I was abducted, shoved in a cell and kept for four months."

Howard softened a little, but his folded arms made his hostility clear. "Abducted by whom?"

"My father. I managed to escape a few days ago. I was just about to get away and then...he was there, my father. He was the one who kidnapped me outside of Bradley's funeral. We got in his way when we took down Hesbani."

"Hesbani? What are you talking about?"

"Someone paid my father for Hesbani's head, but we got there first. We cost him a lot of money."

Howard frowned, kept his arms folded. "What does any of that have to do with any of this? Why were you working with Dr Krenshaw? Do you know what he has done?"

Sarah nodded. "My father said he was taking Krenshaw abroad and handing him over to the South African government for justice. I didn't know he was going to do any of this, I swear. He dragged me along and, before I knew it, I was fighting the MCU. God, how is Mattock? Is he alright? Tell him I'm sorry. I'm so sorry. I didn't mean for any of this. I just wanted to get out, start again."

"Mattock is fine," said Howard, finally unfolding his arms. "He knows you shot wide on purpose. In fact he told me to go easy on you. Not sure I could be so forgiving if somebody shot me."

"Howard I-"

Somebody shouted. "Agent Hopkins."

Howard spun around. An Asian man in a guard's uniform was hailing him from the cafe area.

Howard grabbed Sarah and took her along. He seemed to know the guard calling him. "Tariq, what is it?"

"We have a survivor."

Sarah's eyes went wide and for a moment she hoped that it was Ollie, but she was soon disappointed when she saw it was Krenshaw. Sarah forgot the situation for a moment, filled and driven by rage. She pushed Howard aside and hurried over to the doctor. Krenshaw was shot in the chest, his breathing ragged, but he was awake for now. The wound was clearly fatal; he did not have long."

"What is in that briefcase?" she demanded. "Tell me."

Despite his obvious pain, Krenshaw managed to smile. "With pleasure." He said, before coughing and spluttering. Blood seeped between his lips, but he managed to continue. "Inside the briefcase is my masterpiece, a disease so deadly it will bring the West to its knees and finally bring the world the equilibrium it needs. There will be no more 3rd World, no more elitism; just mankind's united struggle against a virus more powerful than God. This country is about to become a headless chicken. My mission may have failed, but your father will go on to strike at the heart of this country. It will be an example to the world."

Sarah grabbed the doctor and shook him, making him groan. "What is it? What is the virus and how do we stop it?"

"You don't...stop it. It will burn you from the inside. Your flesh will melt away until there is nothing left but bone and fat. I call it...the Peeling." Krenshaw's body clenched and a mouthful of blood spewed out of his mouth. Sarah tried to hold onto him, but he bucked out of her grasp and spread out on the tiles.

"He's dead," said Howard, pulling her away. "What was he talking about, Sarah? What is your father planning?"

"I have no idea. Something's happened to him. He's not the same."

The security guard, Tariq, looked at Howard and said, "Should I take her into custody? Your director has been on the line, he's sending a team to work with the Home Office in clearing this mess up. Seven of my men are dead and the whole airport is on lockdown."

"I'm sorry," said Howard. "Truly. I know what it's like to lose men, but this woman isn't responsible. She wasn't involved in the firefight. She's one of ours."

Tariq raised an eyebrow and looked at Howard with suspicion.

Howard was not deterred. "Sarah's been working undercover for MCU. Her father, Major Stone, is a wanted man and, as his daughter, she was uniquely placed to infiltrate his operation. Now Major Stone's men are dead and we very nearly had him, too. My people from MCU will clear everything up with you, Tariq, but, right now, Sarah and I need to find Major Stone before whatever is inside that briefcase gets out. The airport must be surrounded. There's no way he can get out, surely?"

Sarah glanced at Howard in confusion. What was he doing? He was lying on her behalf, but why?

Tariq stood stiffly for a moment but then shrugged. "You've been given authority here. I can't stop you from doing anything. I'll go find out where Major Stone headed after he fled." The man walked away, speaking into a radio a couple of seconds later.

"Why did you say that?" asked Sarah. "I haven't been helping you."

Howard was still red in the cheeks, but his arms lay by his sides and he no longer glared at her. "Your father is still at large, Sarah. You may still have some use. You are his daughter after all."

"Not sure that will be much help."

"We'll see. Either way, you're going to help me make this right."

Tariq returned a couple of minutes later, shaking his head and blinking slowly. "Your man escaped through a fire exit next to gate 12. He broke a luggage handler's neck on the tarmac and managed to disappear. I don't even know how that's possible. It's broad daylight and there are police officers surrounding the entire airport. Only a ghost could slip away."

"My father was SAS," said Sarah. "He can disappear from a locked room."

Howard took Sarah aside. "You've been working with your father. Where could he be planning to release the virus?"

Something popped into her head and she spoke it before she even understood what it was. "Headless chicken."

Howard looked at her. "What?"

"Krenshaw said the country was about to become a headless chicken, that my father is going to strike at its heart. My father has a grudge against the government for some reason. I think he might attack Breslow."

Howard moaned. "Great. Last year the Queen, this year the Prime Minister. You think he's heading to White Hall, Westminster, Downing Street? Are you sure about this?"

"No, but my father doesn't speak idly. If he's been making comments about the government, it's because he's planning something. Is parliament in session today?"

"I'll find out." Howard turned and made a call on his mobsat, something she remembered doing herself not so long ago. When he turned back again he had a grave expression on his face. "The house is in session all day. They're voting on foreign war policy. Breslow wants to recruit another forty-thousand bodies into the army in order to fight abroad."

Sarah straightened up, hoping she was wrong about her father but pretty much sure. "Infecting an airport with a deadly virus would have been devastating, but wiping out three-hundred MPs will make a good Plan B. We have to stop him."

Howard nodded. "We will. Nobody else is getting sick because of Krenshaw's pet projects. Not on my watch."

"We need to get into the city before my father gets there."

"Mandy is waiting by. He'll be glad to see you."

Sarah couldn't help but smile. "Is he still a talker?"

"Hasn't changed a bit." Howard's expression had turned briefly jovial, but it now turned quickly serious. "You're not off the hook for any of this, Sarah. At the moment, the only thing going for you is ignorance and stupidity, but if I find out you knew what your father was planning..."

"I didn't know," she said, "but I understand. I really screwed up here, Howard, and all I want to do is make it right. Get me to my father and I'll finish this, I promise."

Howard looked at her curiously. "You sure? This is your father we're dealing with."

"He's not my father," she said. "To be honest, he never has been. Even so, it's time for me to emancipate myself once and for all."

CHAPTER FORTY-EIGHT

Sarah followed Howard out through the barricade of flashing police cars and headed over to a vehicle she knew well. It was one of the MCU's black Range Rover Westminsters. Howard opened up the rear door and allowed her to hop up inside, while he slid into the front passenger seat beside another man. Sarah spotted Mandy at the wheel and nodded.

"Hey," she said.

Mandy said nothing but nodded back as agreeably as he was able. The thick-necked driver-slash-pilot-slash-stuntman was MCU's mechanical savant. There wasn't a motorised vehicle in the world that Manny Dobbs could not manoeuvre to within the very limits of its capabilities.

"Get us to the Houses of Parliament," said Howard to Mandy. He didn't need to say 'fast' because Mandy went everywhere fast by default. Without word, he gunned the engine and whipped the Range Rover through the police cordon, which stretched for half a mile around the entire airport. Sarah wondered how on earth her father had got away. To lay siege to the country's busiest airport, killing indiscriminately, before disappearing into dust, was a typical feat of the SAS, but

Major Stone was no longer a part of their ranks. He was even more dangerous.

The city's traffic was stirred up like a nest of bees, since news obviously spread of the terrorist attack on the airport. After Hesbani last year and the rumours of Ebola Reading being part of a deliberate attack, the residents of the capital were skittish, afraid. They had every reason to be.

Britain was a country struggling to find a new identity in the world. It was no longer a world power but neither did it fit well into a host of equals. While Europe came together as one, Britain fought desperately to remain empirical, keeping its pound and taking umbrage with any who dared give it orders. After the recent attacks, Britain would be forced to ask for help from the allies it so often spurned. If parliament were hit, then nothing would ever be the same. Sarah wondered if that was what her father wanted. Not just change, but complete renewal.

It took almost an hour to reach Westminster and Howard chatted to Palu constantly via mobsat. Crossing over the bridge towards Big Ben immediately brought back memories for Sarah, memories of Hesbani and her former comrade, Hamish. Had he truly been working for her father all along? Was his hatred for her part of the reason he had turned away from his own country?

"The traffic has held us up badly," said Howard, turning around to face Sarah in the back. "Your father had a head start on us and Palu just got word of a car theft outside of Heathrow ninety-minutes ago. He might have a ride."

Sarah asked, "Does Parliament know it may be a target?"

Howard nodded. "Special Branch is holding a perimeter, but Breslow won't convene. You know her stance on terrorism, she doesn't bend or respond to threats."

Sarah hissed. "Things that don't bend, break."

Mandy skidded up outside the Houses of Parliament and immediately two armed men approached them. Howard hopped out and showed his badge. The Special Branch officers backed off.

"Follow my lead, Sarah," Howard told her. "I still can't say I trust you."

The comment hurt Sarah, but she could find no fault in its reasoning. She had betrayed Howard, betrayed her country. She and the United Kingdom were in no way cosy companions, but she realised now that it was her home — love it or hate it — and right now it was under threat by her father.

They headed inside the Houses of Parliament and entered Confederation Hall. Immediately, they turned left towards the House of Commons. There were a pair of guards up ahead, sitting in ornately-wrought brass chairs either side of the entrance. Howard called out to them.

"Is Parliament still in session? Have you been fully briefed? Hey, stand up and answer me."

Sarah reached out and touched Howard's arm. "Howard..."

They approached the two Special Branch officers and Sarah noticed right away how their chins lay against their chests. Blood stained the top of their shirts and glistened.

Howard pulled out his gun. "Your father's already here. These men have no weapons."

Sarah stepped in front of Howard and kicked open the doors to the House of Commons, just as the first gunshot rang out. Chaos erupted throughout the tiered benches of the chamber. A flood of MPs tried to sprint towards the doors but many were mown down by automatic gunfire. They fell onto their stomachs, side by side, and formed a carpet of bodies. The remaining MPs, still well over a hundred in total, froze in place, cowering behind benches or lying completely flat on the floor. The Leader of the Opposition tried to stand tall and approach Major Stone, who stood on the Speaker's dais like a towering judge, but Prime Minister Breslow swatted the sallow man aside like a fly. She would be the one to deal with this situation, that much was clear.

Sarah's father spotted her presence and seemed surprised. "Sarah? Be a good daughter and close those doors, would you? I would hate to have to shoot anybody else."

Sarah played along and shoved the doors closed behind her and Howard. Howard had his gun levelled at her father, but it would be little match for the twin MP5s that the other man wielded. Krenshaw's briefcase lay on a table in front of Major Stone on the table in front of the Speaker's chair. He patted it and smiled.

Breslow turned on Sarah and glared. "I know you."

Sarah nodded. "My face is kind of hard to forget."

"You stopped Hesbani."

"I did."

"So why this? Why are you doing this?"

Sarah shook her head. "I'm not here to help my father. I'm here to stop him."

Breslow gave a cat-like grin and turned around to face Major Stone. "Least you raised a decent daughter, Major Stone."

Major Stone was unsmiling. "You know of me, Prime Minister?"

"I was briefed about what happened at Heathrow and warned that you may have been en route here. Bravo on gaining entry, Major. I believed the place quite fortified."

"It'll take more than a few upper-echelon civilians to stop me. If Special Branch is all you have to protect you, it's a miracle you've lived this long."

Breslow continued to smile. "You wouldn't be the first man to underestimate me, Major."

"I'll be the first to kill you, though. A woman has no place running the world of men. What could you understand of war and politics? Women exist to raise men, not dominate them. You are an abomination."

Breslow seemed unfazed by both the blatant misogyny and the pair of sub-machine guns aimed at her face. "What do you want, Major? You have just killed the Foreign Secretary and three members of the shadow cabinet. Despite what one might think, I considered them all friends."

Major Stone waved an arm around the room, making various MPs flinch as the MP5's crosshairs fell over them. "What I want is what you see: the submission of this malignant hive of malefactors followed by its complete annihilation."

Breslow nodded at the two MP5s he was holding. "Do you have enough bullets?"

He tapped the briefcase in front of him. "I have something better."

Howard took a step forward, gun still held up and aimed forward. "Prime Minister, MCU believes that the contents of that briefcase contain a deadly disease engineered by the man responsible for Ebola Reading."

Breslow looked at him. "That would be Dr Krenshaw, correct? Deceased?"

Howard nodded. "You've been well briefed."

"It pays to be, although it would seem one can never be too prepared." She turned back to Major Stone. "So, I return to my previous question: what do you want? If it is merely to kill us all then what's keeping you?"

Sarah felt a twinge of satisfaction as she watched the uncertainty cross her father's face. He obviously hadn't expected such brazenness from the Prime Minister, a woman. He gathered a hold of himself quickly, though, and gave the PM a glare so fiery that it would not have been surprising if she caught fire.

"I want the right-honourable peers assembled here to witness you admit your crimes. The people in this country need to see that our leader is no nobler than Saddam Hussain or Colonel Gaddafi were. I want to see you humbled to the lowly scorpion that you are — you and all those like you."

Breslow actually yawned then. The assembled MPs had crept out from their hiding places and were now enraptured by what they were seeing.

"So that's it," said Breslow. "You're just another disgruntled vet with a grudge against the men and women who commanded them? Did I ever give you an order, Major Stone? You'll have to forgive me for not remembering."

Major Stone spoke slowly. "Syria, September 13th, 2012."

Breslow looked at him blankly.

"There is the problem," he said in a voice more a growl than speech. "On that date, one-hundred-and-twelve innocent people lost their lives on your orders and you don't even remember. You have forgotten the bomb you dropped after I lased a target I was assured was a rebel outpost. But it wasn't, was it? You had me and my men light up a goddamn orphanage just to get one man, who wasn't even there. You wanted Al Al-Sharir so bad that you were willing to kill one-hundred children just to get him."

"You don't strike me as a man who values children, Major Stone."

"That's where you're wrong, Prime Minister. I care very much for children, for they are the only truly innocent of this world. They know nothing of bloodshed and greed, religion or politics. I even had a child myself, once. I tried to be a father for a while, was even pretty good at it. I would hold this child of mine on my lap, each night before putting her down to bed, and sing songs to her. Her beautiful little face would light up and something inside of me would light up, too. That beautiful face no longer exists, just another thing turned to scars and ashes by this damned nation."

Sarah brought her fingers to the scars on her face and suddenly felt weak. It was strange, but some ethereal feeling came over her where she could almost remember what her father was describing. She had brief snatches of sitting on a man's lap and feeling sleepy as the words of a lullaby soothed her. But as soon as the memory came it vanished. For that split-second she had had a loving father, and it had felt good.

Breslow took the floor again. "If the Intel was wrong, then it was your job to report it, Major."

Major Stone lifted his chin, staring down his nose at her. "I did report it. I saw the children thirty-seconds after I lased the building. I tried to call off the strike, but word came from above that my objections were received but overruled. Somebody high up felt that taking out Al-Sharir was important enough to drop the bomb anyway, collateral damaged be damned. That order came from you, Prime Minister."

Breslow huffed. "How could you possibly come to that conclusion? I have no hand in military operations other than sanctioning them."

"I am Major Stone. The men and women of the Armed Forces fear and respect me. I knew within the hour who gave the order. Men I would trust with my life swore that it came from the very top. Number 10 gave the order to continue with the bombing, despite the presence of over a hundred non-combatants. You killed a hundred children, Breslow. No, you have probably killed thousands since you came to power. You are a butcher. Now I will repay you for your sins."

Major Stone reached for the briefcase.

Sarah stepped forward. "Major Stone, stop!"

CHAPTER FORTY-NINE

Her father looked at her. "I need to do this, Sarah. It's time that the right people were finally made to pay, instead of more innocents."

"There are people in this room who are innocent," said Sarah.

"Ha! Do you really believe that?"

She glanced around the room, at the frightened faces of the male and female MPs. All of them wore fine suits and seemed only concerned for themselves. "Perhaps not," she admitted, "but you open that briefcase and the virus kills a lot more people than are in this room. You were going to release it at Heathrow for Christ's sake. It's madness."

For the first time in her life, her father seemed insecure. His voice lost a measure of its authority and his glaring eyes failed to keep still. "Something has to change. Releasing the virus at the airport would have rocked the foundations of the earth. There are a group of powerful men ready to rebuild a better world, but first this one has to tumble."

"You sound insane," she said.

"Not insane, just exhausted. Say what you want about me, Sarah, but I have never done anything in anger or for revenge. Every bad deed I have ever done I have done with a clear head and a sense of duty. I'd never even felt rage until after what I saw them do to that orphanage, and what they did to you."

Sarah pointed to her scars and said angrily, "Hesbani did this to me and I killed him myself. I don't need anyone to feel angry on my behalf."

"A father has no choice, and not everybody is able to earn their own justice. You are one of the lucky ones, Sarah. All that the other victims of this country's militaristic greed have is me. I will bring them their justice."

Sarah headed away from the doors and towards her father at the Speaker's dais, ignoring Howard's warning to stay back. She stood before the Speaker's chair and looked up at her father. "Killing doesn't erase killing. This isn't what you devoted your life to. In the past, you took orders, but now you're making your own decisions, which means that all of this is on you."

Her father smiled at her, then actually began chuckling. It was a sad laugh, one that came before an emotional rupture. "I admit it," he said. "You make me proud, Sarah. That's what you want to hear, isn't it? I've always been proud of you. Somebody tells you that you can't do something and you set out to prove them wrong. The SAS is just the same. I, too, spent my life doing things that other men told me were impossible. You are a lot like me, Sarah. I just wish you'd been a man. Think of what you might have achieved then. Maybe we might have truly served alongside one another. Maybe then you would not be opposing me. It is a shame."

Howard stepped up beside Sarah and lowered his gun. "Major Stone, you have served this country with honour. Don't end your career this way."

"You think history will look upon me poorly?"

"Of course."

"Guy Fawkes once tried to destroy parliament and he is remembered as a beloved martyr. I feel, in time, I will be no different, but if not, I don't care. All I care about is Breslow admitting to her crimes. If she doesn't, I will release this virus and kill everyone in this room. There is no vanquishing the beast inside this box."

Breslow folded her arms. "I have nothing to admit to but doing my duty. My obligation is to the prosperity and welfare of this nation. Every time a country imperils us it imperils itself. The blood of those Syrian orphans is on Syrian hands."

All of the MPs in the room swallowed and grew pale. No doubt they wanted to see Breslow fall on her sword so that this could be over with, but Breslow did not bow down to terrorists.

"I admire men like you," said Breslow. "You do as you see fit, and there is no shame in that, but the problem is that you're a man. You lack any sort of finesse. Like a bull you charge at the red flag and hope to gore it with your horns. You see, a woman does not charge the red flag, she holds it so that men like you can chase it blindly until you are too tired to stand. If you had been a woman, Major Stone, you might have actually been of some use."

Major Stone's face went as red as the hypothetical red flag and he raised both MP5s at Breslow. The leader reacted quickly, running and diving behind one of the benches, managing somehow to keep hold of her heels. Left, standing out in the open, was the leader of the opposition. The gangly man took the full brunt of the dual machine gun fire. His dark, sunken eyes bulged from his head and his slanted teeth turned red as blood shot from his throat. He slumped forwards onto the centre table and knocked the mace onto the floor, the ceremonial staff needed to pronounce the House in session. Sarah watched it roll along the floor at her feet and settle in a puddle of blood.

Howard aimed and took a shot at Major Stone, but missed. Major Stone returned fire and sent Howard into cover. More MPs made for the doors but were quickly gunned down. Their bodies fell and blocked the doors from being opened. Sarah stood in the middle of the flying bullets and screaming MPs and kept her eyes on her father. He had placed the briefcase down on the Speaker's desk as he wielded an MP5 in each hand. He was choosing his shots carefully, picking off the most senior members of the House with single, precise rounds. The Education Secretary lay on her back, clutching her throat and making strangling sounds. Most of the ruling cabinet were dead and a good portion of the opposition, too.

Sarah raced forwards, leaping up onto the centre table and heading towards the raised Speaker's dais at the far end, where she leapt into the air. Her father was distracted, shooting the panicked MPs whilst also keeping one eye on Howard, the only other armed man in the room. Sarah made it onto the Speaker's dais and snatched at the briefcase, grabbing it with both hands. Major Stone immediately turned both guns on her, but didn't fire. Instead he shouted, "Sarah, no!"

Sarah landed back on the floor and immediately started running.

Howard leapt up and fired, suppressing Major Stone from retaliating. Sarah made it all the way back to the doors, where she proceeded to try and drag the bodies out of the way.

"Sarah, is that you?" It was Mattock. His strike team had arrived outside in the hallway.

"Yes, it's me. The doors are blocked. My father has killed half of parliament."

"That sodding nutter. Is it over? Do you have him?"

"No, I-"

"SARAH!"

Sarah flinched, spun around, looked for her father at the dais but did not see him.

Howard was hiding in the benches of the sitting government and he nodded over to the opposite side of the room when her eyes fell on him. On the opposite side of the chamber, her father had an arm wrapped around Breslow's neck and held an MP5 to her temple. The other MPs were huddled in a group nearby.

"Put down the briefcase," he demanded. "I will not be stopped."

Sarah made eye-contact with Breslow, who seemed entirely calm despite her predicament. The huddled MPs beside her were clutching their chests and breathing heavily.

"Just go," shouted Breslow. "Get that briefcase somewhere where it can't hurt anybody."

Sarah nodded and turned back towards the doors. Mattock and his men had taken to barging it and there was a slight opening now that was growing ever wider.

"The briefcase will open as soon as the timer runs out, Sarah," her father warned, his confident voice returned, "unless I put in the code. Put it down and get away from it." He sounded almost concerned.

"This bitch is going to admit to her crimes or the whole of London is going to start bleeding from their eye sockets by nightfall."

For the first time since this whole thing began, Sarah saw fear in Breslow's eyes.

"You were always going to release the virus, weren't you?" said Sarah.

"Of course. Killing the Government isn't enough, but with no one running the country the virus will be unstoppable. The United Kingdom will become a worldwide charity case. Eventually, the virus will spread worldwide, the population will diminish and the world will start over, better."

Sarah couldn't believe what she was hearing. "You *want* the apocalypse? What if this virus wipes out the planet?"

"Krenshaw designed the virus to infect only one out of every two people. At its worst it would merely kill half the world's population, and that's nothing but a good thing."

"No virus would be able to spread unopposed," said Breslow. "We'll fight it, we'll understand it, and we'll win. You cannot hope to change anything."

Sarah heard a whisper behind her and glanced back to see Mattock's face at the door. He was poking something through the gap at her. She took it at once and quickly slid it under her shirt and into the waistband of her trousers. Her father was staring at her but hadn't seemed to have notice the exchange.

"I need you to get away from here, Sarah. That briefcase is going to open whether you like it or not. I never did much for you, but I'm giving you the chance to save yourself."

"I already have a containment unit on the way," said Howard. "We'll secure the briefcase and dispose of it. It's over, Major Stone."

"Is it? I've lost track of time. The virus could be released in the very next minute. How quickly do you think your containment unit can get here?"

Howard swallowed so loud that it echoed in the chamber.

"Give me Breslow and I'll leave," said Sarah. "You want to save me then let all of these people go and I will get far away from here."

"Sarah, I'm not negotiating."

Breslow sniggered. "How novel. A terrorist refusing to negotiate with *us*."

Major Stone growled and let off a shot into the crowd, hitting an anonymous MP in the face. That was the last straw. The group of MPs bolted, leaping over benches and chairs, trampling one another and throwing each other aside in a bid to get to the doors. At that same moment, Mattock's team forced their way through the doors and began gathering the MPs to safety. Howard leapt from cover and joined Sarah in the middle of the chamber by the main table. "It's finished, Sarah. I understand if you want to get out of here."

She shook her head. "No, it's not over."

Major Stone still held the muzzle of an MP5 to Breslow's head. "You want the PM, then hand over the briefcase."

"Why?" asked Sarah. "If it's set to go off, then why do you even want it?"

"To make *sure* it goes off."

"You'll get sick, too. Is that how you want to die? Of a disease?"

"It's nobler than most the deaths I have seen."

"Okay," said Sarah. "I'll give you the briefcase and you give me the Prime Minister."

For once, Breslow kept her mouth shut. The horror had finally broken her resolve and she wore the vacant stare of a frightened hostage.

Her father nodded. "I'll meet you in the middle. I want your man to toss his gun aside."

Howard shook his head. "This isn't happening. You're not getting the briefcase and I am not disarming."

Sarah moved close to Howard and spoke into his ear. "It's okay. He won't shoot me. Mattock passed me a gun. Play along and I'll end this."

Howard looked uneasy, but he threw aside his gun. "Fine, but the moment you try to leave this building, Major, they're going to take you out."

"I'm ready to meet my end. Just hurry this up."

Sarah headed into the middle of the room and waited for her father to meet her.

CHAPTER 22

"Hush now, sweetheart, it's time to go to sleep."

Five-year old Sarah fought to keep her eyes open, because she knew that once they closed she would fall asleep and her daddy would leave. Soon he would be leaving for work and she was going to miss him. How would she fall asleep without him there each night? How could she sleep without hearing him sing to her?

"It's okay to close your eyes, Sarah. I won't be leaving for a few more days and then I will be back home again before you know it. They're sending me to a place called Iraq where it's really sunny and there's lots of sand. I'm part of a very special team that will keep me safe and bring me home to you and your mum. You don't need to worry. You are my angel. The best thing in my entire life, but I have to go away to work so that I can give you everything you need. Just be a good girl and go to sleep and tomorrow we can go and feed the ducks at the pond."

Sarah yawned, but continued to keep her eyes open. Her daddy was the strongest and bravest daddy of them all, and she didn't want him to go. But right now she was so tired.

"Sing to me, daddy."

Her father kissed her forehead. "Of course. *Lullaby and good night, with roses bedight*

With lilies o'er spread is baby's wee bed..."

Five-year-old Sarah was asleep before she knew it.

Her father was gone the next day, his unit leaving earlier than expected. When he came back, he was never the same.

CHAPTER FIFTY

Major Stone stepped out from around the Speaker's dais, dragging the Prime Minister with him. She went willingly, apparently eager to exchange her life for something that might well end it anyway.

"It's your last chance to stop this, dad."

Major Stone looked at his daughter and grunted. "You can't stop a bullet once it's been fired."

Sarah sighed and lifted up the briefcase with one hand. With the other she reached behind her back and gripped the handgun Mattock had given her.

"Hand Breslow over."

"First, place the briefcase on the ground."

Sarah exhaled, wondering if she had the ability to do what she needed to do. She knelt down, placing the briefcase on the ground, and then remained in a crouch, gripping the gun behind her back and willing herself to spring up and unload a bullet into her father's face while she had the chance.

"You probably think I won't shoot you," her father said. "Even when you pull that gun you have. Wrong!"

Sarah raised an eyebrow and managed to utter one word. "What?"

Her father levelled the MP5 at her and pulled the trigger.

Sarah's vision curled inwards and spun. She hit her head on the floor and was aware of nothing but her pulse beating in her temples. She looked to her side and saw Howard running towards her father, but he was shot before getting anywhere close. He pin wheeled around and disappeared behind the first row of benches.

Major Stone looked down at his daughter without sympathy. "I really am proud of you," he said, "but better men than you have tried to take me down and failed."

Then he grabbed Breslow around the neck and began moving away with her, taking the briefcase with him and keeping the MP5 against his hostage's head.

Sarah lay on the floor bleeding while Howard moaned nearby. She heard Mattock shouting, but it eventually changed to an order for his men to back off. There was no chance the cockney sergeant would take a risk with both the briefcase and Breslow's life on the line. Major Stone was well protected, even with a dozen guns aimed at him.

Eventually, one of Mattock's men broke free and came to Sarah's aid. He checked her over with his gloved hands, looking for damage. "You're okay," he said. "You've taken a slug in the shoulder, but you'll be fine."

Sarah didn't feel fine. The pain in her upper body felt like her bones were being pressed. She had been wrong about her father — he would dare to shoot her, but not fatally it seemed. Howard was okay too and he recovered enough to come help her to his feet. His vest had taken the full impact of the slug, which had been fired at him from some distance, and he had only been winded. Thank God they had both heeded Mattock's earlier warning to wear vests.

"We have to get after him," said Sarah, wincing as she held onto her shoulder.

Howard nodded. "Hell yes, we do. This is Wilder," he nodded to the member of Mattock's strike team who had come to their aid. A young man with messy blonde hair and fuzzy stubble — the *Milky Bar Kid* all grown up. "Wilder, this is Sarah Stone. She's with us."

Wilder nodded. "Mattock is already in pursuit. Special Branch snipers have been on the roof for the last hour. Major Stone has no place to go. He can't escape."

"He doesn't want to escape," said Howard. "He's ready to die and wants to take the whole world with him."

Wilder nodded as if he understood. "Then I saw 'a new heaven and a new earth,' for the first heaven and the first earth had passed away, and there was no longer any sea."

Sarah stared at Wilder in confusion until Howard explained. "This is no time for bible quotes, Wilder. The Book of Revelations can wait for another day."

Wilder nodded. "Amen, brother."

They headed back out into the hallways, leaving behind bloody footprints and memories of carnage. Even if they managed to stop Major Stone, nothing would ever be the same. Today would be a bloody entry forever etched in the history books. The Parliamentary Massacre of 2015, committed by her father, Major Jonathan Stone, father of Captain Sarah Stone. Now, Sarah would be ostracised for her lineage as well as her face. Her father was a worse man than she had ever thought him to be. She would be doing the world a favour by being the one to place the full-stop on his life.

They headed out of the building and were met by a Police cordon held by countless officers keeping back the crowds. Blinking flash bulbs went off like disco lights, even in the bright afternoon sunlight. Her face would be on tomorrow's papers — the disfigured daughter of a traitor — but none of that mattered right now. If Krenshaw's virus got out, there would be far more for the papers to worry about than today's bloodshed.

Her father was walking through the crowd, pushing Breslow ahead of him, the briefcase held beside him. No one tried to stop him, for all the officers understood the risk of being the one to pull the trigger.

Wilder let out a whistle. "There must be a hundred fingers on triggers right now, but not a single one brave enough to pull."

"Nobody wants to be the one to miss and hit the PM," said Howard.

Sarah kept back, wanting to see what her father was planning. Was his plan only to ensure the briefcase opened? Was Breslow his insurance to ensure he lived long enough to see it? Was the virus really so infectious that it would spread regardless of where it was released?

Major Stone headed down the road slowly, moving his eyes in all directions and making no sudden movement that might prompt a deadly response.

"Let the PM go," Mattock bellowed from the front of one of the police units through a microphone.

Major Stone turned back to answer. "Sergeant Mattock, you should know most of all what I am fighting for. You've seen."

"Too right," he said. "And I much prefer it to watching innocent women and children dying. You knew the risks when you signed up. War is bloody, but we're working our way out of it. It's men like you and Hesbani who ensure we never get to wash our hands clean of blood."

Major Stone didn't allow himself to be distracted further and started moving faster along the road. He was heading in the direction of Westminster Bridge. The traffic had been halted at the far end of the road and on the opposite bank of the Thames. The way was completely clear. Sarah broke free of Howard and Wilder and headed after her father. The two men went after her, but kept a few feet back, not yet knowing what she planned to do.

Her father was almost in the centre of the bridge when she finally caught up to him, out of breath and still bleeding from the gunshot wound in her shoulder. Helicopters swirled overhead with the black silhouettes of snipers hanging from them. The tops of nearby buildings also sported the tell-tale flashes of long-range rifle scopes. Major Stone would be hit from a dozen directions if he let go of Breslow for a single second.

It had to happen here, Sarah decided, in the centre of the bridge where there were no innocent bystanders.

"Daddy, stop!"

Major Stone stopped and turned around, dragging Breslow along like a rag doll. "Don't force me to shoot you somewhere serious, Sarah. I may be many things, but I wouldn't like to be the type of man who kills his children. Tell your men to back off, too, or I'll execute the PM right here."

Howard and Wilder heard and kept their distance.

"You don't have to shoot me," said Sarah, "and I don't want you to. I just want this all to be over. I understand why you're doing this. I'm tired of the way things are, too. It's all wrong. The wrong people are getting hurt all the time, while the guilty get rich in safety. But don't you see the hypocrisy of this? I don't give two shits about Breslow, but if that virus gets out then a lot more children are going to die than in that Syrian orphanage. Have you even thought about that?"

"I've thought about nothing else, but they will die to ensure a better future."

Sarah tried to straighten up, but her wounded shoulder would not allow her. She settled for taking a knee and facing her father from lower down. "You sound like a fundamentalist," she said. "You sound like the type of men you used to hate."

"Perhaps I do. It's probably because I discovered they are just men and nothing more. That is the great lie the government sells to its public, Sarah. They make the other side seem like monsters, and believe me, some of them are, but many are no different to us. The only thing different is the colour of their skin and the word they use to describe God."

Sarah shook her head. "You're blind."

"My eyes have never been more open. Any moment now this briefcase will open and things will change forever. It's your last chance to get out of here."

"Give me Breslow and I will. There are snipers everywhere, dad. Giving up Breslow is the only way you get to walk away from this."

"I don't want to walk away from this." Her father shoved Breslow in the back, but not towards Sarah. He sent the woman toward the bridge's barrier, keeping his gun on her. There he ordered the PM to climb upwards and once she was perched precariously on the barrier, he vaulted up to join her. It had afforded the snipers the brief opportunity to shoot, but none had.

Major Stone put the MP5 to Breslow's temple and held the briefcase over the Thames with the other.

Sarah got up off her knee and took a step forward. "What are you doing?"

"Any sniper shoots me and the virus goes into the river, along with Breslow's brains. People will be drinking it all in their tea by nightfall."

"If I have my way," said Breslow, seeming to come out of her frightened stupor all of a sudden. "The snipers will leave you wounded so I can take you alive. Then I'll have you tortured and your head put on a spike over Tower Bridge."

Major Stone grunted. "How draconian. Use my head as a football for all I care, once this is over." He lowered his weapon for a second, and began fiddling with the briefcase's dial.

"I thought it was on a timer," said Sarah. "You were bluffing"

Major Stone clenched his jaw, still fiddling with the dial. "You thinking that this thing is set to blow is the only thing that has kept me alive. Don't worry, though. I'm about to open it right in the river."

Sarah made eye-contact with Breslow, who understood immediately. The PM clenched her hands together and swung them like a hammer into Major Stone's guts. He doubled over, more in shock than pain, but was distracted long enough that the Briefcase fell from his hands and clattered on the road. Breslow threw herself from the barrier, landing face-first on the hard surface of the road. "Shoot him," she screamed. "Shoot the sonofabitch."

Sarah raised her gun and aimed it at her father's chest, but she didn't pull the trigger — couldn't.

Major Stone smirked at her. "You just can't shoot your old man, can you?"

"Give up."

"Not in this lifetime." Major Stone pointed the MP5 at Breslow and pulled the trigger.

But not before Sarah had pulled hers.

The shot was close enough that the round went clear through Major Stone's chest and left him tottering on the barrier of the bridge. He looked at Sarah in shock, his lips sliding back and forth soundlessly, his eyes flickering. He placed a hand to his bleeding chest and then removed it to take a look at his blood. With a chuckle he then spoke to his daughter, "Well done, man. Well done indeed."

Then the snipers fired from a dozen direction and sent Major Stone's dancing body plummeting into the Thames where his body floated and went still.

There was no time to think before scores of men came running up the bridge from both banks. Howard and Mattock came and took a hold of Sarah first, making sure she didn't faint and that no one could take her away. But she was okay and waved them off.

"You just shot your old man," said Mattock, although he sounded more than a little supportive of the act.

"Are you okay?" Howard asked her.

"I'm fine." She stood back while a group of space-suited gentlemen scooped up the briefcase and placed it inside a plastic crate with great big seals that clamped down around the edges.

"Did the briefcase go off?" asked Howard. "Did it go off?"

Sarah shook her head. "He was bluffing. The timer was never set after we left the airport."

Mattock huffed. "If I'd known that, I'd have taken his bloody head off myself an hour ago."

"Yeah," Sarah said, walking over to the edge of the bridge and staring down at the water below. Her father's lifeless body was being dragged into a police boat like the rotting carcass of a seal. His illustrious career ended in ignominy.

Breslow approached her with a pained limp, rubbing dirt off her suit and combing stray strands of hair back behind her ears. "You've saved the day again, Miss Stone. Seems like I need to have you on speed dial."

Sarah didn't smile at the comment. Her expression was blank as she spoke. "The men from my past seem to have a habit of causing trouble and dragging me into it. If you had any sense you'd lock me up and throw away the key."

"Nonsense. This country needs women like you to put men in their place. In the House of Commons, I can hold my own, but it's good to know that when things get tough, there's a bitch as tough as me who knows how to use a gun."

Sarah looked down at the gun in her hands and found it to be an ugly thing. "Half of Parliament is dead."

"Yes," said Breslow, followed by another, more thoughtful, "Yes."

The PM was eventually ferreted away by her frantic servants, so Sarah went on over to Howard. She held her wrists out in front of her and said, "I'm ready to face the music. I was part of this."

Howard took her gun from her and placed it into his belt. Then he pulled a pair of handcuffs from under his suit jacket and held them over her wrists, but then he hesitated.

"What are you waiting for?"

He sniffed and put the cuffs away. "As I see it, the only crime you're guilty of is shooting a member of the MCU." He turned to Mattock who merely shrugged.

"I don't hold grudges," he said. "Just buy me a couple beers and we'll call it even."

Sarah chuckled. "How about a dozen?"

"Then it's decided," said Howard.

"You're letting me go?"

"No way. After all this, your arse belongs to me. You want forgiveness, then you can damn well earn it. You're joining the MCU — permanently, this time."

Sarah didn't even need to think about it. She knew where she belonged. "If the MCU can put up with my ugly mug, then there's no place I'd rather be."

Howard surprised her then by grabbing her shoulder and pulling her in for a hug. "We missed you."

Mattock made them both laugh by murmuring the word, "Hippies."

It was all over, and for the first time in perhaps her entire life, Sarah felt wanted. She held Howard in the hug long enough for him to eventually drag himself free. "You've changed," he said with a frown. "You weren't really the cuddly type when we first met."

Sarah smiled. "You have no idea how much I've missed you guys. Never let me get kidnapped by a deranged madman ever again, okay?"

"No promises."

CHAPTER FIFTY-ONE

Mattock took Wilder and re-joined the strike team outside the Houses of Parliament, while Howard and Sarah met up with Mandy and headed back to MCU headquarters on the outskirts of High Wycombe. The Earthworm had been half abandoned when Sarah had first visited it and had been in rubble by the time she left, but Howard assured her that the place had changed a great deal in the last six months. MCU's recent successes had brought an influx of government spending and they were now close to being fully staffed. Their location was still secret, despite the MCU now being a household name in UK law enforcement.

Mandy took the Range Rover off the main road and onto a field where a ten-minute bumpy ride led to a derelict farm. When she saw the big old barn, Sarah knew she was home. She got out of the car with Howard, while Mandy stayed inside and parked inside the cover of the old barn.

The secret hatch inside the old shed opened upon Sarah and Howard's arrival and she allowed him to lead her down the long staircase into the earth. At the bottom they reached the first inner hatch and stepped through into a room she no longer recognised.

The Earthworm's tail section was alive, unlike the previously dead and dusty space she had visited. The previously abandoned space, the size of a football pitch, was now staffed with dozens of young men and women, all of them typing at computers or chattering into headsets. Everyone was so busy that not a single one noticed Howard and Sarah's arrival and they were free to walk right through the centre of the room.

"Told you things had changed," said Howard. "We have several dozen analysts working here now and Mattock has been moved to the senior team along with Jessica, Palu, and me. We have a new guy coming soon from the D.C. office to help us coordinate with US operations. I'm afraid Jessica has gone a little too native to be considered a liaison anymore."

Sarah chuckled. Her relationship with Dr Jessica Bennett had been strained to begin with, two independent women rarely got along easily, but towards the end they had begun to see eye to eye and had even begun approaching the fringes of a friendship. "Is Palu expecting me?" she asked.

"Yes, I called ahead. He was happy to hear we hadn't lost you to the other side. Things looked a little hairy, there, for a while. We thought your father had brainwashed you."

"He did. I was completely lost, even before my father kidnapped me, but now I finally know who I am. This is where I want to be."

Howard nodded. "Good."

They headed through the Earthworm's middle section, which had been a smoking ruin not six months ago, and headed straight for the head section. There, Howard used his thumbprint to open the hatch and they stepped through into the MCU command centre. Palu and Jessica sat there, waiting expectantly. They stood up when they saw her.

"Captain Stone," said Jessica in an accent far less American than Sarah remembered. "Glad to have you back with us."

"I'm glad to be back, and no 'Captain,' please. I'm just a new recruit now."

Palu smiled. He seemed smaller and wearier than she remembered, but the glint in his eyes was vibrant and alive. "You're anything but a recruit, Sarah. Taking down your father can't have been easy. Are you okay?"

Sarah prodded the scars on her face and said, "I have a lot of demons in my past, but my daddy was the worst of them all. If I dealt with him, I can deal with anyone. Yeah, I'm okay. I'm actually feeling kind of good, in a way."

Howard patted her on the back. "Take a seat, Sarah. We can do the debriefing now and then get some sleep in the dorms. There'll be more bad guys to fight tomorrow."

Sarah took the seat. "I just hope the next villain I have to take down is outside of my family."

"Before we begin," said Palu. "I need to introduce you and Howard to our new Intelligence Officer. He arrived an hour ago, having travelled from MCU's newly formed D.C. branch. I'll just give him a buzz and bring him in."

Howard took a seat next to Sarah and looked at Jessica. "What's the new guy like?"

"Handsome."

Sarah laughed. "Are you on the market, Dr Bennett?"

Jessica chuckled. "A single lady is always on the market for the right man."

One of the room's side doors opened and a tall man stepped into the command centre. Everyone stood up to greet him, but Sarah did so more quickly than the others. In fact, she leapt to her feet in shock.

"Thomas?"

Thomas stepped further into the room and smiled at her. "Hello, Sarah. I've missed you."

Howard glanced at Sarah. "You know this man?"

She nodded her head slowly. "Yes, he's my dead husband."

CHAPTER FIFTY-TWO

It had been a long and tiring wait. Heathrow had remained on lockdown for forty-eight hours, which made the delay in Moscow almost unbearable. But he was a patient man and had been waiting for far longer than two days for the journey he was finally undertaking. His imminent plans had been ten years in the making and a delayed flight was inconsequential as a result.

The Russian envoy stepped out of the airport and stretched their legs on the pavement, taking in great lungful's of crisp British air. It was a glorious day, made even more glorious by their arrival. The city of London had been cowed, its hubris dismantled, first by Hesbani and then by one of its own soldiers turned rogue. The United Kingdom no longer trusted in its safety and there were scant politicians left alive to provide the public the succour it needed. The rumours of a great, man-made disease currently being held at a Porton Down laboratory gave the nation nightmares and even the confident bluster of Prime Minister Breslow was not enough to give the country back its spine. The United Kingdom was no longer united. It was crumbling into dust. And very soon, it would be finished.

Yuri was smiling happily. The Russian diplomat had visited the

UK many times in the past and often spoke of his fondness for it. Peter was little different and wasted no time in ordering a Cornish pasty from a nearby vendor. It was disrespectful to love a nation more than one's own and the two Russian diplomats were sickening in their display of affection for the country that was, in many ways, their enemy. It was no secret that Moscow despised the West as much as any Middle Eastern state, but its seat in the global assembly was precarious and came with shackles. As much as Moscow needed to play nice on the world stage, it was only a means to an end. There were more ways to topple the West than by flying planes into buildings or battling over isolated oil reserves.

A sleek black limousine awaited the three men outside the terminal and Peter and Yuri hurried excitedly towards it, further sickening the stomach of their silent companion. At least the man who greeted them was a true Russian. Vladimir Rusev was a portly man with a harsh face that never smiled. Yet, when he spotted the three men leaving the airport he greeted them warmly. "Peter," he said, shaking hands. "Yuri. How are things in Moscow? Glorious I hope. And you, my good friend, it has been too long."

Al Al-Sharir smiled. "Yes," he said. "Indeed it has. But now that I am here, Vladimir, I expect things to move along very quickly."

Rusev nodded and winked. "Very quickly indeed, my friend. Everything you need is in place. We have been waiting for you. Welcome to the United Kingdom."

"Thank you," said Al Al-Sharir. "I came just in time to see it fall."

Continue the story, get book 3 END PLAY now!
CHECKOUT WITH AMAZON

END PLAY: SUMMARY

Old Nightmares and New Threats...

Sarah Stone is finished. The last year of her life has seen her face madmen and terrorists that will haunt her forever. This case will be her last.

The Flower Man is London's worst ever serial killer, putting even Jack the Ripper to shame. Sarah can't quit until she catches the monster and ensures no more innocent victims are killed. A local tip off might just be the break she needs to find her man.

But Sarah doesn't know that an even bigger monster from her past has awoken, settings events in motion that will devastate the city of London. It's already too late.

If Sarah doesn't end the killing, it will end her. She has one chance to get her life back. This is her end play.

WANT FREE BOOKS?

Don't miss out on your FREE Iain Rob Wright horror starter pack. Five free bestselling horror novels sent straight to your inbox. No strings attached.

For more information just visit this page:
www.iainrobwright.com

*Dedicated to my fans
you rule!*

"The war against terrorism is terrorism."
   – Woody Harrelson

"There are many more serial killers living outside the prison walls than inside."
   – Pat Brown

CHAPTER FIFTY-THREE

Sarah dodged the London traffic and descended the muddy embankment beside the road. Even in heavy boots she risked slipping, but Howard's hand against her back kept her steady.

"Remind me what this tip-off said?" she asked, wincing as she nearly twisted her ankle.

"It wasn't really a tip-off," Howard told her. They reached the bottom of the hill, and he let go of her shoulder. "Local bus driver broke down and saw someone skulking around this ditch. When he asked if they needed help, the stranger fled."

Sarah rolled her eyes. She imagined the drivers passing by thinking what an idiot she was tramping about in the mud. "Palu only has us following this because we have zero other leads."

"And two of the victims were found in inner-city ditches like this," said Howard.

Sarah glanced back at the main road. Like most of London in the morning, it was chock-a-block, and exhaust fumes billowed in the air. "I hate this city," she muttered.

Howard stepped up beside her.

"Nothing. Come on, let's check it out fast. It stinks down here."

Howard tugged up his belt, raising his trouser cuffs away from the mud. "You okay? You look pissed off—even more than normal."

"I'm fine. I just don't..." Sarah's words faded. Something about the way Howard looked at her—like he actually cared—made her want to open up to him. She almost spilled herself open: *No, I'm not fine, Howard. Ever since I met you, I've been battered and bruised, almost killed a dozen times, and forced to watch my friends die. I don't sleep. Every loud noise makes me curl up beneath the covers. Oh yeah, and my dead husband just returned and wants to act like nothing happened— like I didn't lose half of my face and a baby back in that desert. I am not fine, Howard. So, help me, please.* Instead, she shrugged. "Better things to do then trudge through mud, Howard. Let's just get this over with."

He shrugged. "All right. You want to take point?"

"Yeah." She examined the way ahead. The ditch cut alongside the road to collect runoff from a row of cement culverts. The ground was a quagmire, thick with scum of iridescent foam where chemical pollution from nearby factories mixed with rain and sewer water. An animal corpse rotted a few metres away, a scrawny grey thing that could have been a fat squirrel or a skinny badger. Sarah pictured a stranger skulking around down here and decided it was unusual enough to investigate—but by some local plod, not a pair of MCU agents. What was Palu doing sending them here?

Thinking of her ex-husband—or *husband again now*, she considered—forced a rush of anxiety into the pit of Sarah's stomach. The sensation was less akin to butterflies, and closer to a swarm of locusts.

"You think these pipes lead into the sewer?" asked Howard, pointing to the line of culverts.

"I don't know," she admitted—plumbing wasn't one of her skills. "I remember playing in pipes like that when I was a kid though, pretending to be an SAS soldier to impress my dad." She nearly laughed at the memory, but it died before it passed her lips. Howard knew better than to prod for details about her childhood, so he remained silent. Major Stone was dead, end of story. Sarah felt no guilt for liking it better that way.

"There's a larger pipe ahead," said Howard, stepping over a fly-tipped microwave. "You see it?"

Sarah did see it. This pipe had a circumference four times as wide. "The bus driver said the person in the ditch disappeared, right? Could have gone in here."

Howard nodded. "Let's be ready."

"Yeah, something killed that squirrel back there, so let's be extra cautious. It could be a stray dog or anything. The fight against crime is never ending."

"Glad to have you on the team." Howard pumped his fist and smirked. She almost gave him back a smile in response. After a year of suffering her abrasiveness, Howard had finally learned to enjoy her bitter humour. She kind of hated him for that.

They trod carefully through the stagnant water until they stood in front of the large sewer opening. Despite her jokes, they both unholstered their guns. In the last year as an agent, Sarah learned something might try and kill you at any moment. That was what kept her awake at night. Along with the faces of the men she had killed.

Rusted bolts dotted the cement pipe's circumference, suggesting a grate once barred access. The midday sun shone inside only a few feet before impenetrable shadows took over. Warm, stinking air flowed outwards. Sarah felt the moisture settling on her face. She fought the desire to gag, muscles beneath her jaw tightened. "Smells like ass," she said. "We don't really need to go stomping around in here, do we?"

Howard raised an eyebrow and stuck out his angular chin. He was about to tell her off. "You want to abandon a lead?"

She sighed. "No, but I swear Palu is punishing us for something."

"You're paranoid. Come on, you said you want to get this over with, so let's look inside quickly."

"I can't believe I'm doing this." Sarah yanked the LED flashlight from the left epaulette of her black utility vest and clicked it on. The high-powered beam sliced through the darkness. The pipe was dirty: a place no person should enter voluntarily. Nonetheless, Sarah fixed the glowing flashlight inside her epaulette and started forward.

Their footsteps echoed as their boots splashed in the water inside the pipe.

Sarah wrinkled her nose as the stench assaulted her. "I really don't think we'll find anyone skulking around in here. Least of all, the Flower Man."

Howard apparently agreed, because in the glare of his own torch, his expression grew glum. "Shame, because I really want to catch that sicko."

Sicko is an understatement, thought Sarah. The serial killer the media had named the 'Flower Man' had killed twelve victims in just two months—a spree putting London's former murderous VIP—Jack the Ripper—to shame. This latest sociopath's MO was the stuff of nightmares. He made gardens from his victims—cutting out their eyes and stuffing the sockets with seeded soil and filling every orifice with aggressively growing plant life and insects. The harrowing part was that it worked. Victims became gardens, sometimes remaining alive for days with plants growing from their bodies. The last victim had been a twelve-year-old girl, discovered in a Lambeth ditch with daffodils growing out of her scooped eye sockets, and a dying Lupin planted inside an incision above her groin. Pain had sent the girl's mind to oblivion long before her body joined it, which took less than twenty-four hours after getting her to a hospital.

The details made Sarah sick.

Like Howard, she would love to get her hands on the Flower Man.

Yet, she also wanted to run away screaming. She was used to terrors by now, but the constant stream of abhorrent monsters the MCU faced was too much to bear. She had faced demons in the deserts of Afghanistan, but what altered her outlook forever was learning there were demons at home. Nowhere was safe, the United Kingdom: a glass palace built on sand. The thick scars on the left side of her face were a constant reminder of man's love of cruelty.

I just want to stop feeling this way.

As they delved deeper into the stinking sewer, *plinks* and *plops* surrounded them; condensation caused droplets to fall from the ceiling. The darkness ahead grew hot and muggy.

"I'm sweating," said Howard, swivelling his torch beam into an excited spiral as he reached up and wiped at his forehead.

Sarah nodded. "Me too. I've never been in a sewer before—I know, I know, what have I been doing with my life—but I'm not sure if this whole tropical climate-thing is normal. Is it?"

Howard shrugged. "Beats me. Sewer gases? I'm trained in under-ground ops, but I don't think this counts."

The deeper they went, the more Sarah was sure the heat was odd. Maybe it was trapped sewer gases as Howard suggested, but it still seemed out of place. Like walking through a greenhouse.

Howard stopped. "You hear that?"

Sarah stopped too. "I hear buzzing."

A corner lay up ahead, and despite herself, Sarah removed the safety from her gun. Without a word, Howard did the same. They both sensed it—something was wrong.

I always like something is wrong, thought Sarah.

She took a deep breath and crept around the corner, her gun raised. She batted at her face frantically. "What the fuck?"

Howard moved beside her and was also taken by surprise. He covered his face with the crook of his arm and ducked. "What is this? Flies?"

Flies were everywhere, but that wasn't what held Sarah's attention. In a wide cavern where the sewer opened into a nexus of separate chan-nels, stood a tall lighting rig. Its warm orange glow, along with the droning buzz of its lamps, suggested it was ultraviolet. Weeds and plant life thrived all around.

"It's a garden," said Sarah.

It was bizarre to find vibrant foliage in a dank sewer, and it trans-formed the entire area into a creepy grotto. Creepy, because it meant the Flower Man had been there.

Or was still there.

Realising the same thing, Howard swept the cavern with his Ruger

P95. He spoke urgently. "If this is one of the Flower Man's gardens, he was here as recently as yesterday. He might still be close by."

Sarah swallowed. Once again, she stood in the den of an amoral monster. Her entire life was filled with wicked men—Hesbani, Al-Sharir, Dr Krenshaw... her father. She felt sick to her stomach, as if the Flower Man had left behind a noxious ooze that she now inhaled. She wobbled and reached out, but there was nothing to hold on to, and she almost fell.

"Sarah, you okay?"

"Let's phone this in. I need some goddamn air."

Howard lowered his gun and moved towards her. "Hey, it's okay. It's just a bunch of weeds. I don't think he's here."

Sarah righted herself and stood straight. "It's a bunch of weeds growing in a stinking sewer, put there by a deranged psychopath who turns people into flowerbeds. Just standing in this place makes me..."

Howard frowned. "What?"

"I don't know." *Vulnerable.* "I just want to get back outside where I'm not breathing in piss and shit."

Howard reached out and squeezed her arm. "Okay. Let's get out of-"

"*Hwah Mah!*"

Howard spun and raised his Ruger. Sarah did the same with her SIG 229. The strange noise had come from a large patch of flowers growing beneath the heat lamp.

"*Hwah!*"

Sarah looked around, searching desperately. Then she saw something. "Oh God, no!" She stumbled over to the centre of the cavern and knelt beside a large flowerbed. Howard tried to move up beside her, but she pushed him away. She wanted an unobstructed view.

The girl was still alive.

"I'll call an ambulance," said Howard, seeing for himself what lay in the flowerbed. His voice thick, nauseous. He pulled out his mob-sat and dialled.

Sarah focused on the victim. The girl's age was indeterminate because of the wet mud and moss caking her face. Sensing Sarah beside her, she shook her head from side to side and mumbled urgently. She could form no words because wet dirt packed her mouth. A pair of rubber tubes ran down her nostrils, allowing her to breathe, and both her eyes had been scooped out and replaced with wilting daffodils. Sarah needed to help the girl.

But there is no helping this girl.

"It's okay, sweetheart," she said. "I've got you now. My name is Sarah. I'm a police officer."

The girl's mumbling became more frantic, suggesting she understood. Victims were often most manic when finally rescued. Sometimes you had to stop them from injuring themselves in the panic. Relief could be even more powerful than fear.

In a panic of her own, Sarah clawed the dirt from the girl's mouth and removed thin root tendrils with her fingernails. Insects scuttled up her wrists. Whatever the Flower Man had planted had not yet sprouted, and with every finger-full of dirt gone, the girl spluttered and moaned a little more. Eventually, she gasped and choked, her throat clear for the first time in... how long?

"Mhwa Har. Mhwa Har."

Sarah stroked the girl's feverish brow. "Okay, sweetheart. Don't talk. Just stay calm."

"Shit," said Howard. "I can't get a call through down here. I need to go outside."

"Then go!" Sarah shouted at him.

"Heev fwear."

Sarah stroked the terrified blind girl's face. "It's okay, sweetheart. Help is coming. You're safe now."

The girl shook her head. *"Nooo! H-h-heeeee heeeeere. He's heeere."*

―――――――

Sarah stumbled. Her SIG trembled in her hand and she almost dropped it.

Shit shit shit.

The blind girl's warning was clear. She mumbled it over and over: *"He's here. He's here. He's here."*

Howard shot an arm out to steady Sarah. "We don't know he's still here. He might have fled when the bus driver saw him."

"He's here. I know it."

Splish splash splish!

Footsteps came from the sewer tunnels.

A beast stalked the shadows.

Howard's hand still gripped Sarah, and for once, she didn't shrug him off. Everything about this felt wrong.

Splish splash splish!

"He's here! He's here!"

The blind girl's shouting jolted Sarah. She looked at Howard and pointed. "Take position!"

He gave no argument and hurried to the far side of the cavern, dissolving expertly against the wall. Sarah stayed with the victim, SIG no longer trembling, finger poised over the trigger.

The blind girl screamed.

"What is all that noise?" came a high-pitched, yet stern voice from the tunnels. "A garden is a quiet place. We'll have no noise. You are... Hmm, yes... oh my..."

The blind girl thrashed and squealed like a stuck pig at the sound of the voice.

What monster can do this to a person? thought Sarah.

The wet footsteps in the tunnel had halted.

The killer knew they were there.

Sarah and Howard peered at one another, jaws tense, eyes wide.

Help me! the victim begged. *Don't let him get me.*

"Quiet," shushed Sarah.

The footsteps in the tunnel retreated. Quickly. The killer was running. The blind girl's mouth had been packed with soil, but now she screamed. Her pleading had given them away.

Sarah raced out of the floodlit cavern and sprinted into the dark sewer tunnel, but was halted as she stumbled into knee-deep water. She had to battle to keep from falling under. "MCU, stop... stop right now!"

Ahead, a shadowy figure tilted around a corner. The Flower Man had got a head start on her. Sarah took aim and fired, hoping to scare him into stopping, but it didn't work. The Flower Man was getting away.

"Sarah!" Howard appeared to her left, at waist height and clear of the water. He reached down. "Get out of the muck. There's a walkway up here."

Sarah grabbed Howard's hand and hoisted herself up. Atop the walkway, the two of the them sprinted side-by-side. Sarah was the faster runner of the two, but her waterlogged boots slowed her down. As such, they rounded the corner at the same time and were met by a long, high-ceilinged tunnel. The Flower Man had not got far enough ahead to escape pursuit. In fact, they were gaining on him.

"He's slow," said Howard, sweating from the heat they'd left back in the cavern. "We're catching up to him."

Sarah increased her pace. Her flesh squirmed—she was about to come face to face with a monster—but the girl's screams echoing through the tunnel behind her was enough to spur her onwards. "MCU!" she hollered. "Last chance. Stop now or I will fucking kill you!"

The suspect kept running—in a strange, limping gait—and didn't look back. Sarah and Howard continued gaining on him, and he was no longer a silhouette. His features had taken shape. Tall. Skinny. With a lame left leg.

"Stop!" Howard ordered. "It's over."

It's over. Sarah repeated the words in her head, enjoying them.

The Flower Man's reign of terror was about to end.

Another monster removed from people's nightmares.

Is that why she still did this, why she still chased bad guys? Would catching this monster allow her to sleep tonight?

She doubted it.

When they reached the next corner, the Flower Man had disappeared.

Howard looked around urgently. "Shit, where did he go?"

Sarah slowed her sprint to a jog and switched her tact from speed to caution. The sewers were a maze—a labyrinth—and the Minotaur lurked.

"Eyes open, Howard. He's hiding."

Howard and Sarah fanned out, Howard dropping back, Sarah taking point. Ahead, the walkway widened as the sewer channel entered a closed pipe underneath. Sarah waited for Howard to catch up, and they fanned out again, moving to opposite sides of the cavern. The smell was foul. Sarah's wet boots slid over the slime coating the ground. This deep in the dark, she feared she might never see the light again. The beam of her torch seemed to get smaller, but it had to be in her mind.

Howard gave a silent signal with his fingers, motioning ahead. *There.*

Sarah saw it and nodded. Up ahead lay an open doorway, a sheet of metal hanging on a pair of hinges. "Might be his office," said Sarah, her sarcasm lacking its usual passion. The cries of the blind girl had faded, but they still echoed in Sarah's head. They abandoned her to give chase; failure was not an option. The room ahead was dark, a black cube daring them to enter. Sarah went inside.

Howard grabbed her. "I'll take point."

Sarah let Howard move through the doorway and gave him a few steps before following. There was once a time when her nerves were gilded steel, but after having to shoot her own father, who had just massacred half of Parliament, her courage had run dry. That was why she trembled all over.

Their flashlights lit up the new room, exposing it for what it was. The floor held a grimy mattress. Crates of bottled water lined one wall. It was a bedroom. The sewer wasn't just the Flower Man's killing ground; it was where he *lived.*

The newspapers enjoyed speculating about whether London's

worst serial killer had a family—kids and a wife—as many killers did, but it was clear now that this monster possessed no humanity at all. No more than a sewer rat.

"Jesus." Howard pulled a face. "He sleeps here."

Sarah threw out a hand. "Howard, look out!"

Howard was caught by surprise. A length of wood cut through the shadows and clocked him right in the chin. He grabbed his face and crumpled to the ground. He still clutched his Ruger, but was in no state to take a shot. Sarah brought her own weapon to bear, but the Flower Man dropped the length of wood and pounced on her. The back of her head collided with the brick wall. Stars danced in front of her.

Despite his lame leg, the scrawny man wearing gardener's overalls was deceptively strong. He punched Sarah and crushed her nose, blinding her with tears. As she bent over, clutching her face, her attacker elbowed her in the ribs hard enough to floor her. If not for the fact she had survived her fair share of beatings in the past, and had grown accustomed to them, she would probably have been out for the count. But her body had hardened in the last year. She bit back the pain and rolled back to her feet.

The Flower Man descended on her again, like an angry wasp, jabbing and batting at her. "You will not come here and spread your pollution," he yelled, his high-pitched voice echoing off the narrow walls.

Sarah chanced a kick, making contact with her attacker's lame leg. He bellowed in agony and backed off immediately. Sarah reached to her belt and grabbed her cuffs. This might be her only chance to get the suspect under control, and she needed to end things now before things turned lethal. Flicking open the cuffs, she lunged forwards, attempting to secure the man's wrists before he had time to recover, but he reacted quickly enough to dodge away. Off balance due to her lunge, Sarah took the full brunt of an uppercut to the face. The Flower Man grabbed her by the throat and squeezed.

Sarah struggled, but the fingers around her throat were like tightening vines.

"Hey, Green Dick!"

The Flower Man turned in time to see that same wooden plank now swinging at his own face. He tried to duck, but the plank walloped his forehead, and he dropped to the ground.

Sarah gasped, sucking in air and choking.

Howard stood over her. He dropped the piece of wood and put a hand out to her. "You okay?"

"I had it," she said, shrugging him off and getting up on her own.

"No, *we* had it," said Howard, ignoring her anger as he always did.

Sarah grunted. She picked up her cuffs and strode towards the moaning serial killer. "Your gardening days are over, arsehole."

The entire room shook.

Howard tripped and fell into Sarah as the world continued rumbling. Both of them fell to the ground in a heap as stone chips rained from the ceiling. Even with their flashlights, it became impossible to see through the dust cloud filling the room.

Somewhere far off, a distant dragon roared.

Sarah reached out and found Howard in the chaos. Their hands met and locked together. "What the hell is happening?"

"I-I don't know. An explosion?"

Sarah shielded her face and clambered to her knees. "We need to get out of here before the roof comes down. We have to get back to that girl."

Howard braced himself against the wall and started to climb. The room had stopped shaking, and the dust was clearing. His left eye had swollen shut where the Flower Man smacked him with the piece of wood. "Let's get sewer man cuffed and secured. Then we'll call for help."

Sarah nodded. She still clutched the cuffs and was unwilling to waste another second. Whatever just happened was secondary to the fact that they had a mission to complete. It might be her final mission, so she was going to make it count. The Flower Man was going to rot in a jail cell because of her.

She had him.

He was down.

Finished.

Sarah stared at the empty space on the ground and cursed a dozen times. In the confusion, in the disarray...

The Flower Man had escaped.

"He's gone," said Sarah. "I let him get away."

Howard stood beside her. "*We* let him get away."

CHAPTER FIFTY-FOUR

Sarah stayed with the girl until help arrived, which consisted of a single ambulance. She would have expected a greater response for a victim of the Flower Man, but other things were going on, apparently.

Howard stood beside Sarah, talking to Palu on the mob-sat. Sarah had wanted to remain inside the sewer with the victim, but needed to get out of the place. The smell... The damp... Like being in Hell. That she had let the Flower Man escape was enough to make her tear her hair out, but instead, she clenched her fists and remained silent. Brooding. She sat down on the grassy embankment and waited for Howard to finish his call. When he ended it, he stared at her.

"What is it?" she asked, already knowing it was bad. The explosion in the sewer had felt like the end of the world.

Howard shook his head like he couldn't believe what he was saying. "Tower Bridge... it's gone."

"What do you mean, *gone?*"

Howard stared off into the distance, his voice weak when he spoke. "I mean, it's gone, Sarah. Shit, this insanity never ends. You think you're making a dent—that there's just a certain allocation of evil in the world, and that every victory brings you a little closer to ending it altogether—but it's not true, is it? Evil never runs out."

"Howard, tell me what happened."

He shook his head as if snapping out of a daze. "Sorry. Palu told me that a group of suicide bombers walked into the centre of Tower Bridge thirty minutes ago, and blew themselves up, with enough force to sink the entire structure. While we were trying to bring down one psychopath, a whole group of them were sneaking up behind us."

Sarah didn't have it in her to offer words of solace to her partner, who seemed like he needed them. There was no solace to be had. Howard was right—evil never ran out. It was that conclusion which led Sarah to want out of the MCU as soon as possible.

Howard sighed. "We need to go. Palu wants us at the scene before the police screw things up."

Sarah glanced over at the sewer pipe. The one that led to Hell. "What about the girl?"

"Nothing we can do for her now. Palu is trying to get a couple of uniforms to secure the site, but for now, we need to leave her with the paramedics."

Sarah reached up and touched the scars covering the left side of her face. "She would have been better off dead. She'll never heal from this."

"Least we gave her a chance to try."

Sarah turned and climbed up the embankment. Because of them, the Flower Man was still at large, free to destroy more lives. They had got their shot and wasted it. Who knew if they would get another.

They both headed back to the car in silence. It wasn't until they reached the jet-black Range Rover parked at the side of the road that the silence was broken.

Sirens.

Ambulances raced past, but were uninterested in the girl in the sewer. They were heading to Tower Bridge.

Or where Tower Bridge used to be.

Sarah slid into the passenger seat. "Let's go," she said. "Let's just go."

If not for their Range Rover's sirens and flashing lights, Howard and Sarah would never have made it to the scene of the explosion. London's veins were clogged with fleeing traffic, but multiple emergency vehicles headed in the other direction. Howard's driving was advanced enough he rolled over the pavement and across verges when needed, but even then, they took an hour to drive four miles.

Howard parked in the middle of the Horsleydown Lane. The Range Rover didn't block access as the road had been cordoned off. When she got out of the car, Sarah witnessed a perverted postcard—an iconic London structure beneath a clear blue sky, spanning the Thames —distorted by billowing smoke and raging fires. Cables and ironwork twisted into the air above chunks of disembodied road that jutted out from both sides of the river. A yacht bobbed in the river, capsized amongst the debris—its dead occupants were being fished out by a pair of police officers in a speedboat. A crowd of thousands huddled around the embankments on both sides of the Thames.

A Met officer strolled up to meet Howard and Sarah as they approached the cordon. "Do you have business here?" he asked.

"Just sightseeing," said Sarah. "Would you take a picture for us?"

Howard touched her arm, signalling her to let him do the talking. "Officers Hopkins and Stone from the MCU. We're part of the first response team."

The officer nodded, but asked for ID. Howard showed his, but Sarah never bothered with hers. Luckily, one set of credentials was enough, and the officer lifted the cordon and allowed them to crouch beneath it. On the other side, Sarah and Howard sidestepped a row of body bags. A cursory glance tallied at least a dozen victims. More casualties floated in the Thames—various corpses missing arms, legs, and faces.

Human flotsam.

"This is bad," said Howard, staring at the river where the two hundred-foot bridge once stood. Both of its towers had fallen forwards into the water. "We dropped the ball."

"This isn't our fault," snapped Sarah, although she was thinking the same thing. How had they not caught this? The MCU had more funding and resources than ever, and they had been on a roll. First Hesbani, then Krenshaw and Major Stone. The wins kept on coming.

But this loss was enough to erase every win.

Tower Bridge... Gone.

Howard shuffled beside the river like a zombie, staring out at the flaming debris. Like Sarah, this last year had taken a toll on him. He was less brash than he'd used to be, not quite so cocky. Although she hated to admit it, Sarah liked him more with the extra weight he now carried—they had a connection grounded by mutual loss.

Sarah grabbed a police officer and asked for a briefing. The stern, older woman grunted, but reeled off the details: Four suicide bombers with a hostage made a speech, then blew themselves up in the middle of the lunchtime rush-hour. A hundred dead at least. Howard and Sarah got into the groove, speaking with witnesses and searching for clues. Hard to believe they'd spent the morning chasing a serial killer only to be met by this.

Chaos.

An hour passed, but they learned little of use, which was why Sarah was relieved when a black Range Rover arrived and parked next to theirs. She was less relieved when it was Thomas who stepped out of the car.

That's all I need.

Howard sensed her distraction because he hurried over to her side. She nodded to him that she was okay. Thomas was joined by Mandy, expressionless as usual, despite the scene of devastation meeting him. Thomas, on the other hand, was all emotion as he passed by the cordon with his hands buried in his thick blond hair. "The bastards," he said in his strange mix of British and Floridian. "Sarah, are you okay?"

She frowned. "I'm fine. The people on the bridge are less well."

He nodded, looking around with wide eyes. "I can't believe this. What is wrong with this world? When does it end?"

"Been asking that ourselves," said Howard.

Thomas ignored him and focused on Sarah. He motioned at her collar, which she realised was stained with blood from her nose. "I heard about the sewer tunnels. Are you hurt?"

"How's the victim?" asked Sarah. "How is the girl?"

"In the best care," said Thomas, "but she's pretty messed up. Too bad we let the bastard get away."

"*I* let him get away," corrected Sarah. "I had him."

Howard touched her arm. "You're not to blame, Sarah. The explosion..."

"Hopkins is right," Hopkins was right. "The Flower Man is on the run now. It's just a matter of time until he's apprehended. We'll address that issue later. Right now, we need to respond to what we have here."

Sarah folded her arms. "Do we have anything from above?"

"Plenty. Mandy, find somewhere we can set up."

They made their way to a cafe at the edge of the blast site. The windows had shattered, but no one inside was injured. The owner kept free coffee on the go for everyone present and the place was full of investigators and reporters. Mandy found a quiet corner by the kitchen and set down a laptop he'd been carrying in a holdall. Mandy was a man of few words, so gave no introduction to the video he opened on the screen.

"Taken from a cell phone," Thomas explained, but then corrected himself. "A *mobile* phone."

"It's okay, we speak American as well as you speak English," said Sarah, not looking her estranged husband in the eyes. In fact, she hadn't looked him in the eyes since he'd returned from the dead a month ago. She had done her utmost to avoid him. She needed time to think.

Maybe a lifetime.

The video played in high quality, taken on a top-spec camera phone. What it lacked was proximity. The spectator had wisely kept their distance from the bridge, and the footage seemed to come from a second-storey window. It showed four men standing in the centre of Tower Bridge, possibly of Middle-Eastern descent. A blindfolded woman struggled on her knees in front of them, fighting to get away but held down by rough hands.

"Who's the hostage?" asked Sarah.

"Maxine White," said Thomas. "UKIP MP for Hendon."

"Any reason she would be targeted?"

"Plenty. She's pretty much the poster child for increasing war efforts in Syria. She's a hardliner for eradicating ISIS through whatever means necessary, including high-yield missiles. There's rumblings she's also been trying to follow France's lead by banning the burka. Farage has been grooming her as his successor and she's been gaining support."

"She might as well have painted a target on her forehead," said Howard. "Anti-Muslim... Right-wing... Misguided."

Sarah winced as the video footage flickered and distorted, a massive blast of light blooming in the middle-ground. The bridge came apart like a bundle of crisp leaves, and a second later the laptop speakers squealed with distortion. The video ended with the spectator taking cover as stone and metal rained down on the Thames.

Sarah chewed a knuckle. When she removed it, she tasted blood in her mouth. "Whatever Maxine White believed in, she didn't deserve this. We need to find out who is responsible."

"We already know," said Thomas.

"It was Shab Bekhier," said Thomas.

Sarah recoiled. "What?"

Howard frowned. "Shab Bekhier disbanded after we took out Hesbani."

"Hesbani never controlled Shab Bekhier," said Sarah. "Al-Sharir does."

"Sarah..." he looked at her. "Al-Sharir is dead. He hasn't been on anybody's radar for years."

"It's true," said Thomas. "I spent five years in the desert amongst a dozen different terrorist cells, and by the time I came out of cover, I had stopped hearing Al-Sharir's name all together."

Sarah gritted her teeth. "Five years is a long time."

Thomas sighed. "Sarah…"

"Thomas!"

"I went undercover to try and prevent things like this from happening. My life seemed like a small price to—"

"We have more footage," Mandy interrupted, breaking the tension before it had a chance to grow. He spoke so rarely that, when he did, it made people stop and pay attention. They turned back to the laptop, and he played another video.

Again, Thomas gave introduction. "The previous footage was submitted to our website by an anonymous witness. This, however, was taken from a news chopper. From the look of it, the terrorists were waiting for the media to arrive, because when they spotted the helicopter, they began their speech. God bless the news crew for having a parabolic mic mounted underneath their bird. They captured it all."

The audio was muffled, like someone talking with a plastic bag over their head—and the screams from the bridge didn't help matters—but Sarah could fill in most of the blanks from context. One of the four bombers stepped forward and opened his arms revealing a torso strapped with chemicals and wires. Some kind of nitro bomb, Sarah suspected. The man stared up at the helicopter as he spoke.

Today we lay waste to your nation as you lay waste to ours. We fight for freedom, rejecting tyranny. Your false idols of security and power fail you. Shab Bekhier will show you the way. Shab Bekhier will lead the world to a new day—a day of truth and enlightenment. This is your warning, heathens. Praise be to Allah.

Once again, Sarah flinched as Tower Bridge exploded. This time, though, she found her anger. "If this is Shab Bekhier, Al-Sharir is behind it. Only he could pull off something so big—so evil."

"We don't know that," said Howard. "Hesbani was behind the last attack we thought was Al-Sharir. This could be another former Lieutenant of Shab Bekhier, or someone using their name."

"Al-Sharir had no other Lieutenants," said Sarah. "Hesbani is dead, so this has to be Al-Sharir."

Thomas reached out to touch her, but she took a step back. He appeared hurt by the reaction, but she didn't care. He exhaled. "Sarah, Al-Sharir is gone. If I learned anything in the desert, it's that."

She wasn't listening. Her hand drifted to her belly where once she'd held a child—her and Thomas's child. Life had been heading in a drastically different direction before she crossed paths with an evil man in the deserts of Afghanistan. Hesbani may have taken her face, but Al-Sharir had taken her life. He wasn't gone like Thomas naively assured her. She felt him. Her skin crawling every time she whispered his name. He was still alive.

Waiting for the time to strike.

Hesbani had done unfathomable damage to the United Kingdom during his attacks, but this felt worse. A London landmark gone in an instant.

What next?

Howard saw Sarah panicking and made eye contact with her as he spoke. "Sarah, listen to me. We'll put a stop to whatever this is, I promise."

She focused on his soft brown eyes, finding a modicum of calmness in the way they gazed at her. "I just need a minute," she said. "Give me a minute."

Howard stepped back. "Okay."

Sarah turned away and started walking.

"Sarah," Thomas called out, but she ignored him and headed for the door.

Outside, the devastation hit her all over again. More body bags had piled up, and shocked victims woke from their stupors and began to weep and moan. Sarah kept her distance, not wanting to stray too near to death. Her soul was tarnished by the evil acts of men like Hesbani. She worried what would happen if she absorbed more misery. Yet, misery came to her in a flood as her mind spun webs of rotting, sinewy despair.

Is Al-Sharir behind this?

Is he alive? Is he here?

Enough.

Enough of this.

The MCU had dragged Sarah into its world to help stop Hesbani— and she had done that. Job done. She had stayed too long, and it had made her sick. Now she wanted out. No more bombs. No more diseases or hostage situations. No more serial killers. And most of all, no more husbands returning from the dead. Sarah just wanted to be left alone, to hide away with her shattered mind and ghastly face. She was a soul destined for solitude, and it was time to admit that. In her pocket rested her mob-sat. One call to Palu and she could end this misery, remove herself from the never-ending nightmare. She could resign. The bad guys might never stop, but that didn't mean she had to keep on going.

She was done.

Like a weight had lifted from her chest, Sarah breathed deeply. Her steps felt lighter. Knowing she was finished, making the decision in her head, cleared away a black cloud that had been hanging over her for too long. She glanced back at the cafe where her colleagues—soon to be former—still huddled in conference, and experienced a slight twinge of sadness. She would miss Mandy and his strange ways. Would miss Dr Bennet and her unwarranted curtness. Howard, most of all, she would miss as a friend. They had become close, and that was precious to her— but not precious enough to keep living each day in terror. Realising you weren't as tough as you thought was unpleasant, but it was also strangely liberating. She was an aged boxer stepping out of the ring.

Beyond the cordon, the crowds had begun to thin, police finally gaining control over the scene. Many spectators wandered away once they realised seeing dead bodies wasn't as entertaining as they'd presumed. Gawkers were often unwittingly affected by the very horrors they were so eager to see, and would regularly turn away with stricken looks on their faces that Sarah always thought served them right. The growing gaps in the crowd allowed her to see that someone was watching her.

She frowned and stared back.

It took a moment to register who was watching her.

Then it struck her. The Flower Man.

"You son-of-a-bitch!" Sarah took off like a missile. The Flower Man bolted too, shoving aside a couple of teenagers and fleeing into the streets. A police officer stepped in Sarah's way, and she thrust a shoulder out and knocked him aside like a skittle. No way was she letting the Flower Man escape again.

I'll shoot him if I have to.

The Flower Man threaded through a row of parked cars and headed into an alleyway between a Polish supermarket and a pet shop. Sarah kept right on his tail, knowing she should call backup, but worried it might slow her down and allow the killer to slip away again. No way was that happening.

She pictured the girl in the sewer.

Screaming and blind—forever changed.

The Flower Man's limp was no match for Sarah's piston-like legs. She was a machine, fuelled by anger and a desire for violence. The killer was a fool for having followed her. He knew it, too, because he kept glancing back over his shoulder anxiously.

Why had he been watching her? Were serial killers really so arrogant? Well, the Flower Man's hubris was about to get him caught.

The chase moved into another alleyway behind a row of shops. The back yards were empty. Nobody was around. A chain-link fence punctuated the end of the road. A dead end.

Sarah gritted her teeth and picked up speed. *Nowhere left to run.*

The Flower Man sprawled against the fence and shook it wildly like a caged animal. Sarah slowed and approached him cautiously with her hand on her SIG. "Stupid, stupid, stupid," she mocked. "Why on earth would you tail the very agents who almost had you in a jail cell this morning?"

The Flower Man stopped shaking the fence and turned to her. He panted heavily, yet somehow managed to look smug. His dark, brown eyes seemed disembodied from his face, as though floating slightly out of their bony sockets. "Your face, it interests me," he said, staring at her scars as though they were a museum painting. "A wasteland beside a meadow."

Sarah scowled. "Trust me, I'm all wasteland. Right now, I'm about to lay waste to you."

He seemed not to hear her. "I wonder what could grow in a wasteland. What seeds might one sow? Your face could be a wonder."

"Down on the ground," Sarah demanded.

"You're tough. Hardy. I could keep you alive for years under the right conditions."

Sarah pulled out her gun. "Ironic, because I will make sure you spend the next fifty years alive in a prison cell under very bad conditions. Now, get on the ground before I shoot your goddamn cock off."

To her relief, the Flower Man raised his hands above his head and lowered to his knees. "I look forward to getting to know you, Agent."

"You'll get plenty of time, arsehole." She strode forward, skin tingling at the proximity to the killer but ready to take him down. She'd encountered evil many times before, but this man was not killing for a cause or a vendetta—not involved in any war, or fuelled by anger or loss, defiance or hate. No, this creature lacked emotion altogether. His face was a blank canvas stretched across a horde of writhing insects. Dark eyes that never stopped assessing.

Sarah stood in front of the kneeling man and reached around her back to grab her cuffs. "One move and I'll put a hole in you."

Her fingers grasped at air. *Damn it.*

Her cuffs were gone, likely still in the sewer where she had last tried to use them.

"Problem, Agent?"

"Just get down on the ground. Face down. Now!"

The roar of a vehicle entered the alleyway behind them and Sarah couldn't help but glance back and see it. A white van careened towards her, a lone man behind the wheel.

What the Hell?

In that split-second Sarah took her eye of the Flower Man, he leapt up, crashing into her and knocking her gun aside. Sarah tumbled backwards but didn't fall. She tried to bring her gun back around, but the Flower Man was too quick and jabbed her in the mouth with a stiff punch. She rocked back on her heels.

The van skidded to a halt, narrowly avoiding Sarah. She caught her balance and turned, hoping for aid, and when the side panel of the van slid open and three men jumped out, she was relieved.

"I'm an MCU agent. I need help to arrest thi-"

The men grabbed her under the arms and around the neck, dragging her towards the van. She kicked and tried to escape, but she was overpowered and off-balance. In front of her, the Flower Man stood startled, disembodied eyes stretched wide. The three men shoved Sarah into the back of the van, hitting her in the head enough times to stop her struggling. She cried out for help as they shoved a hood over her head, but nobody came. The most terrifying thing of all was that the three men then headed back out of the van and grabbed the Flower Man. They shoved him alongside Sarah before closing the door. She could feel the warmth of the killer's body against hers.

Her abductors drove away.

CHAPTER FIFTY-FIVE

Howard squeezed the mob-sat almost hard enough to break it. "Damn it, Sarah, answer the call."

"You should have stuck with her, Hopkins," said Thomas

"I'm not her babysitter. She said she needed a minute, so I gave her one. What should I have done, tied her to a chair? Not sure she would have appreciated that."

Thomas seethed. "She's struggling with the job, and you're her partner. You should have informed me."

Howard had known Thomas for only a month, but already he didn't like the man. The American assumed authority and treated everybody as a subordinate. Who did he think he was? Sure, he was Sarah's husband, which gave him reason to worry about her wellbeing, but where was that concern when he faked his death to go undercover in the desert? Howard was the one who had been by Sarah's side this last year, being a friend to her despite snarling opposition. Sarah was abrasive and rude, but underneath was something else he'd gradually been uncovering. The scars on her face were a mask that had started to slip.

But Thomas had screwed it all up.

Ever since he arrived at the MCU, Sarah's mask had reapplied itself firmer than ever.

"Why would she take off?" Thomas asked Howard, some of his anger gone and his tone more conciliatory. "Did she say anything to you about needing a break?"

Howard leaned back against the plate-glass window of the cafe. "She's burnt out, Tom."

Thomas bristled. Howard knew the American preferred to be addressed by his surname—Gellar—a habit from his days as an Army Ranger. "She's not burnt out, Hopkins. This last year has shown just how strong she is."

"This last year almost broke her," said Howard. "The man who disfigured her in Afghanistan popped up and tried to assassinate the Queen, and then her father tried to wipe out the Government. To top it all off with a nice little bow, her husband came back from the dead to say hi. She's burnt out, trust me. I've been seeing it for a while, but it's not my place other than to have her back. If she took off, it's because she needed to. I'm sure she'll check back again soon."

Thomas scrutinized Howard with glaring blue eyes. "If you believe that, then why do you seem so worried, Hopkins? If you squeeze that mob-sat any harder your knuckles will pop."

Howard peered at his clenched fist and willed himself to loosen his grip. "Just because I'm sure she's okay, doesn't mean I'm not worried about her. She's my partner."

"And she's my *wife*, which is why you should have updated me if you had concerns about her mindset."

"*You're* my concern, Gellar. The reason Sarah is a mess is because of you."

Thomas clenched his fists. "Careful, Hopkins."

"Don't threaten me. You're the new guy around here, Tom. You're the one who turned up and complicated everything."

"Sounds like you wish I'd stayed dead."

Howard huffed. "Sounds like your guilt talking."

"You don't know a thing."

"I know you're an arsehole."

Thomas stepped forwards, chin out. Howard stood still, but his hands rose from his sides. *Bring it on, Geller.*

"You two!" Mandy came running. He'd taken himself off to sit in the car, but was now returning urgently. "I just got off the line with Palu. Sarah's mob-sat just went offline."

"She probably switched it off," said Thomas, sounding unsure.

Howard said, "No. The tracking module never switches off. If it's gone offline, it's because the mob-sat has been destroyed."

"Or tossed in the Thames," added Mandy. "Either way, it seems like Sarah might not be planning on reporting back."

Thomas rubbed his forehead. Howard disliked the man, but he couldn't deny he looked genuinely worried about Sarah. "Maybe she doesn't intend on coming back," he said.

"That's her choice," said Howard. He hoped it wasn't true.

"Or she's in trouble," said Mandy. Anxiety looked wrong on the big man, like seeing a trembling rhinoceros. "She's disappeared on us before, Howard, and she needed us. If this really is Al-Sharir... They have history."

Howard felt the blood flow out of his cheeks. The last time Sarah vanished from the face of the earth was because her father had kidnapped her. Now the man was dead, so what were the odds of something like that happening to her again? Slim? Impossible?

Howard couldn't stand by and do nothing. As much as he might imagine Sarah just taking off, he couldn't imagine her tossing her mob-sat and disappearing completely. She wouldn't do that to them. Not after all they'd been through together. She would at least say goodbye. To him at least. Wouldn't she?

Howard got to work. "Mandy, get back on the line to Palu. I want to know the last location we have for Sarah's mob-sat. We're not losing her again."

Sarah winced as her ribs hit the unforgiving back of a wooden chair. Her captors immediately tied her wrists behind her back before stepping away. Would they leave her in the dark with a hood over her head? Who was doing this? What did they want?

Her kidnappers yanked off her hood and made towards the door. It was too dim to make anything out other than their backs. It looked like they had her in a storage room, little larger than a cupboard. A flickering lightbulb swung overhead and gave off a brief scattering of light—enough to reveal that her chair was the only piece of furniture in the room. The only other source of light was a rectangular window pane above the door. The thin shaft of light highlighted thick dust in the air. Seeing it made Sarah cough and turn her head.

The door closed, and her kidnappers left her there alone.

Minutes passed, and they returned, shoving someone else into the room with her. Sarah squinted, adjusting her eyes, then blinked until she could make out who it was.

The Flower Man.

He wasn't tied to a chair like her, but instead, he lay unconscious on the ground. A patch of blood stained the side of his scalp and suggested he had not gone quietly. Neither had Sarah, but they had not bludgeoned her like that. Had they taken more care with her?

They'd taken several minutes before tossing him in with her. Had they tried speaking with him? Did they know he was the nation's most-wanted man? A twisted serial killer? Would they care?

The Flower Man stirred. From Sarah's vantage point, he did not seem like a monster. Gangly and unattractive, but nothing about him cried 'killer'. It was his eyes that showed his true nature, and right now they were closed.

Soon, he would be awake.

Sarah tried to pull her arms forward, but they were bound tightly to the back of the chair. The chair's legs were bolted to the floor. She wasn't about to stand up anytime soon, so she bit her lip and fought her restraints. Had someone kidnapped her just to leave her at the mercy of a serial killer? What was the point? Would they gain a thrill from returning later to find her strangled to death?

There had to be a greater purpose.

She'd been taken for a reason.

As the seconds ticked by, Sarah searched for inspiration. The floor was carpeted with cheap blue fabric tiles—some of them missing—and the paint on the walls was peeling. Plaster crumbled in several spots where shelving racks might once have stood. It was an abandoned building; Sarah was sure.

Trapped in an abandoned building with a serial killer.

Sure, why the hell not?

The Flower Man gasped and sat up.

Shit!

Sarah gritted her teeth and yanked at her bonds harder. The ropes tore at her wrists, but she felt them give a little. If they had been nylon or wire, she'd be screwed. She sawed her wrists back and forth, working at the knot millimetre by millimetre, as quickly as she could. Each minuscule gain brought agony as flesh shore away from her wrists. The Flower Man remained on the ground staring into space. He had not come-to yet and seemed confused about where he was.

Sarah struggled.

The ropes loosened.

Blood flowed down her wrists.

The Flower Man climbed to his knees, then to his feet.

He looked at Sarah. Saw her.

Shit shit shit.

Time had run out.

The Flower Man stared at her but didn't seem to understand. Then his eyes lit up, and a slippery smile stretched across his lips. "Meadow? I feared we'd been parted."

Sarah struggled. "Stay the fuck away from me!"

"Don't be so coarse." He slunk towards her, long arms and legs swaying like reeds.

"Get the fuck away from me!" she shouted louder, hoping someone would come help her. Wishful thinking.

The Flower Man leered over Sarah, his mouth smacking within inches of hers. Bizarrely, he gave off the scent of fresh cut grass. His teeth glinted pure-white in the dimly lit room. "Silence... petal."

Sarah's neck stiffened, and she struggled to breathe. The ruined side of her face throbbed as blood pumped through the brittle capillaries there. The monster standing over her reached into the pocket of his thick work-trousers. For one terrifying second, Sarah thought he was going for a knife, but then realised it was nothing so large. The Flower Man cupped something in his left hand, but his other seized her face, pressing down over her nose. Sarah grunted, and he shoved his left hand against her mouth, crushing the hidden contents against her mouth, scratching at her lips. She struggled, but the hand clamped over her face was like a Venus Fly Trap, and she couldn't take a breath.

Except through her mouth.

"A true gardener does not seek optimal conditions," the Flower Man whispered into her ear, "he seeks to create life in harsh, unwelcoming conditions. That is the true aim. Your face is barren, but I shall make it grow again—like a meadow."

The word 'barren' chilled Sarah, but she was powerless to fight back. Another second passed, and she could resist no longer. Her lips parted, and she gasped.

Along with air, she swallowed something else. Something bitter.

"Seeds, my petal. *Blue Phacelia*, the perfect flower for a desert like you."

Sarah gagged, spitting out seeds but choking on several that went down her throat. Her attacker was crazy. Did he expect a flowerbed to sprout suddenly from her ears? "You're insane."

"Some might say. The truth is I possess clarity most—if not all—lack. Do you not see the scourge set upon this world by mankind? Take this room for instance—a peeling, insect-laden pit. Unused, yet taking up a patch of land where nature might thrive. Mankind takes what it wants, and far more than it needs. We are spiralling towards our doom,

Meadow, but I am fighting back. I fight for that which cannot defend itself."

"F-Flowers?"

"Nature. Everything that is *not* man, for man is a weed ruining the greatest and most beautiful of gardens."

"You kill innocent people for nonsense," said Sarah.

"No human being is innocent."

"You need help. Actually, right now, we both need help."

He smiled at her, took a brief glance to his left and right. "You're probably correct. I assume our hosts are interested in you and not me, but we shall see. We could have hours together until then—those men seem very busy. Plenty of time to tend to you."

Sarah struggled with her bonds again. "Leave me alone. Just... Please, don't."

"Do not fear. We shall do this together."

He lunged forward, mouth against her neck and biting.

Agony.

Sarah screamed.

The Flower Man took out another handful of seeds and shoved them into the ragged wound he had opened above her left shoulder, grinding them down deep into her bleeding flesh.

Sarah screamed louder.

The Flower Man snarled and went to bite her again. This time, he aimed for the other side of her neck. Sarah's instincts took over, and she dropped her head, catching her attacker's mouth with her forehead. The Flower Man snarled and clutched his jaw—more angry than hurt. Sarah saw blood glisten over his teeth as he sneered at her. Did he enjoy the pain? The blood on his lips? Lifting a finger, he wagged it at her like a disapproving school teacher. "The sweetest roses have the sharpest thorns. You will be glorious in bloom."

He lunged at her again, just as the door behind him opened. The squeaking hinges distracted him, making him spin around. Sarah didn't get a clear view of what happened next, but there was a loud *clonk*, and the Flower Man fell at her feet. This time, a great deal of blood leaked from a wound on his forehead.

"My apologies," said her saviour. "I sought to arrive sooner. Pressing business matters, I'm afraid. I am sure you understand, Sarah. It is good to see you again."

A man stepped forward out of the shadows, entering the shaft of light coming from the glass panel above the door. Clean shaven and suited, he was a different person from the man Sarah had once known.

But it was still undeniably him.

Al-Sharir.

CHAPTER FIFTY-SIX

Sarah's boogeyman stood before her in the flesh. Years of torment, of sleepless nights and panic attacks, all because of this man, swarmed through her brain, yet she could vocalise nothing. She shied away, a frightened girl. The thing she hated most.

Al-Sharir, on the other hand, seemed pleased to see her; a benign smile on his face like a father greeting his kids after returning from work. "Captain Stone, how fateful to be standing in the same room as you again. Allah enjoys playing games, no?"

Sarah's tongue felt thick in her mouth. "W-what are you doing here?"

"I think you know. Business brings me here. Speaking of which, I was impressed with how you foiled my protégé last year. Hesbani always was difficult to control—he allowed anger to drive him instead of justice. Justice is always proper, always constrained by right and wrong, but anger—unbridled—is unwieldy and prone to misuse. It is good to see you, Sarah. I often reflect upon our time together in the desert. You have no child, I take it? Did you lie to me all along?"

Al-Sharir had released Sarah from her captivity in Afghanistan only because she was pregnant. Did he know she had lost the child soon after, or did he think she had lied to save her own life? "My baby died after what you and Hesbani did to me."

"I did nothing. You damaged yourself by entering a country that was not your own and seeking to impose your unwanted ideals on an innocent population. No British soldier injured in Afghanistan is an innocent victim. You accept your fates when you wage war."

"My unborn child was innocent!" said Sarah, thrashing against her bindings. "I was in your country to help!"

Al-Sharir looked at her with what appeared as genuine sympathy. "I am sorry for your loss, truly, however deserved they may be. In your mind, life has rewarded you unjustly. I can only imagine how you feel about that. Angry, I would assume."

"You ruined my life."

"You and your armies have ruined thousands."

"You're a monster."

"I am just a man, and you are just a woman."

Sarah had forgotten how much the man spoke in riddles. She struggled to stay calm. "Let me go, Al-Sharir."

"Perhaps. Perhaps I shall kill you instead. I released you into the desert to be a mother, to turn away from your wickedness and live a decent life—the life of a good woman. Then, last year, I learn of you interfering with Hesbani as part of the MCU—another corrupt agency designed to subdue my people."

"Hesbani killed hundreds of innocent people. He was going to shoot the Queen."

Al-Sharir gave part of a smile and nodded. "Audacious, yes. A child throwing a tantrum, I am sad to admit. He should never have turned away from me."

Sarah was surprised. "You don't agree with what he tried to do?"

"It lacked greater design, but he was defending Allah's will. It is his capture and execution that pains me. His rashness was his undoing and I can blame no one for that. But let us not talk of the departed any longer. You are very much alive, Sarah. Your tormenter too..." he nodded at the Flower Man who was moaning on the ground. His head wound glistened but didn't leak fresh blood. "Should I wake him up and leave you to resume your interaction?"

Sarah still tasted the bitter seeds at the back of her throat. "If your plan is to punish me by leaving me at the mercy of a psychopath, then just get it over with. I won't beg you."

"Ha! Dear Sarah, my plans go far beyond you. You are but a symptom of an immoral world."

"Immoral?"

Al-Sharir nodded slowly. "Nations of sheep who pay footballers millions while 3rd-World doctors operate without supplies. Governments who see war as business and peace as recession. The West is a plague, and it is spreading. I shall be the cure."

Sarah shook her head, tired of the same old argument. "You think your way is better? Sharia law, forced worship?"

"It is not Sharia law, it is Allah's law, but no man should worship unwillingly. That is the problem—man's will is being eroded by an empire of sin. Will you deny He who gave you life?"

"The man who gave me life is dead because I shot him."

"An act of courage without a doubt, but your true father is eternal."

In another time, Sarah might have continued the argument until she had vented her frustrations, but she wanted this over with. "Kill me, I don't care. Whatever you are going to do, just do it, but don't kid yourself that there's anyone up there keeping score. You're deluded, and I feel sorry for you."

Al-Sharir stepped out of the light and knelt before her so that his face was in line with hers. "You truly seek death, Sarah? The last time we met, you begged for life. At any cost, if I remember."

"I've changed."

"I see that. Okay, I shall conclude our discussion." He pulled a knife from a sheath he held in his hand—a slim knife, tapered like a small sword. "I took this from a Russian when I was fourteen years old. Many have tried to take my country from me, Sarah. You are just the latest."

Sarah's death had been inevitable. Ever since leaving the desert, she had known this day would come. Al-Sharir would finish his destruction of her. Part of her welcomed it. She could never heal from the wounds he had inflicted upon her—only fester.

Let it be now, she thought. *Let it just be over.*

Still, Sarah couldn't ignore her fear as the blade hovered closer, moving towards her chest; but it did not pierce her. Instead, Al-Sharir thrust at the gap between her ribs and her arm, sliding the knife beneath her armpit until it was behind her back. Sarah didn't understand what was happening, but then she felt the blade saw at her bindings.

He was letting her go.

Al-Sharir pulled the knife back and placed it on her knee where it balanced precariously. "A gift to you, my dear. This man on the floor is an abomination. A creature born of darkness. Kill him, as I would. Do Allah's work by extinguishing this evil, and I will allow you to go free, to serve Him by my side."

Sarah couldn't help herself and laughed. "Join you? Are you insane?"

Al-Sharir showed no sign of insincerity. If anything, he appeared hurt by her reaction. "Is it so crazy? You and I are bound, Sarah. Allah wishes our destinies entwined, and it is so. You are angry, as I once was. You want to stop the horrors of the world. So do I. But you are fighting on the wrong side. Does it not exhaust you?"

Sarah surprised herself by answering. "Yes."

Al-Sharir nodded knowingly. "The anger will not leave you unless you free yourself from it. You joined the MCU to find justice, but you will find none in its false causes. Join me and truly change the world, Sarah. Let us end the time of soldiers and bombs. Your child could have grown up in a different place. A place where she would not be forced into the desert to risk her life for a false notion of freedom. I do not enjoy violence, Sarah. I do not profit from it. Humanity does not profit from it. Help me bring peace to the world."

Sarah shook her head, but didn't laugh anymore. Al-Sharir was as compelling now as he had been in the desert. What was he planning? How many more must die to incite his version of *change*?

Was he truly trying to make the world a better place? Could he? Could *anyone*?

"Join me, Sarah, and live. I shall leave you alone with this man—this creature who has killed so many. A *serial killer* as you would put it. He would see you dead, so you must act before he has a chance to."

Sarah glanced at the Flower Man and thought about the girl in the sewer—blinded and mutilated like all the other victims. Did a creature such as this deserve the gentle treatment of the British justice system? Was Al-Sharir's way better?

Did she have a better idea?

Al-Sharir walked away, giving her one last cursory glance as he paused in the doorway. "You are unfinished business, Sarah. Whatever choice you make, I shall end our affairs today."

The door closed, and a bolt slid across.

Once again, Sarah was trapped in the dark with a killer.

Al-Sharir had sliced Sarah's bindings and left. The ropes no longer dug into her skin and were becoming looser.

From the floor, the Flower Man grunted. "Meadow? Are you still there, Meadow?"

Sarah scissored her wrists back and forth, working the ropes free little by little. Returning blood flow made her fingertips throb, which only made her movements clumsier.

"Meadow?" The Flower Man stretched the word out as though tasting it. "*Meeeeadooooow...*"

Sarah shifted her body to the side, gaining leverage to free her wrists. Almost free, but her extended movement caused the knife placed across her knee to tumble to the ground. She'd forgotten all about it, but now she needed it more than ever. "Damn it."

The Flower Man rose to his feet. As the recipient of several beatings today, he was resilient to say the least.

Sarah got one wrist free—

The Flower Man rubbed at his head, saw the blood on his fingertips and growled.

—then the other wrist.

The ropes fell away. Sarah's hands were free.

The Flower Man wasted no time and dove at her like a snarling dog. Sarah freed herself in time to throw herself forward and out of harm's way. She slipped from the chair and landed on her knees. The Flower Man collided with the chair.

Sarah scurried towards the knife on the floor. It lay only a few feet away.

If she could just reach it...

The Flower Man fell on top of Sarah, pinning her face down against the dirty carpet tiles. "Time I planted you, petal." He wrestled with her arms, trying to force them behind her back.

"Get off me!"

"Not until I plant my seed in you. You will be my greatest work."

Sarah fought to free her arms, gasping in pain as her shoulder sockets strained.

She was powerless—her attacker too strong.

Her entire life had been spent fighting—fighting to get her father's attention, fighting to make it in a man's Army, fighting to overcome her demons—but now she was just another victim. Like the girl in the sewer, or the innocent people who had been going about their business on Tower Bridge.

Or her unborn child.

Sarah's chin smacked against the floor clacking her teeth together, but her fighting renewed and she strained with everything she had. Managing to yank one of her arms free, she threw it out ahead of her, scrabbling at the carpet tiles. Her fingers found the knife and wrapped around the leather handle.

"Stop fighting." The Flower Man clutched at her belt, busying his hands. "You cannot stop nature."

Sarah twisted onto her side. Then she swung the knife. With his hands busy at her belt, the Flower Man left himself undefended. The knife plunged right towards his face.

Clonk!

Sarah used the blade's pommel and aimed at the Flower Man's left eye, thudding against hard socket. He yelped with pain and fell away like a scalded dog. Courage returning, Sarah rolled onto her stomach and clambered to her feet. Putting her entire bodyweight forwards, she tackled the Flower Man to the ground and straddled his chest, pinning his arms. She used the blade's pommel once more, bludgeoning the Flower Man across his face and splitting the taut flesh above his cheek. His mouth formed a pained 'O' as his arms flopped weakly at his sides. Sarah had him beat.

The power belonged to her.

The knife trembled in her hand, tip pointed up towards the ceiling.

She rotated her wrist until the blade pointed downward. The tip hovered over the Flower Man's panting chest. Sarah could end the sick bastard now and do the world a favour. No waiting for justice, no risk of escape. Instant closure for the victim's families.

Maybe Al-Sharir's way was right. It got quicker, better results.

The knife felt heavy in Sarah's hand.

It would be so easy to plunge it downwards. Just put her weight on it and *pop...*

Sarah tossed the blade aside, sickened.

There was no denying the relief in the Flower Man's bulging eyes.

"I won't play Al-Sharir's games," said Sarah. "The only way to end violence is to trust in the justice we have. You and I are getting out of here, and then I am placing you under arrest to stand trial and answer for your crimes, you sick fuck," she added.

The Flower Man grinned. "Looking forward to it, Meadow."

Sarah punched him in the mouth hard enough make his teeth rattle. "One wrong move and I'll break your neck. This is over for you, understand? If you plan on escaping, think again. Only reason I didn't bury that knife in your chest is because I don't want your blood on me. So prepare yourself to spend the rest of your life in a cell. The alternative is you stay here and die. The man who abducted us is dangerous—more dangerous than you—and he won't have any patience for your brand of lunatic. Get it?"

In a rare moment of lucidity, the Flower Man kept quiet and nodded.

Sarah got to her feet. "Good. There's a glass pane above the door big enough to get through. You are going to hoist me up so I can knock it through, then I'll unlock the door on the other side."

She allowed him to his feet. It looked like he'd gone several rounds with Ivan Drago, but he nodded willingly. "Sounds like a plan."

Sarah stared up at the panel above the door. It didn't look thick, but knocking it through might prove difficult and make noise. Once she got through, she needed to be quick. Like it or not, there was no option not to release the Flower Man. He was the only one with interests matching her own right now. He was a cold and calculating creature, but intelligent enough to realise his fate if he didn't escape with her.

The Flower Man wiped his palms against his overalls. "Ready, partner?"

The wooden chair Sarah had been tied to was bolted to the ground. She took a run up and kicked it, but needed another three attempts to eventually knock out one of the backrest struts. She picked up the fallen length of wood and batted it in her palm. "Now I'm ready. Make a step up for me."

The Flower Man stood in front of the door and laced his hands together. "Giddy up."

Sarah strode forward and hopped up into his clasped hands. He hoisted her with ease—long limbs easily capable of handling her weight. Without asking permission, Sarah stepped onto his shoulders and raised herself up higher. Although he mumbled with discomfort, he obliged and held her ankles for support. His fingers against her flesh made Sarah's skin crawl.

"Hold me still. I'm going to knock it out." She placed one hand against the door to steady herself and raised the chair strut in the other. She held it in the middle like a javelin and smashed the end against the centre of the glass panel. Rather than shattering, the pane popped out whole and tumbled to the other side.

Sarah clucked. "Well, that was easy."

"We make a good team," said the Flower Man, still holding her ankles.

Leaning forward, Sarah peered through the gap she had made. The corridor beyond was lit, but out of the two fluorescent strip bulbs only the far one worked, which left the near stretch of hallway dim. At least no one stood out there—not a single guard posted. Sarah knew it was too good to be true, but she had to take advantage while she could. She wedged her elbows against the window frame and tipped forwards, hanging halfway out the gap. The fit was tight and gave her little room to manoeuvre. Her only choice was a headfirst lunge to the floor—with fingers crossed she didn't break her neck.

It was better than hanging around waiting for Al-Sharir to return.

"Be ready," she called back to the serial killer clutching her ankles.

"I am ready."

Sarah heaved herself forwards through the gap.

And then she fell.

Throwing her arms out, she tried to land safely, but her head hit the floor, and her weight came down awkwardly on her left arm. She crumpled onto her back in a heap. The pain was immediate—a stinging jolt running all the way to her shoulder. There was no time to lie there recovering, though, so she quickly hopped to her feet. Briefly rubbing her shoulder, she flexed her arm to test it. That she could still move it was the best she could expect right now.

"Meadow, are you okay?"

Compassion from a serial killer.

Or concern for his ticket out, Sarah thought.

She looked at the locked door behind her and considered turning her back on the Flower Man. It was a dumb move to free him, but she wasn't willing to abandon him to Al-Sharir's men. He belonged to her now, and she would be the one deciding his fate. For all she knew, Al-Sharir might end up letting him go. A risk she couldn't take.

The lock on the door comprised of a simple bolt, and Sarah slid it across. The door swung open and revealed a smiling Flower Man. "Very honourable of you, Meadow. I assumed you would leave me to rot."

"Not here, not yet." She yanked him by his arm and started him down the hallway ahead of her. He was still beaten enough to remain subdued, but if he got wind of the fact that her shoulder was wrecked, he might risk pouncing on her again. She had to hide her bruises. Just to be sure, she bent down and picked up the wooden chair spoke.

They headed to the end of the corridor. It didn't take long until they heard a voice. The door to the next room was ajar, and Sarah moved up to peer inside. A single man occupied it—he was talking on a mobile phone. Was this the guard in charge of making sure Sarah didn't escape? If he was, she had lucked out, because he had allowed himself to become distracted. Al-Sharir obviously hadn't expected her to team up with the Flower Man, and without him there would have been no escape. She could hardly believe this herself.

Speaking of whom, the Flower Man crouched beside her, following her lead. From the smile on his face, he seemed to be enjoying himself, but he was also squinting as if concentrating. Sarah put a finger against her lips to make sure he remained quiet. He nodded, but then resumed his thoughtful squinting, studying the man in the room.

The guard was not what Sarah expected. He was a white man, not Middle-Eastern, and it sounded as if he was speaking Russian. The only thing that mattered was that he was alone and distracted.

Sarah would get no better opportunity, so she crept up behind the man. He was so embroiled in his conversation he failed to notice her presence. She brought the wooden chair spoke down on the back of his skull and dropped him. There was no need to hit him again.

"Nicely done," said the Flower Man, inspecting her work with an appreciative grin. "One hit and done."

"Not my first time." She checked on the guard and was glad to see he was still breathing. He had no gun or weapons of any kind, which was disappointing. All he had was a walkie talkie. His job had been to radio in if something happened. Maybe Al-Sharir didn't want anybody hurting Sarah except himself.

So far, the escape had been easy. Too easy.

"We don't know what we'll find in the next room," said Sarah. "So be ready to run. We can't be far outside of the city, so we need to get outside and flag down help."

"Or to the nearest sewer."

Sarah couldn't tell if he was joking or not. He looked a sorry state with his head caked in blood and his chest panting, but there was no mistaking the animalistic glint in his eyes—like he might blink sideways at any moment—a lizard dressed like a man. Insanity seemed to ooze off him.

The next room they entered was a reception area with an old three-seat sofa and two empty vending machines. There was another door on the opposite side, leaving them no choice of direction. It wasn't ideal, but Sarah wasted no time. The longer they took, the more likely another of Al-Sharir's men—or the man himself—noticed their escape. The new door was thankfully unlocked, and Sarah opened it cautiously. Her heart thudded in her chest.

Please let this be a way out, or at least some place with a panic room and phone.

Her wishful thinking let her down, and Sarah found herself inside a wide-open warehouse. A dozen dangerous-looking men stared at her.

Oh shit.

The Flower Man grunted. "I think they see us, Meadow."

Sarah nodded. "It's a possibility."

She glanced about quickly, taking in everything she could. The one side of the warehouse was open, with several loading bay shutters raised up on their rollers. A large white van stood parked just inside. In the middle of the warehouse, a large group of men surrounded Al-Sharir, who seemed surprised to see her loose, but also amused by it.

He was the cat and she was the mouse, they both knew it. Only three men pulled out guns, but they all pointed at Sarah.

"Could someone direct me to the toilets, please?" said Sarah, hoping they didn't shoot her right then.

"Sarah, I underestimated you," said Al-Sharir, smiling at her warmly. "I assumed you'd try to escape, but I expected it to take you longer than ten minutes. Did you pull the chair beneath the window? I made sure it was bolted securely."

She shook her head and then nodded to the Flower Man. "I got my friend to give me a boost."

The Flower Man waved. "Nice to meet you all."

Al-Sharir kept his focus on Sarah. "Working with your enemies for a greater purpose. You think much like I do. Have you considered my offer of alliance?"

"I am nothing like you," Sarah spat. "You expected me to commit murder."

"No, I only hoped you would. To have you with me would have been most elegant, but I assume you are choosing option B, which puts us in an uncompromising opposition. I don't play kindly with *my* enemies, Sarah, I shall warn you now."

"You'll always be my enemy, Al-Sharir."

A brief standoff ensued, which surprised Sarah, for she had no leverage. Perhaps Al-Sharir was still deciding whether to kill her. The Flower Man edged away. Sarah would do the same if not for the fact she was locked in a staring contest with the monster from her nightmares. She had no idea what to do, or what was about to happen.

Another moment passed. Al-Sharir sighed, pulled out a gun, and started shooting.

Sarah ducked just in time and fell into a run. More shots rang out, forcing her to duck her head and run blindly. She made for the open side of the warehouse—the only chance for survival.

If she could just make it outside...

The only cover was the truck, so she sprinted towards it.

"Wait for me." The Flower Man raced after her, arms flapping above his head.

Chunks of cement floor bounced up at their feet and ricochets bounced off the walls. That Sarah hadn't been hit yet was a miracle. It would only take a few seconds more before a slug eventually caught her. Then she would bleed out on the floor with her perpetual tormentor standing over her.

She dove towards the van and scrambled up against the side. She'd made it! A few seconds of safety were now hers.

"Stop! Stop shooting." Al-Sharir shouted at his men and the shooting petered out. "Sarah?" he said. "Sarah, we can't escape each other. Why not give in now? All that pain you carry with you. It can end."

Sarah slumped against the side of the van. There was something about this day that wanted her dead, and dread clung to her like a mouldy shower curtain. She wanted out of this life, but it had its talons in her and wouldn't let go. Maybe she should just step out and let a bullet claim her.

It would be so easy.

But Al-Sharir had stopped his men from firing for now.

Sarah frowned. *Why?*

Al-Sharir's men didn't have a perfect line on her, but they could easily suppress her until they had her surrounded. So why weren't they firing?

Because I'm standing next to the van.

What is inside this van?

The Flower Man knelt beside Sarah clinging to her like glue. He had stopped smirking and looked shell-shocked. Oddly, she felt responsible for him. She clicked her fingers in front of his face and regained his focus. He nodded to let her know he was still present.

The two of them were still screwed though.

Silently, Sarah pointed at the van's side door then at the handle. The Flower Man frowned, but seemed to understand her instructions.

He rose from his knees and yanked open the side panel, sliding the door across on its rail.

Sarah staggered away from what she saw inside the truck. "God no!"

The Flower Man shook his head, a look of abject horror on his face. "We have to stop this."

Sarah prodded him. "There's no time. We have to get out of here."

The Flower Man nodded and came back to reality—they were being shot at—and they hurried alongside the van until they were outside the warehouse.

They were nearly free.

The sun was about to lose its grip on the sky. It would be dark soon.

"Sarah, you can't stop me." Al-Sharir called after her. "Nobody will stop me. This world *will* change."

Sarah and the Flower Man escaped the warehouse, and without looking back, they raced across an empty courtyard towards the main road. There was no gate, only a barricade which they ducked under without slowing. The rush of traffic on the main road in either direction allowed them to disappear.

Al-Sharir did not follow. Sarah was safe.

But not for long.

No one would be safe for long.

———————

Now that she was out of the warehouse, Sarah's body gave out. Her injured shoulder sagged, and her tired legs shuddered with every step. By the time she reached the end of the road, she probably resembled a weird imitation of Elvis. The Flower Man followed closely, and he too looked ready to drop. Good thing, too, because if he tried to run, she could do nothing to stop him.

They dodged evening traffic as they fled the warehouse and Sarah noted street names so she could call down hell upon Al-Sharir. If she could find a phone soon, he would have no time to escape. But every time she tried to flag a driver, she was ignored—people did not stop on busy London roads.

She needed to make that call.

What she had seen in that van...

An alleyway led between a closed tyre fitters and a vacant warehouse. It spat them out onto a busy high street, and Sarah almost cried with relief. Night had fallen, but pedestrians still hurried back and forth. Their chattering was music to her ears. Shops still traded—their lights switched on and doors open. Sarah considered grabbing someone for their mobile phone, but then she saw something even better outside a Chinese greengrocer.

"Come on!" she said, grabbing the floundering Flower Man and dragging him across the road. "Don't try to run, because you won't get ten yards in the state you're in. All I need is one good Samaritan."

He glared at her, defying her assessment of him. "I may be hurt, but I have strong roots."

"Perhaps, but that doesn't mean you didn't get your arse handed to you several times today. I don't think you can take another beating. So move it!"

The Flower Man clutched the back of his head tenderly as if remembering quite how beaten he was, then rolled his eyes in resignation. Without further argument, he accompanied Sarah to the other side of the street where she hurried over to the payphone she had seen —an old-fashioned red booth you rarely saw these days. Perhaps it was a sign. Inside its metal confines, Sarah immediately felt safer. The Flower Man held the door and leaned in beside her. In a stroke of fortune, it was one of the few pay phones in London not at all vandalized, and it gave a dial tone without pause. Sarah called the secret number that MCU agents could call in emergencies. It put her straight through to command, which in the last year had become a hive of ten-dozen operatives. She didn't recognise the woman who answered the call.

"It's Sarah Stone. Put me through to Palu."

"Yes, ma'am."

Three seconds later: "Sarah, it's Palu! Where are you?"

Sarah squeezed the phone, wavering body sagging against the side of the booth. "He's alive," she shouted into the receiver. "Palu, Al-Sharir is alive."

"What?"

"He has a bomb. A nuclear fucking bomb."

Palu's voice was grave. "Sarah, tell me exactly where you are."

Sarah turned to find a street name, but a glint of metal caught her eye. She glanced down to see a thin dagger in the Flower Man's hand—the blade Al-Sharir had given her back at the warehouse.

She thought she'd left it back in the room, but he must have grabbed it while they were on opposite sides of the door.

The thin blade slid into Sarah's guts before she could say anything. It felt cold. And yet it burned. The Flower Man whispered into her ear as she fell. "I'm sorry, but I have gardens to tend to. Goodbye Meadow."

Sarah slid down the side of the booth to the floor, clutching the hole in her stomach as it leaked blood. Nobody on the street noticed her inside, and the Flower Man closed the door and simply left.

Yet again, the day wanted Sarah to die.

This time she felt like it might win.

The heat in Afghanistan drove the men crazy, but Sarah kind of liked it. Hamish was a pale Scotsman—so he suffered worse—but Sergeant Miller, with his dark-black skin seemed to tolerate it as well as Sarah did. Right now, Sarah was enjoying a little alone time in Camp Bastian. The place was abuzz with activity, as usual, but she found that it was easy to ignore if she closed her eyes and focused on the sun's rays against her skin.

Four months ago, she had arrived in the country. It was her first real tour after Sandhurst, and prior to it she had only been on low-security attachments in Germany and Poland. It felt good to finally be out in the field, where she could finally do some good. That she had been distracted by a young US Army Ranger was something she was aware of, and trying to fight. Yet, she couldn't help thinking about Thomas.

He was a sergeant attached to the 75th and had arrived in the UK side of the vast military complex that comprised Camp Leatherneck and Bastian to gain assistance with a patrol he was making. Sarah had taken his Intel and offered a small detachment of men on behalf of her commanding officer. Thomas had thanked her with a bootlegged bottle of wine during an evening that had ended with her hands down his fatigues. She still blushed at the thought. It didn't seem like he had been out to take advantage though, and when he said he would be back to see her soon, he seemed to mean it. In fact, he seemed excited at the prospect.

Was that why Sarah had spent her two days off sunbathing in the centre of camp where she could be easily spotted.

She was acting like a teenager.

But it was the first time she had ever felt like this. Her entire life had been dedicated to a military education—almost inevitable with a father in the SAS—and she had wasted no time with youthful frivolities. Sure, she had her share of male interest, but as soon as they met her dad, they always decided she was more trouble than it was worth. So she stopped bothering with trying to make friends or lovers. There were more important things in life. Only now was she finally in a place where she felt grown up enough to relax and live a little life. Sure, she was in a war zone, but she was happy. It felt like she was where she was meant to be.

Helping the local population hadn't been as rewarding as she had expected, and many of the Afghanis seemed to resent her presence. She had fought through it best she could, and her squad had delivered food and supplies to countless children, and offered medical assistance to a dozen villages. Whether the people wanted to be helped or not, they were being given aid. Every day, this country grew closer and closer to liberation, and one day, democracy would rule. Not everyone supported Blair and Bush on the decision to enter Afghanistan, but Sarah felt that the results would eventually speak for themselves. This was the start of something great—a harmonious and peaceful Middle-East. Sarah was proud to be a part of it.

And she was excited about seeing Thomas again.

So where was he?

Please tell me he wasn't just a player—the hot American guy from the other camp. Is he spilling the beans to his pals right now?

Almost like a mirage, Sarah's eyes spotted movement on the edge of the rec area. A man appeared beyond the open-air weights gym, moving between glistening chests and bulging biceps. He seemed to shimmer in his olive-green fatigues, but Sarah knew it was just the heat rising off the sand. Before Thomas came into full view, she had already known it was him. She had been sure.

He's here. Gosh, why is my stomach fluttering?

He spotted her sunbathing and frowned. "Hey, it's er... *Sharon*, right?"

Oh my God. Are you kidding me?

She leapt up from her chair. "Sarah!"

"Thomas. Pleased to meet you."

Sarah felt sick. She stared at the man and didn't know whether to punch him or kick him in the nuts. She might do both.

Thomas burst out laughing. "Your face is a picture. It's also extremely beautiful. Have you always been so perfect?"

Still off-kilter, Sarah wobbled. "Y-you're pulling my leg?"

"Yeah, I'm yanking your chain. I came here to see you, like I said I would. Haven't had a chance until now; you know how it is with the war and stuff."

She chuckled. "Yeah, it's a bother, isn't it?"

"You free today, or do you have orders to sit here?"

"I was... waiting for you," she admitted, then chastised herself for laying herself out so openly. She'd had such a closed-off upbringing, with only the distinguished Major Stone as a parent, but she had somehow ended up as an over-sharer. Often she would speak openly of her feelings and make people uncomfortable.

"So you *are* free?"

Sarah blinked. "Huh? Oh, yes. I'm free. How long do you need me for?"

"Why, do I need to sign a form or something? Let's start with lunch and see where it leads us."

"To dinner usually," she said. *Wow, what a lame joke.*

"And then to supper. May I?" He offered his elbow. Sarah took it, and together, the two of them walked through the military camp in the centre of the desert like a married couple.

Perhaps one day they would be, thought Sarah, then told herself to stop being such a silly girl. She was an officer of the British Army, not a teenager.

Still, maybe he's the one...
Maybe.

CHAPTER FIFTY-SEVEN

Down in the depths of MCU's subterranean base, the Earthworm, Howard's mouth was dry, and he lugged a rotten carcass in his guts. He'd failed her. Again. Maybe it was unwise to care so much for a fellow agent—death was an ever-looming part of the job after all—but it was he who had recruited Sarah.

That made it his responsibility to keep her safe.

Good job, Howard. Really, great job.

The rest of MCU's senior team sat around the conference desk, looking equally sick to their stomachs. Sarah meant a lot to them all. They meant a lot to each other. You couldn't survive hell without company.

"How did we let this happen?" Thomas demanded.

"This isn't on you, Thomas," said Palu, pasty and white. "You just got here. This is my team. My mistake."

Howard nodded. "We're all in this together."

Mandy didn't speak, but he also nodded without hesitation.

Thomas just sighed. "We need to find her."

"It's been twenty-four hours, and we have nothing," said Palu, lacing his hands together in front of him and blowing out air. "How can terrorists blow up a London landmark and leave us nothing? How is one of our agents gutted in the street with no one seeing? This is not what the MCU is about. We do not fail; we do not fuck up. We are the angels that haunt the dreams of bad men. But today..." he shook his head with disgust. "Today we are broken and beaten. I don't understand how this happened."

Howard sighed. "It happened because Al-Sharir is supposed to be dead. Every scrap of intelligence coming out of the Middle-East tells us he has been missing for years."

Palu shrugged, looked angry even though Howard had said nothing to offend. "So what are you saying? Sarah's last words were untrue?"

"No! Sarah said she saw him, and I believe her. She was abducted and escaped—like she always does—but only after seeing something."

Thomas raised his eyebrows. "A nuclear bomb?"

"That's what she said. Why doubt her?"

"Because she has never seen a nuclear bomb up close, nor have any of us, I would imagine."

Howard looked away and grunted. "Perhaps it said *Nuclear Bomb* on the side, Tom, I don't know."

Thomas sneered. "Things need to be that clear for you to do your job, don't they, Hopkins? You are Sarah's partner. How many times has she been hurt, abducted, or threatened in that time? You're not fit for this job. You should step down—join the police."

Palu smashed his fist on the table and stared at Thomas. "Agent Hopkins is a damn fine agent and deserves better than to be spoken to in that way. And I would also inform you that being a police officer in this country is not a lesser calling."

Thomas sighed. "You're right. I apologise, Howard. I'm sure you did your best."

"My *best*? Gee, thanks."

"Enough, Howard," warned Palu.

Howard quieted. As much as Thomas was an arsehole, his words hurt. Sarah had been in constant jeopardy since Howard had brought her in. As partners went, he was a shitty one.

But what could I have done? Sarah is a lioness. She hunts alone. Without her, the MCU might not have done half the good it has.

"I assembled you all here for an update," said Palu, nodding at some of the senior analysts standing at the back of the room. They weren't often invited to senior meetings. "What do we have? Mandy?"

Mandy flinched as if surprised to be called on. He cleared his throat twice before he summoned words. "The Tower Bridge bombers were spotted arriving in a Toyota Space Cruiser, a relic from the 90s. Not many about—a collector's item, really." He cleared his throat again. "Anyway, I set up a team to trace its history and recent locations."

Palu sneered. "So, you have nothing? Thomas, what about you?"

"I've been working with my contacts in the Middle-East, and they all agree that Shab Bekhier has been dormant for at least the last three years—not including Hesbani's splinter group. My current assumption is that a new group has assembled and taken the name."

"So you don't believe Al-Sharir is behind this?" asked Palu.

"How could he be? The man is wanted by every authority in Europe. If he were still alive, we would have flagged him by now. If a nuclear bomb were in play, it's more likely that this is an Iranian plot—or maybe Pakistani."

Howard shook his head. "Sarah used to be your wife, Tom, and yet you dismiss what she said? She said it was Al-Sharir."

"I am *still* her husband, Hopkins, but that is beside the point. Sarah has been under a lot of strain, and the topic of Shab Bekhier has rattled her. We're unable to validate what she told us right now. She may already have been stabbed by that point. Blood loss... panic... she's not a reliable witness. I don't want to get sidetracked by looking for phantoms. Our main concern is a potential bomb—nuclear or otherwise—so I suggest you focus on something other than Sarah, Hopkins. Your attachment to her is concerning."

"Excuse me?" said Howard, shifting in his seat. His hands were sweating.

Thomas didn't flinch. "You know exactly what I'm saying. Sarah is not interested in being close to you, Howard, so back off. She's been through enough."

Howard leapt up from his seat. "Because of you, you jackass! Her head has been all over the place since you came out of the desert like the second coming. She thought you were dead. You *were* dead to her. Notice how she's not been all that keen on talking to you?"

"She just needs some time."

"Don't assume you understand what she needs, Tom. You don't know her."

"She is my wife."

Howard shook his head. "This is her family."

Thomas turned to Palu. "Is this not evidence that Hopkins is unfit to do this job? He sounds more like a love-sick schoolboy than an international agent."

Howard clambered across the table, knowing he was losing control but unable to change course. He grabbed Thomas by the collar. "I'm her partner, you arsehole."

Thomas threw a punch and knocked Howard back across the table. He tumbled awkwardly and sprawled onto some chairs. The analysts at the back of the room gasped. Thomas punched Howard in the ribs while he tried to get back to his feet.

Mandy appeared from nowhere and grabbed Thomas by the arm, swinging him into the nearest wall. Then he dragged Howard to his feet and shoved him away. "You okay?"

Howard rubbed his jaw. "I'll live."

"Suspend him, Palu." Thomas was bright red.

Palu said nothing for a moment, just laced his fingers together and stared at the table. He seemed burdened by more than just the ongoing situation. "If I'm going to suspend anybody," he said, "it will be you, Agent Gellar. Your obvious personal issues with Sarah are causing problems for us all. Agent Hopkins' relationship with Agent Stone has been nothing but professional. Your own jealousy and paranoia is affecting your work. I suggest you take responsibility for the decisions you made five years ago, and stop acting out at other people. You are new to this team, and are very welcome, but if you continue to goad my Agents, or give me orders, I will put you on the first plane back to Disneyland."

Thomas glared at Palu. "If you're referring to my home state of Florida, at least get your facts straight. Disneyland is in California. I think you mean Disney World."

"Wherever the Muppets fuck is of no concern to me, Agent Gellar. What concerns me is the fate of this nation, and right now, you all seem more interested in melodrama. If anyone could see us, we would all be fired on the spot. We have a vital duty. To this country. To each other."

Howard was panting, anger pumping his lungs like a set of bellows. He took a second to calm down, but eventually nodded. "I'm sorry, Gellar. The bad guys scored a victory yesterday, and what happened to Sarah is a little too close to home for us all. I wish I had something that could help us, but the truth is I have nothing. These terrorists appeared out of nowhere and blew up a landmark, taking a local MP and one hundred and nineteen people with them. The MCU exists to keep the gates of hell closed, but today we allowed one of the locks to fall. If we don't act now, the whole thing will blow open."

Thomas stared at his feet and seemed ashamed at his behaviour— maybe he wasn't a *complete* arsehole. "I just want to help," he said. "I apologise for doing anything other."

"Then let's figure this out," said Palu, "so that the next lunatic with a bomb looks elsewhere to make their statement. We will not allow the United Kingdom to become a soapbox for monsters."

The door to the conference room opened, making them all turn. Dr Bennet frowned at the fallen chairs and the fact that everyone was out of breath. "You know, everyone can hear you kids bickering in here. Y'all might want to keep it down. Our patient is awake, but she has quite the headache."

Howard felt a spark up his back. "Sarah's awake?"

Jessica smiled. "That's what I said now. Want me to see if the lady's taking visitors?"

Everyone in the room smiled, and the tension fell away just a little. It was the good news they needed.

Sarah was awake.

Howard entered the quiet space of the infirmary and strode toward a curtained cubicle at the back. Thomas tried to throw out a hand to hold him back, but he missed, so Howard arrived first. He threw back the curtain and smiled to see Sarah awake. "I swear you spend more time in this hospital bed than you do your own."

Sarah managed a weak smile. "That fact you even think about me in bed is weird."

Howard sat on the foot of the bed. "How are you feeling?"

"Like I was stabbed."

Thomas stepped inside. "It's not funny, Sarah. You shouldn't have been in that situation."

She blinked, and for a moment it seemed her eyes might stay closed, but then they drew open slowly. "Situations like what? Trying to stop terrorists and psychopaths? I'm pretty sure that's the exact situation MCU agents are supposed to get into."

"You should have been more careful," he chided. "You could have died."

"Don't worry about it, Tom. Even if I had died, I could just come back from the dead like you."

Thomas exhaled. "Sarah..."

"Thomas."

Howard patted her leg—warm beneath the covers. He didn't want her getting stressed out with the whole Thomas issue. "We're just glad you're okay, Sarah. Jessica said everything will heal fine."

"Except my face," said Sarah, "but hey, look on the bright side— which is on my right, in case you were wondering."

"Glad to see your sense of humour has returned," said Palu, standing by the curtain with Mandy. "I'm sorry to jump straight on your neck, but we need to be clear about what you said on the phone before..."

She nodded. "Before Plant Face stuck a knife in me like a prized pumpkin? I remember: I said Al-Sharir is alive and that he has a nuclear bomb. I wasn't kidding."

The room went silent.

"You're sure?" asked Thomas.

"Al-Sharir was wearing a name badge. And the bomb said *nuclear warhead* on the side."

Thomas glanced at Howard, unsure how to take Sarah's sarcasm. Some husband, if he didn't know her sense of humour by now. It led Howard to consider what she must have been like before he'd met her. *Before she lost half her face.*

And an unborn child.

Howard glared at Thomas. *And a husband. That makes three shitty cards life dealt her.*

"Look," said Sarah, blinking as if her eyes were irritated. "It was Al-Sharir for sure. He's had a shave, and wears a suit, but I've been seeing that man's face in my dreams every night for the last five years—and not in a good, sexy way. It was *him*. I'm certain. As for the nuclear bomb, I don't know for sure, because I'm not an atomic brain cheese, but I saw a cylinder inside an open suitcase with Russian writing on it. I'm leaning towards it being very bad."

Thomas sighed as if relieved. "It could be a chemical bomb."

Sarah nodded. "Yeah, let's hope so. That would be lovely."

"Sarah..."

"Thomas."

"So we have a serious problem on our hands," said Palu, rubbing his face with both hands. Despite his Indian heritage, he'd grown deathly pale. "Al-Sharir must have some serious resources to disappear off the radar for so long. No reason he would be in the United Kingdom other than to launch an attack."

Sarah added, "He blames us for every single death in Afghanistan, including his wife, children, and several cousins."

"Then he shouldn't have been a member of the Taliban," said Thomas.

"There's no proof he was," said Sarah. "Al-Sharir is a monster we made."

Howard groaned. "And now he's here."

Sarah looked at Palu. "So, do you believe me?"

Palu took a moment to answer. "Sarah, you are one of the bravest, most intelligent people I've ever known. You are fearless—reckless even—and sometimes you let your heart lead your decisions instead of your head. But I trust you completely. If you say Al-Sharir is here, then he is here. Relax, Sarah. We'll take care of things until you're better."

Howard patted her on the leg again. She looked beaten in a way he hadn't seen before. Eyes dull and lifeless. "I'm sorry you got hurt. I should have been there."

"No kidding," said Thomas.

Sarah gazed at Howard with bleary eyes. "It's my fault. I ran off half-cocked like I always do. If it had been you, you would have called for backup. I'm to blame, no one else."

"Well, you're safe now," said Thomas. "Get better and we'll figure out the rest later. I don't know what I would have done if you..."

Sarah grimaced. "Don't Thomas. Please don't. There's a terrorist and a serial killer loose because of me. Things haven't even started getting bad yet. I'd be better off dead."

"Do you remember anything that can help us, Sarah?" asked Palu eagerly. He was the only one with his mind on business. Howard did not blame him for that. There were bigger issues than Sarah's injury.

Sarah shook her head. "I don't remember what happened after the phone booth. Al-Sharir has set up in an abandoned warehouse somewhere. Opposite an old garage, I think. *Sherwood Street?* The bomb is in a white van—I didn't get the plates. Maybe a Citroen. I... I'm sorry; my mind's a blur."

"We blanketed the area," said Palu. "We found an empty warehouse, but there was nothing there."

"Mandy found you after we traced your call," explained Howard. "We got to you as fast as we could."

At the back, Mandy nodded solemnly. "I thought you were already gone. But when I picked you up to carry you back to the car, you woke up."

Sarah frowned as if trying to recall. "I don't remember."

"You were delirious from blood loss. It was all over the floor of the phone booth. I can't believe no one saw you. You kept saying something over and over. A name: *Katie.*"

Sarah said nothing, just stared for a moment, then lurched to the side and retched. Howard lunged to keep her from falling out of bed. Jessica came running into the room. She held a cardboard bedpan and shoved it under Sarah's chin.

"Okay, sweetheart. Get it all up. It's just the body coping with shock. Once it's out, it's out."

Sarah stopped vomiting and spat thick wads into the pan for several moments. She let out a painful moan and flopped back into the bed. Howard tried to grab her hand, but she moved it away.

"It's all finished now, Sarah," said Thomas. "You're safe. You don't need to risk your life anymore, you're done. Everything will be okay."

"Let's give her a little peace now, please, boys," said Jessica. "She needs to rest."

Howard stood. Although Sarah's wounds were not life-threatening, she looked like she was scrabbling at death's door. It wasn't only physical—she looked emotionally weak. It hurt Howard to see her. Sarah was so strong, so... *stubborn*. Seeing her beaten and wounded was not how he wanted to remember her.

And he was feeling like these might be his final moments with her. Sarah wanted out. Looking at her now, it was obvious.

"I'm here if you need me, Sarah," he told her. Then left her alone.

Sarah stared at the ceiling, willing the sickness away. It didn't matter how tough you were when you vomited; it reduced everyone to a pleading child. Nausea was the least of her worries though. Lying in bed, alone, was not what she needed.

How many people would die because of her?

How many more victims would the Flower Man claim?

When would Al-Sharir's next attack be? And where?

She was an MCU agent—a guardian—and she had failed to do her job. Worst of all, she was quitting that job. The death toll would be on her, and she wasn't even going to stick around to take responsibility.

I can't stay. I have nothing left to give.

I've been beaten, shot at, stabbed.

And how many people have I watched die? Bradley. Ollie. My father.

I've done more than should ever be expected of a person. I never asked for any of it.

"Your body will be just fine, but I'm afraid I can't prescribe anything to remove that dark cloud hanging over your head."

Sarah saw Dr Bennet standing at the foot of her bed and frowned. "Sorry?"

Jessica took a perch by Sarah's legs, scooping her long white coat beneath her. "You're finished, aren't you, sweetheart?"

Sarah nodded, and the act of admission nearly brought tears.

"That's okay. You wouldn't be human if you could let the last year's events slide off your back. I've watched you do things no one else could ever do. I mean, y'all leapt out of a helicopter in mid-air."

The absurdity of the memory made Sarah smile. The thought she had done something so reckless...

It worked though. I jumped out of a helicopter and lived.

"You'll all be better off without my crazy stunts."

Jessica huffed. "If it weren't for your *crazy stunts,* the Earthworm would have been filled in with concrete months ago. Instead, it's chock full of analysts all working against evil. You did that, Sarah."

"No."

"God made you to be what you are," said Jessica, "and you should never apologise for it. I judged you harshly when you arrived, but now I would be heartbroken to see you leave."

Sarah fought back tears again. "A year ago, I would never have believed you if you'd said I'd have people caring about me."

Jessica smiled.

"It's not enough though. I'm scared—so scared that I feel like my heart might explode in my chest. I don't sleep. I can't eat. Around every corner I expect to see a gun..." She nodded at her mid-section, bandaged and covered by the blanket, "or a knife."

Jessica sighed, reached out and took Sarah's hand. "Sweetheart, let me tell you a story about what it's like to be a frightened woman. Y'all have to go right back to nineteen eighty-eight for a start. Medical College of Georgia. That was where I got my degree. *A fine place for doctoring,* my daddy called it. I hated it. My family was poor, and I was living off the money I made working at a fried chicken shack. I shared a house with four other girls and got on with none of them—you've probably noticed I take a while to warm up to people."

Sarah nodded. "I like to describe you as *socially cautious.*"

"Then you would be most kind. Anyway, being poor wasn't the reason I hated school. I was homesick."

"Understandable."

"Not at all," said Jessica. "I should have been glad to escape. It should have been the biggest relief in the world."

Sarah frowned. "Why?"

"Because I was away from *him.*"

"Who?"

"Uncle Ted. My daddy's brother."

Sarah swallowed. "I'm not sure I like where this is going."

"You shouldn't, sweetheart, because it's precisely what you think. Back home, I was always my daddy's little angel, but Uncle Ted saw me as something different. To him, I was his dirty little niece he could use however, and whenever, he liked."

Sarah's nausea came back like a tidal wave crashing through her guts.

"It started when I was six or seven," Jessica continued. "Living so close, Uncle Ted would often babysit for my folks. I won't go into detail, but when I grew old enough to leave for school, I thought the abuse was behind me. But I missed home. Ain't that the most insane thing you ever heard?"

Sarah said nothing, not sure she understood enough to respond.

Sensing her confusion, Jessica patted her on the leg beneath the covers. "I missed my daddy and my ma. I missed the tyre swing hanging from the maple in our yard and the smell of the country. Worst of all, I missed *him*."

"Your uncle?"

"Don't ask me why, but I missed him like the rest of my folks. I think I missed my small, easy to understand world. School was like being in the jungle. People everywhere competing for grades, jobs, friends, social standing. Boys were sniffing around me every time I went for a drink, and they all seemed to have an agenda. Girls were bitchy—just like I feared they'd be. Essays were hard and ever present, and my job selling chicken at two in the morning to drunks and deadbeats was soul crushing. I was drowning, and I missed home where things made sense."

"But you stayed," said Sarah. "You were strong enough to see it through."

She nodded. "Yes, I stayed and finished my education. Turns out, though, home followed me to college. Uncle Tom took a job in Augusta, a mile away. Turned up one day right on campus to see me. I thought I was hallucinating."

Sarah shook her head. "You're kidding me?"

"Nope. He had ideas in his mind of us being together. I was a woman now, and away from home. No one would know. He had a place—small, but much nicer than the single room I had in a house with girls I hated."

"I hope you told him to piss off!"

Jessica didn't answer and looked away.

"Oh..."

Jessica turned her gaze back at Sarah. They were not weeping, but steely and hard. "I let that monster pervert me. As a child, I had no choice, but as a woman, I could have said no. But I was weak and scared, so I clung to him because he was familiar. Whatever I do, Sarah, for as long as I live, I will always be that weak, incestuous girl who moved in with her abusive uncle just to feel safe. If a heart attack hadn't taken him two years later, I'm not sure how it would have ended. I barely talk to my folks anymore; can hardly face them. Shame is a wretched thing, Sarah. No need to tell you that."

Sarah felt tears on her cheeks, unable to hold them back. "That's horrible, Jessica."

She shrugged. "And yet it's nothing."

"What? What do you mean?"

"It's just a single story in this horrible world we inhabit. Men and women make monsters of themselves every day, and countless victims are used and spat out. If I had been a stronger woman like you, Sarah, perhaps I wouldn't have been a victim. Maybe, if someone brave and courageous like you had been around to protect me, I wouldn't be the cold, mistrustful bitch I am today."

"I'm not courageous, Jessica. And you aren't a bitch."

"Yes I am, and yes you are! Sarah, you are the antithesis of men like Al-Sharir and my uncle. You are part of the other side—the side that protects victims before they get preyed on. You're scared, Sarah, but unlike other people, that doesn't stop you. Don't leave. Stay and stop the monsters. You do that, and I promise it will get easier. You *will* heal."

Sarah closed her eyes and more tears spilled down her cheeks. "How do you know that?"

"Because *I* have healed," she said. "Trust me, being here, doing this... it's the best way to stop being afraid. We have to be stronger than they are, Sarah. It's harder for us because there's more at stake."

"I don't know if I can keep going."

Jessica stood up from the bed. "You don't know you can't, either. Get some rest. I'll check on you again after Breslow leaves."

Sarah wiped her eyes and tried to sit up. Her stomach wound creased and pain flared. "The Prime Minister is here?"

"Not yet, but she's on her way. Nobody knows what she wants, but all senior team members are ordered to attend. You're probably lucky to get to sit this one out. It's unlikely she'll be happy."

"Yeah," said Sarah. "Lucky."

Heads will roll, and it's all my fault.

Jessica left Sarah alone, but she found herself incapable of sleep. Painkillers helped with the pain, but it was persistent enough to keep her from comfort. Her wound, stitched and bandaged, felt hot beneath the covers. Despite her injuries, Sarah's mind was on other things.

Why is Breslow coming here?

Does she blame the MCU for Tower Bridge?

Of course she does. Who else is to blame?

I am to blame. As much as everyone else, I am to blame.

Palu would try to take the blame personally, Sarah knew, but Howard would jump in and share it with him. Jessica would probably stay silent—Mandy for sure. Thomas would...

Sarah had no idea how Thomas would react, and that upset her. Did she even know him anymore? It had been five years.

There had been a time when Sarah thought she knew Thomas better than anyone. A time when she had loved everything about the man. Was he that same, caring person she'd planned to move to Florida with? The man she was going to settle down and live the quiet life with?

How did life get so complicated?

Sarah gritted her teeth and pushed herself into a sitting position. It hurt like hell—took her breath away—but it didn't floor her. She was able to catch her breath. Once she was sure her stitches had not reopened, she rotated her hips and tossed her legs over the side of the bed, sliding forward until her bare feet touched the frigid tiles.

God damn, her stomach hurt.

She stood up slowly, breathing heavily. An invisible hand socked her in the stomach, but she attempted to walk it off. One foot in front of the other, she took a step.

Okay, okay. This isn't so bad.

Sarah shuffled across the infirmary. She wore a hospital gown, but located her boots and stepped into them. Getting into her clothes, though, would be too much, so she headed for the door.

The infirmary lay in the Earthworm's middle section. The middle section also housed the Hive, which was where a majority of the MCU's analysts worked in a giant open workspace. That was where Sarah came out on her way to the head-section. Two hundred analysts stopped what they were doing and stared. A hospital gown was not the most professional dress for a senior field agent.

Sarah cleared her throat. "I want a team working on the location of my clothes, *stat*. I want last known locations, possible associates, the works."

The analysts continued to stare.

Sarah bellowed at them. "All right, get back to work!"

Shit that hurt. Okay, then, no more shouting.

Two colleagues came to help Sarah, but she waved them away. She limped on her own through the Hive and tried not to collapse where anybody would see. The head section of the Earthworm lay ahead, and it was where Breslow would be if she was already in the building.

She took fifteen minutes to get there, by which time she was too weak to push open the heavy door to the conference room. Through the frosted glass silhouettes moved. Words were exchanged.

Sarah knocked on the glass.

The door opened.

Howard's wide eyes peered out at her. "Sarah?"

"I wanted to check if anyone fancied a cuppa."

Jessica pushed Howard aside and appeared in the doorway. "Sarah, what are you doing out of bed? Actually, *how* are you out of bed? I gave you enough painkillers to dope a horse."

"Good thing I'm not a horse then. Is Breslow here?"

Jessica nodded her head to the side subtly. *"Yes, she's inside."*

"I need to be in on this. I'm responsible."

"Sarah, no-"

"Bloody well let her in," came a stern voice. "Stop wasting time."

Jessica sighed and moved aside so that Sarah could step inside the conference room. Sure enough, Prime Minister Breslow stood there with her hands on her hips. The stocky, short-haired brunette was pushing sixty, but she glared as fiercely as any woman in her prime.

Sarah nodded. "Prime Minister."

"Agent Stone. I wish I could say it was nice to see you, or that you're looking well, but alas I seem to run into you at the worst times."

Sarah couldn't think of anything to say, so she went over to the room's large oval table. Thomas pulled a chair out for her, but when he tried to help her sit, she shoved him away and lowered herself into the seat. She wished the back support weren't so rigid.

"Okay," said Breslow. "Can we get back to it, please? I was just in the middle of promising to close down the MCU and drag you all through the muck. Again, I state that Tower Bridge is currently sinking into the Thames. A hundred-and-twenty-two-year-old landmark gone forever because someone here wasn't doing their job." She slammed her fists on the table. "Somebody better have a damn good reason why this was allowed to happen."

Palu placed both his own hands on the desk as if to brace himself. "It's my fault," he said shakily. "The MCU had no knowledge of this attack. That is down to me as leader of this team."

"No," said Howard. "We all work together and if something was missed, we *all* missed it."

"Then you're all murderers," said Breslow. "One hundred and sixteen deaths are on you. Your job is to stop terrorists, and damn did you ever screw the fucking pooch this time."

"Again, I take full responsibility," said Palu.

"It's clear, mistakes have been made," Thomas interjected. "I intend to investigate fully what went wrong, Prime Minister."

On who's authority, thought Sarah. *Palu is the boss, not you.*

"Not now you won't," Breslow told Thomas. "I'm not here to find out who needs lynching. There'll be time for that later. There's going to be another attack, and you have less than twelve hours to stop it."

"How do you know?" asked Sarah. It was precisely as she'd feared; more deaths would be on her hands. If she hadn't turned her back on the Flower Man in that phone booth, she could have brought in a team to take out Al-Sharir before he escaped.

Breslow nodded to an aide who Sarah hadn't even noticed was standing in the room. The man had an obvious talent for fading into the background. Now, he slunk forward and placed a small laptop onto the table. He used a cable to plug it into the media port built into the conference table. The laptop's display came up on the room's 65inch wall monitor.

"The media aren't running this yet—on my orders—but I can only keep it from the public for so long. It took place this morning in front of a police station in Croydon."

Sarah watched the monitor with trepidation. Yet again, she witnessed a video of a London street. This time, the focus was on one man. Light-skinned, yet potentially Middle-Eastern, he wore *perhan tunban*—the traditional dress of an Afghani man. He looked directly at the camera as he spoke, spitting every word with venom.

"Prime Minister Breslow, for a decade you have waged war on Allah's true people. You have reduced our homes to rubble. You have taken our possessions and raped our land. Money is your idol. Greed your weapon. Today, you reap what you have sown. Already your golden city burns, but your empire has only just begun to crumble. Within twenty-four hours, we will decimate your heathen empire. We will inflict upon your golden city a death toll from which it will never recover." The man paused for a moment as if wanting his words to sink in. "The only way to prevent this is repentance. Prime Minister Breslow, accept that your life is beyond saving and end it. You have twelve hours in which to hang yourself to death on national television. Refuse and your empire will burn. One death in exchange for thousands. A true leader loves his people. Are you a true leader?"

Sarah expected the video to end, but instead, the man threw up his loose-fitting shirt and exposed several sticks of explosives wrapped around his bare stomach. Two seconds later, the man's body was replaced by a cloud of billowing smoke. A single sandal remained on the ground.

The video ended. Breslow stepped in front of the television. "As if my day couldn't get any bloody worse. The deadline is 8PM tonight. I'm not intending to hang myself, so I suggest you put a stop to these maniacs before they carry out their next attack. Fail and I will hang you out to dry like you wouldn't believe. You'll go down in history as the most inept group of people who ever lived. I will not condone any more of my public being murdered. Enough is enough. Get your shit together, folks. Palu, I want a word with you in private."

Palu nodded and followed the Prime Minister out of the room like a scalded dog. The PM's aid disappeared with them.

A long moment of silence filled the room while those remaining stared at one another blankly.

Sarah broke the tension, "Has anyone told Breslow about the nuclear bomb yet?"

CHAPTER FIFTY-EIGHT

Three hours and nothing. The MCU's senior team—the country's fore-most counter-intelligence personnel—were without leads of any kind. The minutes ticked by, and soon those minutes would make up hours. Hours they didn't have. Mandy sat in silence typing away, while Jessica anxiously hummed. Howard and Palu conversed over a shared monitor while Thomas glanced periodically at Sarah. Sarah acted as though she didn't notice.

Jessica had given her a pain injection which allowed her to func-tion, and luckily it did little to dull her mind. Unluckily, however, it did nothing to dull her emotions. Her hands trembled.

Palu had returned ten minutes after leaving to talk with Breslow, more rattled than ever. He shared nothing with the rest of them, but he'd clearly been held accountable. A sheen of sweat coated his fore-head, and he cleared his throat constantly as he worked. Unlike the conference room, the war room featured no central table, and instead, featured a circular bank of slimline computers. Any agent could bring up a document on screen and zip it across to another terminal. It allowed the senior agents to work fast and as a team. Howard was zipping something across multiple screens right now.

"I have a background on the bomber in front of the police station," he explained. "Nasir Riaz, twenty-four years old. Comes from a good family. Father's a solicitor. Mother's an estate agent. No siblings. He is a confirmed Muslim, but has no ties to extremist groups or foreign interests. I'm waiting on a search of his internet history, but so far there's nothing about him that cries terrorist. Wait, hold on a second..."

"What is it?" Sarah asked. She sat directly to his left.

Howard frowned at the screen for two seconds before speaking. "I have Riaz's education in front of me. He completed a Modern Language degree at University of Exeter and has been studying a Master's degree at University College London... in Russian Studies."

Thomas shrugged. "Russian, so?"

"It could be something," suggested Howard.

Thomas pulled a face. "Not Russia's style. Think again, Hopkins."

"No, wait," said Sarah, putting up a hand. "Back at the warehouse, right after I escaped, there was a guard. He was speaking into a phone. I swear he was speaking Russian. And the other men—Al-Sharir's men— were not all Middle-Eastern. Some of them were white. They could have been Russians."

Palu knitted his hands together and closed his eyes as if he had a headache. "Okay, okay, that may be something we can use, but... I don't know. Something feels off. Islam and Moscow don't tend to see eye to eye. The Russians shed as much blood in Afghanistan as we did. I can't see Al-Sharir working with them."

"Al-Sharir always thinks about the big picture," said Sarah. "I'm not saying these attacks came from Putin himself, but there's plenty of wealthy factions within Russia that would benefit from a destabilised West. Al-Sharir would have needed money and influence to disappear for years while he planned this. He hasn't been seen in the Middle East at all. Maybe that's because he was in Russia or Eastern Europe."

"Okay. We run with it," said Palu. "Howard, get me a list of all the students taking Russian Studies at UCL. See if you can contact Riaz's tutor. The more we can learn about the kid, the better."

"I'll check flights out of Russia during the last month," said Jessica. "Maybe Al-Sharir came in under an alias."

"Okay," said Palu, "but don't linger on that because it might be a dead end. Palm it off to an analyst quick as you can."

"Should we send a team out into the field?" asked Howard. "We need eyes on the streets."

"I've already sent out everything we have to surveil every London landmark we can think of. I even recalled Mattock from his new recruits."

Sarah relaxed at hearing Mattock was returning. The bolshy Mancunian was as tough as they came, and a calming influence in even the worst of shit storms. He had been off training new field agents in the Brecon Beacons using techniques he'd learned in the SAS. They needed him back now more than ever.

"What should I focus on?" asked Sarah, hating that she needed direction. Her mind was a blur.

"You should go back to the infirmary," said Thomas. "Sarah, we got this. I don't want you injuring yourself further."

"I'm fine."

"You're tough," he admitted, "but you're not invincible. You were stabbed one day ago. Most normal people would be in agony."

"I *am* in agony," she said. "But this is my mess. I need to clean it up."

"This isn't your mess, Sarah." Howard sighed. "Al-Sharir got by us all."

"But the Flower Man didn't. I had him. And if I hadn't dropped my guard, I would still have him and would have called a team in quickly enough to stop Al-Sharir. I screwed up. So shut up and let me *unscrew* things. We have..." she checked her watch, "six hours until we all potentially explode. I just need a place to start."

The intercom in the centre of the room buzzed.

Palu reached forward and pulled one of the handsets from its cradle. He spoke into the receiver. "What is it? Okay... What? Have you verified?" He took the handset away from his ear and glanced across the table, at Sarah.

She frowned. "What is it?"

"We have a phone call. It's the Flower Man."

Sarah reached out and yanked one of the intercom handsets and placed it to her ear. The pain in her stomach seemed far away. "Hello."

"Meadow? Is that you, Meadow?"

"Yes, it's Sarah."

"Impressive. You don't die easy. Strong roots."

"Maybe if you weren't such an idiot, you would have stabbed me properly."

Thomas's jaw dropped, and he reached out for the intercom. Sarah smacked him away. On the other end of the line, the Flower Man chuckled. "You and I have had a taxing experience. You're not the only one licking your wounds. Nature heals though, and so will we."

"What do you want? I know it's not to tell us where you are. Have you been thinking about me? Sorry to hurt your big serial-killer ego, but I'm focused on other things right now, so could you leave a message with my secretary, please?"

"Oh, Meadow, I will enjoy what remains of our time together, but I am not calling because I miss you, my sweet pea. That you're even alive is news to me. No, I am calling about our little problem back there in the warehouse."

"The bomb?"

"Yes, that vile, manmade abomination. You must stop it. London is my home."

"How touching."

"I dislike terrorists as much as you do. So messy and meaningless. I can help you, Meadow."

Sarah looked up and realised all eyes were on her. The call was now on speaker, and an analyst would be running a trace. "Sorry, we're not hiring."

"I know what your friend is planning next."

Sarah gripped the handset tighter. "How could you know that?"

"Because I speak Russian—like that guard did before you knocked him out."

Sarah remembered the Flower Man squinting back at the warehouse as if thinking. *No, he was listening.* "You understood what he was saying."

"Yes. People are going to die, Meadow. Lots of people."

"Tell me what you heard."

"No. I was going to, but now that I know you're alive..."

"What do you want?"

"A meeting."

"Where?"

He told her, and Sarah didn't waste a second agreeing to the time and place.

"But Sarah, I expect you to come alone. If I see anybody else, I will hold onto this information until the next life. If we're going to work together, I expect you to keep your word."

"It will be me alone, you have my word. But if you try anything, or if this is some bullshit ploy, then I'll shoot you in the face."

There was a brief pause, then the line went dead.

The call ended, and Sarah replaced the handset.

Palu called for the trace. The call had been made from a payphone in the middle of Harrow. A team was already en route.

"There's no way you are going to that ambush," Thomas said to Sarah. "It's madness."

"You got anything else? Nope, didn't think so."

Howard sighed. "It's dangerous, Sarah."

"This job is dangerous."

"Okay. I'll be close by with backup. I won't be more than two minutes away." Howard said.

Thomas threw his arms up. "What is happening here? Are you all actually considering this?"

"I don't know," said Sarah. "Are we?" She stared straight at Palu, who had been absent from the discussion so far. Something was on his mind, and it was making him indecisive.

Palu nodded slowly, then addressed Thomas directly. "We have nothing else, Gellar. We can't afford to turn down the only Intel we have."

"You'll get her killed."

"No," said Sarah, rising from her chair "I am choosing to do this, so if something happens, it's on me. I don't need you looking after me, so back off, okay?"

Thomas looked at her like she was mad. "Fine. What do I care? I'm only your husband."

With that, Thomas turned and left the war room.

Sarah rubbed her shoulders as she stood exposed outside of the garden centre. It wasn't particularly cold, but she couldn't help shivering. A symptom of the blood she had lost. She felt weak too, although better than she had. The more she moved about and walked, the less stiff her body felt. With the injection Jessica had given her before leaving, she might almost pass for uninjured. She just hoped she wouldn't have to run or defend herself. It would not end well.

Arranging a meeting inside a garden centre in Croydon was an attempt at irony or the Flower Man held such delusions that he genuinely needed to be around plants. Did he think he was a plant? No, he wasn't that crazy.

Just the level of crazy that makes you torture and mutilate innocent people.

Am I actually about to do this?

Just pop in for a chat with a serial killer, Sarah. What's the worst that can happen? It's not like you're wounded from his previous attempt to kill you.

Sarah cleared her throat and stepped inside.

Mid-afternoon on a Saturday, which meant the garden centre was crammed with people. The narrow aisles of plants and shrubs made it hard to check out the entire area at first glance. People bunched up in several chokepoints as they tried to manoeuvre trolleys around one another. Standing amongst so many colourful flowers, Sarah would have expected perfume, but she only smelled soil. The air dripped with the moist, earthy odour of it.

No sign of the Flower Man.

Sarah chose the first aisle and walked down it, brushing past a row of overhanging hydrangeas. Their pink and blue petals bunched together like a clown's wig. Their beauty was lost on Sarah. People with scarred faces care little about flowers. It was her scars people looked at now, moving to other aisles to avoid her. People didn't trust themselves not to stare, so they avoided the situation by moving away. Nothing Sarah was unused to. People kept their distance from ugly.

Except Howard and the others.

If I leave the MCU, I'll have nobody.

I was doing just fine before I met Howard.

Were you, Sarah? she asked herself, *because I seem to recall you getting into a fight in the middle of a bank.*

Sarah shook away her thoughts and carried on down the aisle. She had a job to do, and she was distracting herself. The odds of her walking out of that garden centre in one piece were slim, so the least she could do was concentrate.

At the rear of the giant greenhouse was an opening to the outside that appeared to be where all the taller shrubs and potted trees were arranged. It was there that Sarah headed, hoping to find room to manoeuvre. The garden centre's interior was muggy, cramped, and made her claustrophobic.

"Meadow."

Sarah turned and saw a figure emerge from the mingling branches of a row of ferns. The Flower Man. His face was yellowed and knotted from his beatings, but he had recovered well—better than she had. He stood straight, long limbs poised. His eyes smouldered fiercely.

"I was beginning to think you wouldn't come," said Sarah coyly. She hoped to disguise her frailty by goading him.

"I always keep my word, Meadow, as you apparently keep yours. I saw no one else arrive."

Sarah, looking around at the shrubs and potted trees. "I have to ask: What is the deal with the whole gardener thing? Did your mother sleep with a daffodil or something?"

His expression darkened.

Sarah noted the reaction and prodded a little more. "Is your mother still alive? Does she know what you do?"

"My mother is of no concern to you, but she would be proud of what I have become."

Sarah noted the words *would have* and *become*. What did he feel he had become? No time to psychoanalyse a killer right now though. "Okay, we can get into it another time, I suppose. Once you're locked up."

The Flower Man smirked. "You came alone as promised, but you don't hide your pain as well as you think. A strong breeze could knock you over."

"It's only a matter of time until we catch you. You've been exposed."

"And like a rose bush exposed to the sun, I will flourish. That is why I must insist you stop your friend."

Sarah snarled. "He's not my friend."

"He seemed to think otherwise. Regardless, he's just another one of you: a destroyer out to reduce the world to rubble. You will stop him. My work is not yet done."

"What is Al-Sharir planning? You said you knew."

"I know the next target will kill ninety thousand."

Sarah wobbled as she heard that terrifying number. *Ninety thousand!* A spike of pain burst through her wounded abdomen and almost floored her. To her surprise, the Flower Man reached out and steadied her.

"Not yet, Meadow. Stay focused."

"You're sure—*ninety thousand*?"

"Yes, I am positive. It must be the bomb we saw."

"Where will it go off?"

The Flower Man frowned, recalling. "I don't know. The guard said something about it being ironic that this country was going to be brought to its knees by one of the false idols it worships."

"What the hell does that mean?"

"Your job to work it out, Meadow, not mine. I've told you what I know."

"Which is nothing!"

"I have faith in you. If you succeed, we will meet again. Perhaps just the once more. I tire easily."

Sarah reached out. "Wait! You're not going anywhere."

He yanked on her arm and kicked her knee, tripping her to the ground. The impact of her ribs hitting the gravelled floor knocked the air from her lungs and sent a shock wave of agony through her wounded torso. She yelled out, but her attacker clamped a hand over her mouth. "You disappoint me, Meadow. You keep trying to end our relationship prematurely. I want to play. You think I missed all your vital organs on accident back in that phone booth? I wanted merely to escape, not end our fun."

The Flower Man fumbled with her belt. Startled spectators called for help, but no one intervened to help her.

"Get off me," Sarah moaned.

The Flower Man pulled her radio free and tossed it into the row of ferns. "And no calling your friends on me. We'll meet again—don't you worry."

Before turning away, the Flower Man booted Sarah in the stomach, making her shriek. Then he was gone, disappearing into the potted ferns.

Her wedding night. Damn, she could hardly believe it. A year in one of the harshest places on earth, and she had found the man of her dreams and married him. It would be difficult, flitting back and forth between camps and trying to plan their down time together, but the ceremony today in front of the Camp Bastian chaplain had been perfect. Too bad her dad hadn't been there to see it. He was currently in whereabouts unknown with the SAS. He had spent half of her life as a ghost. Marrying a military officer might actually have been the thing to gain his approval. The thought of her settling down and being a 'woman' would likely please him. She'd never seen him less happy than when she had tried to gain entry to the SAS to be closer to him. The suspicious part of her wondered if he had been the masked instructor who had put her through the worst hell of her life. She'd almost died going through the assessments, and towards the end, she had become sure she was being put through more than was necessary.

But tonight was not about the past. It was about her future. Her future as both a wife and Army officer. She was a woman and a soldier —and proud to be both. She was living the equality that she sought so desperately to give to the women of Afghanistan. The Taliban would fall, and they would finally get the chance to live their lives.

"You're deep in thought," said Thomas, lying on the bed, naked and sweaty beside her. He ran his finger lightly down her cheek as he looked into her eyes. "Are you really my beautiful wife?"

"Apparently," she said. "Any buyer's remorse?"

He shook his head like she was ridiculous. "Never! Marrying you was my purpose in life."

She rubbed her foot against his ankle. "Don't be silly."

"I'm not. I'm going to love you forever."

"Really?" Something about the thought of having someone care about her—truly care about her—made her flush with happiness and a feeling of safety and certainty that life would always be okay. She'd always be safe.

Thomas kissed her lips. "I'll always be here, Sarah. I promise."

"Good, because up until now, the men in my life have been pretty absent. I need something I can rely on. You make me feel so strong, so protected. I never thought I would ever feel this way, but I love you so much."

"I love you too." Thomas got up from the bed and walked naked around the small bunk-room they had been given for tonight. Sarah's squad had decorated it with a mixture of roses and condoms. Three bottles of champagne sat unopened on the table; they'd been too occupied to make a start on it yet. Thomas went to the bottles now and opened one. Army champagne was not known for its quality, but Sarah's dry mouth cried out for it. Thomas poured them both a glass and then perched on the bed. The desert was freezing tonight, yet both their bodies gleamed with sweat. Their love-making had been wild and fierce, both of them unable to get enough of the other. Sarah knew such passion could not last forever, that marriage was a system of diminishing returns in the sex department, but right now she felt like a higher being, one made of an energy almost too powerful to contain.

Thomas offered a toast. "To our lives together, and our love that will never fade or break."

Sarah clinked her glass. "And to be there for each other no matter what."

They downed their drinks and threw aside their plastic flutes, suddenly thirsty for something other than champagne—thirsty for each other.

CHAPTER FIFTY-NINE

Howard hurried into the garden centre. Sarah had called from her mobsat, but explained that the Flower Man had first tossed it to get a head start. She wasted five minutes searching for it. Howard had parked outside a nearby supermarket, but London traffic meant he took four minutes to arrive. By the time he reached Sarah, the Flower Man had a ten-minute head start.

"Mandy is circling the main roads," explained Howard. "And we have two teams coming in any minute."

"We won't get him," said Sarah. "He picked this place, which means he would have had an escape route already planned. The only reason he didn't just spill over the phone was because he wanted to torment me."

His partner winced with pain, and blood spotted the front of her shirt where her stitches split. She sat with a cup of tea in one hand that a member of staff had made for her. She didn't try to stand.

"Are you okay?" he asked her. "Do you need me to call an ambulance?"

She shook her head. "I'm hurt, but I'll live. There was never any chance of me arresting him. That's not why I came."

"I know. Hold on, let me get Palu on the line." He glanced around. The staff had cleared the yard and left them alone, so he made the call and put it on loud speaker. "Palu? I'm with Sarah."

Palu responded. "Go ahead, Sarah."

Sarah leaned forward in her chair and wheezed as she spoke. "The Flower Man heard something back at the warehouse. The next attack will kill ninety thousand."

"Ninety thousand?" said Palu. "That exact number?"

"Yes."

Howard rubbed at his chin. "An odd number to just throw out there."

Sarah nodded. "It sounds exact. Maybe the population of an intended blast radius? We should check neighbourhood statistics."

"Already on it," came Thomas's voice. Sarah grimaced, and Howard empathised with her. Every time she looked at Thomas, or heard his voice, it caused her pain.

Is it because she still loves him?

How can she after five years?

Howard knew nothing about Sarah's marriage—it was long before they met—and part of him was uncomfortable with that. It felt like he had got to know Sarah so well over the last year, but the truth was he knew so little.

Why did that bother him?

"Thank you, Agent Gellar," said Sarah coldly.

"Are you hurt?" he asked her. "What happened?"

"I'm okay. The Flower Man escaped, but I expected it."

"That's okay, Sarah. We're doing big picture right now. We'll sweat the small stuff later."

"Deadline is two hours away," said Palu. "Is that all you have, Sarah, or is there more?"

Howard chewed his bottom lip. *Two hours.* It already felt too late. Was there really a nuclear bomb? Would he get caught in the blast?

No, don't think like that. There's still time.

"One other thing," said Sarah. "Something about the bomb being delivered by one of the idols we worship."

"The hell does that mean?"

"Same thing I asked. I don't know."

Howard looked up at the sky, hoping for inspiration. Night was falling, and it had grown cold. The sun was still low in the sky, but the moon had already appeared as if eager to get started. Was it only a matter of hours before both would be obscured by a choking-black mushroom cloud? Would it be years before London saw the sun again?

Howard closed his eyes. *Is it time to pray?*

"I'm sending Mandy to come and get you both," said Palu over the radio. "I want you both mobile in case we get a potential location. Stand by."

Sarah tipped the mug of cold tea onto the ground and watched it splash amongst the pebbles. It seemed a somehow portentous gesture to Howard. She looked up at him and said, "This is really bad, isn't it?"

Howard nodded. "About as bad as things get. I'm sorry."

"What for?"

"For dragging you out of your life a year ago, and into this."

Sarah seemed taken aback. She opened her mouth to say something, but a hissing sound interrupted her. "Sarah," came a voice through her mob-sat. "It's Mandy. I'm outside."

Sarah pushed herself up. "We're on our way."

Howard took her arm to help her walk and was pleased when she let him.

Howard was worried. Worried because when they met Mandy outside the garden centre, Sarah slumped across the backseat, bleeding.

"We need to get you looked over," said Howard. "Your stitches are torn."

She straightened up and lay her head back against the rest. "I'm fine. I just need a breather. We don't have time to worry about a couple of burst stitches. How long until the deadline?"

"One-hour twenty," said Mandy, tapping the digital clock on the Range Rover's lit-up dashboard. It was pitch-black outside, and as Mandy pulled onto the main road, they passed into and out of street lights.

"I should've never run from that warehouse," said Sarah.

Howard turned around in the front passenger seat. "Enough with that bullshit. You couldn't have done anything else, other than getting yourself killed."

"I was terrified, Howard!" The outburst surprised him, and from the shakiness in her voice alone, he realised Sarah was risking a breakdown. "I was fucking scared," she went on manically. "I just wanted to run. Al-Sharir got away with a nuclear bomb because I'm a goddamn coward. What's wrong with me? I'm losing it."

Howard looked at his partner and wanted to hold her. A year ago, he had found a strong, stubborn warrior of a woman and turned her into a bleeding, weeping mess. If anyone was to blame for anything, it was him. "Sarah, what you've been through this last year... I thought you were disposable. When I recruited you, I thought you were disposable. I wanted your knowledge of Shab Bekhier, but no way did I think you were strong enough to become an MCU agent. On paper, you were a train wreck: post-traumatic stress, agoraphobia, anger-issues—and that was just the stuff your follow-up psych listed from when they discharged you from the Army. I thought you were a liability the second I came across your file, but I needed your knowledge, so I used you."

Sarah didn't blink or respond in any way.

"Truth is, though," Howard continued. "Without you, I wouldn't be half the agent I am. This city would likely be in ruins. If I hadn't recruited you when I did, the monsters would have already won. I became an MCU agent because a monster killed my father, but you, Sarah... you're the reason I stay. You show me what an MCU agent is supposed to be. You're brave—like, *superhero* brave—and if this whole city goes up in flames an hour from now, the last person I would blame for anything is you. You've already done more than you ever had to. Thank you, Sarah, I mean it. For being willing to jump on a grenade if it means saving a life."

Sarah started to cry, but she kept it silent and turned away, looking out of the window at the passing shops and office blocks. Howard didn't know if his words meant anything to her, but they meant something to him. It felt good telling her how he saw her. Maybe it made him less guilty.

The dashboard comm buzzed and Mandy answered the call with his thumb. "Mandy."

"Mandy, it's Palu. Do you have Sarah and Howard?"

"They're in the car with me. You're on speaker."

"Okay, thanks. Howard, Sarah, we're running simulations on blast radius for a low-yield dirty bomb. It could be anywhere in the city. The estimate is based on far too many variables. There's no way to predict where ninety thousand people would be a likely number of casualties other than it being an area with residential tower blocks or heavy commercial areas like Oxford Street. Only places we can rule out are industrial areas. Please tell me you have something else. I need more data to filter the potential target areas."

"We have nothing," said Howard, a lead weight sliding down his throat and thudding in his lower intestines. His leg shook in the foot well, and he had to place a hand on his thigh to stop it.

"Damn it," came Palu. "This country's blood will be on our hands."

Howard glanced in the rearview mirror and saw Sarah grimace. "Come on, Palu. It's not over yet."

But Palu was gone. Thomas broke the silence by coming on the line. "Sarah? Sarah, are you there?"

Howard glanced back at her. As always, she was pained by her husband's presence. Yet, this time, it seemed to revive her as she sat straighter and became more alert. "I'm here."

"Sarah, get out of the city."

"What?"

"There's nothing you can do. You have an hour left, so get your ass back to the Earthworm, or drive even further."

"I can't," she said, shaking her head and seeming to shed some of her weakness. "You expect me to flee when millions of people don't even know they're in danger? How could I live with myself if I ran now? My job is to protect people, and that means sticking around," she looked at Howard, "and jumping on a grenade if I have to."

"What? Sarah, don't be foolish. I know you want to do the right thing, but so do I. We had something real—our marriage—and I shattered it. I shattered it because I wanted to do the right thing. Thousands of people are alive today because of the intelligence I provided. The sacrifice I made, I couldn't say no to—you wouldn't have either, Sarah. Now I want to make things right. We were on our way, Sarah, ready to settle down with a house and kids. Church on Sunday, football on a Monday. You say you're willing to jump on a grenade? Well, that's exactly what I did five years ago. I jumped on a grenade and destroyed my life because I couldn't stand by and watch innocent people die. Maybe you'll never forgive me, Sarah, but if you die, we'll never get a chance to find out. Loving you was the only thing I had out there in the desert to hold on to. The only thing that was real."

Sarah was frowning, not from confusion, but as if the words hit her hard. Howard had to admit that Thomas sounded genuine, and if it were true, maybe he had done the right thing all along. It took people willing to sacrifice for the rest of the world to be ordinary and selfish. Thomas and Sarah obviously had that in common. Perhaps that was why they'd married. Maybe they would remain so.

"What did you just say?" asked Sarah.

Thomas sounded confused, his voice stuttering for a moment. "What? I don't have time to repeat all that, Sarah, so I really hope you caught it all. I love you. Don't die on me, okay?"

"No, no," she said, seeming to think hard. "What did you say about the house and kids?"

"Erm... Church on Sunday and football on a Monday?"

"Football is on a Saturday," she muttered.

"Not in America, it isn't," replied Thomas. "Sarah...?"

"Shush. It's Saturday today. Is there any football on?"

"You mean soccer?" asked Thomas. "On in the city right now? Why?"

Sarah looked at Howard, but he could only shrug at her. Football wasn't his game. "I only watch Rugby."

Sarah cursed. What was she thinking?

"England are playing Algeria at Wembley," said Mandy. "And it's *football*, Thomas, because we actually use our feet—not our hands."

Sarah and Howard both turned to Mandy in surprise. "You like football?" Howard asked his long-time colleague. He hadn't known.

Mandy slowed for a traffic light. "Not a lot to do when you spend most your day driving. Football on the radio is one of my few joys—especially when Tottenham are playing."

"And there's football on tonight?" said Sarah. Thomas tried to come back through the line, but she shushed him again. "At Wembley?"

Mandy nodded.

Sarah seemed excited. "Do you know the capacity of Wembley Stadium, Mandy?"

"Ninety thousand."

"Shit! The bomb is at Wembley Stadium."

"How do you know?" asked Thomas through the line.

"Because you don't quote ninety thousand unless you mean ninety thousand. Killed by one of the false idols we worship. People in this country worship footballers. We pay them millions of pounds a year—Al-Sharir said it himself when I was tied up. Footballers are untouchable. And one of them is a terrorist."

Howard was about to turn to Mandy and tell him to change direction for Wembley Stadium, but Mandy was already way ahead of him. He blew the red light, zipping between a black cab and a Tesco delivery van—making both beep irritably—then pulled a one-eighty in the middle of the road. Tyres screeching, they sped off in the opposite direction.

"I think we're on our way to Wembley Stadium," said Howard into the radio. "Maybe you should have the bomb squad meet us there."

"I'm on it," said Palu, back on the line and finally sounding like he had some of his fire back. It was long overdue.

Did they really have a chance?

Howard glanced in the rearview mirror and smiled.

In the back seat, Sarah seemed to be alive again.

Sarah still hurt—it felt like she'd stopped a runaway train with her belly button—but the rush of adrenaline had restarted her system. The last thing she wanted was to run headlong into danger, but neither could she run away; something inside of her wouldn't allow it. That was why she'd resigned herself to the nightmare of a bomb crippling London— and perhaps getting caught in its blast. Though she tried not to admit it to herself, death seemed almost certain now.

Perhaps that's why she was doing this.

Death. An end.

There was a chance for her to stop the bomb now though, to prevent more blood being on her hands; a chance to walk away from this with her soul intact. But adrenaline alone wouldn't be enough to keep her going—a virulent spike already fading. Something in her pocket would help her do what needed to get done.

Before leaving the Earthworm, Sarah swiped another painkiller injection from the infirmary's supply closet. The label read: *Ketorolac+epinephrine*. A combined stimulant and painkiller to help injured agents escape the field before collapsing from their injuries. Right now, Sarah needed it to send her back *into* the field. She pulled the cap off with her teeth.

Howard caught sight of her in the rearview mirror and spun around. "What the hell is that?"

"A snack," Sarah told him.

Before Howard could object, Sarah speared her thigh with the injector. A tingling wave flooded her body, but a minute later the throbbing agony in her torso subsided. She let out a sigh. Her body relaxed on the backseat.

"I really hope Jessica prescribed you whatever you just shot yourself up with," said Howard.

"That's between me and my doctor. Just stay focused on what matters. Has Palu run a background check on the players?"

"Not yet. He will get back to us as soon as he finds something."

"It better be soon. We have about forty minutes left until London gets the biggest fireworks show in its history."

She knew Howard understood the stakes. Looking out for her was just one of the ways he coped, even though it never failed to irritate her. "You know, there might not be any attack," he suggested. "You escaping the warehouse might have thrown Al-Sharir's plans into disarray."

"I hope not," said Sarah.

"What? Why?"

"Because if I'm right about the stadium, we have a chance to disarm and confiscate that bomb, but if Al-Sharir moves to Plan B, we have nothing. This way is better, even if we're cutting it close."

He looked at the clock on the dashboard. "That's an understatement. You know if the bomb squad can't disarm the device, there's a good chance we'll have front row seats when it goes off."

"Are you saying we should make a run for it while we still can? Let the Bombies handle it?"

"No, I want to see this through. If they can't defuse the bomb, we can at least report back as much as we can before we're done. We need to be there no matter what, in case there are clues. This is our screw-up."

Thomas came on the line. Mandy turned up the volume. "Bomb squad is outside the stadium. They arrived in an ice cream van."

Howard huffed. "Sorry, what?"

"They turned up in a fake ice cream van to avoid mass panic— apparently, it's something they've been trialling. The vehicle houses a blast container made from Ballistic Fibreglass and coated with flame retardant plastic. If they can't disarm the bomb, they'll remove it to the blast container."

"That's good," said Sarah, "because I was going to throw a blanket over it and hope for the best."

Howard chuckled.

"I've been speaking to stadium security," Thomas went on, "and they are adamant that a bomb could not have made it inside. They almost laughed at the suggestion. Every person through the turnstiles gets searched if they so much as have a purse."

"What about the players?" asked Sarah.

"The players enter through an underground access directly from their coaches. The changing rooms and office facilities are not accessible from the public entrances."

"It came in with one of the players," said Howard. "They wouldn't have been searched."

"Okay?" said Thomas. "But how does a player carry a bomb into the stadium with no one seeing?"

Sarah shook from the stimulant in her system. "D-Damn it, he's right. The bomb I saw was too big to conceal."

Howard rubbed at his chin—now rough with stubble. "Maybe the entire team is involved."

Sarah rolled her eyes. "I can buy one—even two—players being suicidal, but not an entire national football team. Maybe I got it wrong."

"Wrong or right," said Thomas. "It's the only lead we have. Too late for you to get out of the city, so you better pray the bomb squad finds something to disarm."

Sarah sighed. "Then this is either goodbye or see you later."

A pause. When Thomas answered, his voice was thick. "I'll see you all later."

The line went dead.

Mandy parked the car outside Wembley Stadium.

Thirty minutes left.

CHAPTER SIXTY

Sarah leapt out of the Range Rover and approached the three black-clad men that could only have been the bomb squad. Sure enough, an innocent ice cream van was parked nearby on the curb bordering a large, grassy playing field. A large red sticker across the serving hatch read: CLOSED. Wembley Stadium towered behind it majestically, its iconic arch sweeping through the black backdrop of night. The crowd's catcalls echoed out of the stadium's open roof. The cheers were foreboding—ignorance of the potential danger.

Howard flashed his badge at the bomb squad. "Why haven't we evacuated the stadium?"

"There's ninety thousand people in there." The speaker had greying-black hair down to his collar. Stress of the job perhaps. "Stadium security is quietly removing people in sections, but this is one of the largest stadiums on the planet. If the crowd gets wind of what's going on, we'll have a mass panic on our hands. Ninety thousand frightened people is something none of us want. The Prime Minister demands we take care of this quickly and efficiently. If we can prevent stopping the game, all the better."

Sarah gritted her teeth. "Breslow and her secrets. We have twenty minutes left to get these people out, and she wants us to keep things hush-hush."

"If this is a nuke," said the bomb expert, "then an evacuation at this point will do no good. The evening traffic alone will stop anyone escaping the blast radius. If this bomb is going off, there's no way to mitigate it—thousands of people will die. We are here to stop that from happening. Now, where exactly is the device?"

Sarah and Howard exchanged glances. "We don't know for sure," said Sarah. "But we think it came in with one of the players from the Algerian team."

"Jesus. Then let's get in and start looking. Security has opened an exit around the side. Come on!"

They hurried towards the stadium. Sarah wondered if Howard was as terrified as she was. Her skin tingled, like she was running towards a roaring fire. They headed in through a side entrance and entered the clinical hallways of the arena's bowels. Signed posters of footballing legends lined every wall. Sarah recognised none of them. A team of security had assembled, and each of them held radios. Their bemused expressions suggested they thought Sarah and the others were barking up the wrong tree.

Sarah pointed at the one who looked as though he might be in charge—he wore a black cap that didn't match his blue uniform. "Where are the locker rooms?"

The man shrugged. "Staff or players?"

"Players."

"Right down the corridor behind me, but it'll be halftime in fifteen minutes, so you can't go in there. More than our jobs are worth."

Sarah glanced at her watch. The deadline was in fifteen minutes. The bomb was going to explode at halftime. She shoved the security guard out of her way and moved in the direction he had mentioned. "Let's see if it's more than your life is worth, because we might all be sitting on top of a bomb."

The guard stumbled, and before he had a chance to recover,

Howard and the three bomb experts got in his face. Howard gave the man an order: "Start helping."

The guard seemed to weigh up his options then nodded. "Come on, this way."

They picked up their pace and ran down the corridor. Finally, the security team got that no one was kidding. They unlocked the locker-room door and shoved it open.

Sarah leapt inside, hoping to find the bomb in the centre of the room. She looked around. "No, this is the England dressing room. We need the Algerian dressing room."

Howard nudged her. "Do we? I mean, we don't know it's an Algerian player. We're making a huge assumption."

"We don't have time to be politically correct. Racial profiling is all we have right now." She turned to the security leader. "Algerian locker room, now!"

The man didn't argue and took her into the next corridor. He unlocked another door. "In here."

Howard shook his head. "Shit, there must be sixty lockers in this room."

The security leader nodded. "Locked too. Need me to get the keys?"

"Yes, quickly." Sarah looked at her watch. Closer to ten minutes now than fifteen.

"We need to do this now or never," said the greying bomb squad leader, his two men flanking him. "We're going to have to rush any attempted disarmament as it is."

Sarah studied the lockers. The room was large and square, but it wasn't just a locker room. There was an adjacent wet room with showers, too, and a row of large closets full of what looked like bandages and shampoos.

"There's no time," she said. "Get these lockers open any way you can."

Sarah led the way, rushing forward and booting one of the wooden doors. The top half of the lockers were open shelves with hangers over them, but the bottom sections comprised of well-built footlockers. Kicking one was like kicking a tree. "Shit, this is going to take forever."

Working at the locker next to her, Howard pulled out his gun.

"Put that away!" the bomb squad leader shouted. "A gunshot will turn the crowd upstairs into a herd of wildebeest."

Howard spun the gun in his hand and brought it down on the footlocker butt first, smashing it against a padlock. Two more blows and he broke the lock. Once he had, everyone understood and followed his lead, grabbing fire extinguishers or other equipment to use as tools. As the only other person with a gun, Sarah pulled out her Sig and bashed away in the same manner Howard had. Each blow pulled at her stitches, but she was too hyped-up on fear to stop.

But it was taking too long. Four blows to open her footlocker and then met by a large holdall she had to unzip to see inside.

Ten minutes and counting.

Nine-minutes-fifty-five...

The security leader returned with a bundle of keys. He didn't ask for directions and went straight to the first locker and popped the padlock—then the next one—and the next one. His colleagues checked the holdalls. But even with the keys it wasn't fast enough.

Nine-minutes-twenty-six.

They needed to know exactly where to look.

Howard's radio hissed.

"Ignore it," said Sarah. "We don't have time."

"I can't," said Howard. He answered the call and put it on loud speaker. "Talk quickly!"

"Howard, it's Tom. We have a possible suspect for you. *Rabah Slimani*. He plays in the Russian Premier League. In the off season, he does charity work in Afghanistan—every year since 2011."

"The time Al-Sharir disappeared," said Sarah. "He's our man. I know it."

"Slimani's locker is this one," said the security leader, pointing.

The players had a choice of short or long-sleeve shirts, which meant the ones not chosen remained on the hangers. Sarah glared at the bright-green jersey with *Slimani* printed on the back in bold yellow letters. "Get it open."

The man did as requested. His hands shook as he popped the lock, wasting a vital few seconds. When he yanked open the locker, Sarah went to look, but the bomb squad leader pushed her back. "This is where I take over, ma'am."

Sarah nodded, trembling with excitement but understanding that a bomb was not a toy. Instead, she looked over the greying man's shoulder. Like the other footlockers, a large holdall lay inside. The bomb expert didn't pull the bag out, but left it where it was and unzipped it. He gave no reaction as he peered at the contents.

"Jesus, you weren't messing around. It's a fucking bomb," said the security leader, but didn't shame himself by running away. He stood rigid as a statue, and so did his men.

The three bomb experts conferred before the leader addressed Howard and Sarah. "This is a Semtex plastic explosive. It's chemically tagged; you can probably smell the signature. Means I'm pretty sure."

Sarah studied the pile of beige bricks—so mundane, so benign. Could they really explode and cause mass damage? "This isn't the bomb I saw. This isn't a nuclear bomb."

"No, it's not. It's plastic explosive. Not enough to bring down the entire stadium, but it's attached to an aerosol and a chamber full of something nasty—possibly mustard gas. We're right under the main stand. If this bomb goes off, it will take out at least twenty thousand in the blast, and probably as many more with the chemical dispersal. The rest of the crowd will panic and trample more victims to death. It's bad. Ninety thousand people bad."

"Can you disarm it?" Howard asked.

The bomb expert shook his head and appeared to grow even greyer. "Not in six minutes. Best I can do is detach the chemical element of the bomb, but the Semtex is wired to blow the moment anyone tries to tamper with it. This bomb is going to blow."

"Jesus Christ," said the security leader. "Oh fuck me sideways. I need to call my mum."

"Calm down, you," said Sarah. She kept her focus on the bomb expert despite the panicking security guard. "What's your name?"

"Mike."

"Okay, Mike. Detach the chemical for me."

He nodded. "Yes, of course, at least we can do that. Then we need to move as far away from here as we can. We have a portable blast chamber to place over the bomb, but there's no time for anything else."

The man got to work and took less than a minute. He removed the glass cylinder full of straw-coloured liquid and held it in his hands like a kitten.

"Who has the keys to the ice cream truck?" asked Sarah

"I do," said one of the bomb experts. "Why?"

"Just hand them over."

The man gave Sarah the keys but frowned. "There isn't enough time to secure the bomb. The timer is set to blow in three minutes. You won't make it"

"Then move out of my way so I don't get exploded all over you," said Sarah. She shoved the bomb squad men aside and yanked the holdall onto her shoulder.

Howard moved to block her. "Sarah, we need to get out of here now."

She stepped around him. "No one is running but me. We can't get the people out of the stadium, so I'm getting the bomb out instead."

"There's no time," said the bomb squad leader, but she ignored him.

Howard shouted after Sarah, but she was gone, racing out into the corridor and praying she remembered her way. She turned the first corner and passed the England dressing room. A couple of physios had arrived—ready for halftime. They dodged out of her way before she collided with them. In the next corridor, she spotted the side entrance they had come through and realised it was closed. Mid-stride, she leapt up and kicked the crossbar-release across its middle.

It blew open. Thank God for fire safety.

The cold night air slapped her face. The sound of the crowd inside the stadium was a force of nature. They clapped as one organism.

The halftime whistle blew.

The deadline was up.

How many seconds did she have left?

No time to glance at her watch.

Sarah raced towards the ice cream van still parked on the curb. She fumbled with the keys in her hand and found a button on the keyring. When she pressed it, she heard the reassuring *click* of doors unlocking. Heading around back to the large rear door, Sarah opened it and peered inside. She saw a perfectly square box about the size of a fridge. Sarah dropped the holdall inside and pulled down the lid. It clicked into place.

Please, please, please don't go off yet. Just a little longer.

Sarah needed to pee.

She raced around to the driver's side door and hopped up behind the steering wheel. The engine came to life as soon as she shoved the key into the ignition. The bomb squad kept good care of their vehicles. Shifting into first, Sarah stamped on the gas. The van lurched forwards. She steered away from the stadium-side curb and drove across the road, jumping up onto the opposite pavement and continuing onto the grassy border. The playing field ahead was deserted—not even a single dog walker. Good.

She drove right for its centre.

Shifted into second... third... fourth...

Increasing speed.

The suspension bounced and swayed, throwing her about in the seat.

Sarah glanced at her watch. 9.02PM.

Deadline was overdue.

Sarah shoved open the driver's side door and threw herself out.

She hit the grass and cartwheeled. The mud beneath the field was packed and dry, but the surface was lush enough to take the edge off her fall. She remained painfully conscious as she bounced and rolled, flopping like a rag doll. She yelled out in a mixture of fear and pain, tumbling and tumbling for what seemed like an eternity.

Finally, she came to a stop.

She flipped onto her stomach and looked off toward the speeding ice cream truck. At the edge of the playing field was a row of houses. If the van kept on speeding towards them, it would—

The night sky lit up like a sunny afternoon.

A swirling pyre of flames rose in the centre of the field. All air retreated from the fire, buffeting Sarah like machine gun fire. The sudden vacuum took her breath away, and she lay on her stomach, suffocating, as the world violently combusted. A cloud of dirt peppered her face and made her duck down in the grass. She waited for the flames to take her.

Seconds passed, and she could breathe again. Daring to look up, she saw an almighty bonfire surrounded by smaller, dying infernos. Somewhere distant, she heard people scream.

The stadium crowd.

Terrified, but alive.

I did it.

A lance of pain made Sarah grasp at her stomach. Her fingers came back wet. She took one more glance at the bonfire and passed out.

CHAPTER SIXTY-ONE

Sarah awoke to chaos. Sirens pierced the night and car horns honked like an army of squabbling geese. She lay face-up on a gurney, strapped down around the shoulders and legs. The interior lights of a nearby ambulance illuminated her. She tried to struggle; her body failed her.

"Keep still," said Howard, moving into her vision. He had a sooty smudge on his forehead and his eyes were red. "Your stitches have split wide open and your heart rate is through the roof. That's probably from the epi you stole—yeah, that's right, I just got off the line with Jessica. She's going to kick your arse, Sarah—right after Palu kisses it. He's currently doing a jig around the war room from what I hear."

Sarah closed her eyes and took a moment to herself. She felt no pain, only numbness. Her limbs had been through a spin dryer so badly that her brain had decided to pretend they weren't attached to her. It was a mercy. "Is everything... Did I..." The questions were there in her mind, but she couldn't put the words into sentences. Even that was too much effort.

Howard put his hand on top of hers and smiled. "You did it, Sarah. The bomb detonated in the middle of the playing field. Couple of shattered windows in nearby houses, but no fatalities. The crowd panicked when the bomb went off, but security was able to maintain control. There's a tonne of twisted ankles and bloody noses, but again—no fatalities. Nobody died. You stopped it."

"It's not over, Howard. That wasn't the bomb I saw in the warehouse."

Howard nodded gravely. "I know, but we've bought ourselves some time to figure out our next steps. You have to stop doing this, you know?"

Sarah's throat was dry. "Stop what?"

"Saving the day. I understand why you do it—it's who you are—but your luck won't last forever. I'm with Thomas on this one—I don't want you to die. Don't want you to leave either. I'd be sad if you were gone."

Jessica said the same thing.

Nobody wants me to go.

But how can I stay?

Sarah turned her head towards the bonfire still burning in the centre of the field and watched it flicker. A fire engine rolled across the field with two more right behind it. Had she really just saved ninety thousand people? Al-Sharir was trying to bring the country to its knees.

But I stopped the son-of-a-bitch. However smart he thinks he is, I stopped his plan. He failed.

Until he tries again. He's still out there somewhere.

Sarah squeezed Howard's hand and looked him in the eye. "I'm not leaving until this is over. I want Al-Sharir chained up in the deepest pit we have."

Howard nodded. "Good, but there's nothing we can do tonight. I'm heading back to the Earthworm to debrief. Mike from Bomb Disposal said he'll handle everything here. Good guy, maybe I'll try to recruit him."

Sarah grunted. "No, don't. He doesn't deserve it."

Howard chuckled. "I suppose you're right. The ambulance will take you back now. Want me to ride with you?"

"No, you shouldn't leave Mandy on his own; he'll get bored. I'll see you at home," she said.

Home. Is that what she thought of the Earthworm now?

Howard leaned forward and planted a kiss on her forehead. "Good work today, Sarah."

"You too."

Howard left, and a paramedic slid Sarah's gurney into the back of the ambulance. She closed her eyes and could not open them again.

The morning shower was sublime. Ten minutes passed without Sarah so much as moving a muscle. She'd gone to bed dirty and wet, but now the soot and blood slid away from her skin and disappeared down the drain, along with the scalding water. Eventually, she had to force herself to step out of the shower and into the bedroom. Senior agents could reside within the Earthworm if they so choose, and Sarah saw little reason to pay rent in one of the most expensive cities in the world when she didn't have to.

She didn't expect to see Thomas standing there when she left the en suite bathroom, and she quickly pulled her towel tighter around her chest. "What the hell are you doing here?"

He looked away. "Shit, sorry. The door was unlocked. I was calling out. I'll leave!"

"No, just tell me what you want. And next time, *knock*, dickhead."

"I came to tell you we've been asked to send the senior team to Thames House for a meeting with Breslow. I assume you want in?"

"Of course, but I doubt Jessica will sign me back to duty; she only just redid my stitches."

"She's already released you," he said. "You would go anyway, she said, and if the Prime Minister is handing out congratulations, you deserve to be there. She also told me that the strongest pain med you're allowed to take is paracetamol, so if you want to go back on duty, then you have to cope with the pain."

Sarah had woken up on fire, so stiff and in so much pain she thought she was dying. The shower had helped, and now that she was standing, it felt like she might be okay. Her stitches had been reapplied last night, and she slept straight through for eight hours. It hurt to move, but she *could* move.

"Just let me get ready and I'll be right with you," she said.

Thomas didn't leave. He kept looking away, but turned his glance slightly towards her. "You saved a whole bunch of people last night, Sarah. No one will ever know how close we came to disaster. I just wanted you to know how proud we all are of you."

"We were lucky."

"Lucky to have you," he said. "You're not the same person you were before I left. Sorry I didn't realise that until now. This is obviously where you belong."

"No, it's just where I ended up. This was never where I belonged."

I belonged with you. We were supposed to have a life together. Damn you.

Thomas took a step towards her and turned his gaze a little more. When she didn't berate him, he took another step so he was right in front of her. "If I could go back and make a different choice," he said, "I would. I didn't know what I was getting into, or how much you needed me."

"I *did* need you, Thomas. But not anymore. What the hell happened to you?"

"It was your father."

Sarah swallowed. "What?"

"Your father was leading a team of SAS and Delta force. He contacted me the day before I was due to travel to Kabul to raid a Taliban safe house. He recruited me en route, sat right beside me on the bus."

"My father!"

"I didn't know it was him, then—not until later when I put it all together. When I first met him, he asked me if I wanted to truly serve my country and make a difference. I said, 'yes of course'. He told me how I could."

Sarah folded her arms, making sure her towel stayed in place.

"A French Muslim UN agent had infiltrated a local Taliban group in the city, and was looking to 'turn' an American captive over the next twelve months. They would stage a friendly fire incident on the troop carrier I was travelling in and then I would be captured by a local militia, who would pass me off to the UN agent's Taliban group. My involvement would eventually get me inside the inner workings of the Taliban and help my country identify key targets. I had to make a decision there and then. Your father is a hard man to turn down."

Sarah nodded, feeling numb. Her father and Thomas had met? Had her father targeted Thomas specifically? Was the plan to hurt Sarah, or was it just a coincidence?

There was no coincidences when it came to her father.

"I can't believe it. He made you disappear. It was him... My whole life, it was him always bringing me down, smashing everything I ever had for myself. Why?"

Thomas shrugged. "He was in contact with me for the first year, but then I started working directly with Delta Force. I never thought I would be gone for more than a year or two, but I just kept getting deeper. Trying to leave could have gotten me killed. Any time I asked to send word to you, I was denied. Thousands of lives were in my hands, my handlers would always say. How could I argue against that? It wasn't until you struck a blow to Hesbani that all of the local cells fell into chaos. I used the chaos to break my cover and return. Sarah, the things I had to go through out there..."

"I don't care," she snapped. "You chose your misery. I never chose mine."

He nodded. "I understand."

"Let's be mature about this," Sarah sighed, "and work together like adults, okay? I don't want to be mad at you anymore. It's too hard."

"The last thing I want is for you to be mad at me. I can't tell you how much you mean to me."

"Thomas... just don't."

"You're still my wife, Sarah. I still love you."

He leaned in closer.

Sarah swallowed. "Thomas."

"Sarah."

He kissed her.

She kissed him back. And it felt like home. It felt like a different life —one with a house and kids.

But I can't have kids anymore.

Thomas pulled her in close and placed his hand against her face as they kissed—against her scars. Sarah shoved him away. "Don't!"

"I'm sorry."

"Don't be sorry. Just be gone."

He did her the favour of not arguing, and with a sad nod, he turned away and headed for the door. "I'll see you up top."

Sarah waited for the door to close and got dressed. Part of her wished Thomas had stayed. Getting her socks on was a bitch, for one thing. By the time she got everything fastened, she was panting and clutching her stab-wound. It reminded her that the Flower Man was still out there somewhere.

Along with a nuclear bomb.

Which is going to strike first?

They might have won a battle last night, but they were losing the war on two fronts.

Sarah headed into the Earthworm's tail section where the bedrooms and staff areas were located. She carried on to the main elevators that would take her up top. A year ago, the surface of the MCU had been a derelict farm, but after the well-publicised victory over Hesbani and Sarah's father, the Earthworm's location had become public knowledge. That was why concrete walls and towering guard posts now surrounded the entrance.

She exited into the paved compound and headed for the barn—one of the few original farm-buildings left in place after the renovations. It was where the MCU kept its fleet of Range Rovers and Jaguars— British symbols of engineering, making the MCU a patriotic force as much as it was a practical one.

The others all waited for her. Thomas looked away coyly, which made Sarah wonder if she might blush herself. What had happened back in the bedroom? He'd kissed her. And she'd liked it.

Do I miss him?

Or do I just miss being wanted? For a second, my scars were gone. I was a woman again.

But then they came right back. I'll never be rid of them. I'll never be what I was.

Mandy opened the front passenger door of one of the Jaguars. "The lady of the hour."

Palu stood next to Thomas, and they both clapped. Howard joined in. Sarah couldn't stop herself from smiling, which left her disappointed with herself. This was no time to celebrate; not while Al-Sharir was still out there. "Let's just get on the road."

"Okay, okay," said Palu. "Good work, agent Stone. I'll see you at Thames House."

Palu got in a car with Thomas, but Howard came and joined Sarah and Mandy. The two cars set off one after the other, with Mandy taking point. Sarah hadn't visited Thames House before, but its grand archway in the city led to the headquarters of MI5. Breslow probably wanted to meet them there so she didn't have to travel to the outskirts of the city and down into MCU headquarters. She wanted them on her territory, not the other way around.

Despite last night's victory, Sarah couldn't envisage Breslow giving them a pat on the back. The Prime Minister gave praise thinly, and the country was not yet out of danger. MCU still had scant Intel regarding Al-Sharir's master plan or his current whereabouts. They were still chasing their tails.

They had one thing though.

"What happened to Slimani?" she asked from the front seat, turning back to Howard.

"Breslow has him. In fact, he's en route to Thames House as well. MI5 will probably take a crack at him before we do."

"Are you kidding? He's *our* suspect, not theirs."

Howard shrugged, as if he'd already fought this battle and lost.

"Breslow works more closely with MI5, and the terrorists wanting her to kill herself has unnerved her. Palu said she sounds ready to start a full-on war with someone."

"Just what we need," said Sarah. "More violence."

"We can help put a stop to it by bringing in Al-Sharir," said Howard. "We'll put that monster on trial."

"Putting him on trial will be the last thing that will happen. It would do more harm than good."

Howard leaned forward. "Oh? Why do you think that?"

"Because a lot of what Al-Sharir says is right," she said. "We have as much to answer for as the terrorists. I still remember being over there, Howard—the looks on the local's faces every time we walked by. We were never wanted there; not by anybody. We can't keep dictating to the world as though we're better. Has Breslow caused fewer deaths than Gaddafi or Saddam? I'm sure the statistics would make for interesting reading."

"You might be right," Howard admitted. "But maybe don't discuss it at the meeting with Breslow, huh? I understand what you're saying, Sarah, but I disagree. We *are* better. This is a country built on freedom and equality. It doesn't make us wrong for wanting to bring that to places like Afghanistan and Iraq."

Sarah sighed. She hated arguing with Howard—the emotion he put into his responses always made it hard to unleash her true vitriol on a subject. He'd seen as much wretchedness as her, yet he still believed in everything he did. "Perhaps my point is that our methods need to change. What we're doing isn't working."

"I'm with you on that."

"We're here," said Mandy.

Sarah looked out the window and saw the imposing spectre of Thames House. "Are those journalists? They're everywhere."

Howard grimaced. "Guess they want answers. Tower Bridge gets attacked, and then Wembley... the nation is teetering over the abyss. They want us to tell them it's all going to be okay. Either that or they want someone to blame. Keep your eyes forward and ignore them. We don't answer to them, Sarah, okay?"

Sarah's lips were dry, so she licked them. The thought of being caught by a dozen cameras made her scars tingle. *Please don't let me be on the front cover of the newspapers tomorrow morning.*

She stepped out of the car and tried to stride confidently towards the Press. But her legs felt hollow, and she became too aware of her own body. Her approach before the snapping photographers became awkward and stiff.

Palu and Thomas got out of the car behind, and it was to Palu that the journalists congregated with their microphones. *"Director Palu, can you confirm the explosion last night came from a bomb intended for Wembley Stadium? Director Palu, is the nation under siege by terrorists? Does the MCU have any suspects in custody? Is the footballer Rabah Slimani implicated in last night's plot? Is he being held?"*

Sarah expected Palu to stonewall the journalists like he usually did, but he surprised her by stopping and addressing them. "I cannot yet comment on our ongoing investigation," he said calmly, "but what I *will* say is that, last night, the MCU's finest agents struck a blow against terrorism. People live today because of the bravery of a few good people. I will share more when I am able. Thank you."

The journalists shouted out more questions and jabbed at Palu with their microphones like a phalanx of spearmen, but he strode confidently forwards. Seeing they would get no more response, the journalists searched for other prey. Sarah. *"Hi ma'am, I'm Jack Millis with the Chronicle. Were you one of the agents involved in last night's operation? What is your position with the MCU? Could you share any details with the nation? Are we in danger? Will there be more attacks?"*

Sarah found herself pinned, journalists surrounding her. She spotted a camera pointed directly at her and panicked. She raised a hand and covered her scars. The flashes came from all directions. Microphones poked at her face. She called out for Thomas to help her, but he continued on, oblivious to her struggle.

"And what about the Flower Man? Is it true you allowed him to escape after apprehending him?"

Sarah's heart beat faster. Her lips moved. "I..."

"Were you involved in the failure to secure this country's worst-ever serial killer? Another victim was found. She died in the early hours of this morning."

"No... I..." She stopped wavering and stood straight. The girl from the sewer had died. Why had nobody told her? Had anyone been with her at the end? A friend? Family? Sarah clenched her fists. "The Flower Man is on the run. I have seen his face, and we will have him in custody soon."

"You've seen him? Who is he? Where is he?"

"He's a sad little man with mommy issues, same as most serial killers," said Sarah, thinking about the girl in the sewer. "He has been living in London's sewers like a rat. But rats are less disgusting. Soon—"

"There'll be no more discussion," said Howard, yanking her away from the bushel of microphones under her chin. "Please move aside. You're hampering a high-security operation."

He grabbed Sarah by the arm and marched her forward, his hand tight around her arm, his voice a whisper. "They're a pack of piranha. Don't give them blood, and they'll starve to death."

They reached the Thames House archway and were met by two armed police officers. No journalist dared approach this close, and Sarah took deep breaths to recover. Flash bulbs still erupted in the road, but now all the photographers would get was the back of her head. And that was her good side.

"That really sucked," she said. "When I heard the girl we found had died... I reacted."

"You did fine," said Thomas, still not realising what had happened. "It's never easy."

Howard rubbed her back. "They don't get it, that's all. They don't understand what we do or what we go through."

"They deserve answers," said Sarah, still hearing the echoes of questions in her head. *Is it true you allowed him to escape? The Flower Man?*

She died in the early hours of this morning.

Palu turned to Sarah. "The British public deserves answers, not these parasites. We will address the nation directly when the time comes. Leave the journalists to make fun of President Conrad. Anything more complex is beyond them."

Palu exchanged details with the two armed police officers and gained admission for them all. Sarah wanted to get away from the piranhas at her heels, so she headed in directly after him, almost treading on his heels. The polished chessboard floor that met her made her eyes blur. The high ceilings made her feel unbalanced. After a moment, she was able to appreciate the grandiosity of the room.

Breslow stormed down a staircase towards them, wagging a finger and pointing off to the side. "In there now!"

They all looked to where she was pointing and saw a closed door. Thomas headed away from the group and opened it. The MCU agents funnelled inside, Breslow barking at their heels. She was not happy.

Sarah clenched her fists. *Maybe she should take on the terrorists herself if she thinks she can do better. Does she think the job is easy?*

Despite her anger, Sarah knew her arguments were false. Breslow did her job and MCU needed to do theirs.

Breslow closed the door behind them and locked everyone inside the small meeting room. There was a television on one side and a moderately-sized conference table on the other.

"Nobody sits down," said Breslow. "This will be brief."

Palu folded his arms. "Prime Minister, I assure you—"

"Not a word, Palu. Not until I've said my piece." She turned to Sarah. "I've been told you were the driving force behind last night's victory. Seems like you pull the MCU's arse out of the fire on a regular basis. Well done."

Sarah leant up against the wall to take the strain off her aching joints. "I seem to recall pulling your arse out of a fire once, Prime Minister."

Breslow glared at Sarah, but then a smile cracked her face. "I suppose I can't deny that, can I? Although it was your bloody father trying to kill me."

The woman had a point, so Sarah shut it.

Breslow stood in front of the door as if ready to batter anybody who tried to make a run for it. There was a reason the woman had stayed in power for almost seven years—she was terrifying. And that terrifying wrath was currently aimed at the people in this room.

"I started the MCU," said Breslow, "as one of my first acts of Parliament, but to tell you the truth, it was former President Conrad who was the driving force behind it. Then the recession hit, and he abandoned the project and left me with the bill. I am not your biggest fan, and this time last year I was trying to mothball you. Public pressure forced me to reconsider, and I admit your role in stopping Hesbani was impressive. You've done good work, and with the extra funding I gave you I hoped to turn a turd into a topaz. Now Tower Bridge is gone, and the public is demanding blood. Then we almost lost Wembley Stadium and ninety thousand fans. I just want to ask you: WHAT. THE. FUCK. IS. GOING. ON?"

There was silence as everyone fidgeted awkwardly. Palu smacked his lips, unsure whether he could speak. "Prime Minister, this... this is war. I cannot promise you there will never be casualties. That isn't a promise we ever made. Last night, ninety thousand innocent people got to go home to their families because of the bravery of my agents. You blame the MCU, but we are standing in the headquarters of the MI5 who missed it too. We are at war, and the enemy is as strong and as capable as we are. The moment we start lynching each other is the moment they gain a foothold. We kept this country from the precipice last night."

Breslow put her hand on her hips. "Damn it, Palu. Can you imagine what would have happened if the Press got hold of the video demanding I hang myself? The media is running it this afternoon, but I dread to think how it would have gone down if Wembley was a smoking ruin. The rabid dogs would have demanded I actually follow through with it. This nation is terrified. It has been under attack for far too long, and now I hear the maniacs have got hold of a nuclear bomb. Understand this, I will not go down in history as the Prime Minister who let London get nuked. I will not!"

"No," promised Palu. "You won't."

"Promise me," said Breslow, not pleading, but demanding.

Palu hesitated. "I... I promise."

"Then on your head be it. Thomas, do we have any leads?"

Sarah frowned, wondering why the PM would address Tom directly.

"We would like to question the suspect in last night's bombing. We have strong suspicions that Russia is involved in these plots, and would like to get answers to that effect."

Breslow raised an eyebrow. "Moscow?"

"No indication it was government sponsored. It's just as likely a renegade group wanting to weaken the West."

"So, you think Al-Sharir is working with the Russians?"

"That is our theory, yes."

"And do we have a lead on Al-Sharir's whereabouts?"

"Not as of yet."

"Then I think you should bloody well work on getting one. The intelligence community's most-wanted criminal is in our country. If we don't catch him soon, we'll become the laughingstock of the world, or a crater on Europe's backside."

"And we wouldn't want that," said Sarah. "To be laughed at."

Breslow glared at Sarah again. "I see your injuries didn't affect your lip, girl. If not for the fact you remind me so much of myself, I'd wring your bloody neck. Do you have any thoughts about what is happening right now?"

Sarah was unprepared for the question, but the chance to voice her thoughts directly to Breslow was something she didn't want to miss. "I think Al-Sharir has been planning this since the day we took his family. He is fuelled by rage—much like any other terrorist—but the reason he is dangerous is his calm and reasoning. None of this is reactionary. It all leads to a greater purpose. He probably bombed Tower Bridge as a symbol of the damage we have done to his country, ruining it beyond recognition. Wembley was supposed to be a statement about our priorities as a people. He was trying to strike at our obsession with wealth and celebrity—indulgence and sin."

Breslow nodded. "What else is he likely to target?"

Sarah thought for a moment. "You?"

"Me?"

"Yes, Prime Minister. Al-Sharir has attacked our identity, our culture, and I imagine his final intention will be to attack our government. Along with the United States, we have made an industry out of toppling foreign governments with force—Saddam, Gaddafi, our current attempts to depose Assad. I think he will seek to repay the favour."

Breslow sniffed. "This nation is a democracy, not a dictatorship. One cannot overthrow our government simply by killing me. Anyway, he tried to get me to commit suicide last night already."

Sarah shrugged. "I'm not saying I know Al-Sharir's exact plan, but that's my theory. His ultimate purpose will be to punish those he holds most responsible for the strife in his country."

"He should blame the Taliban."

"He blames you."

Breslow sighed. "Yes, I suppose he does. Okay, I suppose we're wasting time. I will give you access to our suspect, but I'm afraid you'll have to keep it clean. Terrorist or not, he is an international footballer. The Algerian government is demanding he is released, and his goddamn talent agent is threatening to sue us all into oblivion. We need concrete evidence he planted that bomb in the stadium, or we'll have no choice but to let him go. A confession would be a very nice start to my day. Do your job, Palu."

Palu nodded.

The Prime Minster unlocked the door and stormed out, leaving them to stand for a moment. Thomas eventually led the exodus, and a member of MI5 was waiting to take them to see Rabah Slimani.

Sarah stared at the monitor in the open security nook off the main corridor. It showed the feed from the nearby interrogation room camera. Slimani sat back in his chair, one ankle propped up on his knee. Relaxed, confident. Like a millionaire footballer.

"Who's going to take a crack at him?" asked Howard, which Sarah knew was his way of asking Palu for permission to do it himself.

"I will start the questioning," said Thomas, before Palu or anyone else could argue. He strode immediately into the interrogation room. Sarah saw him appear on the camera feed. Calmly, he took a seat on the opposite side of the room's small wooden table. Slimani acted as though he didn't notice.

Several microphones covered the room, so it was easy to hear what was being said from the security nook. Thomas started with the friendly act. "I'm a big fan of soccer. It's really starting to take off back home. In fact, we get a lot of players coming to ply their trade in the MLS. We pay the big money."

Slimani said nothing.

Thomas went on. "There's some big Russian clubs too, though, huh? Like the one you're currently signed to. Was it the money that led you there? I hear you're a good winger; could have played just about anywhere. So, was it the money?"

Slimani sneered. "*You* may care about money, but I don't."

"Yeah, I like money. Is that wrong, Rabah?"

"Money is a tool to control men and diminish God's influence."

Thomas nodded as if he understood. "It's the only way to buy a Ferrari, though. That's what you drive, right, Rabah? Does God approve of flash cars?"

"Shut up. I don't speak with fools. My lawyer will have me out of here within the hour. I will be out of this stinking country tonight. It sickens me being amongst you."

Thomas leaned back in his chair. "I'm just trying to have a chat with you until your lawyer gets here. No need to be so hostile. Like I said, I'm a big soccer fan, and it's great to meet you. Back to the Ferrari, or the two houses you own... if money is so sinful, you sure seem to spend a bucket load of it."

Slimani said nothing, just looked at the wall.

"My theory is that it's all a front, Rabah. You've been playing the part of the high-rolling soccer player, throwing around cash, jet-setting here, there, and everywhere. You've even been doing charity work in Afghanistan too, right? The model celebrity athlete. Nothing I found, though, mentions you as being a fundamentalist like you're acting now. You haven't preached about the evils of money in the past. Only now, in this room. Why is that? Is it because you've been pretending, but now the need is over? Is this who you really are, Rabah?"

Slimani said nothing.

Thomas nodded calmly. "Did you meet Al-Sharir during your charity work in Afghanistan? Or did you meet him first and start doing the charity work later as a cover? Did he brainwash you into supporting his little crusade, is that it? A shame because you're obviously a talented guy. Why would you throw your life away for a misguided extremist like Al-Sharir?"

"He-" Slimani growled and stopped himself from saying more.

Thomas grinned. "Oh, I almost got you there, didn't I? Were you going to defend Al-Sharir? Is he some sort of hero to you? What were you going to say Rabah? Tell me. Share."

"I've got nothing to say to you. I want my lawyer."

"Al-Sharir doesn't care about you, Rabah," said Thomas. "You're just a tool to him, like money. He's bred you to be his secret weapon—a rich, talented footballer, untouchable by the rest of the world. I have to admit, it's smart. The exact thing Al-Sharir excels at."

Slimani sneered. "You said he was a fool, so which is it?"

"You tell me, Rabah. What do you think of Al-Sharir?"

"Never heard of him."

"I don't believe you."

He shrugged. "So don't."

Thomas sighed. "Look, Rabah. I want to help you. You planted a bomb in Wembley Stadium. Once we talk to your teammates and check CCTV, we'll have enough to bury you. Your government is only making a token complaint, and will give up on you once you look even slightly guilty. No lawyer, or smarmy talent agent, will help you. Only *you* can help you, Rabah. Al-Sharir used you. Tried to make you a martyr. But you failed your mission, and now his use for you is over. Help us find him."

"I want my lawyer."

Thomas stood up from his chair. "Fine, okay, Rabah. It's disappointing, but I guess your idiocy is why Al-Sharir chose you."

"You'll burn. Allah sees everything."

Thomas laughed. "I imagine he sees far more than you give him credit for."

Sarah met Thomas as he exited the interrogation room. "Is that it? We got nothing."

Thomas put a hand up to shush her. "Easy does it. Breslow said we have to play clean, so that's what I'm doing. He isn't getting a lawyer for at least twenty-four hours, and in that time we'll increase the pressure; make him think we're not observing his rights."

Sarah ground her teeth. "We don't have time for slowly. Al-Sharir's next attack could be in ten minutes for all we know."

"This is what we have to work with, Sarah. We'll do everything we can, but we can't make him talk any faster. There's a hundred analysts back at the Earthworm searching for Al-Sharir. We will find him, I promise you."

Sarah glanced back over her shoulder at Palu. He was speaking on the phone, but didn't seem to be taking charge in the way he should. The man had gone limp, reactive instead of proactive. She looked back at Thomas and glared. "What is going on, Tom? Why are you making me promises and interrogating the suspect without waiting for permission? Why was Breslow asking you personally about the investigation?"

Thomas folded his arms. "Don't worry about it, Sarah. We just need to work together and do our jobs."

Sarah studied Tom's expression, a little of the man she knew coming back to her. He tried to keep a straight face, but the flickering of his lip gave him away. Suddenly, it all made sense. She cursed. "Breslow's putting you in charge, isn't she?"

Thomas sighed. "It's not official until this crisis is resolved, but the Prime Minister feels new leadership is in order. The MCU may have been rejuvenated in the last year, but it still has old blood directing it. Palu isn't the right man for the job anymore—the war is changing. Intelligence is changing."

"You fucking traitor, Tom. Is that why you came back from the dead? To stab Palu in the back?"

"No, Sarah. I came back for you."

"Bullshit. You're thinking of yourself, same as you always did. Palu and the rest of us risked our lives a dozen times over in the last year. You have no right to take over. We're only just getting started."

Thomas shrugged. "It's already done. Breslow will attribute Tower Bridge to Palu's failings and force him to retire. I will take over and renew the public's confidence in the MCU. It makes sense Sarah."

It did make sense, and Sarah hated herself for seeing the rationale. The MCU was bigger than Palu, and it needed a scapegoat to survive. "Tom?"

He frowned. "What?"

"You're a fucking arsehole."

She walked away, ignoring Tom's calls for her to come back. She went over to Howard and Palu, who still stood by the monitor in the security nook. "We need to go harder at this guy," she said. "We don't have time to pussyfoot around."

Palu looked at her, a pained expression on his face. "Breslow said we have to stay clean. There are no hard and fast methods to make a suspect talk."

Sarah looked at the ageing director and had a sudden urge to hug him. He'd always had her back, even when she'd been a liability. Now he needed her to have his back. "I know Thomas is taking over the MCU and just so we're clear, he can suck my dick."

Howard shot a look at Palu. "What?"

Palu sighed.

Thomas hurried over to shut her up. "Sarah!"

She kept her focus on Palu. "This isn't your fault, boss. None of this is any of our fault. We risk our lives over and over to clean up messes long after the damage has been done. Breslow is to blame for this more than we are, along with the long line of war mongers before her. We are the good guys, Palu, and you are the good-guy-in-chief. Thomas can take over if he wants, but I will never respect him like I respect you, and you are still my leader for now. So give me a goddamn order, Palu, please! Let me get answers out of Slimani before it's too late. He's stalling because he knows that's all he needs to do."

Palu glanced at Thomas. Thomas shook his head and glared. Slowly, Palu turned back to Sarah with tears in his eyes. "I'm sorry, Sarah. I... can't."

Sarah clenched her fists. "Then we're all screwed."

"Hey, pigs!" A voice came from the monitor. It was Rabah Slimani. He was standing and shouting at the camera in the corner of the room. "I want my lawyer now! I'll be free and flying home 1st class by tonight while you head home to whatever slum you live in. Hear me? Get my lawyer or you'll be cleaning toilets for the rest of your careers."

Sarah exploded in a snarl. She shoved Thomas out of her way and barged through the interview room's door. Slimani flinched as it smashed against the wall.

"Hey, dickhead!" Sarah was spitting with anger. "I'm the one who found your bomb last night. The one who made you look like an incompetent idiot. That must really aggravate a competitive guy like you. I'm also a woman, which probably makes things worse."

Slimani said nothing, but the nervousness on his face was easy to read.

"Nothing to say to me?" she asked. "Is that because you're a pampered, over-paid footballer, or because you're a pathetic fundamentalist perverting the words of the Quran just so you have an excuse to act like a colossal dick?"

Slimani snarled, but sat back in his seat. Sarah leaned into his face. "Trust me," she said. "Allah thinks you're a dick as well."

"Fucking whore. Just wait and see!"

"Wait for what? You screwed up, Rabah. I stopped you. Tomorrow's papers will be plastered with your face beneath the headline: **Worst Terrorist Ever**. Hopefully, you'll be alive to see it."

Slimani laughed. "Threaten me all you want. I'm leaving here, and you won't be able to do a thing about it."

Thomas and Howard appeared in the doorway, but Sarah swivelled and kicked the door shut on them. She dragged one of the room's two chairs up against the handle and wedged it. "I always wondered if this shit works. Now, you have one chance, Rabah, and I'm not playing around."

The man smirked. "Is this the bad cop act? Because I already got the good guy routine off the Yank."

"Answer my question or I will shoot you, Rabah. Where is Al-Sharir?"

"Fuck you, bitch."

Sarah pulled her Sig from its holster and shot him.

The gunshot was deafening inside the cramped interrogation room. Howard and Thomas shouted from outside and rammed their shoulders against the door. The chair wedged under the handle slid on the tiles. The door opened easily.

Sarah pulled a face. "Guess it doesn't work after all."

Howard gawped at Rabah. His jaw dropped.

"Sarah?" said Thomas, standing equally as shocked beside Howard. "What did you do?"

A scream escaped Rabah as he lay on the floor, bleeding. He clutched his bleeding knee like it was on fire. Sarah pointed the gun at his other knee. "There goes your football career, Rabah. Want to say goodbye to walking altogether?"

"Please, no! You're crazy."

"Yep, pretty much. Now tell me where Al-Sharir is."

"Help! Help me!"

Thomas attempted to grab Sarah, but she pointed the gun at his face. "Don't! You've already died once, Tom—this time you won't come back."

Thomas backed off.

Howard remained in the doorway like a statue.

Sarah turned the gun back on Rabah. This time she pointed at his head. "Al-Sharir has taken everything from me, Rabah, you should understand that." She tapped at her scars with the muzzle of her gun. "Behind this pretty face is a monster he created. I am going to kill you unless you tell me exactly what I want to know."

"Help me!"

Sarah shot Rabah in the other knee. "Next one is in your head."

Rabah screeched like a boiling kettle. "Please, no! No, no, no."

"You have two seconds, Rabah. Then I send you to see what Allah really thinks of men like you. Where is Al-Sharir? One... Two..."

"I don't know," he wailed. "Honestly. I don't!"

Sarah tilted her head and pointed her gun between his eyes. "That's too bad."

"Wait! I know his next target!"

Sarah had been a heartbeat away from pulling the trigger, but now she lowered the gun. "Talk more."

Rabah put a bloody hand out in front of his face, flinching as if expecting a bullet at any moment. "He... He's going to wipe out Parliament."

Sarah glanced at Howard and Thomas. She'd been right.

Rabah carried on, his eyes rolling like he was going to lose consciousness. "He... he has a nuclear bomb."

"Tell me something else."

"He's going to blow up Westminster. Tonight."

"How?"

"I-I don't know."

"Oh dear, now you're dead."

"No, no, no. I really don't know. I haven't spoken to Al-Sharir in a year. He... he has been living in Kazan, in Russia. The... the men that own the team I play for... they helped him disappear from Afghanistan. He is acting on their orders. I work for them, not Al-Sharir."

"Russia is behind all of this?"

"No! Just the men who own my club. They... they want to weaken the United States and its Allies so they can take its oil interests and remove Western forces from Russian border territories. Russian crime syndicates want to gain a foothold in Asia, and they have started working together... pooling their resource. Please, I need help. A doctor, please!"

Sarah frowned. "Al-Sharir wouldn't be interested in helping the Russian Mafia. Are you bullshitting me?"

"He's not working with them willingly, but his goals align with theirs. He needed money and influence to complete his goals, so he made an alliance."

Sarah lowered her Sig and tapped it against the side of her leg while she thought. "You're a pretty smart guy, Rabah. Maybe now that your football career is over, you can be a teacher or something."

"I need help."

Sarah sighed. "I suppose we both do now. Thank you for your time, Rabah. Tell my colleagues everything they need to know, okay? Then they will get you help. If you cooperate, you might still have a chance at walking."

"I'll tell them everything. I swear!"

"Good." Sarah turned to the door, but Howard and Thomas were gone. In their place were two armed police officers come to arrest her.

Sarah threw down her gun and got onto her knees. She knew the drill. "Still totally worth it," she said as they descended on her.

As they led Sarah away, she glimpsed Palu standing over by the monitors. Tears glistened on his cheeks, but when he gave her a subtle nod, she understood he was proud of the sacrifice she had just made. Her life might be over, but at least the MCU had a chance.

It had a chance.

CHAPTER SIXTY-TWO

"Be careful with her," Howard shouted at the stiff police officers. "She has a recent stab wound in her abdomen."

Sarah didn't expect them to care about her wellbeing, and she was right. They hurled her into a holding room so hard that she went skidding onto her face. Her stitches were white-hot—burning eels snaking through her flesh. It was hard to breathe through the pain, so she put her hands on the back of her head and stayed there, face down on the floor, hoping they would leave her alone. They were happy to oblige, shoving Howard out of the room and closing the door.

For the second time that week, Sarah found herself locked in a small room alone. Slimani's blood spattered her trousers, damp against her skin. Who knew knees could squirt. She ended up chuckling, but was aware it was only because her sanity lay on the brink. She'd just committed suicide. Might not be dead, but her life was over anyway. They'd throw the book at her for this. The government was all for torture, now and then, but only when hidden, and only against people unable to cause a fuss. Slimani would cause a fuss.

But Sarah felt good. Her high was amazing, like she'd shed a mangy old cloak to reveal a shining suit of armour underneath. She had stopped being a victim to evil and had attacked it head-on. Her fearful second-guessing ceased, and she inflicted punishment upon one who deserved it. What she had done was not wrong; it was *just*. Slimani had planned to kill and maim ninety thousand people. Two missing kneecaps was the least he deserved.

Slimani would remember Sarah's face for the rest of his life.

Like I remember Al-Sharir's.

I can't believe he is here. I wish he were standing in this room, just him and me.

For ten minutes, Sarah lay on the floor feeling strong, invincible—no longer a victim.

It had been totally worth it.

Clonking footsteps rang out in the corridor and grew louder as the person approached the door. Sarah climbed up off her belly and stood, ready to receive her guest.

The door swung open and Breslow appeared.

"You stupid, stupid girl," the Prime Minister growled as she stepped inside. She turned to an armed police officer who tried to move with her and waved a hand. "Leave us. Now!"

The officer was visibly unhappy, but not brave enough to argue. He left hastily and closed the door.

"I know what you're going to say," said Sarah, "but I don't care. I'm glad I did what I did. We didn't have time to go easy on that son-of-a-bitch. We needed leads, and we needed them yesterday. Fuck Slimani."

"Fuck *you*," said Breslow. "Because that's what will happen now. You are fucked. Fuck fuck fucked."

Sarah remained unflinching, even though Breslow's expression made her want to shrivel up. "If Palu and the others stop Al-Sharir, then I can accept a stretch in prison."

Breslow guffawed. "A stretch? Dear, they will throw the book at you. They might even attempt to try you for war crimes. You shot a prisoner in custody on camera. A high-profile prisoner with enough money to create a media circus. They will lock you up and forget about you, just so they can save face."

"So *you* can save face."

Breslow snorted like a bull. "Girl, don't piss me off. Even if I could keep you out of prison, Slimani's football club value him as a nine-million-pound asset. They will sue the MCU for damages, I promise you. This is a bloody mess of astounding proportions. You've made me look a fool, whatever happens. Saving face is the least of my worries. You think I care about that little shit, Slimani. There is a nuclear bomb in my capital, and it could go off at any moment. That's what matters here, consequences be damned. You got answers, Sarah. Slimani is currently spilling his guts about all he knows, and if his leads help us find and disarm a nuclear bomb, I will make sure the papers know it was down to you. Best you can hope for is that the papers take up a crusade to free you. God knows you're a hero, Sarah."

Sarah frowned. "But..."

"But you're a bloody fool." Breslow reached for the inside pocket of her blazer and plucked out a small black hard drive. "This is the camera and audio footage of Slimani's interrogation room. It contains the whole damn mess. The only copy."

"You're going to destroy it," said Sarah, dumbfounded. The Prime Minister was going to risk everything for her.

"Am I bollocks," said Breslow, betraying her Yorkshire upbringing she hid so well in Parliament. "I will be giving this straight to my Secretary of State for Justice so she can prosecute you for all the world to see. This country does not condone your actions, even if they do get results."

Sarah nodded. "I understand."

"However," said Breslow. "I'm a busy lady and I will be assembling a full Parliament all day today, probably until the early hours. Two-hundred of my peers are demanding to know why our country is under a full-scale attack. I'm not looking forward to giving them answers— because I don't bloody have any. At the very least, I can't see me handing over this hard drive for at least the next twenty-four hours."

Sarah frowned. *Is she doing what I think she's doing?*

The Prime Minister moved towards the door and banged on it. The anxious-looking police officer opened it in less than a second. "Yes, ma'am?"

"Agent Stone is being released. Please return her weapon and return her to Director Palu."

"Soon to be retired, Director Palu," Sarah corrected.

Breslow shot her daggers. Sarah shut her mouth. One battle at a time.

The police officer looked at the Prime Minister like she had gone insane. "Ma'am?"

"You heard me! Release her now. She has a dentist appointment she simply must get to."

The officer nodded and took Sarah by the arm. Five minutes later, she was outside Thames House breathing the fresh air, a free woman.

For twenty-four hours.

Palu stood outside, waiting to pick Sarah up. Fortunately, the Press had caught wind that Breslow was in the building, which meant they paid less attention as Sarah and Palu hurried to the car that Mandy had parked nearby. It had darkened and started to drizzle, making the early afternoon more like evening.

Palu opened the rear passenger door for Sarah without saying a word. After she slid in, he went to the front passenger side and got in. Mandy pulled away from the curb. The London traffic was subdued.

A distance away from Thames House, Palu punched the dash-board. "Damn it, Sarah, what were you thinking?"

"I was thinking we were standing around with our sweaty balls in our hands while a terrorist laughed in our faces. I begged you to make the call, Palu, but you didn't have the spine for it. Ever since Tom arrived, you've lost something. Where's the bulldog who helped convince me that the MCU was worth fighting for? Where's the man who would do whatever it takes to protect people?"

"I'm still here, Sarah, but not for much longer. They're getting rid of me, and I don't want this to be my send-off. The world will already remember me as the man who allowed Tower Bridge to be destroyed. I can't let a nuclear bomb slip through my fingers too. This can't be how my life's work ends."

Sarah sighed. "You're over-thinking things."

"I'm over-thinking a nuclear bomb?"

"Yes! We have been kicking terrorist butt, left-right-and-centre, this last year, so why are you now doubting yourself? Because there's a nuclear bomb? We stop bombs all the time. Because of Tower Bridge? If not for us, there would be a dozen landmarks floating in the Thames. We don't win 'em all, but we win the ones we can. Thomas hasn't taken over yet, Palu, so stop acting like he has. You are the director of the MCU."

Palu sighed. "After Tower Bridge, Breslow told me to step down."

"So step down. After we get Al-Sharir. This isn't Thomas's fight; it's ours. You, me, Howard, Mandy, Jessica. We're family."

"And now you're going to jail," he said. "Breslow told me you have twenty-four hours."

Sarah shrugged. "Give or take."

"What you did was stupid."

"But necessary. You want to help me. Let's catch Al-Sharir. Justice will be kinder if I stop a nuclear bomb from decimating London. That's how you protect me."

He nodded. "You're right. Are you okay?"

Sarah frowned at the question. "Huh?"

"You lost it on Slimani. I've never seen you like that. Are you okay?"

Was she okay? She felt okay, but she was still on a high. It was true she'd lost control back in the interrogation room.

"I'm not okay," she admitted. "This last year... Hesbani... my dad. It's been getting harder and harder just to get up in the morning. I've become so frightened that I see danger everywhere. What happened in that room was me finally snapping, but I don't regret it. Slimani is an evil man, and I needed to confront him. I needed to take charge and be the one in control. Shooting an unarmed suspect is not my finest moment, but somehow it gave me back a part of myself. It gave me whatever it was I needed to see this through. Enough is enough, Palu; one way or another I am finding Al-Sharir and looking the monster in the eye. Then I'll blow his goddamn head off. Whatever happens after doesn't matter. My life already ended in a desert five years ago."

"Your life is not over," said Palu. "It's only just starting."

"Then it will be short lived, and I intend to end it on a high note."

Mandy pulled them into a car park. When Sarah looked out the window, she saw a pub named *Last Orders*. It had several tables outside in a small garden, but with the rain and darkening sky, nobody sat at them.

Sarah frowned at Palu. "We're having a pint?"

"Absolutely. Looks like this is the end of the line for us all, so let's drink to one last hurrah."

Palu and Mandy got out of the car and waited for Sarah to join them. They strolled across the damp car park, the heavens opening above them. Sarah felt her high fading, being replaced by a calm clarity. This was the end of something. Things were going to change. The only question was *what things?*

They headed inside the pub, where Sarah was surprised to see Thomas, Jessica, and Howard sitting at a round table. Alcoholic beverages sat beside each of their open laptops.

"You were right about the pressure," said Palu. "We need to sit back and think things through in a calmer environment."

"What you 'aving?" Mandy asked them both.

If Sarah was headed to prison, her last drink needed to count for something. "Cognac. Double."

She sat at the round table with the others while Mandy went to the bar. The pub was more or less empty besides them, and it was clear why. The fruit machine was dim and no longer working. The quiz machine displayed an error message on screen. The carpet was balding. The barmaid was miserable. It was Sarah's kind of place.

Thomas glanced at Sarah sadly, but he didn't mention what she had done back at Thames House. He might have even been ashamed of her, she considered, but she hoped it was sadness she was seeing in his eyes. He had gone away for five years once; now it was her turn to disappear on him.

"I imagine your stitches have popped open again," said Jessica disapprovingly.

Sarah nodded. "I'll live."

"You okay?" asked Howard.

"I'm good. Do we have any leads?"

Howard beamed at her. "Oh yes. Slimani would have told us his mother's bra size if he thought we wanted to know it. You completely broke him."

"Shooting a man in the kneecaps will do that," said Jessica. "Crude, Sarah. Very, very crude."

Sarah shrugged, embarrassed.

Howard sipped his pint and updated her. "The owner of Slimani's football club is Omar Vankin, an oil magnate from Kiev, currently residing in Kazan. His oil fields in the Middle-East are hemmed in by Western interests, and his attempts to expand in the region have been hampered by ongoing NATO operations along with other factors. We believe Vankin's connections with Al-Sharir arose eight years ago when he built a refinery in Northern Afghanistan. He entered Britain on a business visa three weeks ago, via private plane."

"Are we bringing him in?" asked Sarah.

"Of course," said Thomas, still failing to look at her for more than a half-second. "I have a team searching for him now. He's not the main thread we're following, however. He arrived in this country with one other person—the pilot."

"Okay," said Sarah. Mandy arrived with her Cognac and sat down beside her.

"The pilot doesn't exist," explained Howard. "At least not on paper. His visa was forged under the name, Karl ibn al-Walid. There's no one with that name living in Russia, or anywhere else that we can find. Check the history books, though, and you might find a *Khalid ibn al-Walid*. A friend of the prophet Mohammed who fought against an oppressive Byzantine empire. He led a tiny force of Muslims and defeated an army many times its size. Basically, Islam's biggest underdog."

"Al-Sharir enjoys irony," said Sarah, growing excited by the lead. "And he doesn't do anything without hidden meaning. If he had to choose a false name, he wouldn't have been able to resist making a joke at our expense. Maybe he sees it as honouring his faith. He is an underdog seeking to topple a powerful, unjust regime."

"Sounds like you almost believe that," said Thomas.

Sarah shrugged. "I'm past the point of good guys and bad guys. This is personal."

Jessica sipped her sparkling wine. "Isn't everything, sweetheart?"

"Not *this* personal," said Sarah. "So what else do we have?"

"Omar's plane is parked at Biggin Hill," said Howard. "It's scheduled to take off and depart tonight."

"He might be planning on fleeing," Thomas suggested. "We're not sure."

Sarah shook her head. "Al-Sharir is intending to blow up Westminster. With a nuke, he could hit Parliament from half-a-mile away, but that won't be enough. Parliament must be at the epicentre of the explosion—the exact target—so that his point is made. He'll want to leave it a burning crater beside the river."

"Parliament is in full session," said Palu. "Security will be tighter then it has ever been, in light of recent events. No way is Al-Sharir getting anywhere near it with a bomb."

"By foot perhaps," said Sarah. "But not if he delivers the bomb by air."

"Shit, you're right." Howard tapped at his keyboard. "I'll check flight paths. I doubt any exist right above Parliament, but there may be some near enough to launch a surprise attack."

"I'll ground all flights from Biggin Hill," said Thomas.

"And I'm going there," said Sarah. "If Al-Sharir is planning to commit suicide by plane, then the nuclear bomb might already be on board. We can end this right now."

"I'm coming with you," said Howard

Sarah nodded. "Wouldn't think of going without you."

Thomas grunted, but kept his gaze on his laptop screen.

"Need a lift, luv?" came a masculine voice from over Sarah's shoulder.

She turned to see a familiar face and leapt up to hug the man. "Mattock!" His stubbly chin took a layer of skin from her neck, but it was worth it to see him again.

"Hey, lass. I hear you've been in the wars."

"No more than usual." She eased back and took in Mattock's grinning face. His shaven head sported even more scar lines, and his left cheek had a recent cut. "You, too, by the looks of it. New recruits being too hard on you?"

He grinned. "The green-eared buggers don't know what's hit 'em. I beasted one kid so badly, he shit himself. Other than that, I think he'll make a bloody fine agent. We all shit ourselves to start with if your trainer is doing his job."

Howard stood. "Shall we do the reunions later? We have a capital city to save."

Mattock looked at Mandy who was sitting at the table and about to finish the pint he'd only just started. "Okay if I take chauffeur duty today, guv'na?"

Mandy nodded. "I'll have another drink."

"Cheers! Then it's decided. Let's go and kick some arse."

Sarah grabbed her double Cognac and downed it before slamming the empty glass on the table. Afterwards, she rubbed at her stitches and wondered how much longer they would hold. "I might need you to do the actual kicking though, Mattock."

"No worries, luv. I got two feet."

They headed out of the pub and into the carpark. The rain was hammering down now and forming puddles on the tarmac. A perfect day for the world to end, but Sarah would not let that happen. The sun would rise again on London tomorrow.

"Out the way, please, mate," Mattock told someone walking into their path.

Sarah saw a man in a hooded raincoat and wellington boots. He looked oddly familiar. Gardening overalls peeked out from beneath his dirty jacket.

Sarah stopped. Frowned,

The stranger's jacket opened. "I heard what you said, you bitch. We had something, but you ruined it."

Sarah's eyes went wide. "Get down now!"

The Flower Man pulled a shotgun out of his overalls and pointed it at Sarah. Sarah went for her own gun, but it was too late. She stared down twin muzzles of an antique shotgun. Her death.

Howard barged Sarah aside and dove for the Flower Man's weapon. He grabbed the muzzle of the shotgun as it discharged.

Blam!

A moment of silence, then only the sound of rain on tarmac. Gradually, the rapid *Pitter Patter* disappeared, replaced by a high-pitch ringing.

The sound of screaming.

Sarah snapped back to reality. Howard lay on top of the Flower Man and knocked the shotgun aside. Blood splattered the ground, merging with the puddled rainwater.

It was Howard who was screaming, even as he fought with the Flower Man.

His right hand was missing.

Mattock lunged forward and booted the Flower Man in the head, knocking him out cold. Jessica, Palu, Thomas, and Mandy raced out of the pub and into the pouring rain. Then they stood there, confused.

"Get going," said Howard, attempting to cuff the unconscious serial killer with only his left hand. Rain soaked his face and dripped off the strands of his brown hair.

Sarah reached for him. "Howard, your hand..."

"There's no time. Go! Get Al-Sharir."

Mattock grabbed Sarah and pulled her away. "Come on, lass."

"Go," shouted Palu from the edge of the car park. "We'll take care of things here. Go!"

Sarah looked at Howard and felt sick. That shotgun had been meant for her. He'd jumped right in front of the blast.

"Go," Howard mouthed the word at her. His wet face was alabaster. His lips quivered, wanting to scream.

He doesn't want to do it in front of me, Sarah realised.

She nodded to her injured friend who had just saved her life, and then turned and ran through the rain, heading for the car that would take her to Al-Sharir.

The boogeyman from her nightmares, finally in the flesh.

———

Mattock drove as fast as Mandy did, but with less control. It made the speeding journey through the city a hair-raising experience. Even more so in the pouring rain.

"Now I see why Mandy does the driving," said Sarah in the back seat. She held her stomach, hoping to keep her insides on the inside. She was sweating, and her fingers tingled. After all this was through, she was going to collapse.

Then they'll take me to prison.

She probably wouldn't even get chance to see Howard. *His hand...*

Sarah's situation began to sink in. She was scared. Shit, she was really scared. As awful as things had been since leaving the desert, it wasn't prison. Would they ever let her out again?

Just focus on what needs to be done, Sarah. Worry later.

Biggin Hill was on the southern border of Greater London, and in normal weekend traffic, the drive would normally have taken two hours. As it was, with the traffic being sparser than usual, the drive was looking to take less than an hour. At the speed Mattock was going, it was little wonder.

"There's a team due in place by the time we get there," Mattock updated her, barely looking at the road. "Got to tell you, it feels good to get down from those hills and back in the field. Teaching ain't for me."

"So why do it?"

"'Cus I'm the only one good enough to make sure the new kids know a trigger from a tripwire. No offence."

"Offence taken, but that's okay."

"So," he asked. "Who was the pillock who tried to kill you?"

"The Flower Man."

"That was him, huh? Looked nothing more than a streak of piss to me. Certainly had it in for you, lass."

"I insulted him to the Press. Serial killers and their egos, I guess. I can't believe what Howard did. His hand..."

"How about you?" asked Mattock. "How are you holding up?"

"People keep asking me that. Do I have something on my face?"

"Just a few scars, lass, but nowt all that noticeable."

Sarah scoffed. "Yeah, right."

"I worry about you, lass. You're my responsibility."

"Why?"

"Because I bloody decided you are. We're not going to let 'em lock you up, don't you worry. I'll storm the gates myself if I have to."

"No," said Sarah. "You stay out of it. It's time I started facing up to things. My mess is my mess, okay?"

Mattock declined to comment.

"I said, okay? You bloody Manc!"

In the rearview mirror, she watched his eyebrows rise in surprise. "Okay, okay, lass. I heard ya. We're ten minutes out, so what's the plan?"

"We rendezvous with the field team and run a scout forward, assess things, and go from there. Nobody starts shooting unless absolutely necessary. Last thing we want is a stray bullet setting off a bomb."

Mattock nodded. "If we get a chance to take Al-Sharir without a gun fight, we should take it. Take that bugger in alive and make him squeal."

The car radio lit up. "Come in, unit 2, come in."

"Sergeant Mattock reading. What's happening? Over."

"Team Leader Fogarty. Shots fired. Shots fired. Permission to engage? Over."

Gunfire rang out in the background.

"Sod it," said Mattock. "Permission granted, but Fogarty, I forbid any of your team to die."

"Roger that. Over."

If it was possible, Mattock seemed to press his foot down harder and speed up more. They had avoided using their sirens, not wanting to alert Al-Sharir upon their approach, but now Mattock hit the button and the Jaguar came to life—lights and sirens emitting from both ends.

In the back seat, Sarah pulled out her Sig and checked it.

It was happening. They had Al-Sharir pinned.

She loaded a round into the chamber.

Time to end this.

CHAPTER SIXTY-THREE

The Jaguar's brakes squealed outside the airport gates and Mattock leapt out, pulling his gun and badge despite no one seeking to stop him. The two unarmed security guards trembling in cover seemed uninterested in trying to stop anyone from entering. Gunfire rang out amidst the din of rain on tin roofs. The rain had calmed, but it had left everything sodden.

Sarah's hand tightened around her SIG, but she kept her finger off the trigger. She wanted Al-Sharir alive, to make him answer for his crimes. Whether she possessed the ability to refrain from lethal force when the time came, however, was unknown.

Would shooting the fucker dead be so bad? At least it wouldn't give Al-Sharir the chance to use the trial as his own personal soapbox.

Possessing the most combat experience, Mattock took point and skulked towards the airport's admin building. His Glock 17 sported an extended magazine and lengthened barrel. The sergeant took his sidearm seriously.

More gunfire sounded from the landing strip around back. Had the field team discovered Al-Sharir about to take off and attempted to pin the man down?

Two women cowered behind a parked re-fuelling car. Sarah slid up to them, keeping her weapon low and smiling to reassure them. Her horrendous scars likely worked against her in that regard. "I'm a Government agent. Can you update me on what's happening?"

The older of the two women nodded, her bagged eyes less shell-shocked than her friend's. Pinned to her navy-blue jumper, her name badge read: *Dana*. "They just started shooting at each other," she spluttered. "A bunch of men in Hangar 3, and another bunch who turned up in black Range Rovers."

"The men in the Range Rovers are MCU agents," explained Sarah, wiping drizzle from her eyebrows. "The other men are terrorists. You say they're in Hangar 3? Is there a way for us to approach it without them seeing?"

The woman thought for a second and shook her head. "Not really. Your agents are to the rear of the admin building, but Hangar 3 faces it. You can't sneak around because a fence runs right behind it."

"Okay," said Sarah. "Thank you."

Mattock put a hand on her shoulder. "Looks like we'll have to tackle things head on."

Sarah sighed as the gunfire continued rattling off. "It doesn't sound like that's going so well for the field team."

"What are your thoughts?"

"I'm not sure yet. Let's just get to our people."

They entered the empty admin block and soon exited out the other side. It placed them alongside Fogarty and his team, who were taking cover behind an old RAF Spitfire parked on a grassy patch. Biggin Hill had once been an air force base, but this was probably the first time in half-a-century the old fighter plane had seen war.

Sarah slid down behind a stone obelisk holding the brass plate describing the plane's heroic deeds from days past. It was just wide enough to keep her safe, but the bullets pinging against the other side made her feel like a sitting duck.

Mattock ducked behind the Spitfire's tail where Fogarty was popping in and out of cover with his Heckler and Koch rifle. He had three men alongside him, all firing the same weapons, all up and down like springs.

At the opposite side of the paved taxiing area, muzzles flashed from the shadowy confines of Hangar 3. A small plane took up the centre, big enough to seat only a half-dozen passengers and two pilots. Was it big enough to carry a bomb?

Yes.

Sarah's head filled with the sounds and scents of men trying to kill each other. She found herself back in the desert staring at her fallen, dismembered sergeant. It was that moment, when Miller tried to help the veiled woman—Hesbani's sister—move her fruit cart out of the road, that Sarah's nightmares began. The first time people tried to kill her. They hadn't stopped since.

"We count six armed combatants," Fogarty shouted over the din to Mattock. "No casualties on either side yet. We're pinned down and so are they. No one has the advantage, and it's only a matter of time before we start taking casualties."

Mattock peeked out of cover, then ducked down as a bullet pinged off the top of the plane. The old Spitfire was a relic; its days of being shot at should have been over. It highlighted just how long mankind had been at war with itself.

Sarah wondered if one of those muzzle flashes in the Hangar belonged to Al-Sharir. Would this be the day he died? Or the day *she* died? Somehow, either outcome felt like a relief.

Mattock leapt up on the Spitfire's wing and lay across it, shielded from gunfire by the raised fuselage of the plane. It allowed him to talk with Sarah without breaking cover. "We could call in another team," he shouted, "but I don't like the thought of adding gunfire to a situation with a nuclear bomb. I'll be honest, I don't know if we can accidentally set it off or not, but I don't want to take the risk. I've told Fogarty and his men to stop firing. Maybe our targets will try to make a break for it if they think we're abandoning our assault."

Or they'll recover enough to set the bomb off right here, thought Sarah. *I need to end this now.*

"Don't go anywhere," she told Mattock, then broke cover and sprinted back into the admin building. A stray bullet shattered the glass of the door right behind her. A plan formed in her head.

Mattock gritted his teeth as gunfire clattered against the Spitfire's hull. A bloody travesty to see the noble machine peppered by a bunch of nationless prats. He'd never understood religious fundamentalists. What were they even fighting for? An idea?

A bunch of children demanding everyone agree with them because their daddy said so.

Idiots.

At least fighting for money or power made sense. It might be ugly, but at least it was understandable. The world was for the taking, and those too weak would lose out. That realisation made Mattock the soldier he was today. Be fiercer and bloodier than the enemy and you walked away with the spoils.

Sarah Stone fought for more complex reasons.

Sarah fought to keep the monsters at bay. She fought to keep moving forward, instead of halting to allow her past to devour her. Sarah fought because she was afraid. And angry.

Mattock smirked. *Christ, that girl is angry. I'm not sure she even realises quite how much.*

It was Sarah's father, prize arsehole Major Stone, that forced her into a life she didn't deserve. Underneath the rage, it was possible to see Sarah's soft, empathetic soul, but it was covered by so many emotional callouses that it was often obscured. That guarded, yet caring personality led Sarah to join the Army—to 'help'. Misguided, yet noble, it pained Mattock to see what had become of Sarah.

She didn't know it, but Mattock was one of the SAS trainers who had put her through two weeks of hell almost ten years ago. Her father had come to him and told him to make his daughter's life impossible—to 'break her physically and mentally'. Mattock hadn't liked it, but you didn't defy an order from Major Stone.

So he had tortured and beat that young girl—the promising junior officer attempting to join the men-only elite of the SAS. The Special Forces was not something in which you enlisted on a whim to impress your daddy. Major Stone had not been impressed by Sarah's transparent attempts for approval.

But Mattock had been.

Ten days in, Sarah was broken, her lean body an unending bruise after a thirty-mile march through rain-drenched hills. Normally, forced hikes with a full pack were only half as long, but Major Stone wanted Mattock to keep going until Sarah fell. Out of the nine recruits—eight of them men—Sarah was the only one left standing at the end. The ordeal placed her in hospital, at death's door, but she never quit. Mattock had given in first.

As lead trainer, he had no choice but to recommend her for inclusion into the illustrious ranks of the SAS. He'd been happy to do it. Any reservations about serving alongside a woman had been dashed; Sarah was a soldier he would be glad to have at his side under fire. She had done more than enough to earn her place.

But Major Stone thought otherwise.

Sarah did not qualify for the SAS.

But *fuck* she should have.

Mattock left the regiment a few years later and was glad to see the back of the man who would have his own daughter tortured. He never expected to meet that brave, indomitable girl again, and he never did. The Sarah Stone he encountered last year was a shadow of her former self—impulsive and insecure. Broken in ways Mattock had never been able to inflict on her. Thank fuck he had worn a mask the whole time he'd been her SAS trainer. She never knew who he was.

One day, I should tell her.

I can't keep looking out for her without her knowing the truth.

Where had Sarah rushed off to, anyway? What hair-brained risk was she about to take next? Mattock could not let her get hurt, because he was part of the tragedy that made up her life.

More bullets pinged off the Spitfire. Someone yelled, "Man down!"

Fogarty flew back and landed in the wet grass. Blood bubbled from his neck. Mattock slid down off the wing and scrambled over to him. A few seconds was all he lasted.

"Fuck's sake."

The enemy's gunfire lessened as they started to pick their shots from the shadows of the hangar. Impossible to fight an enemy you couldn't see and couldn't aim at. Mattock had no choice but to call his team into retreat. He ground his teeth. He didn't like backing down— but he liked losing men even less. "Okay, men. It's time—"

Before he had chance to call a retreat, the enemy's gunfire shifted away from the Spitfire and allowed the men to catch a breath. Mattock peeked from cover to see what was happening and was surprised to witness a small vehicle rolling across the tarmac towards the hangar.

Mattock squinted. *It was the re-fuelling car they passed when they'd entered the airfield.*

The small vehicle was boxy with a bulky compartment on the back. A leaking hose-pipe trailed behind it, leaving a slick trail like a slug. It couldn't have been travelling more than 5mph.

When the men in the hangar realised what they were shooting at, they ceased fire at once. Another second and they might have ignited the fuel container. As it was, the little truck puttered along the tarmac unmolested, driving along by itself.

Did Sarah have something to do with this?

The answer to Mattock's question came a split-second later when a gunshot rang out from the side of the admin building. The bullet struck the tarmac and kicked up sparks.

Flames danced along the line of spilled fuel.

The little truck exploded.

That was when a sleek black Jaguar sped across the runway.

Sarah's plan wasn't really a plan. But, she considered fire could only help the situation. *Al-Sharir enjoys blowing things up so much, well here you go, arsehole.*

There had, of course, been the risk of detonating the bomb in the hangar, but she never intended the explosion to occur close enough for it to be a factor. The fire was just a diversion. A distraction while she dove—drove—headfirst into action.

As soon as she shot the tarmac and ignited the spilled fuel, Sarah sprinted over to the MCU Jaguar. Her electronic ID activated all the vehicles in the fleet which meant the ignition roared to life as soon as she pushed the button on the dashboard. Behind the steering wheel, she put her foot down and grinned at the vehicle's ridiculous acceleration.

0-60 in 4.9 seconds.

The wipers flicked left and right, clearing away the drizzle.

The flames spreading across the tarmac formed a wall, and the little fuel truck popped and spat like a dying firework. The effect was chaos on both sides of the paved taxi area. All gunfire ceased, replaced by confused shouting.

Sarah raced across the tarmac in the Jaguar, engine screaming. With the noise of the explosion still ringing in their ears, the men in the hangar did not hear her coming. Nor did they spot her until it was too late. Sarah slammed on the brakes and locked the vehicle into a skid. Yanking the wheel, she threw the car sideways. The tyres screeched and shed skin as they fought to keep grip. The Jaguar skidded into the hangar at 50mph.

Too fast.

Looking sideways through the driver side window, Sarah saw the plane flying towards her. Two armed men screamed as the car mowed over them like ants. Their bodies helped slow the Jaguar down, but it still slid out of control.

It was going to smash right into the passenger plane.

And the bomb inside.

Sarah closed her eyes and gripped the wheel. Her recklessness had screwed things up again. In her bid to get the bomb, she would set the thing off right here in the hangar.

The squealing grew louder.

Then stopped.

The Jaguar lurched. Sarah's head struck the side window.

Sarah opened her eyes and took a single breath, waiting for fiery oblivion. When none came, she chanced a glance out of her side window. The plane's nose sat inches away from the glass.

Startled men surrounded the Jaguar. White men. Russian men. Men with black-market assault rifles. Only one was different. One man who did not match his white, heavily-armed colleagues.

Wearing another crisp suit, Al-Sharir cut through the centre of the group of men, parting them to either side. He glared at Sarah through the window and Sarah glared back. Slowly, not wanting to cause alarm, she raised her hands up away from the steering wheel. And placed both middle fingers against the glass.

Al-Sharir aimed a revolver and pulled the trigger.

Kapow!

The bullet left a blackened scorch mark on the bullet-proof window, yet Sarah flinched anyway and threw herself down across the seats.

A moment of silence while she lay face down against the seat. What was happening?

The rest of the men surrounding the Jaguar opened fire, clattering the windows with automatic fire from weapons far stronger than Al-Sharir's revolver. These weapons caused spider webs to spread throughout the car's glass on all sides. Eventually, the windows would break, and Sarah would be a sitting duck. She clutched her SIG and told herself that she would get off at least one shot—and that the bullet would be meant for Al-Sharir.

One man jumped up on the car bonnet and rammed the butt of his rifle against the windscreen. Each blow sent shudders through the glass and widened a small hole right in front of Sarah's face.

Sarah looked out, seeking Al-Sharir and readying herself for that one, important shot.

The windscreen shattered.

Sarah's protection fell away, and the cold air rushed in. The snarling brute standing on the bonnet aimed his rifle at her face and said something in Russian.

Sarah searched for Al-Sharir. Where was he?

Gunfire rang out, echoing off the cavernous insides of the hangar.

Sarah rocked back in the driver's seat.

The man on the bonnet flew backwards, disappearing beyond the nose of the car. Sarah stared out the missing windshield and spotted a man in black entering the shadowy hangar.

Mattock.

The MCU field team unleashed hell upon the distracted enemy, taking down three in the first flurry and forcing the rest to drop their weapons in surrender. Mattock moved up beside the Jaguar and rapped a knuckle against the cracked driver's side window.

Vision blurry, Sarah elbowed open the door and got out.

Mattock gathered her with one of his thick arms. "I've heard about drawing enemy fire, lass, but parking yourself in the middle of a gunfight is taking things a tad too far. You okay?"

Sarah patted herself down. Her legs felt hollow. "I think so."

Mattock shook his head and grinned. "You have the luck of the Irish, girl. And big brass balls."

Sarah returned the grin. It was over. They had the plane. They had-

She searched the hangar. "Where is Al-Sharir?"

"Looks like he ain't here," said Mattock. "Sod's slippier than a female fish."

"No," said Sarah. "He was here, I saw him. He was inside the hangar."

Mattock's smile faded, and he returned to business. "Field team, fan out. Al-Sharir is here and attempting to flee."

"Er, Sarge?" A grizzled agent called over from the steps of the plane. The man had opened the side hatch and was peeking inside.

Mattock growled. "What is it, Fletcher?"

"There's no bomb on this plane, Sarge. It's empty."

Mattock and Sarah exchanged glances.

Sarah rushed over to the hatch and looked in. Nothing but two rows of seats, all the way to the back of the tail.

"Damn it!"

An engine roared to life at the back of the hangar. Headlights blinded everybody and forced them to cover their eyes. Sarah saw the blurry silhouette of a vehicle picking up speed.

A white van

The white van.

"The bomb is on that vehicle," shouted Sarah. "Nobody shoot! Nobody shoot!"

Mattock and the men stood down, rifles raised but triggers still. They acted confused, not knowing what to do. The van headed straight for Sarah.

Sarah stood firm, facing the speeding vehicle down. In the driver's seat, Al-Sharir stared back at her.

Finally, they would end this.

CHAPTER SIXTY-FOUR

Sarah faced down Al-Sharir and did not move. She did not flinch. The time for running had passed. She would end this now. Al-Sharir must have seen something in her face, because he suddenly seemed unsure of himself. He gripped the steering wheel tightly and aimed the van right at her.

"Sarah," Mattock shouted at her. "Get out of the way."

Sarah stood firm.

The van raced towards her.

After all they'd been through, Al-Sharir intended to drive over her like a stray dog.

Well, fuck him.

Sarah stepped to one side. The van sped through the spot she'd been standing in, missing her by an inch. It carried on out of the hangar.

"Secure the scene, Mattock. I got this." Sarah raced back to the shot-up Jaguar and leapt in. She threw the car into reverse and pulled on the handbrake, throwing the nose around to face the other way. Then she shifted out of reverse and set her sights on the retreating white van.

She sped after Al-Sharir.

This time *he* was the mouse. And she was the mother-fucking tiger.

Al-Sharir's van teetered to one side and clipped the wire fence as he raced out of the airfield and onto the main road. Biggin Hill lay in the countryside on the south side of London. Traffic was thin here and the roads long, so the chase picked up speed. In a high-powered Jaguar, Sarah had the best of things, but Al-Sharir was desperate and pushed the van to its breaking point. Every time Sarah tried to pull alongside him, he swung into the other lane, or broke hard and almost crashed them both. The few other cars on the wet roads made things even more precarious. Sarah had no way of stopping the van without endangering innocent drivers.

But there was a nuclear bomb in that van. She had to do something.

The Jaguar's missing windscreen allowed the wind and rain to buffet Sarah's face, making it hard for her to focus. What if she crashed?

She punched the dashboard. "Damn it, what do I do?"

It was time for her to admit something. She needed help.

Switching on the dashboard comms, Sarah did the one thing she always felt uncomfortable with. "Agent Stone requesting assistance. I am currently heading north from Biggin Hill airfield in vehicular pursuit of Al-Sharir. I have eyes on a possible bomb and need help. I need backup."

"Sarah! It's Thomas. I have you. What's happening?" His voice was hard to make out through the whistling wind coming in through the missing windscreen.

"Biggin Hill is secure. Mattock is still on site. Al-Sharir got away, but I am in pursuit. Damn it, Thomas, the bomb is still in the van. He has the bomb."

"I have your GPS. Stay on him, and I will send backup to your location."

"As much as you can, Thomas. Send the guy who changes the tampon bins if you have to."

"Roger that. Do you have any idea where Al-Sharir might be heading?"

"Westminster. It's the only place. This is it, his last chance. He'll be heading straight for Parliament. Breslow is there with every MP worth a damn."

"Okay," said Thomas. "I will have all the entries to Westminster secured. Just stay on Al-Sharir's tail."

"You just try to shake me loose," she said. "This ends today."

"Be careful, Sarah. You're finishing this in one piece, you hear me?"

"Too late for that," said Sarah, then ended the call.

Al-Sharir dodged in front of an old Rover pulling a caravan and caused it to swerve. If it was meant to cause a crash, it failed, because Sarah zipped around the slowing vehicle with ease and kept right on Al-Sharir's tail as promised.

You just try to shake me loose, she thought. *I'm as much a part of your nightmares as you are mine.*

Arsehole.

The chase took them back into the city, and here the dangers multiplied. Whether stressed and erratic, or simply a poor driver, Al-Sharir's van careened and bucked like a branded bull, shunting aside other vehicles and mounting the pavement frequently. Sarah allowed herself to fall back, to drive more safely as she navigated traffic and tight turns, but not once did she allow the white van to escape her sight. At one point, its front-left hub cap knocked loose and went whizzing into the air. Just like his plans, Al-Sharir's van was falling apart. And his frustration was obvious, as with each mile of road his driving became more aggressive—more dangerous. He took turns later and attempted greater and greater risks. He was trying to shake her loose, but he couldn't. He wouldn't.

Yet, despite Sarah's dogged pursuit, she could do nothing to halt the van's progress, or that of the bomb. They were now within miles of Westminster, and another twenty minutes at such speed would see them there. What then?

Would Al-Sharir detonate the bomb as soon as he caught sight of Parliament?

Thomas came back through on the dashboard comms. "Sarah, we have roadblocks set up on all approaches to the City of Westminster. Keep distance and proceed carefully."

Sarah dodged around a post office van attempting a turn in the road. "How far ahead?"

"You should hit it in about five minutes. Palu is leading the team."

"Palu is in the field?"

"I tried to stop him, but this is personal to him too. With Howard injured, he insisted on being on the ground with you. Just keep Al-Sharir heading in the direction he is, Sarah. We will do the rest."

Al-Sharir's van blew a red light, jinking through traffic. Sarah had to kick the brakes to avoid crashing into the swerving cars. "Damn it."

Thomas panicked. "Sarah, you okay?"

She manoeuvred the beat up Jaguar carefully through the two lines of traffic. Al-Sharir pulled ahead, but she still had him. *Nice try.*

"I'm fine," said Sarah. "I just need to concentrate."

The road ahead was closed. Traffic thinned. Sarah would have expected a jam of beeping traffic, but she saw a man disguised as a construction worker forcing cars to detour left or right. Sarah recognised the man from the Earthworm. An analyst in the field. Everybody was working to end this safely.

Al-Sharir ignored the road closure and sped toward the bridge spanning the Thames.

Westminster lay on the other side.

The road block was set up at the bridge's entrance, leaving three choices—either plough right into it, or swerve either side and end up in the river.

Al-Sharir realised too late he had entered a dead end. With Sarah tightening his tail, he kept going at full speed.

This was going to end badly. Al-Sharir would not surrender.

Sarah spotted Palu at the side of the road. He shouldered a rifle, and other agents lined both sides of the road. Two police riot vans formed the road block ahead, but Al-Sharir never made it that far. An almighty *bang* and the van's tyres exploded, torn to shreds by stingers stretched across the road. Sarah flinched as the vehicle hitched up on two wheels and bounced up into the air. How fragile was the bomb?

Coming back down on its rims, the van lost speed rapidly. It righted itself just as it was about to tip over, and swerved into the curb. The front axle snapped and dropped the front bumper into the road. The metal strip grated against the asphalt and threw up a cascade of sparks.

The van came to a stop three feet from the roadblock, rain *pitter-patting* against the roof of the now still vehicle.

Palu and his men sprang into action, rifles pointed at the van.

The driver-side door opened, and a dazed Al-Sharir staggered out into the drizzling rain. He held something in his hand and lofted it above his head towards the darkening sky. "I hold the detonator. Point your weapons somewhere else, or I will reduce this city to ashes."

Palu put a hand up to his men. "Stand down."

Al-Sharir slumped back against the van, panting, but kept his hand in the air. "A wise move. Anybody moves and I press the trigger."

Sarah got out the Jaguar and marched down the road. Al-Sharir saw her coming and smiled. "Ah, Sarah. How fitting you should be here."

Sarah ignored Al-Sharir and headed right for the van. She had to know the bomb she'd seen was real. There could be a timer counting down or a chemical leaking... or there could be a hostage inside. She had to know, and if Al-Sharir was going to detonate the thing here, he would have already done it.

So what was he hiding?

"Sarah, step back, or I will detonate the bomb," he sounded worried, not at all like the man Sarah had feared for so long.

She continued towards the van, grabbing the handle on the side panel.

"Sarah! I order you to step back from there."

"Sarah, what are you doing?" shouted Palu.

"I'm ending this," she said, then threw open the van's side door. She was horrified by what she saw.

Like the plane at Biggin Hill, the van was empty.

"Where is it?" Sarah spoke in a yell. A yell of anguish, and of anger, that once again she'd allowed herself to be made vulnerable by this man —this monster. Al-Sharir smirked at her, even as Palu and his team surrounded him. Night was approaching, and it felt like when it got there, their chance to end all this would be gone.

"Come no closer," he said, or you will never know where the bomb is.

Palu stopped his team, but approached with his rifle against his shoulder. "It's over Al-Sharir. Just give us the location. No one else needs to die."

"Oh, that is where you are wrong. Some people most certainly need to die." He frowned. "You are Indian, yes?"

Palu nodded. "I am Sikh."

"A people made slave by the British Empire."

"The Sikh are a warrior people, not slaves."

"Warriors without land or rights are still slave. Even now, your homeland struggles to right itself after so long under the foot of this country."

"My homeland is here," said Palu. "And you blame it for sins long past."

"Not so long as to be forgotten."

"The British have never revelled in death. They have caused it, yes, but at least it has not become a way of life. This country is free and welcoming. That is the only reason you have been given a chance to try to ruin it. The men and women of this country are good and decent. They deserve better than to be murdered by a monster like you."

"Monsters are created," said Al-Sharir. "Usually by those with the best intentions."

"Just end this, Al-Sharir," said Sarah, pulling her SIG and aiming it at the man's chest. "Your plans have failed. Be happy that you took a bridge from us. You'll be remembered for it. That's what you care about, right? To stop feeling like that insignificant man I met in the desert."

Al-Sharir raised an eyebrow at her. "Insignificant? I believe I made quite the impression on you."

Sarah touched her face. "What, this? This was Hesbani. He always was the one who got things done. You prefer to talk."

Al-Sharir scowled. The jibe had struck him. "I let my actions do the talking, girl. Did Tower Bridge not teach you that?"

Sarah shrugged. "If that was even you. It could have been your Russian benefactors. How much of a leash have they kept you on? Obviously a long one if they entrusted a nuclear bomb to you. Too bad you fucked it all up. Where is the bomb now? Somewhere at the airfield?"

Al-Sharir laughed and seemed pained by it. "The bomb is where it is supposed to be. Do not count your enemy dead before you see his blood."

"Where is it?" urged Palu. "Just end this now. You will go on trial for what you've done, and the whole world will be watching. Make your statement on the dock where innocent lives aren't at stake."

"I shall take no more innocent lives, I promise you."

Palu nodded and seemed hopeful. "Good. Then tell us where the bomb is and all this can be over with. I'm an old man, but I promise that I will stay the course and see you are given a fair trial. Let's make a true statement today and choose something other than violence. Tell me where the bomb is, Al-Sharir."

"Okay, I shall tell you."

Sarah stepped up and pointed her gun in Al-Sharir's face, blinking against the rain as it leaked into her eyes. "Where?"

He pointed up at the grey sky. "I believe it is here."

Sarah looked up, and her hair blew in her face as a small helicopter whizzed overhead. Nose down, it zipped across the river.

Palu's eyes widened in horror. He lowered his rifle and grabbed his mob-sat. "Command, come in. Aerial threat to the Houses of Parliament. Immediate counter-measures needed…"

Sarah's ears honed in on the whirring of helicopter blades, and she watched as the aircraft cast a weak shadow across the Thames—a sparrow in flight.

Al-Sharir stood at the barrel of Sarah's SIG, a serene smile on his face. "It's been so good seeing you again, Sarah. Truly."

Sarah watched in terror as the helicopter rose up momentarily, before tilting forwards and dropping into a dive. It crashed against the south side of the Houses of Parliament and disintegrated in a shower of fiery debris.

The City of Westminster lit up in a blast. Sarah—along with everybody else—was thrown to the ground.

CHAPTER SIXTY-FIVE

Sarah's body was weightless, and her senses merged into a confused blur. She didn't know which way her body was facing when she hit the biting surface of the road. All around her the world screamed in terror, high-pitched and without end.

She ended up face down, forehead pressed against the loose grit of the road. She lay there; no way was she about to get up, wasn't even sure she could. Her shoulder wailed, yanked from its socket. Her stomach sloshed, hot and wet, stitches torn and blood drenching her clothes. Was she dead? She felt dead.

The bomb.

Al-Sharir had played her. The high-speed pursuit from Biggin Hill to Westminster had been a distraction, to keep her and the MCU from realising a helicopter had taken off from the airport. Sarah had chased the wrong goose.

"Sarah? Sarah, are you okay?" Sarah's body felt weightless once more as powerful hands peeled her off the road. Her boots found the ground, and her knees struggled to take her weight.

Palu stared at her, tears wetting his cheeks. "He did it, Sarah. The bastard did it. I let it happen."

She leant into him. "*We* let it happen."

Across the river, the Houses of Parliament were ablaze, much of the water-side structure transformed into a blackened hole. The evening sky buzzed with helicopters, but these belonged to police and journalists.

London had been attacked again.

The team Palu had assembled at the road block stumbled around now in confusion; many had even dropped their weapons. Al-Sharir stood in the centre of the road, observing the destruction he had wrought. The sight of him still standing turned Sarah's blood to ice. Ignoring the pain flaring from every inch of her body, she charged forwards. Crunching glass and debris heralded her approach, and Al-Sharir turned in time to see her coming. It did him no good.

Sarah clocked Al-Sharir in the face with everything she had, punching him so hard in the mouth that the bones in her hand shattered. It knocked him off his feet, and he splatted against the van. Sarah kicked him in the ribs and rained more punches at his head. He curled into a ball, trying to protect himself, but she reached down and grabbed him like a child, pulling him back to his feet. "I'll kill you. I'll fucking kill you."

She continued beating him until his face was a mess, and she had lost her breath.

Spitting blood through broken front teeth, Al-Sharir managed to smile. "Thank you for being here with me at the end, Sarah. My work is done"

"I am going to fucking kill you and anyone you care about."

His gaze flicked upwards at the news choppers. "I suspect you shall. By all means, get your petty revenge. You cannot undo what I have done. Those I care about are revenged."

She grabbed Al-Sharir by the throat and squeezed. Harder... Harder...

Palu shouted from behind her. "Sarah, stop!"

Al-Sharir's eyes bulged in his head. The bastard was still smiling.

Sarah squeezed harder still. He began to fade, and it delighted her.

She was playing right into his hands.

Damn you, Al-Sharir.

Sarah let go of his neck and fell away into the rubble. "I won't make you a martyr, you son-of-a-bitch."

Palu took her hand and pulled her back to her feet. He had regathered his rifle, which led Sarah to search for her SIG. She'd been holding it before the blast.

Palu pointed his rifle at Al-Sharir. He was crying freely. "More innocent blood-"

"I already told you," said Al-Sharir. "No innocent blood has been spilled today. The men and women in that building were corrupt. Your Prime Minister has refused to remove her invading armies from foreign lands. She assisted President Conrad in removing dozens of legitimate heads of state, and I have merely returned the favour. Now it is the United Kingdom that will be rudderless, vulnerable to the anarchy it has inflicted upon others. Today, a corrupt government has been toppled, and you are free."

Palu shoved Al-Sharir back against the van. "Enough! Your words are vomit. There is no honour in what you have done." The road-block team recovered their wits and raised their rifles as they saw their boss in an altercation. Palu told them to stand down and kept his glare on Al-Sharir. "You are a murderer. A stain of our world."

"As are you, Director Palu. You serve your own oppressors, and your negligence allowed me to succeed in my life's work."

"Russia will get the credit," spat Sarah. "You're a puppet, Al-Sharir. You've always been a puppet—first to God now to Vankin."

"I am no puppet," he said without anger. "Vankin possessed means I did not. *He* was *my* puppet. Look around, what do you see?"

Sarah frowned, and looked back at the Houses of Parliament burning and crumbling into the Thames. Yes! It was so obvious. She turned back to Al-Sharir and shook her head. "The bomb... it wasn't nuclear."

"It was," said Al-Sharir, "but I removed the core and replaced it. You give me too little credit. Vankin sought to make London a smear on a map, but I kill only as many as I need to meet my goals. The men and women in that odious building deserved death. The rest of this wretched city will be given a chance to change. You may thank me for my mercy."

"Fuck your mercy. Where is the core?" Palu waved his rifle in Al-Sharir's face.

"Don't worry. It shall be surrendered shortly via an anonymous tip off. Weapons of such destruction are not of God, and I have no wish to retain Vankin's property."

"You'll testify that Vankin was behind all this?" asked Palu.

Al-Sharir lifted his chin arrogantly. "Oh, do not worry, Director. I will expose the sins of many men in the days ahead." He turned to Sarah and pointed to the rubble at her feet. Her SIG lay against a brick that had flown all the way across the river. "Perhaps it is best to shoot me."

"I won't make you a martyr," Sarah reaffirmed. "You'll face up to what you've done."

Al-Sharir smiled, said nothing, but then shocked them by pulling a revolver out from beneath his shirt. Palu and the other armed men lifted their rifles in panic.

"No," Sarah shouted. "Stand down. This is what he wants. He wants us to gun him down in sight of all these choppers overhead. His dream is to die at our hands."

The men lowered their weapons, Palu included. They seemed extremely unhappy at allowing a terrorist to wave a gun at them.

"We know each other well, don't we, Sarah?" said Al-Sharir.

"Yes."

"Then perhaps you should have seen this coming." Like a striking snake, Al-Sharir whipped the revolver up and pulled the trigger.

Palu dropped to the ground.

Sarah bent and grabbed her SIG, acting on instinct as she pulled the trigger so fast that she shot from the hip. The bullet struck Al-Sharir's face and dropped him in the middle of the road. But the damage had been done. She dropped to her hands and knees beside

Palu and pulled him into her arms. His head was heavy in the crook of her elbow. The hole in his forehead was bright red against his light-brown skin. Al-Sharir had taken away any chance for final words.

Sarah still held her SIG. Now she gripped it more firmly than ever. Springing into the air, a twisted wraith, she marched over to Al-Sharir. The man lay on his back, staring at the blackened sky. He coughed and spluttered as blood escaped his lips. Her bullet had sliced off part of his cheek and ear, but was not fatal. "Ouch," she said, with a hateful grin, "that's going to leave a scar."

Al-Sharir peered up at her. Suddenly, he seemed like an old man, grey stubble and dull, lifeless eyes. The man really was finished. He had not thought of his life beyond this moment. Taking revenge for his family had driven every inch of his soul, and he was now at peace. The Houses of Parliament burned so close that the heat reached across the river. Palu's illustrious career had ended in abject failure, and the MCU's future was all but over. The United Kingdom was forever changed.

Al-Sharir had won.

Sarah too was changed because of this monster at her feet. Her scars were deep, her blood thin. Yet her skin had grown thick as bark. She was a warrior now. Like a Sikh. Like Palu.

Al-Sharir swallowed blood and found words. "Finish it, Sarah. Point your gun and erase me from your nightmares forever. Gain back your life by giving me my death."

Sarah pointed her SIG over his heart. He placed his arms out to the side, not wishing to defend himself. His sleeve pulled back to reveal a tattoo of a dagger—its tip pointed upwards. Sarah still remembered the first time he had shown it to her back in Afghanistan when she had been a prisoner at his mercy. A prisoner he had eventually released.

Sarah lowered her weapon. "You will stand trial. Good men and women will dedicate their lives to poking holes in everything you stand for. History won't remember you as a martyr; it'll remember you as just another lunatic with a messiah complex."

Al-Sharir sprung up and lunged for Sarah's gun, but she smashed it against the side of his head and knocked him out cold. It fell to her to give orders to Palu's strike team, so she gave them. "Get the prisoner in cuffs and don't take your eyes off him. He has a lot to answer for and would rather die than face up to what he has done."

The agents nodded, but one stared at her, concerned. "Ma'am. You're bleeding."

Sarah looked down at her stomach and saw she was drenched. Blood dripped as far as her thigh. "Now would be an okay time to pass out, right?"

The agent looked at her with concern.

Sarah dropped to the ground.

CHAPTER SIXTY-SIX

Sarah lay on a plastic board beside the road. It was dark, and a man she didn't know pressed both hands against her stomach. When he saw her eyes open, he tried to calm her, and did such a good job that she went back to sleep.

When she next opened her eyes, she was in a hospital ward. It occurred to her that she spent far too much time in hospital beds. She tried to sit up, but failed. Her limbs were heavy, but the feeling was sublime. Although she was awake, the calmness of sleep spiralled around every nerve ending. She barely noticed when Dr Bennet stood over her.

"J-Jessica? Am I...?"

"No, sweetheart, you're not at the Earthworm. You're at the hospital."

"What's the damage?"

"You have a fractured collarbone, fractured fingers, dislocated shoulder, sprained ankle, and severe bruising. You've lost two pints of blood. Oh, and your stab wound is infected. They have you on Morphine and antibiotics. You'll probably live."

"How is Howard?" Sarah didn't know why the thought came to

her, but his absence reminded her just how much he had been by her bedside during the last year.

"His right hand is ruined." Jessica sighed. "Lost his index and middle finger. He's being treated at Bart's. You're at the Royal London. He was asking about you."

"It was my fault. He got hurt-"

"Doing his job," said Jessica. "Howard got hurt protecting a fellow agent. He doesn't regret it, so you shouldn't either. You would have done the same for him, and we all know it. You're both alive, Sarah. Be thankful."

"I... am." Sarah's memory offered her something terrible. "Palu! Oh God."

Jessica blinked, and revealed that her eyes were red from crying. "He's gone, Sarah. That bastard, Al-Sharir. You think he would have been content with the deaths he had already caused."

"Did anyone survive?"

Jessica got a hold of herself. "Parliament? A few MPs escaped with injuries, but so far they've pulled almost two-hundred bodies from the wreckage—including Breslow."

"The Prime Minister is dead?"

"Yes. Al-Sharir completed his mission."

"He didn't use a nuclear bomb, though. He could have."

Jessica frowned. "Are you defending him?"

"No. I suppose I'm just thankful the damage isn't worse."

"I've never known you to look on the bright-side. You'll also be glad to know that Al-Sharir has been detained with enough security to ensure he doesn't so much as fart without a witness. He'll stand trial for what he has done."

Sarah took a breath and almost fell asleep. Images of death swirled through her mind, but she didn't allow herself to mourn. Tragedy would fuel her for the mission ahead. Al-Sharir was one general in a war without end. Sarah would see more like him fall. Bradley, Palu, and all of the innocent victims taken by evil men and women would not be forgotten. Palu's career had not ended in defeat, for he had saved more lives than anyone would ever know, and had inspired a team to carry on his work.

His family.

Sarah's family.

When she opened her eyes again, Jessica had gone.

The ward was dark.

CHAPTER SIXTY-SEVEN

Sarah's first funeral had been her mother's—having died in a sudden car accident when Sarah was six—but she never thought the next would be her husband's. As much as the assembled mourners looked at Thomas's cedar coffin, they all stole sideways glances at her face. The scars covering the entire left side of her face still glistened where they continued to heal. That she was even well enough to attend today was a point of contention with the Army's doctors who had been reluctant to discharge her.

Everything had changed in an instant. She had awoken from a beautiful dream to find her face missing and her husband dead, killed by friendly fire on the same day she had been taken prisoner by a member of the Taliban. The worst blow of all was that she had lost their baby—the only part of Thomas she could have held onto.

She would have been called *Katie*.

Thomas had often spoken of taking Sarah home to Florida to meet his family, and they had formed a plan to settle down in the sun there, but she never wanted to be here like this, standing beside his coffin next to a weeping old woman who couldn't believe she was outliving her only son.

The minister went on about God's plan for them all, but Sarah wasn't listening. Her eyes were fixed on Thomas's coffin; her sick mind wondering what he looked like inside. The American flag on top of the wood seemed like a cruel taunt, for it was in service to his country that he had died.

Time seemed to slide by in fits and starts. Sometimes a single, agonising minute would seem to go on forever as tears streamed from the healthy side of her face, while other times an hour would whizz by in a dazed blur. This was one of those times, for before she knew it, the funeral was over and Thomas was lowered into the ground, gone forever. Her scars burned constantly, but the pain in her heart obliterated all other sensations.

"I've been so excited to meet you," said Thomas's mother as they headed to the funeral cars. "But I never wanted it to be like this."

"I had the same thought," she said glumly. "Thomas was a good man. You must have been a wonderful mother."

"Ha, never had to be with Tommy. He was such a good boy that he practically raised himself right. Always planning on changing the world. The biggest tragedy of this is all the big ideas he never got to act on. I'm just happy he found love while he was alive. Will you be staying?"

Sarah swallowed. "I don't think so. I... have family to get back to."

A lie. When did she start being so closed off?

Thomas's mother seemed sad, but she nodded. "I'm not quite sure how I'm supposed to go on now. He was my boy. I'm a mother without her son."

"Are you... are you going to be okay?"

"No, not really, but I won't do anything stupid. I'll just go on, I suppose. Until I stop going on. I'm an old woman, that's my only mercy. Thank you for loving my son, Sarah. You made him happier than I ever could have hoped. I know it's hard, but you're young. Live your life. Thomas would want you to be happy."

Sarah reached up to her face. "Live my life? My life was just buried in the ground."

"Yes, I understand that, but Thomas never left you on purpose. He would be here with you if he could, so just remember that. Hold him in your heart and keep being the woman he fell in love with."

"That woman is gone."

"Perhaps for now, but don't let her die, and one day, she will be back. Well, it was nice meeting you Sarah. You ever find yourself stateside again, don't you dare not call on me. It would be lovely to get to know you properly when times are brighter."

Sarah hugged the old woman, feeling awkward. Yet she held on for a long time. Eventually she moved back and smiled. This old lady would have been Katie's grandmother, but now she would remain a stranger. Life had changed course in an instant, and Sarah would have preferred if it had just ended. "I loved your son, Mrs Geller. I will never forget him."

The old lady smiled. "Then one day the two of you will be reunited."

Sarah smiled at the thought. "I can't wait."

Three days since the Houses of Parliament had been blown into the Thames and the nation remained in a state of unrelenting shock. In an unprecedented act, the interim government placed the United Kingdom into an official period of mourning—all non-essential businesses closed for a full seven days. The economic impact would be high. But the country's soul needed time to recover.

Sarah stood at the back of the hall as Lord Alfred Pugh took the microphone on stage. No clear chain of command remained, so he had taken it upon himself to manage the crisis by acting as interim Prime Minister. The man had worked tirelessly in the last few days to put the country at ease, and despite his sixty-six years, he barely looked north of fifty with his thick black hair and a bushy moustache.

Lord Pugh cleared his throat and began. "Ladies and gentlemen, thank you for coming. It is my burden, once more, to have to speak to you, but I have some good news. We stand here at our own Ground Zero, where our symbolic structure of democracy stood for over one hundred years. I am here to tell you today that a new House of Parliament will be constructed in its place, and will honour those this country has lost to madness and bloodshed. It will be a beacon of hope to this nation and will stand for the remainder of its history. Long may that be."

The assembled crowd of Press, union leaders, and surviving MPs cheered.

Lord Pugh put up a hand and gained immediate silence. "The perpetrator of this nation's torment is in custody and will stand trial for his crimes, but there are more like him. More sharks in the muddy oceans of freedom. I pledge to you all that we will hunt these men down, evict them from their hives, and put them in shackles. We will put a stop to this senseless terrorism that has come to define our place in history."

More cheers.

"But we will not do so by repeating the mistakes of the past. We will not engage in further incursions on foreign soil. Our priority is to protect our homes—our families. It is not a human right to be a member of the United Kingdom and Great Britain. It is not a right that we will welcome all and solve the world's ills. The time has come for us to look out for ourselves—to protect ourselves. With that in mind, I am pleased to introduce the new head of the MCU, Thomas Gellar."

At the back of the crowd, Sarah sighed. Al-Sharir would get his wish. The United Kingdom was pulling out of foreign territories and focusing on its own affairs. Sarah couldn't help but feel that was a good thing. Yet, the rhetoric behind Lord Pugh's speech worried her. What did the man actually plan on doing?

Thomas stepped up on stage smiling and waving to the crowd as they applauded him. Sarah also heard a couple of jeers. The MCU was not popular right now.

Thomas straightened his tie and leaned into the microphone. "Thank you. I would just like to start by apologising—apologising to this nation for failing to protect it. The MCU was created to stop men like Al-Sharir before they act, not after their devastation has been wrought. In this, I and my colleagues have failed. But this will be my final apology. I will not apologise for casualties in a war, because such things are not useful. What is of use is Lord Pugh's interim government diverting funds from international peacekeeping operations to domestic peacekeeping. The MCU and associated organisations will be better funded and more highly staffed than ever before. Our failures are behind us, and the next man like Al-Sharir who seeks to shed our blood will be met with unrelenting and irresistable force." He caught sight of Sarah in the crowd and faltered for a moment. "Ahem, excuse me. As the new head of the MCU, I will not make my predecessor's mistakes. We will not react to threats already in motion or chase monsters already in our midst. We will annihilate them in the womb. My pledge to this nation is to make it the safest sovereign land in the world. The citizens of Great Britain will once again sleep easily in their beds. It will take time, but we *will* win this war."

The room fell silent, not because people didn't believe Thomas's words, but because they absolutely did. This was a new dawn for the fight against terrorism, and the change in leadership was needed. That Thomas had negotiated the MCU's inevitable closure into a rejuvenation was perhaps testament to his suitability for the role as Director. That he had done so on top of Palu's corpse meant that he was Sarah's leader in name only. However, she wished him success all the same because his failure would see the country broken forever. After the horror the United Kingdom had faced in the last twelve months, this was its last attempt at survival.

Thomas concluded his meeting with a brief security manifesto and then exited the stage. Sarah chose that moment to leave as well, limping outside into the afternoon sun which had risen high above the Thames to cast its sparkle on the water. The sun had risen on London again, as she'd hoped, but it was a different city—a frightened city. She was prepared to work hard to dispel that fear, but it would not be easy, and it would not be quick. Now that her own fears had finally evaporated,

Sarah could focus on what mattered. Protecting good people against bad.

"Gives quite the speech, doesn't he?"

Sarah turned gingerly, holding her ribs, to see Howard perched on the bonnet of a black Jaguar. Mandy sat in the driver's seat and gave her a wave. Sarah gave Howard a hug. She had not seen him since he took that shotgun blast for her. "I didn't see you inside."

"Mandy and I were listening on the radio. I don't think I could have bared watching it live."

Sarah laughed, which hurt immensely. Her left hand was in a splint and she used it to push against the bruising on her ribs, "Yeah, Thomas was pretty smug. I hate to say it, but I think he might do a good job."

Howard shrugged. "At least the MCU has a future. I hear Pugh might be made full Prime Minister. The nation loves him."

"There's no one else left to do a better job, so I say let him." She nodded to the bandages on his right hand. "Your fingers?"

"Still gone. I'll live though. It was my hand or your life. I'd do it again. Anyway, you look like you took enough of a beating yourself, so don't worry about me. I'm just glad you're healing."

"Thank you."

"I hear the Flower Man is some kind of Climate Change Scientist."

Sarah chuckled. It was a surprising conclusion to the Flower Man's terrible reign. "His name is Michael Black. A meteorologist, apparently. He worked at a weather station in Greenland with a Russian science group until four years ago when he suffered some kind of psychotic break. He went to live with his mother until she died last year of lung cancer. I'm not sure what he has exactly, but it's some kind of delusion brought on by his informed fear of climate change. When his mother died, he blamed the pollution humanity is causing. I don't know, it's a whole thing, but the worst part of it is that he's better now."

Howard frowned. "Better?"

"Yeah, they're treating Michael at a secure hospital. Gave him the pills he needed and brought him right out of the psychosis he was in.

Got him to give up the location of three more victims before he went into some kind of daze—won't say a word now."

Howard shook his head in horror. "Can you imagine it? You lose your mind completely, then they bring you back and tell you you've tortured and killed a dozen innocent people. No wonder he's checked out."

"Yeah, I almost feel sorry for him," said Sarah. "Tell you the truth, I haven't had time to think about things. I only returned to work this morning."

"I'm glad you're okay, Sarah. Not being able to have your back at the end... Palu..."

"You were with me, Howard. What you did for me..." She looked at him and sighed. "It gave me what I needed."

"Sarah?" Thomas appeared and joined them. "Thank you for coming. I saw you at the hospital, but you were pretty out of it."

"Morphine," she said. "Because I'm worth it."

Thomas didn't laugh. "I'll be putting a new structure in place at the Earthworm, and of course, I expect you to sit at the very top of things. Not like you haven't earned it."

"Will it take me out of the field?"

"Of course. I'm not having you risk your—"

"Then I don't want it. I'm a field agent. I want to look the bad guys in the face. Give the office jobs to somebody else."

"Sarah."

"Accept that, or I'll leave."

He nodded. "Okay. Hopkins, you have earned a place at the table too, of course. And with your hand..."

Howard sighed. "Sorry, Sarah, but I think an office job is the only way for me to go. You'll need a new partner."

Sarah patted his shoulder. "Don't apologise. There's nobody better to sit in the war room and make decisions. You'll have my back even more than usual."

He nodded. "I will."

Thomas cleared his throat. "I also wanted to talk to you alone about other things, Sarah."

"You mean you want to talk about *us?*"

He stared into her eyes, acting as if Howard was not there. "Before everything went crazy, we shared a moment, Sarah. The spark is still there. I would like to talk about what that means."

Howard swallowed.

Sarah shrugged. "It means nothing."

"I don't believe that. You still love me. What we had—"

"Is over! I buried you, Thomas. Don't you get that? The only thing I love is the memory."

"I didn't die."

"You may as well have."

"If I could make the choice again—"

"You would make the same decision," said Sarah. "And you should. The sacrifice you made was selfless and brave. You gave up your life, your safety, in order to do what was right. People are alive because of your courage, Thomas, and I don't blame you for any of itl."

Thomas looked at her, staring deep into her eyes. "I never stopped loving you, Sarah."

"But I stopped loving you. You did what you had to, and you made a brave decision. Now it's time to face up to your actions and accept the consequences."

"I thought you'd wait..."

Sarah sighed. "It wasn't just me, Tom. I watched your mother break down at your funeral. You don't get to do that to people and expect things to be okay."

"Sarah, I had no choice."

"We all have a choice. You're my boss now, Thomas, nothing more."

"I'm your husband."

"Until we divorce. I'm in love with somebody else."

Thomas blanched, but looked more aggravated than upset. He had truly expected to get his own way, hadn't he? In his mind, he had foreseen returning a beloved hero.

Howard seemed confused by her statement, and he was visibly shocked when Sarah reached out and grabbed his waist. He offered no resistance as she kissed him. In fact, he kissed her back for what seemed like a wonderful eternity. He reached up and took her face in his hand, and she let him. When she was with Howard, her scars did not exist. She wasn't a soldier or an agent; she was a woman. He made her just a woman, and that was why she loved him.

Sarah pulled back and stared into Howard's eyes. "Meeting you was the worst thing that ever happened to me."

He laughed. "Thanks!"

"But it was also the best. I lost myself after Afghanistan. You pulled me back from the darkness."

"For God's sake, Sarah," said Thomas. "Will you think about what you're doing?"

She turned on Thomas. "You chose the job, Tom—the toughest job in the country—so I suggest you focus on what's important. I will help you all the way, but we are just colleagues. I want to be able to exist without you constantly reminding me of what I lost, so that I can appreciate what I have. Move on, Thomas. You have a job to do."

Thomas pulled at his tie as if he couldn't breathe. He grew red in the face. Eventually, he turned and left without another word.

Howard touched her arm. "You okay?"

She nodded. "No, but I'm healing."

They kissed again, and Mandy beeped the car horn in a merry tune.

Thomas turned down the side street where he'd left his car. The black Range Rover sat parked outside a carpet warehouse, out of the view of any CCTV cameras. He slid in behind the steering wheel and nodded to the man waiting for him in the passenger seat. "Thanks for meeting with me."

"Caught your wee speech on the radio," replied the man. "Had the eejits eating out yer 'and."

Thomas smiled weakly. He thought little of his current handler, but was forced to tolerate him and his barely legible speech. "I am in control of the MCU as promised. Am I to proceed as planned?"

"Aye. The bosses are very happy with you. Al-Sharir let the side down by ditching the real bomb, but Vankin isn't ready to give in just yet. Slimani spilled the beans enough to put Vankin away for eternity, so he's had to go into hiding, but the company is still in good shape. Our bosses still want the same thing."

Thomas nodded. He should have been feeling jubilant at his victories, but he couldn't help but be sickened by his loss of Sarah. She had loved him so much once. He had assumed that love would have lasted, and that his return would have been welcomed. Once, the thought of her no longer wanting to be with him would have been absurd. Now, she didn't even like him. It was all Hopkins' fault. He'd gotten to her in Thomas's absence. And now Sarah thought she was in love with the man...?

Absurd. She's my wife.

"We have a problem," Thomas told his handler.

His handler raised his chin curiously, exposing a thick scar across his jugular. "Oh?"

"Agent Howard Hopkins needs removing."

"Is he on to us?"

"He will be. He's smart, and entitled to a high position within the MCU. I hold no authority over the man—at least none he will respect. I want him dealt with before he becomes a problem."

"No bother. I'll inform our bosses. Can they rely on you to keep things tickin' in the meantime?"

Thomas grunted. "Of course. I await their orders."

"The money has been wired to yer account. Makes you quite the rich fella."

"Thank you, Hamish, but this is not about the money."

Hamish chuckled. "Aye, not for me either, but it certainly 'elps. I'll contact you soon." He climbed out of the car and turned, limping on a crippled leg. Before he closed the door, he winked at Thomas. "Bring on the New World, brother, huh?"

Thomas nodded. "Bring on the New World."

Hamish closed the car door and Thomas drove away—off to his new job as head of the MCU. The fate of the nation lay in his hands. And his hands would gladly shape it.

WANT FREE BOOKS?

Don't miss out on your FREE Iain Rob Wright horror starter pack. Five free bestselling horror novels sent straight to your inbox. No strings attached.

For more information just visit:
www.iainrobwright.com

Iain Rob Wright is one of the UK's most successful horror and suspense writers, with novels including the critically acclaimed, THE FINAL WINTER; the disturbing bestseller, ASBO; and the wicked screamfest, THE HOUSEMATES.

His work is currently being adapted for graphic novels, audio books, and foreign audiences. He is an active member of the Horror Writer Association and a massive animal lover.

For more information
www.iainrobwright.com
Author@iainrobwright.com